PRAISE FOR

MORE THAN DREAMS

"Highly entertaining . . . Bullard's dialogue is crisp and believable, and the relationships of her characters are meaningful and lifelike. . . . Put this one down as a novel to curl up with on cold winter nights."

The Chattanooga Times

"Mixes journalistic ethics, political power plays, cocaine-dealing, sex, feminism and romance. It is a page-turner, with a violent and dramatic conclusion."

The Commercial Appeal, Memphis

"Takes the reader behind the scenes of TV news shows—and into the board room of the station . . . It offers a fascinating study of a woman who will do everything, except, fortunately, compromise her integrity for power."

The Virginian-Pilot

"Whirls readers into the frenetic off-screen world of fictitious Boston TV station WLYM. . . . The intriguing main characters and spicy, fast-paced dialogue create an exciting narrative."

Publishers Weekly

MORE
THAN
DREAMS

Pamela Bullard

IVY BOOKS • NEW YORK

Ivy Books
Published by Ballantine Books
Copyright © 1987 by Pamela Bullard

Library of Congress Catalog Card Number: 87-9701

ISBN 0-8041-0402-6

This edition published by arrangement with Random House, Inc.

Manufactured in the United States of America

First Ballantine Books Edition: July 1989

Consider the lilies of the field, how they grow;
they neither toil nor spin;
yet I tell you,
even Solomon in all his glory was
not arrayed like one of these.

—Matthew 6:28

Acknowledgments

This book was written at a time of transition in my life, and is therefore a product not only of the experiences and observations of my years as a journalist, but of personal reflection on the priorities of life and my hope for a future of quiet peace and continued strengthening insight. Throughout this journey, the love and support of friends and colleagues have been a guiding, nourishing force. My gratitude extends to many. Among those . . .

Thank you to John Langone, Jeanne Hanson, Penny Harrison, Nancy Stone and Pat MacDonald, for their early belief in this manuscript.

To Adie Moore, Marc and Kay Hamilton, and Judy Stoia, thank you for the unselfish, understanding love you have always held out to me.

To Liz Mehl, thank you for always being there through twenty years (and still counting) of a beautiful friendship.

And finally, thank you to Dr. Edgar S. Miller and his wife, Jackie, Dr. Donna Moore-Ede, and Dr. Jennifer L. Rike without whose expertise, compassion, and loving support this manuscript would never have reached publication.

BOOK ONE

KATE

"That she bear children is not a woman's significance . . . but that she bear herself, that is her supreme and risky fate."

D. H. Lawrence

1

APRIL 1982

KATE'S HAND REACHED IN THE DIRECTION OF THE BUZZING alarm clock. Feeling along the top, she found the button she wanted, pushed it, and slowly opened her eyes to a gray dawn that barely lit the frame of the bedroom window. 5:02. That meant she had gotten her usual five hours' sleep. She grew more alert. Jonathan. He had had an emergency surgery. She had gone to bed alone. But now her senses followed the awakening of her mind, and she felt the pressure of Jonathan's leg resting on top of hers. She turned her head toward him, smiling at her handsome, still youthful looking husband. Pushing at the sheets and quilt, she rolled her nakedness against his. He responded with a mumble of recognition, put his arm around her and pulled her closer. He then returned to his rhythmic breathing and she knew he was fast asleep again.

Lying there against his warmth, she felt the familiar arousal in her body and wondered if she should disturb him. It never failed to fascinate and please her that after almost twenty years of marriage, the sexual draw between them had not slackened in the least; if anything, it had grown stronger. Kate smiled to herself, thinking also that in all those years, she had never once woken in her bed without her legs entwined in his, or in his arms. Except for the nights when one of them was traveling, or Jonathan was in an all-night surgery. That was the price she paid for being married to Dr. Jonathan Laurence Marchand, chief of neurosurgery, New England General Hospital.

No, she would not awaken him. He needed his rest. And she should get in the pool, swim those laps, and get her day moving. She gently kissed him on the neck, then picked her robe up from the chair next to their bed. Slipping it on, she winced as the problematic right arm went into the sleeve, then quietly walked into the large bathroom, closing the door behind her.

Jonathan's note was stuck to the bathroom mirror: "Good Morning, Beautiful. The good guys won, but I've got to be suited up for another round at 8 A.M. so please wake me for breakfast together. I love you. J."

Good. The surgery was apparently successful. He wouldn't be berating himself this morning, asking the endless question: "Where did it go wrong?"

She brushed her teeth mechanically as the computer in her mind clicked into a different mode: work and today's agenda. The Wednesday morning meeting with the sales department, news briefing, proposal for public affairs to be completed, and all the other significant and insignificant details of running what was hailed as the finest television station in America. Oh, yes, the interview with *The New York Times* was today. "Damn," she said as she pulled on her bathing suit. "I don't have time to be charming today."

She walked slowly and a little stiffly back through the bedroom and down the broad stairs to the floor below. Christ, this house seems huge early in the morning, Kate thought. And it was. One of the largest single-family dwellings on one of the most beautiful estates in Dover.

They almost didn't take it. It seemed foolish for just the two of them, and it meant a thirty-five-minute drive to downtown Boston. But the property had a large lap pool that Kate needed to strengthen her weak back, and an all-weather tennis court for Jonathan's "third love." He maintained Kate was his first, operating his second, and tennis his third. However, on Sundays when the entire day might pass with Jonathan on the court, Kate wondered about that order.

Walking cautiously down the steps Kate glanced into the living room and smiled. They rarely used the room, and Jonathan often threatened to put a basketball hoop at each end of the long space. But Kate loved the antiques she'd filled it with, and the gleaming Oriental rug.

Beyond the living room was a much smaller room, comfortable, with well-worn leather chairs, a long couch covered with pillows, and a small nineteenth-century marble fireplace. Adjoining that room was Kate's elaborate but cluttered study.

Kate looked at her desk and saw the lengthy documentary proposal on top of numerous other papers. She had not finished reading it last night. She must do that today, for the proposal needed work. The idea was sound and she wanted to get the project rolling as soon as possible.

Pushing open the study door, Kate walked out onto the Italian tile that covered the pool area. The air was cold and she walked quickly to the bathhouse to pick up a towel and her goggles. As she unzipped the flap to the bubble that covered the pool, she was grateful for the warm rush of air that hit her. She zipped the flap back up, and slowly descended into the water, grateful for the warmth that would loosen her muscles and pull back the pain. Heating the pool year-round and putting up the bubble in the winter was an extravagant expenditure, but she and Jonathan agreed that what it saved in potential medical bills was worth it. And swimming at a club was out of the question. Privacy. Yes, that had been a major factor in buying the estate. They had their privacy. That was essential.

As she swam now, she began with her usual pacing technique. She was a perfect five-beat stroker, and from the day she had met Jonathan she had said to herself as she swam, "I love Jon-a-thon." It was the essential five beats: "I love Jon-a-thon," breathe. . . . She swam lap after lap after lap but her body was used to the routine, and as if by a silent alarm she stopped, knowing when it was enough.

As she reached for her towel, she heard the sound of a car moving up the gravel driveway. That would be Bridget, the cook-housekeeper. She headed back to the house, her back eased, her step brisk now.

"Morning, Bridget, looks like a beautiful day," Kate shouted in the direction of the kitchen.

"Spring at last, I hope," answered Bridget. "Will Dr. Marchand be joining you for breakfast?"

"Oh, yes, thank you for reminding me," said Kate. When she got upstairs to the bedroom, Jonathan's face was turned away from her. She leaned over him and firmly pressed her wet lips against his. As he responded and his mouth opened to welcome her tongue, she brushed her hand through his hair.

"My own little mermaid," said Jonathan after she stood up again. "Do you suppose in another life you were a fish?"

"What, and not have these legs?" she laughed as she walked into the bathroom. "God wouldn't deprive the world of these gorgeous gams."

She started the shower and pulled off her suit. "Congratulations on last night. Thanks for the note. I love you, too," she yelled above the sound of the shower.

"How much do you love me?" She was startled as he opened the shower door and nonchalantly stepped in, taking the soap from her hands, lathering his hands and slowly moving them over her breasts.

"Oh, Jonathan," she felt her nipples immediately respond. "More than the flowers love the sun." She turned to his kiss, and began moving her hand in circles around his stomach, reaching an already erect penis. She felt herself contract as she pushed his penis against her.

"I've got so much to do," she murmured, "and you have to get to the hospital. Oh, Jon." His mouth was now on her breast and as she watched the water beat on the back of his head, she heard herself moan.

He reached down and turned off the water, never moving his mouth from her breast, then kicked open the door, picked her up, walked into the bedroom and gently laid her on the bed. Kate was amazed at how wet and ready she was for him, and she smiled as he slipped inside her.

Within moments, she was thrusting her hips against him, her legs locked around his buttocks, feeling the familiar urgency and the passion that flared up whenever they came together. She felt a twinge in her back, and Jonathan noticed, placing his hand underneath her to support her.

She moved his other hand to her breast, as her own hands pulled him deeper and deeper into her. She arched her back and, at that signal, Jonathan's breath became deeper, carrying a deep groan as he responded to her voice. Her own last "Darling" was almost a scream as she felt the tremor move through her stomach and back up and down her legs. And then the soft fullness as Jonathan groaned and let himself free inside her.

She was moving her hands up and down his back, soothing him, when she looked around the room. "Oh Christ, Jonathan, the damn door's open!"

"What's the big deal?" Jonathan got up on one elbow. "So Bridget knows that the great Katherine Marchand is a screamer when she makes love. You *are* with your husband, you know."

"Oh, you. . . . " She tried to push him off her.

"Wait a minute, I'm not through."

"Jonathan, look at the clock, it's almost six-thirty!"

"I just wanted to say I love you, and you're the most beautiful woman in the world." He kissed her gently.

"You forgot one thing. I'm the luckiest woman in the world. I have you."

"But will I always be enough for you?"

"What a strange question." She looked at him quizzically. "You know that I never ever had even the remotest interest in another man. You're all I can handle, Doctor." She paused, remembering the one time she, apparently, had not been enough for him, then buried the thought and said, "Now would you please lift that hunk of a body of yours so I may return to the shower?"

Fifteen minutes later, showered, her makeup in place, she stood in a satin teddy in the middle of her very long closet, surveying it as if she were a General inspecting her troops. She knew the *Times* would be taking pictures. What should be the image . . . elegant, businesslike, expensive? She chose a white wool Ungaro suit but as she looked at herself in the mirror she frowned a bit. Too reminiscent of Jackie Onassis? Then she shrugged, not wanting to take the time to change.

Jonathan was already downstairs, drinking coffee and reading one of the numerous papers spread on the large table.

"Morning again, Mrs. Marchand," said Bridget. Jonathan winked at her and Kate picked up a paper and hit him over the head with it.

The television at the end of the table was on, as usual, and Kate half paid attention to the national news while reading the local papers. She had flipped through the *Herald* by the time her eggs were placed in front of her, and had digested the essentials of the *Globe* by 7:25, at which point she gave her full attention to the Channel 3 local news cut-in.

"Jonathan, I want you to watch this," she grabbed his arm as he was preparing to leave the table. "I'm thinking about replacing Lynn."

"But I thought you liked her," said Jonathan. "She's been on the early morning news for over two years."

"Well, I wouldn't get rid of her. I'm thinking about moving her to the six and the eleven."

"Contract negotiations not going so well with Ann?"

"No, not really. Her agent's demanding too much money, and frankly, I think Ann's time may be past in Boston. She's been anchoring for five years, but, more important, the ratings are slipping. We're number two and I don't know if she's worth the aggravation.''

"Number two? Kate, you didn't tell me. When did this happen?'' His concern was genuine. He knew the ramifications.

"The latest Nielsen. I got the advances on it last night. It's only one point, well, two points on two days. But it's the first time since I became general manager that the station has slipped to number two in news.''

"So you think Lynn replacing Ann could give you that boost?''

"It's just a thought. What do you think?''

"I think I'm going to be late for surgery.''

"Oh, Jonathan,'' there was exasperation in Kate's voice, "they don't move without you. What's the big rush?''

"Because I'm going to be using the laser in a new technique inside the brain. And you know how people love to watch new procedures. I'll have the head of the hospital and a lot of other people there.''

He leaned down and kissed her but Kate, out of the corner of her eye, was watching Lynn's broadcast. "Good luck, darling. I know you'll be splendid.'' She didn't move her eyes from the set.

Shrugging, Jonathan walked out, knowing that anything he said now would be lost on her. The switch had been made, as it was every morning. She was no longer his wife, lover, friend. She was the general manager—the youngest and the only woman in the country—at what was regarded as the finest television station in the country.

When the news went to the weather, Kate abruptly got up, went into the study, placed folders and papers in her briefcase, and walked back through the kitchen. "I'll call you later, Bridget,'' she said.

When she got to the garage, she patted the car's side as if it were indeed a live animal, not the sleek black Jaguar sedan she was a little embarrassed to love as much as she did. She drove quickly and deftly through the rolling green exurbia that led to the highway. Traffic wasn't bad and she came roaring out of the Mass Pike toll gates as if it were the start of a race. As she saw the city approach, she thought about the prospect of shuffling her talent around. Could Lynn handle the six and eleven? Would she be a good match with Bill Halliday, the co-anchor? Would they be strong enough together?

Suddenly, she recalled something Jonathan had said. "A new technique. People love to watch new procedures." Maybe it was time for a completely fresh face at Channel 3. A fresh look. Pique the audience's interest. She had arrived at the front of the station. It always amazed her. So lost in thought was she every morning, she never remembered the drive into work. It was like magic. Poof! And there she was. As she pulled in front of the large building on State Street, she saw Mickey Merriam come through the revolving doors at a run.

"Morning, Mrs. Marchand." He grabbed the door handle as it swung open. The son of the head of sales, he was certainly polite enough, and treated her courteously. More than she could say for his father, Steven. Yes, good old Steven Merriam. It was no secret that Steven had gone after the general managership. And in many ways, he was still in there, pitching his case. As director of sales, he had considerable clout, but so far, Kate had beaten him at every turn. She knew she was still in a testing period, and no doubt, Steven Merriam was taking delight in the drop in ratings.

Glancing briefly at the WLYM/CHANNEL 3 brass inlay shining across the polished granite, Kate strode determinedly through the revolving doors and into the elevator on the end, the express to eleven, her floor, home of the general manager, vice presidents, and some department heads. She waited impatiently for the doors to close. It was 8:15. She'd been up for three hours, but now her day began to really matter, and she was hungry for every critical minute of it.

2

$\mathbf{D}$IANA ROWLAND HAD WORKED FOR WLYM FOR THE PAST eleven years and for Kate Marchand for the past six. A conscientious secretary, she was fiercely protective of Kate, personally and professionally. She was also very proud to be Kate's number one secretary, for Kate was regarded as one of Boston's most powerful and influential leaders. There were times when the job, and Kate herself, were very difficult, and Diana had more than once thought that at the age of forty-six she might be ready for a calmer atmosphere. But Kate regularly increased her salary . . . and, well, it was exciting. The only problem was keeping up with Kate, and because she knew she needed a head start, she always tried to be in the office before her boss. This morning she was listening to the dictation Kate had left the previous night and was making notes as she saw Kate come through the door to her office.

"Diana, I can't bear those god-awful overhead lights in the reception area," said Kate, agitated, as she headed past Diana's desk towards her own office. "I don't suppose in this whole bloody building we could find some decent lamps." She was at her desk now, taking papers out of her briefcase. "I'm going to need the news demographics from two years ago this spring for the sales meeting. Also the recent news budget. Please get a copy of Ann Resnick's contract from the attorneys as soon as possible. Also Lynn Mallory's. Tell Andrew I'd like a meeting with him this afternoon. And why aren't the final Nielsens and Arbitrons on my desk?"

"Because I haven't received them from sales yet," answered Diana, making notes on her pad.

"I still don't understand why those reports go first to sales and not straight to me," said Kate angrily.

"Because that's the way Steven Merriam insists it be done . . . so sales can report to the general manager."

"Well, this general manager is more than capable of reading the reports herself, so would you please see to it that in the future as soon as those ratings are out, my eyes are looking at them?"

"Yes ma'am," said Diana, turning towards the door. "Oh, and good morning, Kate."

Kate looked up, wincing. "Didn't I even say good morning? I'm sorry, Diana. I'll say it twice tomorrow."

At that point a secretary from sales had come up to Diana and handed her the two ratings books. Diana took them and put them directly into Kate's outstretched hands. She then quietly closed the door and headed for the ringing telephone.

"Katherine Marchand's office." She grimaced as she heard the familiar syrupy voice on the other end of the line. It was Nora Jevile, a talk show host for WLYM's *Boston Live!* afternoon program.

"She's behind closed doors right now, Nora, and I see nothing in her calendar that indicates a luncheon date with you." When was Nora going to realize the whole station saw through her manipulations, wondered Diana, as she listened to Nora explain it wasn't written down because it had been a confidential arrangement.

"Please hold, Nora." With hesitation, she buzzed Kate. "Did you make private luncheon plans with Nora Jevile?"

"What are you talking about, Diana? You know I try to do everything possible to avoid the woman."

"Well, she's maintaining she has luncheon plans with you and that it's very important."

Kate tapped her pen on her desk. She knew that Nora would not be put off. She would insist upon a meeting, threatening to call her attorney if Kate did not at least see her.

"Do I have fifteen minutes at all today?"

"Yes," responded Diana slowly, "if the sales meeting doesn't go too long."

"All right, tell Nora to be in my office at eleven-fifteen, but also make sure you get Phil Bernelli in my office at ten-forty-five. Oh, and tell her that if she is five seconds late, the appointment is cancelled!''

Diana relayed the time, also the message about being late to Nora. The response was an angry click. Diana laughed as she punched Phil Bernelli's extension.

"Hi, Phil. Kate wants to see you at ten-forty-five."

"Oh oh . . . what did I do wrong now . . . or what is old Nora claiming I've done?"

"Funny you should ask," Diana said. "Nora's insisting on seeing Kate, but Kate wants to see you first, find out what's really going on."

Phil replaced the phone, thinking of the numerous times Nora had gone after him since he had been made producer of *Boston Live!* She hadn't been successful yet, mostly because no one pulled the wool over the eyes of Kate Marchand. But Christ, it was time-consuming. He also remembered today was ratings day. Maybe Kate would have more to say to him than business about Nora.

At that moment, Kate was busy making notes on the ratings of *Boston Live!* A distant second in the time slot, just a point away from number three, *Boston Live!* and Nora Jevile's days might very well be numbered.

Kate continued to study the ratings. Overall, it was a very good book. The station itself was still number one. Its public affairs and programming shows, with the exception of *Boston Live!*, placed well ahead of the competition. But news—there it was in black and white. Down one and then two rating points.

There was a light knock on the door and Diana entered. "Here's the information you wanted for the meeting. I'll have those contracts ready for you when you return. Andrew said the best time for him is three o'clock, but you've got a screening scheduled for three."

"What screening is that?"

"The network documentary on rape. You know, some affiliates are refusing to air it because they believe it's inflammatory. You wanted to screen it."

"Right, and that's okay, I can talk with Andrew at the same time . . . and I may want his opinion. Set up the screening for my office."

"Steven Merriam also said he was interested in screening it. He wrote you a memo about the station's image, remember?"

"He is not invited to this screening, Diana," said Kate, getting out of her chair. "If we left the image of this station up to Steven, we would lose our license for insulting the public's intelligence." She picked up the papers and strode rapidly from her office, heading for the sales meeting and Steven Merriam.

In the conference room, Merriam was using graphs to depict the nuances of the ratings. In his early fifties with dark hair that held no trace of gray (he has to dye it, thought Kate), Steven Merriam was a handsome man. Tall, with no sign of a paunch, it was clear from his fitness that he did not exaggerate his proficiency at handball. And now his hand was gripping the pointer as it made a downward tilt.

"This is our bad news . . . the news. We're slipping." Kate could have sworn she saw a smirk on Merriam's face. "And you all know what this means," Merriam continued, sounding more forceful than was necessary, "a drop of just one point means a thirty-second spot can drop five hundred to a thousand dollars."

He rambled on, telling salesmen point spreads they already knew. Occasionally, one or two of the twelve men and one woman would look in Kate's direction, but she kept her customary appearance of being aloof, if not bored, with the proceedings. She had learned long ago that "keeping them guessing" was worth far more than open debate, especially in the television industry. At most meetings or confrontations, she held her cards until the end, let her opponents wear themselves out, while she steeled herself for the showdown. She also knew that she was far more intelligent than anyone at the station and that she held the winning ace, one that very few in the industry could boast. Kate was clean. There were absolutely no skeletons, no scandals in her life. Looking around at the people in the room, she thought of the mistakes each of them had made. The outright absurdities. The affairs. The drinking. The conflicts of interest.

Men can be such fools, thought Kate. They never see beyond the immediate, they don't understand that life is a series of attachments. Steven Merriam couldn't afford, at this moment, to cut himself off from Kate so radically. She understood that but he did not. That would take an emotional as well as a strategic perception and, like most men, he was weak in dealing with issues that had an emotional base.

She leaned back in the chair and recalled that Freud had said that women were less objective than men because they were often influenced by their emotions. Initially, Kate was put off by this analysis, but then she decided to use it to her advantage. She learned to back up her instincts with knowledge, intelligence and insight. This gave her an edge over most of her male competitors, who relied solely on facts and figures. There were men in the business who managed to be more than number crunchers, but there were no such men in this room.

She looked at the one other woman, Janet Ryan, vice president for programming. Kate had brought her in from San Francisco six months earlier. In her early forties, Janet was attractive and had in this short time endeared herself to everyone from Steve Merriam to the cameramen. She was grateful to Kate for her position because in California she'd been having an affair with a network executive that was destroying both her marriage and her career.

Kate had taken a chance on Janet because her work had been so innovative. But in Boston she was still being too cautious and Kate wondered when she'd begin getting from her some creative broadcasting.

Merriam was now talking about potential slippage in the six o'clock news ratings and Kate knew it was time to make her move. She placed the gold pen down on the legal pad in front of her, and gently pushing back her chair, stood up at her place at the end of the table opposite him. The effect was as if embers of a slowly burning fireplace suddenly caught fire on the bark of a new log. All heads turned towards her. Merriam stopped.

"Continue, Steven, I'm just going to freshen this coffee." Kate walked towards the silver coffee pot on the side table. She knew she had accomplished what she desired. No one was listening to Merriam any longer. Instead, they were watching her. She felt all the eyes in the room on her back. She knew the power she had. At forty-two, and despite serious back problems, Kate Marchand could easily be mistaken for a model in her early thirties. She was five feet ten inches, with dark brown hair that fell in layers down her head to rest on her shoulders. Her eyes were deep brown with light golden flecks in them. They were always bright and clear, and they always seemed to be watching. Until five years ago, when the doctors had finally said no more, she had been a long-distance runner. Now she swam, and there wasn't a muscle in her body that was not in perfect tone. Her complexion was always flawless, the high cheekbones keeping her skin taut, but soft. It was not uncommon for people to tell her she looked very much like Jennifer O'Neil. She disagreed. She had far better carriage than Jennifer O'Neil.

Now, as she moved back to her chair, as if on cue, the room

fell silent. Kate placed her coffee to the side, sat down, and looked straight at Merriam.

"Steven, if I were to take all you have said literally, I would have to say, 'Well, gang, pack up your offices, we've been beaten. Let's shut down the number-one television station in America.' "

She smiled and everyone in the room laughed. Except Steven Merriam.

"Kate, this is serious."

"Steven, I agree we have a problem with the eleven o'clock news," said Kate just as firmly. "But why be the prophet of doom? One or two points at eleven o'clock does not alter the fact that this station is currently running the highest profit ratio of any station in the country. It is also the fastest growing. It is doing more local and syndicated programming than any other station, and at an extremely high profit. In the last two years, our profits have increased dramatically—need I remind you, any of you?" She looked at each face. It was essential that not one of them forget what she had done in the two years she had been president and general manager.

"We are journalistically, and managerially, the most re-spected broadcasting outlet in the United States. Have you so quickly forgotten that *Broadcasting* and *Fortune* magazines now refer to us as the fourth major network because of our extensive and expanding syndication?"

She paused. She had completely deflated Steven Merriam. It was he who now walked over to get a cup of coffee. No one noticed, and Kate continued. She did not want anyone to think that her power was not complete.

"All that does not mean that we should not be concerned about these ratings. We know that if we start to lose the eleven, the ratings at six may also be eaten away. We cannot afford that. Financially, of course, we could survive, but our strength is in the quality of our news, the quality of our anchor team, and the fact that our news stories are syndicated and fed by satellite throughout the United States. News is always a first priority."

She called down the room. "Steven, if I'm reading my rating book the same way you are, we're down two nights on the eleven o'clock."

"Yes," replied Steven, pleased to be back in the conversation. "One point one night, two points a second night."

"Well, I think I can see why we went down two points that second night. WZYN had the last night of the playoffs, and with

Boston in them—well, I don't need to point out what a tremendous lead-in that was for their news.''

"Yes, but they've had strong lead-ins before, and we've usually been able to come out ahead. We obviously pulled a lot of people over, why not that extra percentage?''

"Andrew?'' Kate looked at her news director, Andrew Davis. In his early fifties, he was the top of the line in news. He had come up through the ranks from copy boy to directing one of the biggest news teams outside the networks. Kate and he understood each other. They trusted each other.

"Nothing has changed, Kate. I don't believe anyone would say our quality has slipped.'' He said it in a tone that reminded you he had been a war correspondent. "I know we're not getting as much promotion as we had been.''

Kate turned to look at Peter Worijik, her head of promotion.

"We had a special we wanted to promote, and sales said they needed a few more slots to sell.'' He said it matter-of-factly, the way he knew she wanted to hear it.

"A prime time thirty-second spot is now going for over five thousand dollars. I remember when we were having trouble filling them locally and had to put in self-promotion or public service announcements. Hmmmm. . . . '' Kate made some notations on her legal pad.

"We got the IRC account, that big personal computer firm in town,'' Steven announced.

"Wonderful,'' said Kate. "That certainly more than makes up for losing a rating point and a thousand dollars at the eleven,'' she smiled, but just as quickly was stern again. "But I still don't like it. I don't want any of our news to be number two. Peter, find room for some more self-promotion of the eleven. Steven, I don't want you to lower the cost of the thirty-second spot yet.''

"Kate, you know those guys at the ad agencies look at these books as closely as we do. It's expected,'' Merriam said.

"We also have a different class of audience than ZYN,'' Kate replied. "Remind our advertisers and sponsors of that. I think they'll stay with us, certainly till the next book.'' Kate was thinking of the stock, the image. No, she wasn't going to drop the price. "And I'll talk with Marty at the network and see if we can steal a few of their self-promotion slots.''

"Ah, Kate,'' the tone of Merriam's voice was questioning, so Kate knew he was about to come forward with a suggestion. She did not look up but kept writing and quietly said, "Yes?''

"I think it might be worth considering, over the next few

months. . . ." His voice was hesitant. "Since we're so worried about news ratings, maybe we should have a stronger five-thirty lead-in. That five-thirty news is not too strong. It makes a profit, but we could draw a larger audience with, say, *Family Feud*."

Kate took a deep breath before she raised her head and bore down on Steven Merriam.

"You want to replace the five-thirty news with a witless game show?" Kate's voice rose as she did. "We have the only five-thirty news in the city. It wins its time slot. It has won two Emmys. It provides a service for those who cannot watch the six. Sure, we'd make more money with *Family Feud*. We'd also put some people out of work. And we would do serious damage to our reputation as a leader in news in New England and the East Coast. No. Do not even consider it. Don't any of you waste a moment's thought on that suggestion."

Kate flipped through the other sheets of paper she had brought along. She stopped and studied one, then again looked up at Merriam. "Steven, I want you to know, I screened those tapes of that new cooking show, the half-hour one with that aging actor and actress. I can't remember their names, but it's unimportant." She could, in fact, remember the names, but wanted to definitely undermine Steven's advocacy. "You suggest putting that in and pulling out one of the network soaps in the afternoon. I believe you referred to it in your memorandum as 'innovative' and 'bound for syndication.' Well, nothing could be further from the truth. Julia Child and the quality that PBS puts into her program, perhaps, but not this amateurish bullshit, and *never* to replace a soap. You know the network would be livid. The audience would be livid. And cooking shows are just not what the audience is after anymore."

Merriam's face was red with anger, and he slammed down his fist. The others sitting around the large conference table were shocked. No one behaved that way around Kate Marchand. Kate said nothing but waited for Merriam to speak.

"You don't make any sense sometimes, Kate." He saw the bolt in her eye and heard the groan from Andrew Davis, and tried to retract. "I mean, it's not you. It's the system. You say we have to stand by our reputation for news and information. This show is information, but in this case you defend a soap opera." By the time he was finished, his voice was almost inaudible. He felt his vocal chords were being slashed by Kate's eyes.

Kate paused and leaned back in her chair. "I did not want to bring this up, because I thought it unfair to you, but from your manner I'd guess you require an additional piece of information. You have always underestimated me, Steven. You must stop doing that. My colleagues,'' Kate gestured around the table, ''perhaps Steven is interested in cooking. But I wonder whether his enthusiasm for this particular show has anything to do with the fact that it is produced and put on the market by Dolfo-Kelly Associates, his brother-in-law's production company.''

''That's not the only reason. That's not even a factor,'' Merriam said. ''They're good, very good.''

''They're shit, Steven. And you know, and I know and probably everyone at this table knows that. At this station we know how to call them. That's why we're number one. We go for quality, not because we want to help out a fledgling production company—that by the way, cannot even guarantee ten shows.''

She leaned forward on to the table, crossing her arms. ''And to answer your question on why I defend the soap operas: I don't defend them all. Some are trash. The writing—and sometimes the acting—can be the equivalent of a second grade play. But they give people a chance to care about somebody and to think about something other than their own lives. They're like a dream machine for a lot of people out there, glitzy and glamorous but also dealing with hard issues. The networks push the soaps on us, that's true. But, as long as they don't completely control daytime programming, there's no harm in it.''

She sat back, and began assembling her notes. ''After Steven's briefing, and then our discussion here, I think we've covered everything. Overall, you can all see the Nielsens and Arbitrons keep us solidly ahead in the market. We are a very, very strong number one in most categories. We should be very proud. I certainly am very proud of each of you, and the sales team that keeps those profits up.'' She nodded to Merriam and then said, ''I'll be calling another sales meeting soon to announce new proposals and some exciting news.''

3

BACK IN HER OWN RECEPTION AREA, KATE PULLED A TINY tape recorder from her jacket pocket and placed it on a clean spot on the typist's desk. "I'm only interested in transcribing the very end of the meeting . . . say the last twelve or fifteen minutes. Begin the transcription where Steven Merriam begins arguing for replacing the five-thirty news with *Family Feud*. Diana, would you come in, please?"

Diana followed Kate, closing the door behind her. Kate immediately headed for the couch and lay down. She took several deep breaths, cursing the chairs in the conference room with every exhalation. Diana sat in a chair opposite, notepad ready. She was used to Kate's having to pause several times during the day, and now she watched as the sharp pain slowly began to pull away from her boss's face.

"Diana," Kate's voice was calm and exact, "I want you to call all the major—and maybe some of the minor—talent agencies and agents in every major market city. I want you to talk to everyone from Abrams in New York to Samson in Los Angeles. Chicago. Dallas. Miami. Hit them all. Tell them that WLYM is looking for a good female journalist who wants to become the star of America's best television station. And let it be known I'll offer big money. Keep it confidential please. But please, please, Diana, spare me those good-looking airheads who have done a few decent reports and now think they're ready for the big leagues. You know, the ones in search of all the 'glamour.' "

As if suddenly angry, Kate pushed herself up from the couch. "Glamour! That's what they expect, isn't it, all those starry-eyed communication students—male *and* female?"

Kate walked to her desk and flipped through a few folders. "It's not glamorous to work sixteen hour days, seven days a week. Not glamorous to be constantly questioning, demanding, researching, learning. . . . Yes, learning. And feeling, and then learning not to feel."

Diana thought, though she did not say it, that the woman before her had paid her dues in a cut-throat industry but that most people would view Katherine Marchand's life as glamorous indeed. If they only knew . . .

Kate looked up, returning Diana's gaze. "And you don't get paid for listening to my tirades on the delusions about this industry. Forgive me, Diana."

"Oh, it does me good to hear it every once in a while," Diana said lightly. "Even if you are dashing the dreams of thousands."

"Dreams. It takes a hell of a lot more than dreams to survive—really survive—in this industry. More than dreams to survive with class and influence. More than dreams to command the public's respect and attention. . . ." And with that, Kate smiled and winked at Diana. "Please keep this search for new talent confidential."

"Of course," said Diana, back in step. "Is this wonder woman supposed to be black or white?"

"Diana, we've already got one black anchor, and it's a miracle Boston has accepted him. Let's not push our luck." She paused. "Are you going to turn me in to the NAACP for discrimination?"

"No, I'm just going to have my black brothers and sisters start spending a lot of time at your place in Dover." Diana laughed.

"Okay. Keep me posted on your progress. You can send Phil in." As Kate watched Diana leave the office, she gently touched the small bronzed eagle that sat on her desk. The inscription read:

> You are most brave
> like an eagle soaring in a cloudless sky
> the wind blows and all return to their nest
> but you continue into the wind

The thunder clamors
you challenge with your song
The lightning dances
You never swerve from your flight.

Diana had given her the eagle, with the inscription by Bette Bao Lord, during her battle for the presidency and general managership. Diana had never let her faith in Kate falter, nor had she allowed her to believe that the board would choose Steven Merriam over Kate.

A few minutes later, Diana sent Phil Bernelli in to see her. Kate gestured toward a chair and came from behind her desk to sit close to Phil. She sometimes found her desk an intrusion between herself and her guest, and frequently, a barrier to the truth. As she sat down, she clicked her mind into the computer that would call up the name of Phil Bernelli. In his middle thirties, he had been recruited from New York to produce *Boston Live!* and to increase its ratings. He now seemed older, more haggard than she remembered. An attractive, olive-skinned man, there were dark circles under his eyes, and he was nervously tapping his fingers on the armchair.

"Is there a reason why you feel nervous, Phil?"

"Oh," he looked at his hand, "an old habit." He didn't offer any more information.

"All right, Phil, what the hell's going on down on the eighth floor with *Boston Live!*?"

Phil looked surprised. "Nothing. Everything's fine. I take it the ratings reflect otherwise?"

"The ratings haven't changed, and that's not the reason for this conversation." Kate was puzzled by his defensiveness. "Nora Jevile is insisting on seeing me. I know Nora. I know what a troublemaker she is. I like to be prepared before she starts making charges—which she no doubt will."

Phil leaned forward. "The problem is, very simply, that I'm not willing to put up with Nora Jevile anymore." He had almost shouted the last four words, and immediately regretted it. "I'm sorry. It's been a trying week."

"Don't apologize, Phil. I don't pay you to put up with Nora. But could you be a little more specific?"

Phil looked down to his hands. What he was about to do was very risky. Producers had to be very careful of what they said about their talent. Talent was usually much stronger than any producer. Talent had the clout: the viewing audience. Producers were easily replaced, talent was not, especially when you considered contracts worth hundreds of thousands of dollars.

"Well, Kate, for starters, Nora can't even show up on time for interviews in the field. Last week, we lost the interview—an exclusive—with Joan Kennedy. Nora was forty-five minutes late, said it was the traffic. Joan split after waiting a half hour." He hesitated as he saw Kate's back stiffen. Although he had had few encounters with the general manager, he knew her reputation for honesty and fairness. "And then she's late in the studio. The director can't go through the show without her, and so it gets hurried, and camera cues are off. Then Nora blames the director. And you know Jenny, she's one of the most dedicated directors in the building. And one of the best."

"Yes, I know. Go on." Kate had moved from the chair to behind her desk, where she sat down and started making notes on a yellow legal pad.

"Nora's unprepared. I don't think she even goes through the material the associate producers put together for her. And it shows on the air. And there are all the petty things. I found out she uses the limousine service for personal friends, and bills it to *Boston Live!* Or uses it to cab her son to school, or for deliveries from the pharmacy and liquor store. And when I bring up any of this stuff, I get hysterical calls from her at two A.M. where she cries and begs my forgiveness and says it will never happen again, and she just needs my support. And I say okay . . . and then it starts all over again."

Kate was about to speak when her buzzer sounded. "Yes, Diana."

"Nora Jevile is here, Ms. Marchand." Ordinarily Kate would have laughed at Diana's formality, but she felt a rising anger inside her, and was in no mood for frivolity.

"I'll be free in a minute, Diana." She looked at her digital clock: 11:14. Just barely, thought Kate.

"Can I slip out the back entrance?" Phil wished to avoid an encounter with Nora coming out of Kate's office. He also didn't know how Kate was reacting to his information.

"Oh, no, Phil," said Kate sternly, "I want you right here when I talk to Nora. I want to make sure that she knows you have heard every word I have said." She walked over to the door and opened it briskly. "Come in, Nora." Diana stepped forward and handed Kate a letter from the morning mail. "Letter from a viewer I thought you might be interested in." Kate thought it was a strange time for Diana to bother her with a viewer comment, but she realized Diana must have good reason.

As soon as Nora noticed Phil she said, "Oh, and what brings *you* here?" The hostility in her voice cut the air like shards of glass.

"*I* asked him to be here." Kate sat behind her desk, quickly scanned the letter Diana had handed her, then raised her eyes and looked directly into Nora's eyes.

It was as if Nora Jevile had been struck. She was visibly thrown back in her chair. Phil Bernelli had never seen a look like that. He was grateful he was not on the receiving end.

"So, Nora, you wanted to see me?" Kate's voice was solemn.

"Well, I did want to see you alone."

"Is this of a personal nature, or a professional matter?"

"Well, professional."

"Then there's absolutely no reason why your producer should not be here."

"If that's the way you want it, Kate, it's fine with me." Kate watched Nora straighten herself in her chair, and found herself critically assessing her appearance. A former model, Nora had in recent months let herself go. The layered brown hair looked too teased and ragged. Her complexion, despite a great deal of makeup, was that of a pizza-loving teenager. Her lipstick and nail polish were too red, and the pants she was wearing accentuated the pounds she had gained.

Kate got up and walked over to the window, placing her hand at the back of her neck and stretching slightly.

"I love that blouse, Kate. Where did you get it?" Nora asked.

"I don't remember. Maybe at Filene's basement. But let's get going. I have a busy day, and I'm not sure this meeting should even be happening."

"Well, I disagree. I would think you would very much want to know when your talent is being mistreated."

"Mistreated?" Phil looked at her astonished.

Kate ignored Phil's remark. "Would you care to elaborate, Nora?"

"Well, Kate, you know how hard I have always worked, and I still don't get paid anywhere near what other people around here get paid."

"You get paid a hundred and thirty-five thousand dollars a year plus a clothing allowance of $10,000, although most of your clothing is on a trade from Saks. We pay for your dry cleaning, your makeup, your parking. It is adequate. And you're right, it is not equivalent to what we pay our anchors and others. But you do not work the hours they do or, may I remind you, command the ratings they do.''

''Well, the ratings have only slipped in the last couple of years. Four years ago we were number one. And perhaps the ratings would be higher if the talent was treated a little better.'' Nora glared at Phil, who was still in shock that this menace to an entire staff was being paid over $135,000 a year.

''Is that what brings you here today, Nora?'' Kate had returned to her desk.

''Yes, Kate, I'm being nickled and dimed to death. It is absurd. I can't even take a cab to shoots, I have to take my own car. I have important speaking engagements and Phil is not allowing me to use the limousine service. My expense accounts are being questioned. I am just not being treated with the proper respect. And how can someone do their job properly when they don't feel they have the support of the producer . . . or management?''

''Phil, what's this about speaking engagements and the limousine?'' Kate didn't look up and Phil wondered if the tide had turned against him.

''Well, I don't know anything about speaking engagements. I just have receipts from the limousine service where they chauffeured Nora and a companion between her home and a downtown theater. Her home and a restaurant. And then apparently just a leisurely drive one Sunday down to the Cape.''

''Nora?''

''Well, those were all people important to Channel Three.''

''Like who?'' Kate doodled on the legal pad in front of her.

''Well, I'd rather not say. My private life is confidential.''

''*Not* when you're in a company limousine!'' Kate now stared at Nora. ''Do you know the last time *I* was in a limousine? When the Vice President of the United States was in town last summer. And it was *his* limousine. Other people, management and talent, do not ask for that kind of special treatment. Why do you think you're entitled to it?''

''Well, I always was, until Phil came along.''

Kate put down her pen and looked directly at Nora. ''I am sorry, Nora. Apparently in the past you have not had competent producers.''

''Well,'' Nora said, rising from her chair, ''I never thought I would lose *your* support, Kate. I thought friendships meant more to you.''

"Sit down, Nora. We haven't gone through my agenda for this meeting yet." Kate hit a button on her intercom. "Diana, would you come in here, please?"

Diana quickly came through the door, her notepad in hand. She took a seat to Kate's right.

"Please take notes." Diana nodded, hearing the ice in Kate's voice and knowing that what she really wanted was a second witness to whatever was about to happen.

Kate crossed her arms and cleared her throat, saying, "You have a real problem, Nora. You don't seem to be able to deal with time—other people's time. You keep your director waiting, your producer waiting, cameramen waiting, Joan Kennedy waiting."

"I had a family emergency," Nora interrupted.

Phil jolted his head. "You told me you were stuck in traffic."

"Oh, I can't remember every shoot," Nora slammed her hand down on the arm of the chair.

"There is to be no more lateness on this show. Phil, I hold you responsible for seeing that everyone is ready exactly when they should be. This is a business that runs on the clock and anyone who isn't professional enough to know that isn't professional enough to work for us." Kate paused and then said, "And Nora, start learning your material. You have a whole staff that does all your research, lays out all your questions, does everything—so *you* can look good. And lately you're blowing it. I saw an interview last week where it was clear you had no idea what you were talking about." Kate had nothing specific in mind, but knew it wouldn't be hard to find one. When Nora didn't ask her which show she meant, Kate knew she was hitting the mark.

"What I'm saying is, you're slipping, and what may be worse," Kate leaned towards her, "you're becoming abusive— and I will not allow *anyone* in this station to be abused or to be abusive. I remind you, you are a representative of Channel Three."

Kate took a deep breath and walked to the windows. She moved her hands along the grates, and then stopped, as if to study the large diamond on her right hand. Diana saw Kate's back straighten and thought, "Oh, oh, she was just warming up."

"Phil," Kate spoke very quietly, her back still to the group, "do you recall the remote you did two weeks ago from the cardinal's private residence?"

"Yes, of course."

"Was Nora on time for the taping?"

"Well, no. She was late."

"Did you see her when she came into the residence?"

"Yes, Jenny and I had been standing there, waiting."

"Was she drinking when she arrived?"

"What's going on? What's all this about?" Nora was on her feet, almost shouting.

Kate turned. "Sit down, Nora. Why don't *you* answer these questions?"

Nora stared at Kate. "I was just having some orange juice," Nora said, now calm. "It had been a very long day. You know how they can be, Kate?"

"Combined with vodka, I understand." Kate went to her desk and picked up the letter Diana had handed her earlier. "Do you recall any particular conversations you had that day at the cardinal's residence?"

"Well, no, we just did the show."

"Maybe this will jog your memory." Kate looked at the letter. "This is from a Sister Mary Catherine, secretary to the cardinal. I'll just read the last two paragraphs. 'I find it very disrespectful that Ms. Jevile was drinking on the grounds of His Eminence's residence. When I mentioned to her that perhaps she should not, she replied, "I'll do what I want, where I want." I then told her that I was going to write a letter to you, adding that I was certain that a woman of your stature in the community would never allow such behavior. She laughed and said, "Who do you think I just came from drinking with? Who do you think is my best friend and my best drinking companion?" Ms. Marchand, I find it hard to believe that what this woman says is accurate, but if it is, you are violating a trust and a respect that thousands of aspiring women have in you. I am going to file a formal complaint with the FCC concerning Ms. Jevile's behavior. As for your role in this, I suggest some spiritual introspection. I have discussed this with the cardinal and he has told me to inform you that Channel 3 will no longer be welcome at the cardinal's residence.' "

Kate gently put the letter down and walked in front of her desk again, crossing her arms and staring at Nora.

"Well, it's not true," Nora said. "That bitch. I wouldn't act that way. And she can't keep the press out of the cardinal's residence."

"It's a private residence. The cardinal can keep out Jesus

Christ if he wants." Kate realized she was raising her voice, and immediately calmed down. "You admitted you were drinking, and if you expect me to believe you over a servant of God, you are sadly mistaken. Now, get this straight, Nora. I will not allow you or anyone else to dirty the name of WLYM. This station has fought too hard to be respected and trusted and you've abused that trust. And you have also implied that the woman who runs this station is a pathetic drunk who keeps company with rude, arrogant egocentrics."

Kate turned to Diana, who handed her a photocopied page, with a section underlined.

"Your contract, like all contracts in this station, has a clause allowing for it to be revoked with a ninety-day notice on grounds of 'drunkenness, insubordination, or repeated inability to live up to the terms' of said contract. Just about fits this situation to a T, doesn't it?"

Nora's head shot up. "You can't, Kate. Please. It will never happen again."

"I certainly hope not. To make sure, though, your contract is revoked. We'll be willing to put you on a month-to-month contract, but you will be reviewed by Phil and me at the end of every month. If you want to prove yourself, now is your chance. Diana will contact your agent this afternoon and if he agrees, a new contract will be drawn up."

"But, Kate. . . ."

"It's either that, or nothing, Nora. Let Diana know your decision this afternoon."

Dismissed, Nora left the office as Kate said, "Phil, please stay a moment."

When Diana closed the door behind Nora, Kate said to the producer, "I want this entire conversation to be kept confidential. It is not good for your staff or this station to know Nora's problems."

"But certainly she will say something."

"Oh, yes, but it will be something like how I told her how valuable she was and offered her more money. That's her style. Anyway, keep careful documentation on her and thank you for your help."

"Thank *you*." When he left the office, Diana said, "After I read Sister Mary's letter, I thought that would be the end of Nora."

"No, like it or not, that woman still has a following and I can't afford any negative publicity right now, especially if I'm going to replace Ann. But don't worry, Diana, Nora will do herself in. Now, would you please get Sister Mary Catherine on the phone for me so I can make a personal appointment with the cardinal? And by the way, check where I was that day."

"I already did. You were speaking in New York . . . to B'nai B'rith."

Kate put her head in her hands. "Shit, why couldn't it have been the Catholic Youth Organization?"

As she was arranging an appointment with the cardinal, Kate turned in her chair so her legs could rest on the edge of her desk. Not very ladylike, she thought, but it kept the back pain down. Pain was a poison that sometimes fogged her mind, and that she could not afford.

Kate's private phone rang a few minutes later.

"Is this a bad time, Mrs. Marchand?"

"Not at all, Doctor. I was just arranging to run off with the butler."

"We don't have one. Have you noticed?"

"Hey, I thought neurosurgeons were supposed to be rich. Let's get one."

And then, laughing with her husband, Kate said, "I've got a *New York Times* interview coming up, Jonathan, and I've got to prepare."

"Right, ma'am. I'll meet you at Maison Robert. Seven o'clock?"

"Seven-thirty?"

"Seven twenty-eight. And that's final."

When Kate replaced the phone, she was smiling. She looked out her windows, beyond the buildings, and out where the ocean and the horizon joined. You are a lucky woman, Kate Marchand, she thought, watching a tanker move out to sea. You have everything you want. You're one of the most respected businesswomen in America, a leader in international communication networks. You are blessed with a few good, loyal friends. You have a husband who, in his own right, is one of medicine's guiding forces. And you love him very much, to boot. And he loves you. Very much. Of course he does . . .

Abruptly, she pulled her feet off her desk, swiveled her chair around, and studied the latest ratings and sales figures so that she would recite them spontaneously and exactly during the forthcoming interview. Then Diana's voice came over the intercom, informing her that Mike Colby of the *Times* had arrived.

She straightened the scattered papers on her desk and went to greet her visitor.

Mike Colby was immediately struck by Kate's poise and sleekness. Like a leopard moving across its own turf—beautiful, fearless, with a silent but very real power—that's how he saw Katherine Marchand.

"Mike, you look splendid," Kate was saying. "It's been so long. You look younger than you deserve to." She stretched her hand forward, smiled broadly and then winked.

"Kate, Katherine, television and Boston certainly do become you. Are you still running around with that doctor?"

"If you're still as fine a reporter as you were, you know damn well I am, and you can probably also tell me his salary and the name of his secretary's baby."

"William."

"I knew it." She threw back her head and laughed. "Enough, you've met Diana and Judy. Let's talk, and you can tell me what this is all about."

In her office she went to a cabinet in the corner. "Can I get you something to drink?"

"I'll just join you in anything, Katherine."

"You sure you want a Diet Pepsi?"

"Sounds fine."

Kate poured the drinks, watching Mike peruse her office. He commented on the painting across from her desk, a large and powerful city scene by a successful Boston painter.

"It must be a relief to look from those screens to the painting," said Mike softly, pointing to the three TV sets whose screens flickered incessantly.

"You know, sometimes I have trouble figuring out which is more real, the Boston in the picture, or the television screens."

"Can I quote you on that, Katherine?"

"Oh Lord, Mike," said Kate, choosing this time to sit behind her desk. "What's this 'Katherine' stuff? Relax, and remember, I was 'Kate' on the streets and I still am. I haven't changed."

"For Christ's sake, Kate, you're the most powerful woman in the American media. Everyone knows you're shaking up WLYM, the network, and its subsidiaries and affiliates more than anyone likes. Don't tell me you haven't changed. You've been on the cover of *Time* and *Fortune*."

"I haven't made *Newsweek* yet," Kate laughed. She made the gesture of a toast towards Mike who responded with his own raised glass.

"Well, *The New York Times* would like to get in on the act—do it better of course."

"So that's what brings you to my door. And here I thought it was just a friendly affair."

"I grabbed this job for myself. You know I don't do much writing any more, as a senior editor. I thought I might be able to add something to this story that would escape my colleagues."

"Well, there's no doubt about that. You and I go back quite a while. I hope you'll be discreet, though. I'll give you all the firepower you need to do a damn good piece, Mike."

"I understand, Kate," he said. "I just want the old 'what makes Kate run and where is she running to?' "

"Well, I take it that in that briefcase is a tape recorder. Might as well get it out," she smiled warmly. "No sense being misquoted." She set down her glass, and pointed to her own recorder. "Okay with you?"

Mike nodded. "I guess we begin at the beginning," he said.

"Well, as you know, because you were there before me—and snubbed me—I joined the reporting staff of *The New York Times* early in the sixties."

Mike interrupted. "Now, Kate, I didn't snub you."

Kate laughed. "Well, not as badly as some of the other guys."

"In any case, we're getting ahead of ourselves. I've got to go back to before that . . . you know, the childhood and Mom and Dad and favorite puppies."

"Oh, for God's sake."

"Come on, Katherine O'Shaughnessey, you know what people want to know. Now, do you cooperate, or do I have to go talk to Mom and Dad?"

Kate sighed, and turned to look out towards the horizon. "I wish you could," she said softly. She leaned her head back, pushing her shoulders into the firmness of the leather, and tried to let her body relax.

"Margaret Ann O'Shaughnessey gave birth to Katherine Marie O'Shaughnessey on May first, 1940, at St. Luke's Hospital in Chicago. Daddy, Lieutenant William Paul O'Shaughnessey, was serving his country in Italy at the time. I grew up on the South Side of Chicago, not exactly poor, but my father was a meat packer and his salary wasn't what you'd call extravagant. But his love was—and my mother's. I was an only child and my parents doted on me. Even when the sisters at St. Mary's com-

plained about my unladylike behavior and how I'd read the
newspaper in class.''

Kate suddenly started to laugh. "Remember how I would
always hang out at the Cedar Tavern in New York, reading newspaper after newspaper?''

"How could I forget? You were the most unsociable person
in the bar.''

"Well, that's a habit that probably began when I was around
nine or ten.'' She saw Mike's head tilt. "Not the drinking. Every
Thursday and Friday, my father would get out of the plant early,
around three, and he'd go to O'Toole's and sit with the other
men and drink beer and talk. Well, O'Toole's was on my way
home from St. Mary's. And one day, Daddy saw me walking
past, and came out and got me and sat me on his lap and introduced his baby girl. It eventually became a ritual. Every Thursday and Friday, Daddy would save me a seat at the bar, and I'd
come in, with my parochial school uniform on and all, and I'd
have a Coke and pore over every newspaper I could find in the
bar. Then around five, we'd head home for supper. At first
Mother had a fit, but my father was very bullheaded. He got his
way. So my history in bars goes back a long way.''

"Oh God.'' Kate sat forward suddenly. "I should never have
told you that story.''

"Why, for God's sake? It's innocent enough.''

Kate told him, off the record, of her problems with Sister
Mary Catherine's letter. Mike was laughing. "So wait until the
cardinal reads you began barhopping at age nine.''

"It was just one bar, and you could phrase it a little differently. It was also a great educational experience—I learned all
about boxing and which champions were really Irish—and that's
come in very handy throughout my life . . . I just don't remember how.''

Mike interrupted. "You don't remember? You never forgot
anything in your life. Are you still a walking computer?''

"The truth is, I don't forget, Mike, for whatever that's worth.
Some things, of course, you remember far more vividly than
others. Often things you wish you didn't remember quite so well
. . . like my last time at O'Toole's.''

"It was just before my twelfth birthday and I came bouncing
into the bar as usual. It didn't seem as crowded as usual and
then I noticed my father's stool was empty. We always sat in the
same place, the corner by the windows. I plopped onto my stool,
swung my book bag up on the bar, and turned towards the door,

expecting to see Daddy coming in right behind me. Paddy gave me my Coke, then walked down to the other end of the bar, and talked quietly with two other men who worked with my father. Just then the paperboy came to the door of the bar with the afternoon edition. He was shouting, 'Wall collapses at packing plant. Over thirty dead.' I looked at the stool next to me, jumped down, grabbed a paper from the startled paperboy, and went running home, screaming, crying and trying to read the paper at the same time.''

She stopped talking, and allowed herself, as she rarely did, to watch the image of the frightened, screaming girl, running under the El through the streets of the South Side of Chicago.

''My grandparents came from Nebraska to live with us for a short while after my father died. After a couple of months, they decided that we were pretty well set and they could go home. I said goodbye to them one morning, and then couldn't understand why, when I came home from school that afternoon, they were still there.''

Kate took a sip of her soda. Placing it down thoughtfully, she began to pace the wall by the television sets, trailing her hand across the top of them.

''From what I understand, because my grandparents rarely spoke of it in later years, Mother had gone to say goodbye to them at the train station. As they were walking up to the platform, my mother stopped, said she was dizzy, and then collapsed. She was dead when they got her to the hospital. Cerebral hemorrhage. Right out of the blue. Died instantly. So I grew up in Lincoln, Nebraska, with Grandma and Grandpa, who did a wonderful job, whom I love very much, and who, by the way, both passed away four years ago.''

''Jesus, Kate, that's a bitch,'' Mike said. ''I never knew any of that.''

''Well, there were no more surprises. I went to high school in Lincoln. My grandparents were pretty well off. I was president of my class, valedictorian. Wanted to go West, so I went to Berkeley for two years, then transferred to Columbia. Worked from midnight to eight A.M. on the copy desk of the *Daily News* in New York. Graduated, went to the *Times*, got my master's from Columbia . . . and you know the rest.''

''Hold on, hold on, hold on. We just went through ten years of your life in ten seconds.'' Mike jumped up.

She walked back to her desk and sat down. ''And what type

of person have I become? What was the influence of all that? I'll bet you can answer yourself.''

"Determined. Hard. Tough," Mike said. "Some might say cold, even ruthless.''

"I'm sure they do," smiled Kate. "People have trouble dealing with power.''

"And do you enjoy your power?''

"Yes," Kate said firmly.

Mike didn't know how to respond, or to pursue the question. "What brought you to New York?''

"I wanted the big city. New York was where a lot of the newspapers were, and I had never been in the East. At first, when I got there, I was amazed at how cold Easterners were, unfriendly.''

"Unfriendly?" inquired Mike.

"Well, I told you that while I was in college I worked the night shift on the copy desk of the *Daily News*. I was the first woman ever to do that, and those men really didn't like it. Never once in two years did one of those men speak to me as a person. They'd just toss copy at me and yell what size headline. Occasionally, they'd put cigars out in my Coke or ginger ale. Now, that's a little unfriendly, isn't it? And need I remind you how outright hostile some of my male counterparts on the *Times* were? And despite three years of busting my ass and working my way up from a street reporter to a political reporter, only three men congratulated me when I won the fellowship to Yale Law School. You were one of them, I'm proud to say.''

"No, I'm proud to admit it. Remember, that fellowship had never gone to a woman before, and people didn't think you had enough experience.''

"That's the story of my life, Mike. No one has ever thought I've had enough experience. So far, I've proven them wrong at each turn. And it began at Yale Law School. A dean later admitted to me that he had to really push for me to be chosen. The arguments against me were the proverbial too young, not enough experience. He kept saying, 'but she has talent, vision.' Sixteen years later, when I was fighting for the presidency and general managership of WLYM, those same arguments came up.''

The hardness was in her brown eyes again and Mike thought he'd hate to be one of those men, or women, who went against Kate.

"So now you've got two degrees from Columbia, one from Yale Law School, and you're a *Times* reporter.''

"Right. And then I got into television. I took a job at NRB's network affiliate in Chicago."

Kate watched as Mike went through what looked like her extensive vitae. When he spoke again, Mike said, "Within six months, the network had pulled you out of Chicago, and you were reporting nationally on camera. I've gone back through the files and found some reviews of your work. There wasn't a critic who didn't think you would become the goddess of the airwaves." Mike looked up at her, expecting to see a smile.

Kate said sternly, "I worked hard, Mike, against heavy odds. The network had me all over the country, and outside of it, even Vietnam. And on the other side of it, I was among the privileged reporters who got to feel a cop's nightstick up the ass in the 'sixty-eight riots at the Convention. Eventually I got myself into more documentary work and did modestly well at it."

"Modestly well!" Mike said. "Two Emmys and the Edward R. Murrow Award. I'd say that wasn't exactly modest."

"Excellent preparation, sir. Do you also know that in nineteen-seventy, I went for the slot of associate producer of the evening news, and with the producer, Marty Rathjens, took it from number three to number one? Then Marty got a chance for the vice presidency of the network. He went for it, and it was assumed that I'd replace him." Kate rose from her desk, and hit the side of it with her hand.

"Oh, yeah, I remember that. One of the most obvious cases of discrimination against a woman. They pulled in the head of the sports department instead. The Network certainly took flak for that. A lot of people resigned, too, didn't they? Out of loyalty to you?"

"Yes, bless them, and so did I. It was a very difficult time." Kate clenched her fists as she remembered. She was now pacing again and her footsteps were not gentle on the floor. "I couldn't believe it had happened, that it *could* happen."

Kate's buzzer snapped her back to the present. "Yes, Diana? Oh, you're right," she looked at her watch. "Could you come here for a moment?" She replaced the receiver and turned to Mike. "I'm temporarily out of time. We can move on from this later, but in the meantime, why don't I have Diana give you the old chef's tour?"

"Diana, I'm sure Mike would like to talk to people," Kate said when her secretary entered. "He is to have access to whom-ever he wishes . . . from gofers to vice presidents. And if people are busy, tell them I said to make time for him." Kate paused. "And you don't have to listen to his questions."

"You're opening up everyone in this station to say whatever they want to me?" asked Mike, incredulously.

"Of course. Why not? I told you I have nothing to hide. And I don't think you will find many complaints here that I don't already know about and am trying to do something about. Just do me the favor of rebutting any comments like the station is being sold to an Arab sheik or something like that."

Mike laughed, Diana ushered in Andrew Davis, the news director, and as she closed Kate's door again, Mike said, "That woman's either flawless, or very foolish."

"She may be many things, Mr. Colby, but one thing she isn't, is foolish."

4

ANDREW DAVIS SAT DOWN QUICKLY AND IMMEDIATELY BE-
gan shuffling through the pile of papers on his lap. "Don't rush,
Andrew, I've got to get my own material together here," Kate
said, as she pulled folders toward her.

Again, Kate had reason to be grateful for the small white
button underneath the front lip of her desk. While Mike Colby
was in her office, she had hit the button gently, thereby lighting
a blue disc on the side of Diana's telephone. The light stayed on
until Diana hit another button on her telephone console. It was
a system Kate had set up over a year before and it meant Diana
was to do whatever was necessary to bring to a halt the meeting
Kate was in. She rarely had to use the system, except with the
overzealous or in meetings that were frivolous and a waste of
her time. In this instance, Kate's summons was based on self-
protection. Colby had been getting into an area about which
Kate was still very vulnerable. She wanted time to catch her
breath and assemble her thoughts. Otherwise, Kate knew there
was the chance she might say something she would regret.

"Kate," the sound of Andrew's voice jolted her back to the
present, "I know this isn't what you want to discuss, but Christ,
don't tell me you're one of those secret soap watchers."

"You mean because of my defense of the soaps in the sales
meeting today?"

"Yes, very eloquent, Kate."

"Andrew, look at these screens right now. All the major net-works are carrying soaps in the middle of the afternoon." One screen showed a couple kissing. One showed two men chasing a young girl through an empty theater. And the last showed a woman lying in a hospital bed, sobbing, a weary man beside her, caressing her cheek.

Kate turned up the volume from her remote control desk top as she spoke of each one. "Exhibit A, two people, obviously in love. The viewer watching is in love, too, and believes in love, and has hope. Exhibit B. You can bet this young woman is a favorite on this soap. She's in trouble, and right now there are millions of people rooting for her, and unlike in real life, you can be sure she'll make it to safety. Some hero will come out of the shadows and save her. Exhibit C." Kate again turned up the volume on this set. The man was saying how much he loved the woman in the hospital bed, stroking her beautiful face, and that although she was leaving him, she would always be with him. "Heart-breaking, isn't it?" Kate said as she and Andrew con-tinued to watch the screen. "Now, if you and I were faithful watchers of this soap, which by the way is ours, we'd be bawling like little kids right now, because those script writers would have already had us fall in love with both these people. So, we get to cry, we get to release some emotions. And then, you know what the best part is? The viewers may have learned how fragile hu-man life is but they can wipe their tears and comfort themselves with, 'She's not really dead. It's just a soap opera.' As for me, don't you think I have enough intrigue and trauma right here, without watching it on TV?"

"Yeah, but not enough sex." Andrew grinned.

"Glad you brought that up. Tell me, is it helping or hurting their work that Betty and Warren are investigating each other's libido?"

"Shit! You don't miss a trick, do you?"

"I try not to," answered Kate, "but I also keep a very strict policy of not giving a damn about romance unless the work suffers or it begins to reflect on the integrity of Channel Three. I don't throw stones, but I do throw boulders at people who don't work."

"I think we're okay. They're both working well and the affair seems to add a little spice to their performance."

"Right. So, what the hell is that investigative team doing, Andrew? There hasn't been anything out of them in over three weeks. Not even so much as a pollution scoop. I didn't say anything in this morning's meeting when you talked of quality, but to be honest, I think we are slipping a bit. We've always had something special going on. Is it my imagination, or do I detect a bit of lethargy in the newsroom?''

Andrew sighed and leaned back in his chair, throwing his head back and looking at the ceiling. Kate crossed her hands in back of her head and waited.

"As usual, you're very perceptive," Andrew began, his voice heavy. "I can't really put my finger on it, but it's like we're just coasting. On the day-to-day stories, we're right there and the reporting is still the best in the city. But we're missing that creative push."

"We're missing that risk-taking, going out and digging hard for a story that matters," Kate said.

"It's like everyone's too comfortable," said Andrew, leaning toward her. "You know the old story about why change a winning formula? They all believe they're number one, which they are, so why rock the boat?"

Kate felt herself growing agitated, and picked up the ratings report on the side of her desk, just a few feet from Andrew's face.

"Because we're no longer number one!" Kate shouted. "I didn't push it in the sales meeting this morning, but I'm damned concerned. If ZYN can get at our eleven, they can get at our six. You know that. And look at our six o'clock numbers." Andrew was shuffling through the Nielsen report, trying to find the right page. "Steve Merriam only saw the bottom line on the six—that we're still number one. But look at it, Andrew!" A finely manicured finger pointed to a line of numbers. "Our lead is down to only one and two points. We used to carry 15's and 16's, compared to ZYN's 11's and 12's. Now, look. We're 15's and 14's, they're 12's and 13's, and even JTH has gained . . . 7's and 8's. We're losing viewers to the third-ranking station in town. And their news is a joke!"

"Well, JTH just got that new anchor and you know there's always initial curiosity. Scott Shepherd certainly has the ladies' attention." Andrew was defensive.

"I know that," snapped Kate. "You're not talking to a beginner. Let's just hope the curiosity is going to wear off."

Andrew continued to go through the rating book, his expression perplexed.

"Andrew," Kate said in a calmer tone, "you talked about

rocking the boat. As you can see, this boat of ours is not sailing along as nicely as it should. There's no room in this industry to feel safe. And I think it's not only the reporters and anchors who've been feeling safe and comfortable. I think you have too.''

Andrew did not respond but sat waiting for Kate's tirade to end.

''You know I call them as I see them, and what I haven't seen and heard recently is that determined ex-drill sergeant pushing his troops into new territory. Whatever happened to that list of things I thought worth checking out? Remember the state's juvenile justice system? The nursing home in Malden that had been cited by the feds? The controversy over people crossing the border to New Hampshire to buy cheaper liquor? Do I just talk to myself when I say these things? Or perhaps I should become a reporter for a couple of weeks and remind you and your staff what quality reporting is all about?''

Andrew looked down at his hands. He knew she'd be bold enough to do exactly that. He also knew she could out-report anyone on his staff. Kate Marchand would always be regarded as one of the toughest and best journalists anywhere.

''Andrew, come on, talk. Any problems at home? Any problems anywhere I should know about?'' Kate waited for his response.

''No, no, the family's fine,'' he answered quietly. ''But you're right. I'm being a little slack. Not pushing like I usually do. And I guess I'm letting Ann get to me more than I should.''

''What's going on with Ann?''

''Well, Kate, you know she has never been that easy to work with, and I've always had trouble getting her to do stories.''

''I know,'' said Kate a little sadly. ''She wants someone else to write the copy, she'll just read it, and that's it.''

''She's damn good at it, Kate, and we know the public likes her. And God knows *she* knows it!'' Andrew sounded exasperated. ''Her attitude is not doing wonders for the morale of others.''

''Anyway, it's a strange time for her to be playing prima donna. We're in contract negotiations with her now, and I wouldn't say they're exactly going her way.''

''What do you mean?'' Andrew stiffened in his chair. ''You can't cut back her salary, or any of the perks. Her agent and the union would never allow it.''

Kate watched a 747 make its graceful ascent from Logan and disappear into a cloud bank. She then turned and with her hands behind her leaned on the window sill. "I'm not thinking of cutting her salary," she paused, "I'm thinking of cutting Ann . . . completely."

"What!" Andrew jumped up, genuinely shocked. "We may be slipping a few points, but we're still number one. You don't replace the number one anchor. That's suicide. Forget what I said about the aggravation. I'll get her back under control."

"Andrew, this isn't a spur-of-the-moment suggestion." Kate walked towards the television sets and put a cassette tape into the recorder beneath the middle set. Immediately the image of Ann delivering the news appeared.

"Look closely, Andrew, and listen." They were both silent, hostage to the woman on the television. After about a minute, Kate leaned forward and pushed the freeze button. Ann stared back at them, her mouth half opened.

"She doesn't pull you in. She's lost her magnetism. She doesn't make you want to listen or sound like it's important for you to listen. The sparkle, the draw—it's gone."

Andrew protested but Kate stood up and walked towards the television set. She seemed to be taking one last look, and as if she had just made a final decision, determinedly turned off the cassette recorder, and adjusted the television set back to the soap opera.

"Are you thinking of pulling someone from in-house?" asked Andrew.

"Initially, I was giving Lynn some thought, but something my husband said this morning, and what you later confirmed, has altered that." Andrew looked at her questioningly. "Jonathan did a new procedure with the laser today and you can bet the gallery was packed. You said JTH may be rising in the ratings because of their new anchor."

"I see," said Andrew. "Go for something brand-new. A new look." He paused. "But Ann's been here for over five years. The public's used to her. There will be some anger if she's just dumped."

"At first, but remember how quickly the public forgets—and forgives. And especially when we replace her with someone who wins their hearts and minds immediately."

"Well, you know how to call them, Kate." Andrew sighed. "So if you've found the right one, let's get on with it." He punctuated his enthusiasm by clapping his hands together.

"Did I mention anything about having found that person yet?" asked Kate.

Andrew wondered if he'd have any say at all in her new choice. As if reading his mind, Kate spoke, "And you think I'd hire someone without your approval? Never." Andrew smiled. He knew that was true. He also knew he had not disagreed with one reporter she had brought on board. They were all superior journalists.

"So where are we going to find Wonder Woman?" Andrew inquired.

"Well, Diana's contacting agents today, and we should have some candidates by the end of the week," Kate said. "And I want this kept very quiet. Just you, me and Diana. Then suddenly one night, Ann Resnick will not be sitting next to Bill Halliday. It'll be this, yes," Kate squinted her eyes at nothing in particular, "Wonder Woman."

Kate's mind shifted gears and Andrew had to chase to keep up with her, as she asked a question concerning the completion date of the new mobile unit, a series of new editing suites, and a cable link-up with a highly acclaimed health network.

"Dammit, Andrew, they put a man on the moon in less time than this mobile unit's taking," said Kate. "The editing suites were supposed to be completed three weeks ago. Why did we lease an additional floor of this building—at thirty dollars a square foot, I'll remind you—to expand our editing facilities, give the reporters more time with their stories, and make room for the documentary producers? Certainly not to find out that by the time the editing suites are finally put in, they're no longer state of the art. You know I'm also anxious to get started on the reception room that will be able to handle my little satellite feeds. It's going to take time to place our microwave dishes on the roof. We're in the sixth largest market and we can't function without all that."

"Kate, it's not taking that long. The suites are not going to be outmoded," Andrew protested.

"No?" She tossed a magazine onto his lap. "Have you read that Sony has finally worked out the bugs with the half-inch tape? We're still using three-quarter and one-inch. Those suites may already be old-fashioned. And with those electricians' rates, we've already put every one of their kids through college." Kate was now angrier than she expected to become. Why was she telling her news director about the state of the art in videotape? And why was he allowing a two-month delay in the editing suites?

"Come with me, please." She opened the door and hurried

through the reception area, startling Judy and a delivery man who jumped out of her way. They walked down the hallway, Kate nodding curtly to those who passed her. She reached the exit, and soon she and Andrew were going down the back stairway, Kate's heels clicking loudly on the cement steps with an echo that seemed to carry throughout the building.

At the seventh floor, she opened the metal door, and looked upon a room strewn with wires and cables, editing machines, microphones and haphazardly placed dividers. The only person visible was a man in a far corner laying carpeting. Kate walked over to him, stepping over the debris. The man was busy with his staple gun and Kate intentionally walked right in line with it. The man first noticed the very expensive shoe, then moved his eyes up the leg, the skirt, blouse, to Kate's very unfriendly stare. He tried an innocent smile but was ignored.

"Who is the chief electrician?" Kate snapped.

The workman pointed at a partition. "Mr. Pearson," he mumbled. "He's in there."

Kate set her stride in that direction, and feeling the eyes on her, suddenly turned. "Please resume your work. You don't have much time."

In the cubicle to which the man had pointed, three men were standing over a table, discussing the blueprints in front of them. At the sound of Kate's entrance, all three turned. It was obvious from the look on their faces that a tall, elegant woman was not what they expected to see.

"Which one of you gentlemen is the chief electrician? The man accountable?" Kate's tone was pleasant. The tallest man, older than the others, and Kate thought, deeply tanned for this time of year, stepped forward.

"I am. I'm Ed Pearson. Why?"

"I'm Katherine Marchand." The tone was stern and the effect almost comical as each man brushed off his pants or straightened his collar.

"Mrs. Marchand," Pearson said. He knew her name, her reputation, and had seen her picture in magazines and newspapers, but she was far more stunning in person. He couldn't wait to tell his wife. She had been thrilled when he got the contracting job at Katherine Marchand's station. "I didn't expect you down here."

"I'm certain you didn't, Mr. Pearson. And as charming as you men are, I had hoped I would not *have* to come down here." Kate looked out the doorway of the cubicle. "Tell me, Mr.

Pearson, why am I not seeing my reporters, producers, editors, out there working? Why am I seeing this mess?" Kate's fury was slowly mounting again. "You've been working on this for three months. You're now three weeks behind. Has anything really been accomplished? Perhaps it's time for a new contractor."

Pearson paled. He didn't know much, but he knew no businessman, no person in his right mind wanted to be on Katherine Marchand's blacklist. He began a very rapid, very nervous explanation about delays in equipment, the extensive wiring required, how painstaking he and his crew were trying to be, trying to make it sound as if he and his crew were going to special lengths for Katherine Marchand.

"Hold on, Mr. Pearson, spare me the violins. I'm interested in only one thing. The fulfillment of a contract. When will these ten editing suites be completed?"

"Hopefully, within a month."

"Unacceptable!" Kate was livid and she didn't hide it. "Do you know I'm sending programs to New York to be edited at seven hundred dollars an hour because these facilities are not ready? And that's saying nothing of hotel and living expenses."

On most jobs like this, Pearson thought to himself, you never saw the head person, and delays were anticipated, even expected, especially in the high-profit business of television. He did not quite know what to say.

"Mr. Pearson," Kate continued, "I have a board of directors that I am accountable to, a board of directors that, quite honestly, was not thrilled at the expenditure of over four hundred thousand dollars just for the editing equipment, never mind the cost of leasing this floor, never mind the cost of installing it." Kate lowered her voice. "At the board meeting in three weeks, I have no intention of telling them that the new editing floor is unfinished.

"I'm going to proudly parade the board through this floor, and show them the completed suites, with reporters and producers eagerly at work. I'm going to show them what a splendid investment we've made."

"But. . . ." started Pearson.

"No buts, Mr. Pearson. By the end of this week, I want at least two editing suites up and running. By the end of next week, six, and two weeks from today, ten."

"But I don't think that's possible."

"Mr. Pearson, hire more men, work around the clock. Do

whatever is necessary." She waited, looked at her watch, and then back to Pearson. "Or are you saying you can't do it?"

"No, no, no," Pearson protested. "We'll do it."

"Andrew, I want you to relay this entire conversation to Stan Wolton, and tell him that I expect him, as chief engineer, to make certain these deadlines are met. Let him know my displeasure. And that this Friday I expect him to report to me that at least two suites are operational." She then turned back to the contractor. "Tell me, Mr. Pearson, how big is your company?"

"What do you mean?" he asked.

"Let me put it this way: How seriously would it affect your profits this quarter if I put into effect the penalty clause in your contract?"

The penalty clause! Pearson had forgotten about that. Few companies request it in their contract, but WLYM had. It meant the more overdue the project was, the less the payment. You could even get into a situation where you were working for nothing, or worse, paying back money. "Ah, it wouldn't be good." Pearson was growing pale. "I mean we're already over three weeks."

"I know," Kate hesitated, and it was clear she was calculating something in her head. "I can understand delays in equipment, but you say you have it all now. I will not put the penalty clause into effect for the past three weeks. But as of now, it is in effect. And if you meet the deadline, you will still come out with a very nice profit. However, if all the suites are not *fully* operational within two weeks, I will back up the penalty clause into those earlier weeks."

Kate stepped forward and smiled her brightest smile. She extended her hand. Pearson took it in his, not surprised at how strong the grip was. "I'm certain you won't disappoint me, Mr. Pearson, and this floor will be humming in two weeks' time. And one last favor? Don't just pack up your tools and walk out. Please come up to my office and say goodbye, so I can say thank you." She released his hand, smiled, turned and stepped gracefully over the cables, the silent Andrew right behind her.

Pearson found himself standing there, smiling. One of his co-workers finally found his voice and said, "What was that?"

"That," said Pearson, "was proof that the legend known as Katherine Marchand is very, very real. Now, let's give the lady what she wants. Maybe even earlier." He was still smiling as he turned back to the blueprints.

5

"**D**AMN IT, ANDREW, SOMETIMES I FEEL LIKE WE'RE TRY-ing to put out a Rolls-Royce in a Volkswagen factory," Kate said as they walked back to her office.

When they rounded the reception area, Kate saw Diana with Mike Colby. "Back so soon? Has everyone gone to lunch? Did my television station shrink?"

"No," answered Mike. "I spoke to several people and got the grand tour. Unfortunately, I can't find anyone, even off the record, who does anything but sing your praises."

"There's a contractor on the seventh floor who might be just perfect for you," Kate said absently, as she went through the messages Diana and Judy handed her.

"Is that where you've been?" asked Diana. "You might let someone know where you're disappearing to."

"Yes, I'm sorry." Kate finished going through the messages. "When am I going to have time for all this?" She was exasperated.

"Kate," Mike stood up from his chair, "Diana told me you were screening that network documentary on rape this afternoon. I thought it might be good to watch your decision-making process and see whether you decide to pick the program up."

"Oh, that's right. Another thing on our agenda, Andrew." She looked at Andrew, then at Mike. "Sure, no problem. But right now, give me fifteen minutes to dictate a few things to Diana. Andrew, could you get the new lineup for tonight for me? And you might also use this time to talk to Stan Wolton."

She pushed open her office door and headed into her bathroom, that also held a refrigerator/freezer. She extracted a large blue ice pack and wrapped a linen towel around it. Unbuttoning the back of her skirt, Kate walked over to the couch, and gently let herself down, positioning the ice pack at the base of her spine. She closed her eyes, aware only of the cold and of Diana in the chair next to her.

"I suppose you didn't take the elevator and insisted upon strutting up and down four flights of stairs. Does Jonathan know how severe the pain is becoming?"

"It's not that bad, and anyway, you know he just wants to get his laser into me."

"Maybe it's time, Kate."

"And while I'm recuperating for those months, who's going to run this television station?"

Diana didn't answer. This was a common conversation. She had yet to find an answer to that question.

"So," Kate said, her voice strong again, "do you want me to use the machine, or do you feel speedy with your shorthand today?"

"You're a little tired. I may be able to keep up with you. Anyway, my hand needs the exercise." Diana crossed her legs and positioned her pad.

Kate took a deep breath and immediately began with a memo to Wolton on the status of the construction. She then dictated a letter thanking Columbia University for its decision to award her an honorary doctorate of letters; a letter to the National Academy of Television Arts and Sciences saying that although she was deeply honored, her schedule did not allow her to take the time to judge this year's Emmy nominations; a letter agreeing to speak to the League of Women Voters; a memo to the editorial board firmly stating that she wanted to begin a campaign calling attention to the federal cutbacks for the blind, disabled, and elderly; a note to Bill Halliday commending him on a heart transplant story; a memo to promotion, telling them to begin thinking about a new slogan for the station; a letter to the vice-president of the network, NRB, asking about the possibility of additional satellite time so LYM could feed more of its programs to syndicated stations.

"That's all for now. I guess it's time to screen that documentary." Kate gingerly got up from the couch, replaced the ice pack in the freezer, pulled a brush through her hair and freshened her lipstick. As she passed Diana's chair, she placed her hand on her assistant's shoulder. "I think I've got it all down," said Diana, confidently. "Now what were you going on about after the editing suite part?"

They both laughed. Kate walked to her desk. Diana moved to the door. "I suppose now you want these typed?"

"Anytime before the end of the day."

Diana opened the door. "Gentlemen, the ever-so-laid-back Katherine Marchand will see you now."

Andrew and Mike walked in and sat down opposite Kate. "Mike," Kate said, "there's one thing you should know for your article. That woman out there, who just let you in? She really runs this station."

They laughed and Andrew walked over to the recorder, inserted a cassette, and returned to his seat. Kate pushed her remote control and the tape began.

She asked Andrew, "What's the latest count for this documentary?"

"Over thirty percent of the affiliates are not airing it," he said.

"Where's the major opposition in our area coming from?"

"The usuals. The responsible television groups. Also, Aronson at JTH told the *Globe* he thought we'd be irresponsible to go ahead."

"Since when does the president of another station have a say in what's aired on Channel Three?" she asked.

Kate angrily pushed the remote button so it would fast forward through commercials, then began watching. Just when she was about ready to pick up a memo pad and let her mind switch to other matters, she saw a very riveting, very dramatic, but frighteningly real, rape. Shot with multiple cameras, the viewer was moved from the beautiful, very young face of the screaming, terrified victim, to the face of the not unattractive man who was obviously getting great delight out of what he was doing. For a second, Kate thought, "No, they wouldn't dare take it to the point where he reached orgasm." And they did not. Fade to black. Commercial.

Kate pushed the stop button and looked at Andrew and Mike. They were both flushed. Goddammit, she thought. I bet they both have erections. They did not look at her. Kate hit the button with the fist of her right hand clenched.

As the program unfolded, it took the victim through all the humiliations to which the police and the legal system subjected her. It showed how the victim was ostracized by her friends. Her father would barely talk to her. Her brother was embarrassed by her. Her father did not want her to testify. Her mother, and the police, did. He was a known rapist; this girl could pin him. She decided to testify, and the night before, in a dream, relived the rape. Kate was furious. In its entirety, the program replayed the rape. After her dream, the victim decided not to testify. A female detective changed her mind. Then came a phone call to the victim, threatening her if she testified. Her family asked for police protection. It was denied. "It's only a rape case," said the town's chief of police.

Despite increased pressure not to, the victim did testify. The young man was convicted, but sentenced to only six months, then probation. End of program. Kate snapped off the television.

"Well, gentlemen?"

Mike actually spoke first. "I can see the problem. That rape scene is downright inflammatory."

"Yeah," said Andrew. "A lot of young men . . . and older men too, will get off on that. Think it's a lot of fun."

"So, do we air it?" Kate looked at Andrew.

"Christ, I don't know, Kate. It may not be worth the aggravation."

"Damn it, Andrew. Where *is* the fight in you?" Kate pushed the intercom. "Diana, please come in."

By the time Kate removed her hand from the intercom, Diana was in the room. She took her seat next to Kate.

"Okay," Kate began, "here's my decision, Andrew . . . and Mike," nodding in his direction. "And Diana, you'll need to give this information to public relations, so they can do a press release on it. But make sure I see the release before it goes out." She leaned forward in her chair, crossing her hands on her desk. "I agree that there is a portion of this program that can be regarded as inflammatory. It is the very accurate depiction of a rape. For psychologically unstable males, it could conjure up fantasies and incite future crime. But that is not the message of the rape scene. The message is how ugly, detestable, degrading and frightening rape is. This program carries a young woman through the agonizing process of dealing with the rape and shows very clearly the inadequacies in our police and our judicial systems as well as the very antiquated, prejudicial, and often inhuman attitudes of today's society. Because it is the belief of

WLYM that this program can enlighten the public about a growing problem in this community, and that it should encourage legislators, law enforcement officers, and the public itself to rethink their views and policies, the program will be aired. However, WLYM will make two changes. First, the program will be edited. There is a replay of the rape scene that is unnecessary to the purpose of the program. Also, immediately following the program we will present a special half-hour show, hosted by Bill Halliday and Ann Resnick, which will feature a panel of experts from psychologists to legal experts with open lines to answer any viewer questions, and to tell people where they can go for help or additional information.''

"The network's not going to like your editing one of their shows,'' Andrew said quickly.

"The network will like it less if I refuse to air it at all,'' Kate said, turning to Mike. "Like all affiliates, we have to—most of the time—play by the network's rules. They supply us with sixty percent of our programming and in return we get the profitable local commercial spots. So it's in our best interest to go ahead with this documentary. Financially, our sales staff will pull in up to ten thousand dollars in local spots. And ethically, it's an important program. Public service. Isn't that one of the things television's supposed to be all about?''

When Andrew nodded Kate said, "While you're here, do you have tonight's news lineup with you?''

Andrew, accustomed to Kate's interest in the details of programming, said, "Sure. Once a reporter, always a reporter, right, Kate?''

"Okay, Andrew,'' Kate said. "Sermon's over and I guess we're done for the day. You look tired. Get a good night's rest.''

He walked towards the door. "Some of us are just human. We're not bionic like you, Kate.''

She smiled at Andrew as he closed the door.

Kate looked at the clock on her desk: 4:27. "If you think I go home at five, you're very wrong. I don't really get rolling until my tenth hour into the day.'' She laughed, but Mike had seen Kate's appointment book on Diana's desk, and knew she probably wasn't kidding.

"We were up to your leaving the Big Apple for Boston in 1974, to become executive producer/managing editor of the news at WLYM. In 'seventy-four, well, you were still only thirty-four. Pretty big title for a woman.''

"Yes, it was," reflected Kate, "but I had been no slouch in New York, old friend."

"I know, I know."

"So, what's the question? Yes, it's true I was fucking the general manager." She ignored Mike's "Aha . . ." and said quickly, "No, that's not fair. Larry Sloan is a very honorable man. I respect him immensely. In 1974, desegregation was about to begin in Boston. He knew it would be one of the most traumatic events in this town's history. He also knew there was no leadership that could get the city through it without violence. He believed the absolute worst could happen—death, riots, everything.

"He was discussing this while the two of us were attending one of those god-awful awards dinners in New York. I told him he should open up the airwaves. Let the media be the leader. Provide information throughout the day. Set up a central headquarters, bringing together the school officials, police, parent and student leaders—so all false rumors could be quelled and information would be constantly delivered to the people of Boston, and all those who had an interest in the future of the city.

"Larry asked me right then and there if I would leave NRB and put this all together. At that time, I thought I was destined for the news slot with the network, so I said no. Two weeks later, the network set their new high in discrimination, and when Larry heard about it, he called me and renewed the offer. I still declined, thinking I wanted to stay at the network level, and not go local."

"Why did you change your mind?"

"Jonathan and I discussed it, and decided that we wanted to give it a go. We were ready for a change so Jonathan looked into New England General. It turned out they wanted him. I called Larry back, and he still wanted me. So, we packed our bags and headed north."

"And WLYM welcomed you with open arms?" inquired Mike.

"Hardly. Boston had its own kind of discrimination and there were a lot of people who let me know that they were not happy I was here, that I was a woman, and I was about to run the news. No, it was very unpleasant, and they fought me at every turn, every decision. Only a few stood by me.

"But it's like the saying goes—everyone loves a winner. Soon it was obvious LYM was beating out all the competition. We were acclaimed nationally for literally walking the city through the desegregation crisis. Partly thanks to us, violence was minimal, and people had a place to go for facts. For truth. Of course there was more to it, but we had something to do with the good outcome. And that something brought us up to number one and has kept us there. We're known as the station that tells the truth and plays no favorites, and then lets the public make its own decisions. We keep the public's trust and that is the key to this entire operation.'' She took a deep breath and allowed herself to relax slightly.

Mike now got up and stretched. "And so, for the next four years, you basically made television history in news. People in the business in New York refer to you as a brigadier with one of the most finely tuned news armies ever assembled. You win Emmy after Emmy, Phillips Awards, unprecedented prestige. . . .''

"I'm waiting for another Peabody. They're my favorites,'' Kate interjected, smiling. "Television's equivalent to the Pulitzer.''

Her eyes moved along her bookshelf, and stopped. Mike watched the movement and walked towards the bookshelf. "What's this? One that didn't make it to the museum?'' He picked up the elaborately framed award.

"That one doesn't belong to LYM,'' said Kate softly.

Mike read the inscription: "The George Foster Peabody Award, in recognition of the highest degree of excellence in journalism, is proud to honor Katherine O. Marchand for her reporting of the war in Vietnam and its effect on the people of Vietnam as well as the people of the United States of America, whom she so unselfishly served. April 1969.'' He placed it gently back on the shelf.

"I remember when you were over there, and I remember seeing your reports on the network. You didn't exactly go the easy route. I mean you were slogging through those rice paddies, living with refugees, even behind enemy lines. There was speculation when you weren't on for a couple of nights that either the North Vietnamese or one of our generals had silenced you for good.''

"Mike, you exaggerate.''

"You know I don't, Kate. You were a hero—a heroine—even to us reporters back home. You went into situations and reported things that no one else did. You defied both governments. It's no surprise that Nixon was screaming at the network to get you the hell out of there. He was spending most of his time trying to explain the injustices you were exposing.''

''There was no way he could explain.'' There was a flash of anger in Kate's eyes, as she remembered the pleading looks in the eyes of the children before they were massacred. ''Please, Mike, don't take me back to that time. To be honest, I still have terrible nightmares about it.'' She rose from her chair and began pacing the room, pausing to place her hands on her hips and arch her back.

''Is it true that the injury to your back is from being a little too close to an incoming mortar?''

''Mike, most of my war wounds are in my heart and mind.''

''You didn't answer my question.''

''I answered it as much as I will,'' Kate snapped at him. What she could not afford in the television business was anyone thinking there was a serious problem with her back. No, in this cut-throat business they do shoot horses.

She sat back at her desk, ready to hit the secret buzzer when Mike said, ''Kate, I know you're getting sick of this, and I do admire your patience. Just a few more questions and I'll disappear.'' He looked down at his notes. ''Okay, so then in 1978, you were made a vice-president in charge of public affairs and programming, and you started a lot of new programs. Health, law, a daily children's hour, a weekly forum with management, a weekly talent show, a weekly teenage problem show, a segment on women's issues.''

Kate said, ''Yes, but the important thing is that we set up the LYM syndication network. We used a major sponsoring house and started pushing these programs into markets all across America, and even in Europe.''

''You keep saying 'we,' '' Mike commented, ''but if my research is right, it should just be 'I.' You did all this, from the program ideas to the syndication.''

''But I also had very fine—and still do have, thank God—producers who deliver.'' Kate reflected for a moment. ''That's the hardest part in this business. Everyone wants it so bad, and so few are really good at it. It's hard to push through the mediocrity. And the bullshit.''

''Well, obviously,'' Mike began hesitantly, ''you have a board that was able to pick a winner. Tell me the inside story there, and I promise to leave.''

Kate laughed. ''There's no inside story. It's all in the minutes of the board meeting, and we're a public corporation, so the FCC requires us to keep very careful accounts.''

"Kate, come on. *You* took this company public, *you* incorporated its syndication and satellite network, *you* made it one of the fastest climbing stocks on the Exchange.''

Kate did not reply.

"Everyone assumed that when Larry Sloan had his stroke, Steve Merriam would replace him. It was the New York scene all over again. You were obviously the more qualified, Merriam had even had some conflict of interest charges raised when he was at another local station. But it's a conservative board, and despite the fact that your credentials ran circles around him, no one expected you to be chosen. You were a woman, and you didn't have a business or sales background. Merriam did.'' He paused. "Am I right, so far?''

"Right on target, Mike,'' said Kate with a quiet smile.

"So what happened in that board meeting?''

"Why don't you ask the members of the board?''

"Don't you think I've tried? I've asked every blasted one of them. They all say to ask you. They're very loyal.''

As well they should be, Kate thought.

"The most I could get out of them was that they believed, after your presentation, that you could lead the station more adequately than Merriam,'' said Mike. "Oh, and that Larry Sloan had informed a member of the board that you would be his choice.''

"Well, as you know,'' Kate began, "I was in London at the time of Larry's stroke, setting up our European syndication. Leonard Mankin, chairman of the board, called me with the news that Larry had resigned from his hospital bed. The station was in the midst of big changes and it would not be wise to be without a leader. Mankin called an emergency meeting for two days later, announcing that the choice was between Merriam and me. We would both make presentations to the board.

"My first response was a deep sadness for Larry. He is a good man. I then pulled myself together and got on the phone to reach Jonathan. Where was Jonathan? In surgery. Who was the patient? Larry Sloan. I knew the surgery would be long, and the best thing for me to do was get back to Boston.''

"Was there ever any question in your mind as to whether or not you'd go for it?''

"Of course not,'' said Kate. "And I wasn't going to be beaten this time. Naturally, I got fogged in at Heathrow, but finally in the air, I took two first-class seats and started making charts and graphs, and management schedules and of course, profit calculations. The fog that delayed me in London was also in Boston, so we landed in New York. It was six o'clock at night. The board meeting was at ten the next day. I called my office and asked Diana to let Jonathan know what was going on, then to be prepared to work through the night with me. I finally arrived in Boston at ten o'clock that night, twelve hours till blast-off.''

Kate closed her eyes, remembering the fatigue, but also the exhilaration. ''I walked into my office and both Jonathan and Diana were there. I was a wreck. I hadn't slept in over forty-eight hours. I almost collapsed into Jonathan's arms. Actually, I think I did. But then I went to work, and Diana and Jonathan did everything from connecting the dots on my graphs to pouring coffee into me to keep me awake. Once all the graphs and charts and proposals were done, and Diana was typing, I began working on how to present my material. Jonathan stayed for moral support, dozing on the couch, and then left for surgery at six.''

''What were you putting together, Kate?''

''The game plan for the future of the station—at least for the next ten years.''

''But what was it?''

''Oh, God, Mike, it covered everything from engineering, management, sales and promotion programs, advertising, new programming—every detail that makes a television station,'' she paused, ''and a network.''

''So, obviously, you blew their socks off.''

''Not that easily. Leonard allowed me to go after Merriam, since I had just flown in. Merriam had underestimated me, and did not figure that I would have had the time to put together anything meaningful. He apparently had done a fairly decent presentation, because when I walked into the boardroom, he was leaving with a big grin, and the board looked as if they had made their decision already.''

''You must have been dragging.''

''Oh, Mike, you know how it is. When push comes to shove, and you want something bad enough, you're able to reach inside and pull out a reserve of strength. Well, I pulled it out and used every bit of it. You talk about a performance! You talk about organization! You talk about pummeling a board for two and a half hours with plans and figures and proof, and doing it with basically the force of a nuclear explosion . . . well, that's just what I did. Diana will attest to the fact that afterwards I walked from that boardroom into my office, lay down on my couch, and just passed out cold.''

''Jesus!'' said Mike. ''But at least you knew you won.''

''That's the fun part. The board had decided before even hearing Merriam or me not to take the vote until a meeting a week later. So, the hell was just beginning.''

''I can just imagine. A week of lobbying.''

''No, that's not my style. Merriam lobbied. I kept working, knowing the only things I had going against me were my age, barely forty, and that I was a woman applying for the job as head of a television empire—or at least a potential empire.''

Kate wondered how much she should tell Mike Colby. Would it hurt or help her for the world to know the card she had played? She decided it could only help her, because she had played it successfully.

''The week passed, and around noon on the fatal day I was sitting at my desk when Diana buzzed that Mr. Leonard Mankin was here to see me. I told her to tell him I was busy.'' Kate laughed out loud. ''I wish I could have seen Diana's expression, because there was just silence from her end. She still threatens to kill me for doing that to her. The poor woman had been a wreck all week. Finally, I said, 'Okay, let him in.' Leonard's a good fellow, and he came in laughing. And I knew from the sparkle in his eyes that I was now the general manager and president of WLYM. He extended his hand, said 'Congratulations, it was unanimous.' I thanked him, and he turned and said, 'You're really going to pull it off, aren't you?' I said I was just beginning.''

Mike interrupted. ''What did he mean, 'pull it off'?''

Kate sat down in the chair next to Mike. ''Well, you see, there was a bottom line to my presentation. I told them I would take a two-year contract and if I had not increased profits by two hundred percent, then I would step down.''

Mike was shocked. Two hundred percent! But then he squinted and grabbed her arm, ''Kate, that was over two years ago, you're now on an unlimited contract. You did it. I mean, you did give that board a two-hundred-percent profit increase?''

''No,'' she winked at Mike, removed his hand from her arm, and leaned toward him, ''I gave them almost a four-hundred-percent increase!''

''Jesus,'' Mike said. ''You made them an offer they couldn't refuse. With their stock options, you made all of them million-aires, many times over—in two years.''

Diana came into the room and Kate said, ''Get the man a drink, please. He's great at mental arithmetic.''

''No thanks,'' Mike said, closing his briefcase. ''By the way, Kate, what did you do that day after you found out?''

''Well, I called Jonathan, and then Diana, and I sat on the couch and laughed and cried. Then I took the day off, drove to the Cape, and walked for hours along Nauset Beach on the Cape.''

''Alone?'' inquired Mike.

''Yes, alone, why do you ask?''

''Well, Kate, you have the reputation of being a very driven woman; that you will get what you want at all costs,'' he hesi-tated. Kate was staring at him. Diana was staring at Kate. ''A hypothetical question: Say a mandate, an ultimatum from the heavens came down. Which would it be, this television station or Jonathan's life?''

''I hate hypotheticals, and I hate ultimatums,'' Kate an-swered.

''Is that your answer?''

''No, Mike,'' and with a voice that cracked with anger and tension, ''I hate to disappoint you, but the life of Jonathan Laur-ence Marchand is far more important to me—and far more valuable—than any television station or any network.'' Men-tally, she crossed her fingers, knowing that was the right thing to say for publication, but holding the real question for herself, for later.

''Got it,'' said Mike quickly.

''Cheap shot, Mike,'' Kate answered and waved to him as he left. She snapped her remote control, pushing the volume up on Channel Three.

''Oh, right,'' said Diana, louder than usual. ''I knew I had something else to tell you.''

''About my new anchor, I hope.''

''Don't you ever forget anything?''

''On occasion. Then I call you at home. Be thankful I don't forget more often.''

''Abrams says he has a perfect candidate for you. She's in New York.'' Diana sounded excited. ''He says she's ready to explode into the industry, and will soon be network if you don't act fast. Her contract isn't up for six months, and she may be reluctant to leave New York. But I told him to inform her that

you would like to meet with her as soon as possible." Kate
raised her eyebrows. "Well, you said you wanted this done right
away, and I figured if she was as good as Abrams said . . . I
mean, he gave us Bill Halliday."

Kate held up her hand. "It's okay, it's okay. Yes, fine. What
about a tape?"

"It should be here by Federal Express tomorrow morning."

"Well, then we'll see exactly who it is you and Abrams have
picked out," Kate said, smiling. "And I thought I was kidding
when I told Colby you really ran this television station."

"Well, running this television station is wearing me out, so
if you're finished with me, I'll head for the Red Line and
Quincy."

"Please, with my blessing, and thank you for everything today." Kate went back to the papers on her desk, with one eye
watching Ann Resnick and Bill Halliday. Diana poked her head
in and called goodnight and Kate said, "Listen, I just remembered I'm eating in town with Jonathan tonight, and we'll use
his car. Why don't you take mine, so you don't have to hassle
with the subway?" Diana started to protest and Kate interrupted, "I'm sick of this same old argument. If you're going to
run this station, then act like it."

"Don't worry, I'll put it in the garage, so it won't get ripped
off."

"It's insured. And it's just a car, Diana."

Kate wished that Diana and her husband could afford a second car, but she knew, even with the large salary the station paid
her, every available cent went to putting four kids through college. She stared at the camera close-up of Ann Resnick. To think
I pay you five times what I pay Diana, and Diana's probably the
highest-paid secretary in Boston. Kate gritted her teeth at the
image and out loud she said, "You can be damn sure, honey,
that the next woman who sits in that chair is going to work her
ass off."

As she continued to work at her desk, Kate found her mind
wandering back to the interview with Mike Colby. Recalling the
events in New York had brought back old ghosts. What Mike
Colby didn't know was that when she lost the job in New York,
her marriage was also in bad trouble. Jonathan had been having
a full-blown affair with one of her own news correspondents—
a well-kept secret, until Kate got sick one day and came home
early. The classic sordid scene, only this time the wife walks in
on the husband.

Kate was devastated. She trusted Jonathan. She adored him, loved him more than anything else in the world. And she had been carrying his child, in her third month.

Pregnant with his child, she stood watching his bare ass move over the brunette beneath him. She remembered how she had felt something go cold within her; she felt something die. Then there was the scream that caught in her throat, finally spewed forward. She ran from the room, ran from the apartment. She walked the streets. All night. Around three A.M., she passed a newsstand in Times Square, picked up the *Times*, and went into a luncheonette for coffee. As she read the paper, she saw on the front page of the business section an announcement of the new producer for NRB's *Evening News*. The head of the sports department. Not Kate. For the second time in twelve hours, Kate couldn't believe what she was seeing. She kept walking, heading for the East Side. All her work. All her love. She had failed at both.

It wasn't until she was walking along Second Avenue and she noticed people staring at her that she realized blood was dripping from between her legs. She hailed a cab, screamed for the nearest hospital. No, she wasn't going to lose this, too. Damn them all. But not her baby.

Kate walked across the room and closed her office door. She put her head against it, and sobbed.

She had lost the baby.

For days, she had stared at the hospital walls. Jonathan would sit by her bed for hours, pleading with her to talk with him. She never spoke. She made one phone call. To resign from NRB. Unable to sleep, she left the hospital in the middle of the night, and took a very long taxi ride out to Long Island. She checked into an inn by the ocean, and spent days and nights with no end and no beginning, walking the beach. She called to let Jonathan know she was alive, but didn't tell him where she was. He begged her forgiveness, promising to love only her, insisting that he couldn't live without her. She hung up the phone.

As the days passed, she knew something was changing inside of her. The light was going out and she was shifting the blame from herself to Jonathan and NRB. A part of her wanted revenge, but how to get it?

She made up her mind. She called Boston. She then called Jonathan and told him where to meet her. She watched from her window as he stepped from the car. Her blood was still, her heart without movement.

She laid out the terms. She would take him back. They would start all over. In Boston. He could certainly get an appointment there. She would try her best to forgive him, but made no promises. He was grateful. He felt like he had been spared a death sentence, for he loved Kate deeply.

They had moved to Boston, and over the years, she had fallen back in love with him. Laughter and joy returned to their marriage. She could not have children any more and, if the truth be told, she was glad. Because, although she and Jonathan had almost come full circle, they never really would make it all the way back to where they'd been.

Jonathan was faithful now, Kate told herself. She knew it . . . it was just her own neurosis that made her so carefully check his American Express bills to make sure there were no hotels she'd not stayed at; that made her sometimes amaze herself as she sniffed at his jacket for traces of another woman's perfume. Crazy, she sometimes thought she was. But there was no doubt that that experience had had a permanent effect. She remembered the last walk she took on that Long Island beach. She vowed that nothing, and no one, would ever stand in her way of building her television empire. She would reach the pinnacle of television excellence. And no child, no person, no Jonathan Marchand would ever again be more important than that achievement.

6

WHEN SHE WAS STEPPING OUT OF THE CAB AT THE RESTAU-
rant, her long legs caught the attention of a group of business-
men walking along School Street. One of the men was about to
make a comment, when the light fell directly on her face. The
comment was suppressed and a quiet, "Evening, Mrs. Marchand" replaced it. Kate smiled, handed the cab driver some
bills, and with a nod of her head acknowledged the greeting.

She hurried up the walk and then the steps of what used to
be City Hall, but was now converted into a bank and also one
of Boston's finest French restaurants. As she entered the lobby,
she slowed her step, and the maitre d', recognizing her immediately, slipped her coat from her shoulders.

"Good evening, Mrs. Marchand, how are you tonight?"
Marcel's French accent was so strong that Kate wondered if he,
like Henry Kissinger, went to special Berlitz classes to keep it
in tune.

As Marcel led her through the elegant dining room toward a
corner table where Jonathan already sat, several men greeted
her, and she stopped at the table of the chairman of Boston's
Redevelopment Authority. After he had elaborately introduced
Kate to the other people at his table, the chairman stressed to
Kate the urgency of their getting together to discuss some important matters before the authority. Kate knew he was playing

a game of "impress the guests," and she played along, assuring him she would call before the week was out. As she walked away, she thought to herself that he would have called *her* by ten o'clock the next morning to get her attention.

Jonathan studied his wife as she approached. God, he thought, she can stop a room dead. But then, when she saw him, her attention fell fully on Jonathan. She smiled deliberately and Jonathan put both arms around her and gave her a passionate kiss.

"Jonathan Marchand," Kate whispered, pulling back slightly, but not removing her arms from his neck, "we both have reputations to protect."

"I know," smiled Jonathan. "Just think what all these people are thinking—a married couple kissing in public!"

Kate sat down. "This is Boston, remember. They may have a blue law against it." She reached over and caressed his leg. "Might make it more fun if they did, right?"

Jonathan laughed softly. "Had a difficult day, dear? Want to release some tension?" He pulled down the top of the menu she was studying and said, "Your husband would like very much to have the honor of a little lechery with his wife. Would you prefer before or after dinner?"

Kate put down the menu and gave him that long, entangling look that Jonathan both feared and loved. It was a look of complete mystery. He would often ask her what she was thinking at those times, but she never answered him. Finally, she spoke, "After dinner, darling."

"Fine," he said warmly. "I ordered you a vodka on the rocks."

"No surgery tomorrow?" she asked when the waiter arrived and she noticed he had ordered a martini for himself.

"No, I get to play tour director tomorrow," said Jonathan, not too happily. "We've brought in a new neurologist, a Christopher Cerci from Cedars-Sinai, and I'm to be guide and general introducer."

"Is he any good?" asked Kate.

"Supposed to be a rising star. He's in demand on both coasts."

A comfortable silence followed as they sipped their drinks and ordered dinner. This was how it usually was. At the end of their difficult days, they would either flirt or fight with each other, then go through the ins and outs of the day, sharing the emotion, the facts, the problems, the worries. And so they went through the meal. Kate learned about the success of the new laser procedure, an interesting new patient, Jonathan's triumph over a bureaucratic mess . . . and he, in turn, learned about all the nuances of her day. She did not tell him about Mike Colby's last question and her response. She hoped that portion of the interview would never see print, that no one would ever put her to the test: Jonathan or her work.

Kate smiled to herself. Yes, in the last eight years, she had gotten everything she wanted, and more. And she wanted still more.

BOOK TWO

KIM

*"It's the chance of a lifetime in a lifetime of chance.
And it's high time you joined in the dance."*

"Run for the Roses"

1

K**IM PUT HER NOTEBOOK DOWN ON HER LAP AND TURNED** to look out the window as the lights of the cities and towns of upper New York State glittered beneath the small jet. Her story for the eleven o'clock news was just about complete. The videotape of the Albany legislature balking at more funds for New York City had been sent back to WNRB earlier in the evening, and should, by now, be edited to her specifications. The plane would land at La Guardia by ten, and she'd be at the anchor desk in plenty of time with the lead story along with a scoop on the governor's plans for a new maximum security prison.

As the jet approached La Guardia the small houses of Queens were visible through the clouds. As she did whenever she was flying, Kim thought that behind every light is someone laughing or crying, making love, sleeping . . . dying. The chill she'd known since her husband's death flowed through her veins again and she deliberately turned away from the window.

What was this madness of Harry Abrams all about? He had made such a fuss about reaching her today. A job opening in Boston, at WLYM? She had been called out of a legislative session to listen to him ranting on the phone that this was her golden opportunity. What was wrong with him? He knew she didn't want to leave New York, and even if she wanted to, the terms of her contract would not allow it. And she was not about to uproot her son Jason now that life finally seemed to be returning to an even keel.

What was the line Harry had used? Oh yes. She'd be working for "a pioneer in electronic journalism." Kim had laughed and told Harry he should have been a salesman. Of course everyone knew the reputation of Katherine Marchand, and there wasn't a reporter, male or female, who did not have the highest respect for her. But it was also known that Marchand was building an empire—some said at all costs—and Kim didn't want to get in the way of an empire-building bulldozer. She was quite happy where she was.

The plane came to a rather rough landing and taxied to the private holding area. As she was about to step through the narrow door, the pilot came to hold out his hand to help her down.

"Sorry about the bumpy landing, Miss Winston," apologized the pilot.

"No, that's okay, Pete," said Kim, smiling. "I liked them—all three of them."

On the ride into Manhattan, she completed the final paragraphs of her story, trying to write as legibly as possible, knowing there would be no time to type the script or get it on the TelePrompTer. She automatically began memorizing as she went along.

Mumbling her story to herself, she stepped into a waiting elevator and checked her watch: 10:54. Very tight. Even though the limousine driver had really hurried, there was still not much time for makeup. She hoped the tape was ready. She ran off the elevator into the crowded and frenzied newsroom. The night editor shouted at her, "Thank God! What did you do, walk?"

"I had a chance to get some more information out of one of the governor's aides, so I took off later than I planned."

"I hope it's worth it. You're aging me, Kim."

"Stay tuned," she ran a brush through her hair, thinking that was another reason not to leave New York—the friendship of Gary Kincaid. Although he was her boss, he was also her best friend, and Jason adored him.

"Move it, kid, you're on," shouted Gary.

She literally ran out of the newsroom and across the hall, across the studio floor, and was attaching her microphone, just as she heard, "And now, with an exclusive report on events in Albany today, chief correspondent, Kim Winston."

"The Albany legislature, not exactly renowned for its ability to look into the future, today. . . ."

Her delivery was flawless, her report complete, and the videotape had been edited as she instructed. She walked off the seat to a smiling Kincaid.

"Great job. Can I buy you a drink?"

"Sounds wonderful, but let me check my messages, okay?"

"Sure," said Gary. "You're going to find several from your agent. He says he must talk to you tonight."

Just as Gary had warned, there were several urgent messages to call Harry Abrams. Well, he had been a very good agent. She could at least humor him. She punched out his number.

"Looking for me, Harry?"

"Kim! Great report tonight. You scooped everyone." Harry was genuinely enthusiastic. He was a wonderful cheerleader.

"All in a day's work, Harry."

"Well, did you think about the Boston offer?"

"Offer? When did it become an offer? When did I say I was interested? I told you I'd think about it. And I have. And no, Harry, I don't want to leave New York. My life's finally coming back together again."

"Kim, listen to me. I've sent a tape up there. I know that as soon as Katherine Marchand sees it, she'll want to talk to you. And you're perfect for her, for WLYM and also her big syndication. She's got a fourth network going up there."

"Listen, Harry, with a reputation like Katherine Marchand's, I'm sure she has a select committee pick her talent, and I'm just not up to going through one person after another. No thanks."

"Kate Marchand isn't that way. She handpicks her talent."

"Okay, Harry. What's going on? What's the hidden agenda here? I mean, you're asking me to get out of a contract that *you* negotiated. How's that going to make you look?"

"No problem, sweetie. If WLYM wants you bad enough, they'll buy out your contract. You don't owe NRB anything."

"Harry, have you been drinking? There's six months to go on my contract. They're not going to buy it out. And I do owe NRB something. They stood by me. My friends are here."

"Kim, they've gotten more than their money's worth out of you." And then, in a softer tone, he said, "Listen, maybe it's time for a change of pace. Get away from all the craziness of New York. Free yourself from all the memories. Get yourself and Jason some fresh air."

She was silent as she doodled on the notepad in front of her. "Well, it might be interesting to take a look at LYM, and I guess I would like to meet the great legend."

"Now, that's more like it," Harry said. "If she looks at the tape tomorrow, I'm sure she'll want to see you on Friday."

"What? You know I'm working Friday, and I'm tired, and you know I have to get geared up for these things. What's the big rush, anyway?"

"Calm down, calm down. It's just that when Katherine Marchand moves, she moves quickly. I don't want you to lose this."

Kim's eyes narrowed as she gripped the phone. "You know, I'm starting to really dislike this woman already. She seems to be manipulating me, and I don't even know her."

"Kim, please trust me on this one. If she wants to talk to you, will you go . . . even if it's on Friday?"

"I don't know, Harry. Things are moving too fast. And it's been a long day. I don't believe in making decisions late at night. Let me sleep on it, okay? I promise to think seriously about it." Without waiting for Harry's response, she hung up.

Gary walked over to her desk. "I love to hear talent scream at their agents."

Kim picked up her coat. "You won't believe this one, Gary. Come on, I really need that drink now."

Outside, they found a cab and Gary gave the driver Kim's East Side address, knowing that although Jason would be asleep, she would want to check on him before anything else. He would wait at the small neighborhood place on Madison Avenue, around the corner from where she lived.

She crossed the restrained but elegant marble lobby of the apartment house and exchanged pleasantries first with the doorman and then with the fresh-faced young Irish boy who ran the elevator. Maybe there's very little discrimination in New York, Kim thought, but in the more expensive co-ops, it's always whites who man the front door. It made her think of moving to the West Side, where life was less homogenized.

Upstairs, she put her key in the lock, and heard the sounds of a television. Margaret, who had been Jason's nanny since he was two months old, was watching an old movie in her room. Kim walked down the hallway, towards the sound, and gently knocked.

"Kim, I didn't hear you. Come in." Kim walked into the small, neat room and plopped into an overstuffed chair.

"Well, how did my two favorite people do today?" asked Kim.

"Just fine. No problems at school. No problems with homework. Jason found a new friend at the playground in Central

Park, and he told me to tell you that he will, quote, 'spank you' for missing supper with him twice this week.''

Kim smiled at Margaret. What would she ever do without her? In her late forties, and widowed, she had provided the only way Kim could continue her career and not scream with a guilty conscience every time she left Jason. "Well, I may be in for more punishment, I'll probably have to go down to Washington tomorrow. Another late one." She rose from the chair, suddenly remembering something. "Maggie, do you still have relatives in Boston?"

"Kim, you know better. On my vacation, don't I always visit my sister in South Boston?"

"Of course, I'm sorry. I don't know where my mind is."

"Out to lunch, it looks like. But what brings up Boston?"

"Nothing," shrugged Kim. "Oh, Maggie, have you seen any of those promotional pictures of me around? The doorman's asking for one for his grandchild."

Margaret got up to follow Kim. "I think I can find one in that mess you call a study. Go see the wee one and I'll fetch it for you."

"Thanks." Kim pushed open the door to her son's room and saw the sleeping blond five-year-old, with Herbie, the kangaroo, tucked under his chin. Then her eyes went to the night light he kept on until she came home. Underneath it was the framed picture—the three of them, holding each other, standing in the center on an elaborate, moated sand castle on a beach on the New Jersey shore. It was a picture of promise and love. She pulled her tear-filled eyes from it and knelt down to kiss the soft, beautiful face of her child.

As she walked back into the hallway, she heard Margaret saying, "Here you go."

"You are a wonder, Maggie," she said, taking the eight-by-ten promotional picture. "And what's his granddaughter's name? Patty?"

"Very good, for someone whose brain's out to lunch."

"I'm not going to take this abuse." Kim pulled a pen from her purse and scrawled something across the bottom of the picture. "I'm going to the Peachtree for a drink with Gary for an hour or so."

"Ah ha! Gary again."

"No ah ha. I just need a drink, and someone who won't push me around and call me names."

* * *

"So what's the big deal with Harry?" Gary asked as soon as Kim had settled into the back booth where he waited. "He's not going to take you away from me, is he?"

"Gary, what do you know about Katherine Marchand?"

Kim might have hit him in the back of his head with a two-by-four, so suddenly did he jerk forward, spilling his drink.

"Did I say something wrong? Does that name always get that reaction?" Kim asked, startled.

"What does she want?" he asked angrily.

"Well, I don't know for sure. Harry seems to think she may want me."

Gary signaled for another drink, and then said, "Sure I know her. Who doesn't? I worked with her years ago, before she went to Boston. She's a dynamo, a powerhouse. You must have heard what she's done with that station."

"Funny, you never mentioned that you worked with her. And I know her name has come up in conversation."

"Well, it's complicated. Are you familiar with why Kate left New York and NRB?"

"No, I've heard talk that it was discrimination, but I never paid much attention, I guess."

"It *was* discrimination. Blatant. She was co-producing the *Evening News*. This was after she had become one of America's most renowned journalists because of her coverage of everything from Vietnam to local race riots. She was a hell of a producer. It was well known that the guy she was working with was basically riding on her coattails."

"She was that good?" inquired Kim.

"She was that good. She took NRB to the number-one slot. Then Marty, the guy she's working with, gets a promotion to vice president. He leaves and it's assumed that Kate will become the producer. But the network screws her, brings in the head of sports over her." Gary took another large gulp from his drink.

"What a bunch of bastards!" exclaimed Kim, loudly enough that a few people who had, as New Yorkers do, carefully avoided staring at a celebrity, now turned her way. Lowering her voice, she continued, "What a rotten thing to do. I hope she sued them."

"You didn't do things like that back then."

"So what did happen?"

"Like I said, the head of sports came in, and he can't handle it. Within six months NRB is number two, then number three. He's canned and ends up in the local affiliate." He paused, and looked into Kim's questioning eyes. "Where he manages to hold his own, do pretty well."

Kim put her drink down, and stared at him. "You?"

Gary nodded.

"Why did you do it? Why did you even take the job, when you knew you were stealing it from someone as qualified as she was?"

"Because the guys on top gave me the hard sell, told me I'd be perfect, have all their support. I protested. Kate was my friend. But they convinced me. They said she was too young. It was a man's job."

"And then she went to Boston?"

"Not as fast as that. She kind of disappeared for a while. It was rumored there was marriage trouble; actually, that her husband was having an affair with one of her own correspondents."

"Poor thing, she was getting it left and right. No wonder people say that she's got iron in her heart, after that experience. Did she divorce him?"

"No, it was just suddenly announced that she and Jonathan were moving to Boston. He's a big neurosurgeon and switched from New York to New England General," Gary explained. "Anyway, once she got to Boston, she pulled off some major news coups up there, then became the general manager. When did you do your Nieman Fellowship at Harvard?"

" 'Seventy-two."

"Oh, you just missed her. She went up in 'seventy-four."

Kim digested all that Gary had said, tapping her fingers on the table. "Well, when I meet this phenomenon, I guess the last thing I should do is mention your name."

"Quite the contrary. Katherine Marchand is a fair woman. She knew it wasn't my fault. I know you'll find it hard to believe, but I had dinner with her just a few months ago. I often do when she's in New York."

"This doesn't make sense," Kim said. "I guess all it proves is what a small world television is." Kim sighed and signaled the waiter. "Because you have managed to utterly confuse me, you can pay for these drinks and walk me down the block to my lovely home where at least everyone's sleeping and I won't have to talk anymore tonight."

At home, Kim took a hot shower and then pulled on a man's soft shirt. As she crawled into bed, she realized that the one blessing of her day was that it had left her so tired, she might fall asleep before the loneliness put its stranglehold on her.

* * *

It seemed like only moments before she felt the familiar tussling of the comforter and sheets and the small warm body settle beside her. As usual, she did not open her eyes, and tried to hold back the smile that inevitably rose from her heart. She felt his breath on her face, and waited for the warm hand to rest on her face and a small finger to pull open her eyelid. She dutifully opened only the eye called upon, and then the other.

"Hi, sleepyhead," he said, his own beautiful aquamarine eyes sparkling at his mother's.

"Hi, Chase." She put her arm around him and pulled him closer. "I missed you yesterday."

"I missed you, too," he said softly, "I guess."

"What do you mean, you guess?"

"Well, I'm not gonna miss you if you're not gonna be around."

"Hmmmmm?" Kim was confused again.

"Well, if you're not going to be around, why should I miss you? If you're not around?"

Kim knew that somewhere there was logic in what her son was saying, but she was too old to understand five-year-old logic. "Maggie warned me I'm to be spanked."

"That's right," said Jason, remembering, and immediately pulling free of her grasp and starting to whack her. They jostled for a little bit until she wrestled him under the covers and into her arms.

"How about if I promise we do something *real* special this weekend?"

"Like what?"

"I don't know yet, but it'll be a surprise, and super. Okay? Friends again?"

"Yeah." He squeezed closer to her. "I love you, Mommy."

"I love you, too, Chase, more than you know."

"Tell me again why you call me Chase," he demanded.

"Again?" Kim knew why he liked the story, and began to recite the familiar words. "Well, as soon as you could crawl, you would chase your daddy all around—under tables, over couches, everywhere. You'd chase after him when he left for work, you'd chase after him when he came home. You were always chasing after him. And one day, I just started calling you Chase."

"And so did Daddy," the little boy said.

"Right, darling. Right. And so did Daddy."

"And he loved for me to chase him, didn't he?"

"Yes," said Kim, pulling him closer.

"And he'd always pick me up and hug me and squeeze me and all that stuff."

"Yup, and all that stuff. He loved you. He still loves you." The last sentence was choked.

Chase stared into her eyes that were filling with tears. "Do you cry a lot, Mommy?"

"Not as much as I used to. How about you?"

"Sometimes when I go to bed and you're not here. Sometimes when I see other kids with their daddies. Sometimes when I look at his picture. . . ." His voice trailed off.

"Maybe it's time to put the picture away," she said, holding back her own tears. "I've put mine away. It makes it easier."

"I keep thinking maybe he'll come back, and he'd be upset if I didn't have his picture out. Like he'd think I'd forgotten him or something." He sobbed openly into her chest.

Kim rocked him gently, letting him cry, and whispering the words she knew he hated to hear, but must accept. "Daddy's never coming back, Chase. He's never coming back. But he'll always be with us. And he'll always love us, just as we'll always love him." He continued to sob between mumbles of "no, no, no." She held him tightly, holding herself together too.

There was a knock at the door. "Hey, are you two going to sleep forever? I've got some French toast cooking and someone's going to be late for school."

Kim pulled her head away from Jason's. "We're coming, Maggie. Make that French toast special." She knew that Maggie would be able to tell by the sound of her voice and the request to make it special that Chase was having a tough morning. That they both were.

"Come on, Tiger," she said to her son. "We've got to keep moving on and remember, a special surprise this weekend." She wiped his cheeks and began kissing him all over his face and head and blowing in his ear until he was giggling a little and then skipping off to get his breakfast.

In the dining room, Maggie had the situation well in control. Jason had told her about the special surprise, and she was making up all kinds of possibilities that had him laughing. As Kim poured her coffee she said, "It's a nice day, Chase. If you can finish your breakfast in time and get dressed pronto, we'll walk to school."

Kim was in the bathroom, putting the final touches on her makeup, when she heard Maggie's gentle knock.

"Honey," Maggie said when she'd settled herself at the edge of the bathtub, "do you think this weekend is the right time to do something special? I mean, it'll be exactly a year since David passed on. Maybe you should just let the day be like any other. Don't make it stand out so you'll keep remembering it year after year."

"Oh, Maggie," Kim stared at the brush on the side of the sink, "I don't know what to do. I thought it might make the day pass quicker."

"I don't think anything's going to make the day pass quicker," said Maggie.

"It's been the longest year of my life, Maggie. It feels like ten endless years. Anyway, I promised Chase we'd do something special. I've been away a lot this week. And you know I don't break my promises." She kissed Maggie on the cheek and headed out the bathroom door. "Chase, are you ready?"

As they walked down Second Avenue towards the private school where Jason was enrolled, Kim nodded hellos to the people on the street who recognized her or thought they knew her from somewhere, but couldn't remember where.

"Does everybody know you, Mom?"

"I think there are quite a few people who don't, sweetie."

"Did everybody know Daddy?"

Kim answered as best she could and shook her head. The child would go for days, sometimes a week, without thinking about his father. Why so much today? Could his mind possibly feel the sad anniversary approaching? Could he possibly know what she had been going through a year ago at this time?

"Thank God children are resilient," she thought, as they rounded the corner and Jason began running toward the other children in front of the school. She walked along slowly, watching him pick out his best friend, Josh. She knelt down beside them and gave Jason a big hug. "I love you, have a good day."

He headed off toward the open school door, then turned. "Don't forget about the special surprise!"

Kim smiled and waved, and walked to the corner to hail a cab. When she settled into her seat, the driver, recognizing her, said, "To the station, Miss Winston?"

"Yes, please," she answered and opened up the newspaper she'd carried from home. On the first page of the business section, her eye caught a headline in the right-hand corner, MAR-

CHAND ENTERPRISES TO LAUNCH OWN SATELLITE. Kim carefully read the article, which revealed WLYM's plans to put up its own satellite to handle transmission throughout its syndication network. There was a quote from Katherine Marchand explaining that there was not enough transmission time on the network satellite to handle the growing demands of her syndication.

Kim finished the article and shook her head. Everywhere she turned in the last twenty-four hours was the name of Katherine Marchand. Well, one blessing, thought Kim. With this announcement and the demands it would put on Marchand's time, she wouldn't have to worry about any Friday interview.

2

KATE WAS SITTING AT HER DESK, SHAKING HER HEAD. "I want to know who leaked this to the press?" She was looking angrily at the head of her public relations department, Richard Blistick. "You know it is not good timing. The board wanted to have statements prepared, and I sure as hell didn't want to announce it when the market is so edgy."

"Kate, a lot of people knew about our satellite plans," Richard said.

"But who would leak it before we were ready?"

"I just don't have any idea," Richard said apologetically.

"Well, get hold of your contact at the *Times* and find out. That's part of your job, you know, timing what gets to the press."

As Richard left the office, Diana came in holding a couple of pieces of paper. "You're not going to believe this."

Kate interrupted her. "I'd believe anything today. It's been one disaster after another. From jammed elevators, Andrew saying he can't speed up work on the new mobile unit, to the leak to the *Times*, to the cardinal being out of town, and news screaming because the archbishop is holding a press conference and we can't get in. Now, what are you going to tell me, the engineers are striking?"

"I'm not going to tell you a thing until you decide to calm down and be civil." Diana stared at Kate sternly.

"I'm sorry." Kate took a deep breath. "What's up?"

"The Federal Express package arrived from New York but all it has is the résumé."

"What package? What résumé?"

"Kate? Your mind really is elsewhere. What was your number-one priority yesterday?"

"Of course." Kate hit her own forehead with the palm of her hand. "My new anchor . . . your new anchor. What do you mean, a résumé, where's the tape?"

"I've called Abrams, he's not in yet."

"Figures," said Kate. "Agents can afford to sleep late. Well, let's see the résumé." Diana handed it to her, and was not surprised when she saw the frown on Kate's face.

"I don't understand," Kate said. "I thought Abrams said this woman was the greatest thing since Barbara Walters. It's not a very strong résumé."

Kate's phone buzzed and Diana reached to pick it up.

"Yes, Judy?" Diana listened. "Okay, I'll take it here." She smiled at Kate and pushed a button on the telephone. "Mr. Abrams, this is Diana Rowland. We're a little confused up here. We seem to have gotten only a résumé of your client, no tape." Kate went back to studying the résumé. "Oh, I see, we'll look for it. Hold on a moment, would you?" She put Abrams on hold and looked down at Kate. "He says they went in two separate packages because at first he couldn't find her résumé reel, but he did send it, and it should be here shortly. Do you want to talk to him? Or do you just want to forget it?"

"I'll talk to him." Kate took the phone. "Hi, Harry, it's Kate. How are you?" Diana left the office as Kate began to explain that she didn't see much promise from the woman's résumé. Diana saw the light on the phone go out a few minutes later and wasn't surprised when she was summoned back to Kate's office.

"Harry maintains there's a lot more to this person, so we won't close the book on her until we look at the tape," said Kate firmly. "In the meantime I would like to talk to Gary Kincaid in New York."

Diana gave Kate a sideways glance. She knew what Gary Kincaid's name meant in Kate's history.

Kate continued, "I think he's on a night editor shift right now, so you'll have to get him at home." She suddenly looked up. "He works at NRB with this woman. He must know her, if she's any good."

A moment later, the call came through. "I hope I didn't wake you," Kate said. "But don't I remember you're on a night rotation?"

"As usual, you remember correctly, and no, you didn't wake me. Strange as it seems, I was waiting for your call. Oh, and congratulations on the satellite. You know no limits, Kate. Out there in space now."

"As long as I'm not spaced out, we'll be okay, Gary. Anyway, how are you? And why, may I ask, did you expect this call?"

"I'm fine, and I assume it has something to do with one Kimberly Winston."

"Then you know her, and obviously Harry's spoken to her."

"Right on both counts, Kate."

"Well, talk, Gary. I just have her résumé, I'm waiting for a tape. And to tell you the truth, from the résumé, I don't know what Harry's so excited about."

There was a pause at the other end of the line. "Kate, would you be upset if I told you that, in my opinion, Kim Winston has the potential to be another Kate Marchand?"

"Want to explain?"

"The only other reporter I know who is in the same league as Kim Winston, as far as integrity, hard work, insistence on excellence, and a great delivery—well, the only one is a reporter from the late sixties known as Katherine Marchand."

"Now, that's what I call a recommendation. She said with great humility."

"Kate, look at her tape. Think potential. Think how you can mold them. Given the right chance, the woman will be a superstar."

"Okay, Gary, but Harry tells me she may not be that easy to lure. Do you know anything about that? *If* she is all you say."

"Actually, that could be a problem, Kate, for anyone other than you."

"If she's as tough as you say she is, it could be a problem, Gary, even for me. Any tips?"

"Well, I owe you a lot more than a few tips, Kate. Just keep insisting, but you didn't get it from me."

"Of course not. I don't even know you."

"Can't use that one. She knows you know me."

"She knows the story?"

"Yes," Gary said, "not that I go around publicizing it. And it sure didn't do much for me in Kim's eyes."

Kate interrupted. "Shit, Gary, can't she see it wasn't your fault?"

"She thinks I could have been stronger, had a little more integrity."

"It's past, Gary, forget it. Don't live with one foot back there," Kate said. "Now, what about her?"

"Well, she has a son. He's five years old."

Kate interjected. "Oh, hell, Gary, I don't need a woman who's tearing her hair out over leaving a kid to go to work."

"Kate, don't jump to conclusions. She has a nanny for Jason. In fact the nanny, Margaret, is originally from Boston, I believe."

"That's my lure? The nanny?" Kate was getting discouraged. "What about her husband?"

"That's the thing," Gary said. "A year ago, Christ . . . I think it's a year ago this month. Yeah, it is," he paused.

"Gary?"

"Yeah, Kate, sorry. I was just remembering him. David Winston. Great guy. He was in a freak accident, ended up in a coma, brain dead. Kim traipsed all over the country trying to save him but there was no hope. Against his family's wishes, she enacted his living will, and had him taken off the machines. He died almost immediately."

"Oh, Gary, I am sorry. But you don't paint a picture of someone who is going to be very stable." Kate's voice was gentle.

"That's the point, Kate. She went through all this without shedding a tear in public, or missing more than a day's work. Every moment she wasn't at work, she was with him, but the strength she showed was absolutely mind-boggling. And the day after the service, she was back at work. And don't misunderstand, Kate, she loved that guy."

"And that's the bait, Gary? Give her the chance to get away from her past, start fresh. I know the feeling myself."

"I'd miss her a lot if you decided on her, but I know how you get what you want."

"Okay, Gary, I'll look at the tape with all your appraisals and information in mind. Thanks for the time. Be good to yourself."

Diana had slipped into the office and was inserting a tape into the recorder. "Here she is," Diana said. "What did Gary say?"

"He toasted her all the way up to our new satellite." Kate watched Diana put the tape in the machine. "Diana, I'm going to freshen up for a minute, and then I'll look at the tape."

"You've got a meeting with Peter Worijik in fifteen minutes," warned Diana.

"Back it up for me, please. I'll let you know when I'm ready."

Kate knew that Diana loved to look at new talent and also wanted to know more about what Gary Kincaid had said. But for the time being, Kate wanted to protect Kim Winston's privacy. It puzzled her that she didn't really know why. Perhaps if this was another Katherine Marchand, she wanted to see her first.

She returned to her desk, and still standing, picked up the résumé again. Texas A&M, transferred to New York University; *Newsday*, then a Nieman Fellowship; a New York independent station, then to WNRB. If she was as good as Gary said, why hadn't one of the networks grabbed her? She's thirty-four, good network age. Kate placed the résumé back on her desk. Maybe they just hadn't seen her yet.

"Well, let's see if this Kimberly Winston has it." Kate pushed the button to begin the cassette machine, and adjusted her remote control. She leaned back, sinking into the deep but supportive leather.

As always when she screened a tape, Kate turned off the volume. First, she had to look. As the tape steadied, she found herself watching a radiant, energetic, almost sculptured golden-haired woman walking along what looked like the Atlantic City boardwalk. Her clothes were almost surely Ralph Lauren, and her carriage was as proud as it was elegant. The camera moved to a close-up and Kate saw the high cheekbones, the sensitive curves of the lips, and the animated movement of the eyebrows. Most of all, she was struck by the piercing, azure-blue eyes, the same blue as Chris Curle's on CNN, but more vivid. The color was arresting, the camera seemed caught on it.

Kate realized she was leaning almost across her desk to get closer to the screen. She froze the image. The expression the recorder caught at that moment seemed to be almost challenging Kate. She quickly hit the rewind button, and went back to the head of the tape. Now to put the voice with the picture.

The sound, the tone of the voice, physically shocked her. The beauty of the woman had made Kate think she would hear a voice somewhat removed, maybe demure. But then, she thought to herself, after looking at the physical image, this woman did not strike you as actually demure. No, the voice was commanding, compelling, filled with expression. It was powerful. The woman was powerful. And now as Kate listened to the contents of the report, she realized something else. She could also write.

She was covering a story of government mismanagement resulting in harm to the boardwalk and the beaches, and she made you care. Kate found herself drawn in, attentive to every word this correspondent uttered.

The piece ended and Kate looked at the date that flashed on the screen. September, 1981, *after* the husband's death. Kate found herself wondering if Kimberly Winston had been stronger or weaker before that tragedy.

Next on the tape was an interview between Kim and the charismatic governor of New York. Kate listened approvingly to the questions. She knew how to interview. And she listened to the answers, and did the appropriate intelligent follow-ups. Smart.

Kate flipped off the set and rewound the tape. She very rarely sought a second opinion, and never had to look at more than a few moments of a journalist's work to know if he or she was good. But she was afraid the reaction in her gut to this woman was too strong. The dynamism could be misdirected. She buzzed for Diana. "Get Andrew in here and come in yourself, and let's look at this specimen from New York."

Diana came into the office quickly and when Andrew arrived, he said, "Diana said this was urgent, but wouldn't take long. I hope that's right because I'm trying to get the helicopter over to a gas explosion in Lynn."

"Is it on its way, with a crew?" asked Kate.

"Yes," replied Andrew.

"Then there's nothing you can do. You can't talk it there any faster. And I'm sure our reporters and cameramen know what to do." She smiled at Andrew, sympathizing with his need to be on top of a breaking news story.

"Sit, Andrew, take your mind off the explosion for a minute. Remember how I told you I was already on the prowl for Ann's replacement?"

"Oh, yes, the wonder woman you said you were after. Found her so soon?"

"I don't know," said Kate, trying to sound uncertain. "I just received a tape from someone who comes with high recommendations."

Kate pushed the remote control button but this time, instead of watching the screen, she watched Andrew and Diana. When the image came up, Diana raised her eyebrows and leaned forward. Andrew squinted and leaned forward too. So far, so good, thought Kate. Then she saw Diana begin to smile, and she realized Diana was responding to the reporter on the screen. Kate wondered if she had done the same thing. Andrew had a quizzical look, and then she saw him nod his head to something the reporter said. He was involved. The reporter had already pulled him in. In a matter of seconds. When the close-up came, she saw Diana's fixed stare, and this time, Andrew raised his eyebrows. Both of them leaned even further forward. The first report finished, and Kate pushed a button to freeze the image.

Andrew and Diana were silent, then Andrew spoke. "Kate, I'm usually slow to decide, but even if she can't write or interview, just to have her read the news is enough. I can't really explain it."

"Diana?" Kate asked.

"I love her. I just love her. I want her in my living room every night."

Both Andrew and Diana looked at Kate, their eyes questioning. "She's a magnet," said Kate finally. "And Andrew, I hear she can produce, write, and interview. And she's got an iron will."

"Hmmmm," said Diana, "I don't know if we can take two of those around here."

"I'm going to ignore that," Kate said.

"Why hasn't she been picked up by the networks?" Andrew asked.

"I don't know," said Kate quietly, but in fact she did know. She could guess exactly why. Kimberly Winston had probably just been rising in power when tragedy struck her life. Now the networks were afraid to touch her, at least so soon after the trauma, for fear she was going to crack. But they didn't see what Kate saw. The indomitable will of the survivor.

"Diana, get me Harry Abrams," said Kate decisively. "Andrew, back to the explosion. Don't be afraid to break in live to the network if the story's strong enough."

"Don't worry, Boss, I've got my blood going again. I'll handle the news. You just see to it that you get her." He pointed to the image still on the screen. "By the way, what's her name?"

"Kimberly Winston. Kim Winston. She's a street reporter someone will make an anchor if we don't get her first."

"Well, get her," said Andrew. As he rushed out of Kate's office, her intercom buzzed.

"Abrams on one."

Kate pushed the flashing button. "I want her, Harry."

"I knew it, Kate, but how about an interview? As I told you, she's a little reticent, and I'd have to get her out of her contract."

"How much is it?"

"With fees, just over five hundred thousand."

"Jesus, Harry. I had forgotten how much you guys get in New York. How much will it cost me to buy her out?"

"NRB will ask for the full remaining two hundred thousand."

"And if she wants a raise in salary, we're talking about almost a million-dollar baby here," Kate calculated.

"Wait until you meet her, Kate. You'll see she's worth every penny."

"Nobody's worth that much money. It's just a question of what ratings she can command." Then shifting gears, Kate asked, "Anything else I should know about her?"

"Well, to tell you the truth, Kate, I'd feel a little uneasy if I didn't tell you she's just getting over some major upheavals in her life."

"Unless she's just been released from prison for a murder charge, I'm not interested."

"No, nothing like that. She's completely clean."

"Then there's nothing more to discuss, Harry. Can you get her up here tomorrow?" She was not about to let on that she knew about Kim's tragedy, lest he warn Kim. She wanted to see how Kim would play it on her own, without time to prepare herself.

"I'll try my best," Harry said.

"Of course you will, Harry. Get her up here. Earn your money."

As soon as she hung up, Jonathan called. "Hi, Gorgeous, can you get by without me for dinner tonight?"

"No, but I'll try. Actually, it's after dinner that I'll miss you the most."

"How about Saturday night, then? Do we have any plans?"

"Not that I can remember."

"You know the new neurologist I'm touring around today? I like him and he's new in town . . ."

"Sure, let's have him over for dinner. I feel like cooking, anyway. Do you want to invite Deborah and Bob?"

"Sounds great. I have to rush. I love you."

"Hope it goes well, darling. Wake me if I'm asleep." She heard him hang up, and thought of the long hours he had ahead of him. She also knew he wouldn't wake her. Once her back allowed her to sleep, he would not disturb her.

Her next call was from Richard Blistick who told her what she had already assumed, that the leak about the satellite was from Steven Merriam. What she did not look forward to right now was another confrontation with Merriam.

3

KIM WAS IN THE PRESS ROOM OF THE HOUSE OF REPRESEN-
tatives in Washington when one of the other reporters called her.
She reached for the phone, and, with a strangely sad resignation
heard the jubilant voice of Harry Abrams.

"She wants you, kid, she wants you."

"Who wants me?" asked Kim, pretending not to know.

"Don't fool around with me, little one. You know who I'm
talking about."

"Harry, I am not your little one, and I'm trying to do my job,
and I can't do it jabbering with you on the phone every day."

"Kim, I just spoke with Kate Marchand. She's seen your
tape. She wants to see you, in person, tomorrow."

"Harry, we've gone through this. I don't respond to the snap
of someone's fingers. I'm here covering a story on a proposed
cut in antidrug funds in New York, and I happen to work tomorrow too. If she wants to see me that bad, she can wait until
I have some spare time."

"Kim, don't make this mistake," Harry warned.

"What mistake?"

"The mistake of losing the opportunity of a lifetime."

"Oh, Harry, I'm so sick of this. I have a perfectly good job.
Tell Katherine Marchand I'd like to talk to her but not necessar-

ily about a job and certainly not on Friday." Kim said goodbye and hung up.

"Did I hear the name of Katherine Marchand?" asked Henry Rogers, the Washington correspondent for a wire service. "She's one woman I've always wanted to meet."

She looked up at him elfishly. "Do you mean, Henry, there is a woman left you haven't met? To say nothing of bedded?"

"As to bedding, just two. You and Marchand, honey." He winked at her as the phone rang again.

"Kim Winston."

"Kim, I'm begging you. You don't fool around with this lady. What have you got to lose by just talking to her?"

"Harry, please give up. And let me do the job you set up for me. I like the people. I like the city. Boston can't match my money. And you know I'm getting better every day." She tried to be softer, trying to get Harry to understand.

"You've got nothing to lose by talking to her."

Kim lost her patience. "Harry, I am working tomorrow. I'll be busy with my son tomorrow night and over the weekend. I could go to Boston next week, but there's absolutely no reason for this big emergency. I'll talk to you next week."

Kim went back to the typewriter, putting together the different pieces of her story, hoping she would be able to have it on the satellite to New York within an hour, so she could get the five o'clock shuttle home for supper with Jason. Her phone rang and she just stared at it, furious. She picked it up, yanked it to her ear, and losing control, said, "Harry, enough. Go find someone else to bother."

"He probably would if he could."

Kim was surprised to hear a woman's voice on the end of the line. And despite her surprise, she allowed a slight laugh to slip out before she said, "Excuse me. This is Kim Winston."

"I know. I recognize the voice. This is Katherine Marchand."

Kim felt the breath pulled from her and, for once, she had no idea of what to say.

"Ms. Winston, I usually let the agents handle such things, but when they fail to communicate exactly what I want, it becomes necessary for me to step in," Kate said. "And I know you're terribly busy, probably trying to get out of that stuffy press room and back for the six, so I apologize for bothering you like this."

Kim found her voice and also her doggedness. "Mrs. Marchand, I don't think there *is* a problem in communication. Harry told me," she felt her voice growing bolder, "that you wanted to meet tomorrow. Unfortunately, I have an obligation to work tomorrow and I intend to meet it."

"It's not only an obligation, it's a responsibility to the public, Ms. Winston," Kate interrupted. "And with this Congress, the public needs all the enlightenment it can get."

Kim was surprised at the softness of tone.

"I would very much like it if you, your son Jason, and your housekeeper would be my guests in Boston this weekend." She did not wait for a reaction. "It seems spring has finally arrived. It promises to be a lovely weekend and you may have missed a bit of Boston and Cambridge since your Nieman days. You could fly up Saturday morning. We'll have a suite for you at the Ritz and you can tour the city. I hate to sound silly, but the swan boats go in the water this weekend. On Sunday, perhaps you could all come out to our house. It's in the country and Jason might enjoy it. And of course you know that I have a very strong professional interest in talking to you."

When Kate paused, Kim digested what she was saying. She wouldn't miss a day's work. Jason would end up doing something very special indeed. He loved to fly. She still had a few friends in Boston. Maggie could visit her sister. Oh, hell. . . .

"Ms. Marchand, I just happened to have promised my son we'd do something special this weekend." She hesitated and, her voice politely cool, added, "I think you may have just provided that something special."

"Good. I'll have a car pick you up at your apartment in New York at nine o'clock Saturday morning in plenty of time to make the ten o'clock shuttle. All your arrangements will be taken care of. The Ritz will let us know when you've checked in, and I'll give you a call." There was a finality to her tone.

"Then we have a deal to . . . talk, Ms. Marchand."

"I'm very pleased."

In Boston, Kate Marchand buzzed Diana and said, "Kim Winston will be arriving, with her son Jason, and his nanny, Margaret, on Saturday morning. I've got a list of all the arrangements that need to be made. Order a bottle of fine wine. Make sure the Ritz knows she is to be treated royally. Please give Gary Kincaid a call and ask him what Jason's favorite things are. You know, things that we could get him. They'll be coming out to the house on Sunday. Oh, and please find out whether the swan boats are in.''

"They are. It was on the noon news.''

"Thank God,'' sighed Kate. "Oh, and one more thing, what's that flower that means eternal life, eternal friendship, love, everything?''

"I don't know what you're talking about, Kate.''

"I know, I know,'' Kate said. "The rubrum lily. Order a dozen rubrum lilies for Kim's suite.''

4

KIM LOOKED OVER THE BOSTON PUBLIC GARDENS AS JASON
ran through the four rooms of the elegant suite. Furnished in a
blend of antique furniture and excellent reproductions, with rose
velvet chairs and a pale damask couch, the suite's sitting room
was more like a resting place for nobility than a commercial
hotel space.

"Mom, this is one of the best surprises I ever got. This place
is neater than our real house."

"Look, Jason," Maggie was standing by another window.
"See over there? The swan boats. See the swans in front of the
boats?"

"You mean that bird thing?"

Kim laughed. Katherine Marchand had certainly been true to
her word. It was a beautiful spring day in Boston. The arrangements had been perfect, flawless in fact, even down to a lovely
flight. Jason couldn't be happier. There were no memories for
him here. Margaret was going to visit her sister. Kim had a few
friends still in Cambridge. The suite was grand, complete with
a bottle of Château Lafite-Rothschild, '69. And there was a
bouquet on the glass-topped table by the windows of surely the
most exquisite lilies she had ever seen. White and pink, with
strains of rose rising through their tender petals. Kim touched

one of them gently and wondered to herself how high a price she was going to have to pay for all of this.

At that moment, the phone rang. Kim stared at it and let it ring several times. Despite the fact that one extension was near her, she turned to Maggie. "Would you get that for me?"

Maggie looked at her strangely. In all her years in Kim's home, she had never been asked to answer the phone. Not when Kim was available.

"Kim Winston's suite."

"Hello, this is Mr. Hennessey of guest relations. Mrs. Marchand has requested that Miss Winston give her a call when it is convenient. I have her private number for you." Maggie took the number and assured Mr. Hennessey that the arrangements were fine and that, yes, they knew Mrs. Marchand had put the Ritz at their service.

Maggie was standing by the phone, glaring at Kim. "It's not like you to play these games. Why didn't you want to answer the phone? And are you going to tell us what this last-minute trip is all about?"

"I told you." Kim walked towards her with an arm outstretched and rubbed Maggie's forehead. "The station here, WLYM, is apparently interested in talking to me. It's owned by a giant in the industry—Katherine Marchand. I feel pressured being here, but it was also the chance to do something special. Fill the void of this weekend." She turned and looked at Jason who was talking to no one in particular. "So, let's just make the most of it."

"Well, Katherine Marchand, whoever she is, must want you pretty bad. Look at this place. And the services?" Maggie began walking around, rubbing her hand over the marble mantel. "I was just informed that the Ritz is at our service."

"I take it it was not Madame herself on the line?"

"No," said Maggie a little testily. "She apparently was considerate enough not to want to bother you. She wants you to call her at your convenience. That doesn't sound like pressure to me."

"You don't know this woman, Maggie. That's her kind of pressure." Kim's voice was harsh.

"As God is my judge, you sound like you hate this woman. Do you even know her?" Maggie's voice rose.

"No, and I don't hate her. I'm just edgy. I think it's this weekend. I can't forget."

"Of course you can't. No one's expecting you to forget. But

it's over. There's nothing you can do. Just move on, dear. Now get a smile on. Here comes Jason.''

Jason suddenly flung himself over the top of the couch where they were sitting and Kim grabbed him and flipped him over as she tickled him. She also wiped tears from her eyes, and fought back the pain in her head. They were soon both exhausted, and sitting together quietly.

''So what are we going to do first, big boy?'' inquired Kim.

''Well, Maggie and me are going on the funny boats.''

''Maggie and I,'' corrected Kim. ''But what about me?''

''I thought you'd want to see your friends, and I could at least keep Jason occupied,'' Maggie said. ''Then when you get back, I'll go to my sister's and you two can go off.''

''That makes sense,'' said Kim, now relaxing. ''I'll make some calls, then take a cab over to Cambridge.''

''Aren't you going to use the limousine, Mom?'' Jason made it sound like a criminal offense.

''No, darling,'' said Kim, laughing, ''but you and Maggie can.''

''Oh, neat, Mom. Where will we go, Maggie?''

Maggie turned to Kim. ''You know, it's been a long time since Rosemary has seen Jason . . .''

Kim smiled. ''And wouldn't it be nice if you and Jason arrived on old H Street in a stretch limo? Give Rosemary and all of Southie something to talk about for a long time.''

''Now I didn't mean it that way, Kimberly.''

''Oh, Maggie, do it. It will be fun. Life is too short not to.''

''Oh, neat. Let's go.'' Chase jumped off the couch and grabbed Maggie's hands.

''First, you'll go to the bathroom and change that shirt you already engraved with your cocoa, young man,'' said Kim sternly.

''Yes,'' said Maggie, walking towards the phone, ''and that will give your mother time to make a phone call.''

''Why don't you call her if you're so damn anxious to talk to Mrs. Marchand?''

''I think I will,'' Maggie said, picking up the phone. ''Lord knows someone's got to treat this lady nicely.''

''I'm sure she has a whole militia of servants that she makes treat her nicely; I doubt you'll get through the first line of troops.''

''We'll see.'' Maggie fumbled as she punched out the numbers. ''It's ringing.'' She turned to Kim, who was watching with an impish grin. "Hello," Maggie stammered, looking quizzically. "I'm trying to reach the residence of Katherine Mar . . ."

"chand," said Kim.

"Katherine Marchand." Now Maggie appeared to be listening, then she was smiling, then laughing. "No, that's quite all right." Maggie was smiling at Kim with a very triumphant look. "Perhaps this is a bad time." She was interrupted, then laughed again. "Well, thank you. Thank you very much. We'll hold."

She stuck her tongue out at Kim, who had risen from the couch and was walking toward the phone. "Army of servants? You are wrong on this one. That was her husband who answered the phone. He picked it up down at the tennis court, because he could hear music from the kitchen and knew his wife was trying to—quote—massacre a piece of veal, and wouldn't hear the phone. But he apologized, said he could tell who I was from my accent, and he's right now running into the house to get his wife."

Kim waited a few minutes while Maggie chatted about tenderizing veal. Finally, she said, "Well, I'm looking forward to meeting you too, and thank you. Here's Kimberly." Maggie handed Kim the phone. "It's Kate." She smiled at Kim mockingly.

"Hello," Kim said. "I'm afraid we've interrupted you and your husband."

"No, no," Kate said firmly. "It's my fault. I didn't hear the phone ring, and I didn't expect a call so soon. I thought you might want to get settled. Is everything all right?"

"It's lovely, thank you."

"Kim, I was wondering," said the voice at the other end, "We're having some friends over for dinner tonight. Actually, just Jonathan and me and our close friends, the Falkensteins, and a new colleague of Jonathan's from the hospital."

Kim thought she knew what was coming. Katherine Marchand was moving in on Saturday and not just Sunday as she'd originally arranged.

"Well," Kate was saying, "would you think about joining us? My friends have children Jason's age and I'm sure Margaret could give me some tips on the veal."

Kim felt her headache returning, and thought, here we go, now we start paying the price. "I'm afraid that's impossible, Mrs. Marchand," said Kim coldly. "I was planning to stick to the agenda you spoke of on Thursday, and that would bring us

out to your home tomorrow. Margaret is visiting relatives tonight, and Jason and I are committed to some friends and a
movie tonight.''

"That sounds like a lot more fun, Kim. Sorry for trying
to impose,'' Kate said lightheartedly. ''We'll keep it as is for
tomorrow. George will bring you out around eleven. I look
forward to it. I hope you enjoy your day in Boston. Until
tomorrow then. Goodbye.'' The phone clicked and once again
Kim was left holding a silent instrument. Maggie was staring
at her.

"She wanted us to come out tonight, that's all, and I said
we'd see her tomorrow.'' Kim hung up the phone, not sure why
she felt confused.

"She couldn't have been more pleasant.'' Maggie turned to
find out why Jason was making gurgling sounds in the bathroom. "I hope you get hold of your feelings before tomorrow.
I'm looking forward to it. I wonder what she looks like. Sounds
so simple, down to earth, and homey.''

Maggie walked into the bathroom and Kim absently looked
down at the magazines by the phone. She laughed as she saw
the cover picture of *Boston* magazine. An elegantly dressed
woman, with vivid green eyes, a model's figure, and perfectly
coiffed brown hair, was sitting on the edge of a huge dark desk
with the Boston skyline in back of her. The power she exuded
was unmistakable. The banner across the cover read, "Boston's
Best: WLYM's Kate Marchand.'' And underneath, "Her Dynasty Grows.''

Without opening the magazine, Kim lifted it from the table
and walked towards the bathroom. She rounded the corner to
watch both Maggie and Jason playing with the Jacuzzi controls
on the side of a very large, ornate bathtub.

"Maggie,'' said Kim quietly, "you were wondering what that
dear little housewife and homemaker you were talking to looked
like?'' Kim showed her the magazine cover.

"No, that's not her.'' Maggie stopped as she read the banner.
Then she took the magazine from Kim and studied the face. "I
never thought that's what she'd be like. There's something about
her, Kim, that I've seen before.''

"Well, she used to be an anchorwoman.''

"No, it's not that. It's that look. I've seen it before.''

"Probably on a man-eating tiger.'' Kim took the magazine
from Maggie before she could start looking for the article.
"Don't you two have a date with some swans?''

* * *

The sun had lowered in the New England sky, taking with it the warm spring breezes that had accompanied Kim as she walked along the Charles River. Now, as she picked her way past the seemingly endless MBTA construction at Harvard Square, she pulled her jacket more tightly around her. The moment she entered Harvard Yard, the memories of her Nieman year came rushing back to her.

She had chosen to study philosophy and religion and, unlike many of her colleagues who were more interested in the ongoing parties that surrounded the Nieman activities, she took her studies very seriously. She remembered now how often she would rush across this yard en route to another stuffy classroom. But the brilliance of the professors and many of the students had inspired her to an intellectualism she did not know she had within her. In so many ways, she reflected, what she learned at Harvard had reinforced her personal values. The intellectual, as well as the social atmosphere, had made her a much more aware, more diversified, more demanding woman.

Now, ten years later, she felt she had accomplished many of the goals she had set while a student here. At first, she had felt unworthy of the fellowship. The Nieman was one of journalism's highest honors. When she applied, she had not thought she had had a prayer of receiving it. After an intimidating interview with the trustees, she was convinced it had been a mistake even to try. But her editor had encouraged her, and then, amazingly, she was accepted. The first month she was intimidated by the arrogance of the place, but soon she was questioning professors, even arguing at times. She was taken seriously.

Now, a student and professor passed her without so much as a turn of their heads. Kim thought how pleasant it was to be anonymous again, as she rarely was in New York. She felt like just another woman walking through Harvard Yard. Well, not quite. She still received the looks, the glances, the stares, but that was something that had been going on her entire adult life. Her appearance was something she could only mask after days of neglect, and it had been years since that had happened.

She had lunch with her favorite philosophy professor and visited later with a Nieman colleague who was now in Boston working for the *Globe*. These visits were, in themselves, pleasant but unremarkable. What she had found so interesting had been her friends' reaction when she said she was here at the request of Katherine Marchand. Elliot, her professor, who was usually cynical about anything involving the media, had only high marks for Marchand and her operation. He called her programming "daring" and "uncompromising." And Martha, who had interviewed Marchand, had called her "fascinating," "charming." But, Martha had said, there was obviously a side to her that was "outright ruthless." When Kim had asked why she felt that way, Martha's answer had been, "You don't do what she's done without leaving some bodies behind."

Kim thought about that remark now, as she sat on the steps of the Widener Library and watched the shadows lengthen across the Yard. Just because the woman had accomplished some astounding feats in the industry did not necessarily mean she "had left some bodies behind." And, anyway, Marchand didn't seem to think she was superhuman or above everyone else. Hadn't Maggie had a conversation with her about tenderizing veal? Didn't Maggie end up calling her "Kate"?

What am I *doing*? Kim got up and strode across the Yard. Now I'm defending the woman, she said to herself. Well, enough of the games. Maggie's right. Let's get on with this. I came here to meet Katherine Marchand and that's what I'm going to do. She and Chase would accept the Saturday night dinner invitation after all. It was time to meet the legend. It was time the legend met her. She walked into Harvard Square in search of a taxi to get her back to the Ritz.

5

KATE SAT AT THE COMPUTER TERMINAL IN HER STUDY, CALL-ing up the latest expenditures and projected sales income. Then she picked up a small portable recording machine and dictated a lengthy memo for Diana to transcribe. Halfway through, Jonathan walked into the study and put on the light over her shoulder mumbling something about the darkening of the room, and the harmful effects of staring for hours at the computer display screen. She tried to dismiss him with an irritated wave of her hand, but that only egged him on, and she completed the dictation half giggling as Jonathan brushed back her hair and ran his tongue around the perimeter of her ear.

"Jonathan, stop!" said Kate, not too convincingly. "I have work to do."

"And so you've been doing it for four hours this afternoon, and this morning after your swim," said Jonathan, moving his hand across her breast as she leaned into his waist. "All work and no play makes Kate a dull girl."

"You're so original, darling," Kate whispered, as she wrapped her arms around him and burrowed her head into his stomach. He stroked her back, and she ran her hand up his leg and began fondling his penis which quickly responded to her touch.

"I'm all sweaty," he said with a slight catch in his breath as she pulled his jogging pants and his shorts down to his knees.

"I love it when you're sweaty." She took his penis into her mouth and began fondling it with her tongue around its tip. She could feel him deep inside her mouth, smell and taste his muskiness, sense how she was controlling him. As her hands kneaded his firm buttocks, he pulled her down onto the Oriental rug, stripping off her velour pants, excited to find she was wearing no underwear. His penis never left her mouth as she opened herself now to his searching tongue. As his tongue flicked at her already hard and demanding clitoris, she let out a moan and then a deep sigh. Her own mouth moved up and down, her own hands increased their pressure. She heard him calling her name and then felt his cry deep within her. Afterwards she kissed him softly several times, then moved her kisses up across his stomach, twisting her body around, as she sucked on one of his nipples and then kissed him gently on the mouth and eyelids. Jonathan wrapped his arms around her tightly. With her head in the soft hollow of his neck and shoulder, they lay quietly, whispering their love.

Eventually, Kate began moving herself against Jonathan's leg. He responded by turning her gently on her side and sucking her breast. He moved his hand down her body, fondling her. Just when Kate began to moan, the telephone ring shattered the air like an explosion.

"Shit!" she said.

"Don't get it," Jonathan mumbled.

"It's the private line, so it's got to be Deborah. I told her I'd get back to her about bringing the kids."

"Call her back."

"Oh, Jonathan, hold on." She pushed him aside and reached for the phone.

"Can't a woman even fuck her own husband without being interrupted?" she said into the phone in her actress-stern voice.

"Ah . . ." the voice at the other end paused, "some days, nothing's sacred."

Kate laughed, then flushed as she realized that the voice was not Deborah's.

"Well, now it's my turn to have answered the phone too hastily," said Kate, angry at herself. "My apologies, Miss Winston."

"No, it seems *I* should apologize. And in light of that, I'll be brief." Kim was now matter-of-fact. "I was wondering if I could exercise a woman's right to change her mind and accept your dinner invitation for this evening?"

"It's not just a woman's right. I'd be delighted and so would my husband."

"Thank you, it will be just my son and myself, if that's all right."

"Of course, but what about Margaret?"

"She has plans with her sister."

"Well, this won't preclude tomorrow, so we'll get to meet her then," said Kate, winking at Jonathan, who was impatiently rapping his knuckles on the rug. "Anytime after seven is fine. I look forward to it, Miss Winston."

"So do I," said Kim. "Meanwhile, well, give my best to your husband." Kim laughed, and was pleased to hear Kate respond.

"I'll try." She hung up the phone and turned to Jonathan. "That was the mystery woman."

"So I gathered." Jonathan was pulling her towards him.

"I've got to call Deborah and tell her to bring the. . . ." Jonathan's mouth was on hers and soon they were on the floor, their bodies lit by the sun pouring in through the study windows.

A half hour later Kate whispered in Jonathan's ear, "Do you think there's something wrong with us?"

He picked his head up and looked at her incredulously. "Something *wrong* with us?"

"Yes, we seem to have such a healthy sex life. I mean, all those studies about women who never have orgasms, and men who don't enjoy their wives."

"Well, there is one thing irregular," said Jonathan, rather matter-of-factly.

"What?" demanded Kate, trying to push him off her.

"We're too damn happy. I'm the luckiest man in the world." Kate smiled and continued to caress him, watching the lawn outside grow dark. Eventually, they began to talk about the need to get off the rug and act like grownups.

Kate was in the tub before she remembered her call to Deborah. She picked up the phone on the wall behind the huge tub, and pushed the button that would automatically ring Deborah's home.

"Deborah, I almost forgot," Kate said hurriedly.

"You're in the tub again," laughed Deborah. "I can hear the echo. Why do you always call me when you're taking a bath? Don't you think there's something kinky about it?"

"I think there's something kinky about you. Can I help it if this is where I spend my free time?"

"No, Kate, I'm flattered. But what did you forget?"

"Well, I didn't think that New York reporter I told you about was going to come out tonight with her son. But she changed her mind. So how about bringing Kathy and Joseph?"

"You know they love to come to your house and play with all your video toys."

"Great. Thanks, Deborah. See you around seven." She lowered herself into the foaming bath and closed her eyes for a few moments of relaxation. Kate found herself slipping into a light sleep, listening to Jonathan from the shower hum rather badly, but softly, the theme song from the movie *A Man and a Woman*.

Kim was just stepping out of the shower at the Ritz, wrapping the huge hotel terry cloth robe around her, when she heard Maggie and Chase come through the door of the suite. She was relaxed and felt good. After talking to Kate and hearing Kate's own embarrassing indiscretion, she felt on more even ground—and almost unbearably envious. At first she had missed David so much that the sexual part of herself had seemed forever dead. Now, these past few months, she could hardly contain herself, so urgently did her awakening body need some relief.

"Mom, Mom. . . ." Chase came running into her arms and began a recitation of the events of the day. From the swan boats to lunch at Quincy Market—"best fried dough I ever had"—to the drive in the limousine to South Boston, to the walk down to the water where people were digging for clams—"just like we used to do with Dad."

Kim hugged him and laughed, allowing the tug she felt in her heart. Maggie was quick to change the conversation.

"And how was your day? How was the old campus and lunch with your professor? And why are you all squeaky clean?"

"My day was fine; and Elliot's fine, and I didn't think I usually walked around covered in dirt," Kim said.

"Oh, you know what I mean. You have a look in your eye that means you must be awfully excited about going to the movies with your son. Find some old flame at Harvard, maybe?" Maggie took off Jason's coat, then her own, then headed for the bathroom near her room.

"No, there's just been a change in plans."

"Oh?" inquired Maggie, stopping and turning back towards Kim.

"Yes, I've decided to take Katherine Marchand up on her offer. Jason and I are going out there for dinner."

"Oh, Mom, I thought we were going to a movie. Why do we have to go to some stupid dinner?" wailed Jason.

"Stop whining, young man," said Kim sternly. "There will be plenty for you to do and other children will be there too."

"Well," said Maggie, "for one, I'm glad you've come to your senses. But do you think maybe Jason would be happier with Rosemary and me tonight?" Kim told herself how necessary it was to keep some distance and privacy between herself and Maggie. She did not need, or want, a mother. But she held back her annoyance and said, "We'll still be going out there tomorrow, so you'll have plenty of time to meet Mrs. Marchand. And Maggie, I want to be with Chase tonight. You do understand?"

"Of course I do." She gave Kim a warm smile. "You know, even Rosemary knows this Kate."

"Personally?"

"No, don't be silly. She just knows all about her. Everyone seems to like her." Kim brushed her hair as Maggie told what she knew.

"You know, she used to be a big deal in New York. That's what it said in the magazine, and she took this Boston station from nothing and it's now supposed to be one of the best in the United States. Can you imagine, a woman doing all that? But they do say she gets everything she wants."

"And you think if she wants me, she'll get me?"

"No," Maggie answered. "You don't do anything you don't want to do. I've certainly learned that. All I'm saying is that this might be something you would want to do."

They'd been talking in the bathroom where Kim was getting ready to go. Now she impatiently set down the hair dryer and, taking Maggie's arm, she walked to the living room. "Maggie, please. I know you like Boston and that you would like being closer to your sister. But at the moment, we both live in New York City, where I am employed and under contract and, might I add, where I am very happy with my work." She paused as she pulled aside the cream-colored curtains and looked out the window.

"We are in Boston, and I am going to meet Katherine Marchand because I as well as my agent do not believe it is advisable to say no to her, at least not without talking to her first. But I don't want to relocate. I don't want to upset Jason's life or mine, just when they're finally returning to normal. Maybe in the future we'll think of Boston seriously, but not now. And I don't want to feel pressured. Aren't you happy in New York with Jason and me?'' Her voice was stony.

''No, no, Kim, and I'm sorry I stepped out of line. I guess I'm just impressed with the deluxe treatment we've been getting and the magazine article and all.'' Maggie looked down at the wrinkled cover of *Boston* magazine she'd been carrying around all day. Kim's eyes followed Maggie's and she couldn't help herself. She, too, was drawn toward the figure that seemed ready to jump out of the photograph.

''Would you get Chase out of the tub?'' Kim asked. ''Maybe you could get him dressed while I finish getting ready. I'll call the limousine service and ask how long it will take to get us to wherever she lives.''

''She lives in Dover, about a half hour from here,'' Maggie said quietly.

''I should have known,'' laughed Kim, walking past Maggie, and tousling the older woman's gray hair. ''We'll drop you off at Rosemary's along the way.''

''Oh, wonderful, will you come in?''

''Of course, if there's time,'' Kim said.

As Maggie left the room, she glanced again at the picture of Katherine Marchand. She realized suddenly why the woman seemed familiar, where she had seen that look before, that look of intimidating beauty, power, and determination. It was Kim's look too.

After visiting for a few minutes with Maggie's family, Kim and Chase were on their way to the Marchands'. Jason sat up front with the driver chattering about cars and Kim quietly closed the glass partition that separated the front of the car from the back. She leaned against the seat and turned the stereo on high, luxuriating in the peaceful comfort. Kim blessed the instinct that had made her bring along a dress—maybe she had prepared subconsciously for this dinner. She looked down at the slightly flared skirt of the dress she'd almost not bought when the saleswoman at Bergdorf's described it as ''Dynasty Blue.'' Well, the color was just right, even so, echoing her eyes, its brightness highlighting the streaky blond of her hair. She felt ready for the beautifully groomed fashion plate she was about to meet.

The car pulled off the turnpike and traveled through Wellesley, past homes that were like mansions. Kim had forgotten how wealthy the suburbs of Boston were, similar to the old North Shore of Long Island, except you didn't have to travel very far from the city to reach them. Soon they were on a dark winding back road, and then an even darker road that seemed to handle, just barely, the width of the limousine.

"Is this the driveway?" asked Chase, beating Kim to the question.

"Oh, no," the driver replied, "this is just a local road."

As Kim looked along the headlights at the unkempt roadway, she opened the partition. "I hope they don't pay a lot in taxes for road maintenance."

George laughed and told her it was "private." Kim realized then that the road was kept like this to discourage curiosity-seekers and to insure that only the residents would use it.

Finally, George turned the limousine to the right, through two large stone pillars.

"Here's the drive," said George.

Here goes nothing, or everything, Kim thought to herself. Well, I'm just going to be myself. She can take it or leave it.

They seemed to be driving through a forest and again Chase spoke. "This is still the driveway?"

"Yup," said George. "And we're just about halfway there." A short distance further, George brought the car to a complete stop.

"What are we doing?" asked Kim nervously.

"Oh, sorry, ma'am, don't be alarmed," the driver said quickly. "This is where the sensors are. They set off an alarm in the house, letting the Marchands know someone is coming up. When they're not here, or they don't turn it off, it rings at the police station. We have to wait a second while the cameras take a picture of the car and us."

The car resumed its uphill climb and after several hundred yards came through the forest. They were facing a large circular drive lit with tall wrought iron, glass-encased gas lights. In the fading light Kim could see the beautifully curried lawn and a large house whose windows beckoned them with light. It was like suddenly coming upon a fairyland. She looked at Chase and laughed. His mouth had dropped open.

"The tennis courts and pool are over there but you can't see them. The stables are out back," George said as they drove through a high stone archway. The limousine stopped, the door opened and a man stepped out of the house. Kim felt as if someone had hit her squarely in the stomach.

"Mommy!" Jason screamed. He had already opened the door and seemed to have flown out of the car before Kim could pull herself together and grab him. He was running across the drive screaming at the man. Kim scrambled after him.

Upstairs in the large screening room where Kate was playing with her godchildren and talking to Deborah, the conversation fell silent as they heard the child's screams. Kate went to the window quickly, saw the limousine, and the little boy running toward Jonathan, who looked rather bewildered. Jonathan crouched down and let the child fly into his arms. Then Kate noticed the blur of blue and blond running after the boy. When she reached him, Kim caught hold of him and crushed him to her. He was now sobbing and she was trying to comfort him. The three of them stayed crouched down, and Jonathan had his arm around the blond woman as well as the little boy.

"What the hell's going on?" Kate wasn't aware that Deborah had come up beside her, and was also watching the drama unfold.

Pulling Deborah from the window, Kate said, "I'm not sure, but I can guess. The child lost his father recently. Maybe Jonathan resembles him."

"Oh, God," said Deborah, collapsing into a leather chair.

Kate paced the room nervously. "I think we'll wait up here until things calm down a bit."

She was wearing black silk pants with a heavy white silk blouse open at the throat. Around her neck were pearls and crystal beads, a strand of rough-cut jade, and brightly gleaming gold coins from Mexico. The effect was careless, but opulent.

Kate looked at her watch and when five minutes passed, Jonathan came in looking a little shaken, but talking nonchalantly with the absolutely handsome blond boy holding his hand. Jason's face was still a little swollen, but his eyes lit up when he saw the huge video screen.

"Kate, Deborah, I'd like you to meet Mr. Jason Winston." The small boy now seemed very sure of himself. He stepped smartly towards Kate and held out his hand. "I saw your picture in the magazine."

Kate shook his hand and laughed. She had an urge to pick him up and squeeze him. It was a reaction she seldom had. Jason was now shaking Deborah's hand. Kathy and Joseph, Deborah's four- and six-year-old, came over to greet the newcomer, then pulled him away to the assorted toys and video games. The adults were soon forgotten.

"We had a little misunderstanding when Jason and his mother drove up," Jonathan said softly. "He thought I was his dad, poor kid. He must have forgotten for a minute that his father's dead."

"I thought that's what must have happened," Kate said, taking his hand and kissing him on the cheek. "You seem to have handled it beautifully. Thank you, darling."

"I feel bad for them," said Jonathan sincerely. "His mother, Kim, is putting her face back on, or whatever it is women do."

"Where's my husband?" inquired Deborah.

"In the kitchen, arguing with Ralph about the wine, where else?" answered Jonathan mischievously.

Deborah muttered something about getting her husband into line and left the room. With a few words to the children, who were now far too busy to deal with grownups, Kate and Jonathan left the screening room and went downstairs. Jonathan took Kate's hand and they walked in silence. Halfway down the staircase, Kate spoke. "Well, did you have a chance to look at Kim?"

"To tell you the truth, not really," replied Jonathan. "I was really thrown off, and she was trying to comfort her son." He paused. "But I did get to put my arm around her. You know how I love to fondle your talent." He said it jokingly and unthinkingly.

They were at the bottom of the stairs, and Kate tore her hand from his. She turned and stared at him with a look that would have knocked a weaker man down. Immediately, Jonathan understood what memory he had brought to the surface.

"Oh my God, Kate," his voice was shaking. "I'm sorry. I wasn't thinking. Oh, God, Kate, I'd never hurt you. Never again. I promised. Please, darling." Her eyes softened slightly, and she looked away from him. "I love you, Kate. I could never, and will never, love anyone else. You must believe that." His voice was adamant and strained. "Let me love you, better and better." He turned her face to him and kissed her on the lips, pulling her into him with all his strength and passion. Slowly, she responded, her hand pushing through his dark hair.

Suddenly, they heard someone coming and they withdrew from each other slowly.

"Oh Lord," someone said, "I seem to have done it again."

Jonathan stepped back with a laugh, and Kim found herself face to face with him. She felt the breath taken from her again as Jonathan's hauntingly familiar eyes gently fell on hers. And then she looked at Kate and saw one of the most stunning, and at the same time, provocative faces she had ever laid eyes on. Katherine Marchand had exactly the same thought, gazing at Kim.

"Katherine Marchand."

"Kim Winston."

Jonathan stood back confused. He did not know who had spoken which name. He also felt, as he saw their hands come together, that he was standing too close to an operating table where a patient was being revived by electric shock. Their hands were locked—Kate's deeper tone against Kim's fair color—as fiercely as their eyes were. Finally, it was Kate who broke the moment, dropping her hand and turning to Jonathan.

"I believe you've met my husband."

"Not properly, I'm afraid," responded Kim, extending her hand. "I apologize for the earlier confusion and thank you, Dr. Marchand." She felt her heart trembling.

"Please, it's Jonathan."

"And I'm called Kate. Thank you for coming . . . Kim?" Jonathan thought it was one of the few times he had ever heard Kate sound tenuous.

"Please. And again thank you for all the arrangements."

The polite small talk was interrupted by the loud entrance of Bob and Deborah who were arguing about wine and looking for an intermediary. At the sight of Kim, they halted. As Kate observed them, she remembered the real reason for Kim's presence, and her hunch was reinforced by their obviously strong reaction.

Introductions were made as they entered a very large room whose walls were hung with several very important modern paintings. In one corner a polychrome wood Buddha sat on a marble pedestal, knee crossed, one leg dangling down in the "Royal ease." The furniture was traditional, but all the upholstery was of a pale beige—wools and silks perfectly matched to provide a quiet background to the splendid art. A table in the corner was covered with small bronzes—an exquisite horse, a fierce bull dog, a rifleman taking aim.

"Kim, these are our friends Deborah and Bob Falkenstein. Actually, Bob helps me find these pieces," Kate said, pointing to the bronzes. "He's an antiques dealer."

"That's right," Bob said. "I fear that if it were not for me, this place would be furnished in late Bedford-Stuyvesant. Kate has pretty good taste but she doesn't exactly have a lot of time.

Neither does the good doctor.'' He nodded in Jonathan's direction.

A man passed through the room serving hors d'oeuvres, and Kim heard Kate say to him, ''Tell Bridget eight o'clock is fine.''

Kim, who was standing next to Jonathan, said softly, ''For some reason, Maggie had the impression your wife was a one-woman show. I'm relieved she has someone to help.''

''What do you mean?''

''I'm sorry. I don't mean to be sarcastic, but when you talked to Maggie, she thought Kate was cooking dinner and running her home all on her own.''

Jonathan took Kim's arm and walked her over to a pair of eighteenth-century chairs positioned in the corner for a tête-à-tête. As they sat down and the shadows from a lamp fell across Jonathan's face, Kim saw again the resemblance to David that both she and Chase had seen from the limousine.

''Not that it matters,'' Jonathan began casually, ''but Kate and I take our private time very seriously. We have so little of it together. The only time there is any help around here is when we're out of the house, or when we're entertaining. My wife did prepare most of the dinner for this evening, but Bridget, who comes in every day to clean, and helps us when we entertain, will do the final preparations and serving and cleaning up. And Ralph does everything from handling the gardeners to being what you might call a butler at gatherings like this.''

Kim felt as if she had been rude and intrusive. ''I'm sorry to seem nosey,'' she said.

''I understand, Kim,'' said Jonathan, smiling. ''I know my wife's reputation and I can see that you wouldn't know what to expect. But she wants you to know what to expect from her, and that's why she's invited you into our home.''

At that moment, a splintering noise screeched through the room, and seemingly the entire house.

''God damn it, Ralph, why the hell isn't that thing turned off?'' Kate shouted above the siren, and put her glass down angrily. She stormed out of the room and the noise stopped. In the sudden silence the guests could hear the conversation between Kate and Ralph.

''Ralph, it shouldn't have been turned back on. I told you there would be three cars.''

''I'm sorry, Mrs. Marchand. I thought the final party had arrived.''

''Call the police and tell them there is no emergency,'' replied Kate. "and call quickly because I didn't make enough veal to feed the Dover Police Department." With the lightness returning to her voice, she reentered the room, apologizing for the damage to eardrums.

Meanwhile, Jonathan had gone to the front door.

"You didn't tell me you lived on the other side of the Black Forest, Jonathan," came a strong male voice from the entranceway. Jonathan laughed and told the guest his arrival had caused everyone to go deaf. He then introduced the well-built but slight blond man to Kate. Kim was now standing by her chair and was amused to see the man's reaction to Kate. He was instantly taken aback.

"I'm afraid your photographs don't do you justice, Mrs. Marchand," he said.

"Thank you. I hope you didn't have too much trouble finding the house." Kate turned him by the arm, deliberately, so he was facing Kim.

His eyes had caught Kim's and once again he was visibly startled by the woman before him. Kate watched and smiled to herself.

After the introductions were over, the two doctors went to the bar and Kim studied the newly arrived guest from a distance. He was of a much less rugged build than Jonathan and he seemed very young, but that could perhaps be his tan and golden-blond hair. He looked more like a California surfer than a doctor.

As if he knew she was watching him, Chris left Jonathan's side and came to stand beside Kim. "This room seems to be full of beautiful women," he said. "I didn't expect that in New England. Where are all the blue-haired Brahmins?"

"I wouldn't know," said Kim calmly. "I'm from New York myself." At that moment, there was a burst of laughter and shouting as three children came running into the room. Two of them seemed to be in a not too serious argument and went up to Deborah. The third searched the room anxiously and Kim rose. "Chase?"

Jason came running over to his mother. "Mom, I thought you were gonna come up," he said, trying to sound disappointed. "There are all types of neat things up there."

"I've been busy down here, Chase." She pulled the scruffled blond head against her hip. "I want you to meet a friend of Dr. Marchand's. This is Dr. Christopher Cerci. Doctor, this is my son Jason."

"Please, call me Chris," he smiled and knelt down next to

Jason. "You, too. What type of neat things are you playing with?" Jason began an explanation about huge video screens, video games, tapes and computers.

"I think I've got to see this for myself. Will you show me?" Chris was obviously at ease with children.

"Sure," responded Jason immediately, then looked up at his mother. "Okay, Mom?" Before Kim could reply, the doctor had suggested she join them, and Kim found herself being led out of the drawing room by Jason, followed by Christopher.

"Jesus, can you believe this place?" asked Christopher.

"It certainly isn't your average bungalow," Kim responded. They walked down a long hallway in what seemed a rather awkward silence. "So you're new to this area?" Kim broke in.

"Yes, California born and bred. But now I'm to be a colleague of the renowned Dr. Jonathan Marchand at New England General."

"I don't know that much about Jonathan. Is he renowned?"

"He certainly is. In neurosurgery, they don't get much better. But to the general public, his medical reputation is somewhere in the shadow of his famous wife."

When they got to the viewing room, Christopher said, "I guess this is what you would expect from the power behind a television dynasty—more space age than you'd expect in this old mansion."

"She needs it for her work," Kim said.

"Are you in the business, too?"

"Yes, in New York."

"Old friend of Kate's?"

"No, not really. I met her a few minutes before you did."

"Oh?"

"There's really no need for secrecy," said Kim, adjusting a cassette player for Jason. "There's a rumor that she is interested in me professionally for her station. She brought me and my son up to Boston to consider me for a job."

"I'm sorry. I hope it didn't sound like I was prying," Christopher said.

"No, and to be perfectly honest, I'm glad you're here too. Another newcomer to join me on display."

"You mean the old clothing on the rack routine? Getting the once over?"

"No, I'm making it sound too cold," said Kim, her voice softening. "So far, Kate and Jonathan have gone out of their way to make Jason and me feel comfortable. And I also have to admit, it is an experience meeting this journalism legend.''

"There is something about her; I have the feeling she's not a woman you want to be on the wrong side of," Christopher said, walking around the room and touching the various pieces of electronic and video equipment.

Kim noticed the thick cables coming out of the walls that interfaced with the records and computers. Obviously, she thought, the roof must have a maze of microwave disks so Kate could monitor all network and cable transmissions.

Kim said, "I hope all this stuff doesn't give Jason big ideas about what he needs in his room."

"You keep on talking about you and Jason," said Christopher hesitatingly. "Are you separated from his father?"

Kim was very used to the question. It came every time she and Jason were together with strangers. For some reason, people automatically assumed a separation, divorce. Jason now looked up at her, his eyes growing sad. "No, I'm widowed. Chase's— Jason's father died about a year ago."

"A year ago, Mom? Was it a year ago? How long's a year?" The small boy had tears in his eyes.

None of the three were aware of it, but Kate had come into the doorway, and was now watching Kim and her son silently.

"Yes, it's a year," said Kim gently, pulling the boy close to her. For the moment, she was alone in the room with her son. "A year's a long time; it's twelve months, three hundred sixty-five days." Her voice fell into a whisper. "It's a long time, my angel, a long time." A sob came from Jason and she held him tighter.

Kate watched as Kim comforted her son, noticing that Kim herself did not succumb to the emotion of the moment. Her back grew stiffer, and her voice stronger as she talked Jason back away from his tears and his memories. Christopher had turned and was looking out the window. Kate stepped back from the doorway and walked quietly down the hallway. She remembered Kim's words about having promised Jason a special weekend and realized she was dealing with a woman on the first anniversary of her husband's traumatic death. Well, thought Kate, it's a hell of a way to test someone's strength, but it's a way.

"Darling," said Jonathan, coming up to her. "Ralph says Bridget can serve anytime. Personally, I'm starved."

"Wonder why?" asked Kate, smiling mischievously. "Why don't you call your friend the doctor to come down. He's with

Kim and her son. I'll tell Ralph we're ready." Kate went into the kitchen where Deborah was helping Bridget with the children's dinner—a combination plate of spaghetti and pizza. When Kate joined them, Deborah said, "She's what you've been looking for, Kate."

"Is that the great advertising and marketing mind talking?"

"Absolutely."

At that moment, Kim and Jason came into the kitchen. "Jonathan told us there might be some pizza in here." Kate looked at Kim. There was no sign of any emotional trauma. Kim seemed one-hundred percent in control.

They settled the children and then the three women joined the men at a dining room table that mixed silver and crystal with pottery plates and daisies in bud vases before each place. Christopher took a seat beside Kim, facing Bob and Deborah, with Kate and Jonathan at each end. Kim learned that Deborah was the head of one of Boston's largest advertising agencies; Jonathan, she knew, was a prominent neurosurgeon; that Christopher was an up-and-coming neurologist; and that Kate was many things—charming, disarming, commanding and compassionate. But above all, she was controlled; power personified. And she knew it and seemed to enjoy it. Strangely, Kate's demeanor did not offend Kim, as those same characteristics might have in a man. Kate pulled it off with class and ease. She wasn't overbearing. She didn't make herself sound like she was better than others. She listened, laughed, and seemed to care about everyone at the table, asking the right questions at the right time. Her skill as an interviewer came forward, but along with the touch of gentleness was the definite indication that you did not toy with Katherine Marchand.

It was Deborah's husband, Bob, who triggered the situation that made this clear. "Kate, what's this I read? Your news has dipped in the ratings for the first time?" As soon as the words were out of Bob's mouth and he looked in Kate's direction, he regretted having spoken.

Kim saw the ice fly from Kate's eyes.

"Now we know you can read, Bob." There was an uneasy silence, as Kate put down her wine glass. "And you're right. The eleven o'clock news, twice in the last five years, has dropped a rating point. Two nights, out of five years."

"Of course. It was silly of me to even mention it."

Kate's voice rode over his, as if he hadn't spoken. "Two nights, Bob. One of them the night of the playoffs. The other

network had them. You know that game you love where boys
try to be men by hitting each other with sticks and ramming
other bodies into walls?''

Deborah and Jonathan had started to laugh. Christopher was
smiling, as was Kim. No, thought Kim, you don't make mistakes in front of this woman.

They had coffee in the small study, where a quiet fire burned.
The conversation turned to the increasing role of religious leaders in national and international politics. It was a well-informed,
interesting discussion, and Kim was once again pleased and
intrigued by the caliber of her companions, and, in particular,
with Kate's insight. Jonathan stood beside Kate's chair, his hand
on her shoulder. Kim noticed how Kate would from time to time
lean forward slightly and Jonathan would move his hand down
her back in a massaging motion. On one of these occasions,
despite the fact that she was listening intently to Christopher,
Kate moved her head and brushed her lips across Jonathan's
hand as it returned to her shoulder.

Kim thought she was studying Kate secretly, but Kate was
also examining the woman she now was sure she wanted as her
new anchorwoman, her new star. There was no question that
Kim's physical appearance, the way she handled and carried
herself, was exceptional. But what pleased Kate most was that
Kim showed an intelligence and awareness about political and
social issues she knew she could never find on her own current
staff. And she had one of the best staffs in television. No, *the*
best. Except, apparently, for this one person. And that would
soon be rectified. She was going to get Kim Winston.

As if Kim could sense what Kate was thinking, she suddenly
turned to face her. For several seconds, their eyes held until Kim
turned away sharply, as if pulling out of a trance. When she
looked up again, Kate was discussing with Deborah the role of
the Vatican in international finance.

Christopher soon announced he had early morning appointments with realtors and had to begin to find his way ''out of the
Black Forest.'' Kim took this as a cue to go upstairs and get
Jason. She said good night to Christopher before she went and
when he said he hoped they would meet again, for the first time
in a year, Kim hoped a man meant it.

As she turned to walk up the stairs, he bolted past her. ''Forgot to say goodbye to Jason and the others.'' It seemed only
seconds before he passed her again on the way down, grabbing
her arm and saying, ''Don't rush, the Muppets are babysitting.''

She laughed, said goodnight again, and headed for the large video room. Christopher was right; the Muppets were babysitting, and all three children were sound asleep. As she went to kneel by Jason on the couch, she was joined by Deborah.

"Well, no wonder they were so quiet," said Deborah, hands on hips. She went over to where Jason lay and said, "Usually I only like my own children, but your son is adorable. Have you thought about letting him do commercials?"

"Oh, no," laughed Kim. "One person before the camera in a family is enough."

Deborah sat down at the end of the couch. "Sit, relax for a moment." Kim responded to the woman's affectionate tone, and sat down at the other end of the couch, lifting Jason's head onto her lap. Her son was sprawled out between them and Deborah nonchalantly retied one of Jason's shoelaces.

"You've known Kate a long time?" asked Kim finally.

"Since college. Watched her climb, through the good and the bad."

"It doesn't seem like there's been much bad for her."

Deborah eyed Kim warily. "You're too smart for a comment like that, Kim. Or you're too much like her. You both hide yourselves very well." An uneasy silence followed. "I didn't mean to be reproachful," said Deborah, softening her tone considerably. "Go ahead, ask me about her, everyone does."

"But you won't tell me anything," said Kim, now feeling equal in the game. "Katherine Marchand would not have a close friend who would talk glibly about her or in any way jeopardize her privacy."

"Kim, let's stop dancing. Kate would be ashamed of both of us. I know she likes you. You know she likes you. We both know she wants to hire you. She wants you on her team."

"She has not been that direct with me, although my agent tells me there is sincere interest," Kim said directly.

"Oh, come on, Kim, not just anyone passes these portals. Kate's time is too important to her. She doesn't invite many people here, and she doesn't waste a moment."

"Well, you know Kate, and you know her business," Kim began in an interviewing tone, "what exactly does it mean to be 'on her team,' as you put it?"

"Let me explain it this way. If I were to do a commercial for Kate's enterprises, it would resemble a rocket, breaking through into a different universe. She's moving into new space every day. She is going to make her mark."

"But she has already made her mark."

"She'll always want more, Kim, she'll never be content. She'll be running full blast as she takes her last breath, even though all the odds will still be against her."

"What do you mean against her?"

"Well, we all know the odds of dealing in a man's world—still. And then . . ." Deborah paused. "Kate would not approve of me telling you this, but I'm going to anyway, because I think you're going to need all the information you can get about Kate Marchand to make the right decision for yourself."

"Yes?" said Kim, somewhat hesitatingly.

"Physically, she has already made history, and makes it every day. She doesn't let anyone know that except her few close associates. She lives with a back injury and resulting back pain that would have crippled the strongest man. But she's a person who will not be stopped." Deborah paused. "To tell you the truth, my gut instinct is that you are of much the same mettle."

"I don't know if we *are* of the same mettle, as you put it, but I've never met anyone like her in my life. And I'd like to know her better."

"Well, you've come closer than most, being invited here."

Kim was puzzled. "So why did she have me here? Why am I coming here tomorrow? Why has she opened herself to this? Especially when she knows I'm already under contract?"

"Kim, I learned long ago never to underestimate Kate. She apparently thinks you're worth taking the risk. She knows what she's doing. Be sure of that."

Kim thought about Deborah's words. "What *is* she doing?"

"In my opinion, if you buy the analogy of the rocket, I think she wants you to be the cone of that rocket. She needs you to carry her rocket through that next atmosphere. And I don't mean to sound so calculating, but you know the stakes in this game. Kate is acting with good reason. As a professional, I see you are uniquely marketable. Like a fine racing car." She weighed her next words. "Kate could provide the ultimate race."

"But maybe I don't want the race." Kim's tone was cold.

"Kim, I'd be doing you and Kate an injustice if I didn't tell you how I feel. If you join Kate's team, you will meet the challenge of your life. It will also be the chance of your life. I don't know the circumstances of your life in New York, but if you choose to climb with Kate, you will have to work harder than you have ever worked, and make more sacrifices to her demands than you have ever had to before. In return, she will also make you a legend. You will be fulfilled and stimulated professionally beyond what you can imagine.

"And be assured, Kim, that good or bad, your life will never be the same again."

The two women were silent as Kim thought about Deborah's words and looked down at Jason still sound asleep on her lap.

"I keep hearing people say Katherine Marchand gets whatever she wants."

"In a way, that's true."

"So, if she wants me, she'll get me?" Kim inquired.

"Don't be foolish, that is entirely up to you."

"Even though she has decided she wants me as the 'cone of her rocket'?"

"She wants you, Kim, but if you decide not to come, Kate will suspect you wouldn't have worked out anyhow, because you didn't have the ambition or the imagination to become a superstar."

There seemed nothing else to say. The two women gathered up their children and went downstairs.

"I thought we had lost you two," said Kate as the group of them came awkwardly down the stairs.

"Nope, just commiserating with the Muppets." Deborah winked at Kate.

"Yeah, I'll bet." She turned to Kim. "George has heated the car for you and Jason, and is waiting for you. Thank you again for coming out. We'll see you tomorrow morning, with Margaret, of course."

"Yes, and thank you again." Kim stepped back and watched while Chase offered his own sleepy thanks. Before they left, Deborah took Kim's hand, and leaned forward and kissed her gently on the cheek.

"It was a pleasure, Kim—no, a delight."

When everyone had left, Kate listened to Jonathan sing Kim's praises. He couldn't stop talking about her beauty, her intelligence and—that word again—her magnetism. Kate knew with certainty that she wanted those qualities for her station.

6

KIM DIGESTED HER USUAL DIET OF SUNDAY MORNING NEWS-
papers, *The New York Times* and the *Washington Post*. She
glanced through the Boston papers, the *Globe* and the *Herald*,
but they didn't hold her attention for long. The remains of breakfast lay on the small round table of the suite's dining alcove.
Maggie had gone to Mass, Jason was in the bedroom, still in
his pajamas, watching the hotel's cable channel that seemed to
be running his favorite cartoons, one *Superfriends* episode after
another. He was still a little tired and Kim was letting him rest.
In fact, she was relieved when, checking on him a few minutes
later, she found he had fallen back to sleep. She began a shower,
leaving the bathroom door open, in case he awakened. The ritual
of the hot water, then the cold, was followed. And as she did
every morning, Kim hoped it was indeed true that cold showers
were good for the skin. As the water pounded on her shoulders,
she once again went through the events of the night before—
from the luxury of the estate to the kindness of Dr. Jonathan
Marchand, to the comfortable presence of his colleague, Christopher, to the conversation with Deborah. She reviewed all these
but thought most about the contradiction that seemed to be part
of Kate Marchand. Strong, yet very warm. Powerful and intelligent, yet determined to take a chance on someone who seemed
set against moving to Boston, and had a contract.

114

She began to dress, feeling a bit like she was preparing for an interview—where not her work clothes, but her Saturday country casual style would be judged. She'd brought a Calvin Klein skirt, cut something like a divided riding skirt. It was a color close to khaki—but deeper and with a cut of the fabric that was definitely not government issue. She wore with it a ribbed beige turtleneck sweater and planned to sling over her shoulders a tweed hacking jacket she'd bought at Kaufman's riding supply store in New York—but which had never been closer to a horse than in a taxi briefly paralleling the bridle path in Central Park.

As she was dressing, she heard a familiar song come over the radio. She knew it was silly to be so open to the sentiments of a popular song, but she went to sit in a chair, looking out the window at the early spring morning in the Boston Public Gardens, to listen to the words of how someone wanted to keep someone else from the rain. And, oh, how she wanted that.

The tears flowed easily, as Kim went back to a time when she did not feel so alone, a time when she allowed herself to be taken care of, to be kept from the rain. When it was all right, in his arms, to be vulnerable. The tears grew bitter as she felt the demanding "why" begin to flow into the back of her throat and put its hold on her. She told herself it was time to get herself in check. She was not going to relive the events of a year ago. She didn't have to; the images, the pain, were all still fresh. The crowded church, the endless stream of faces. David's hysterical mother, Chase's uncomprehending silence as he pressed his body against hers. And then the walk alone that night, along the beach, as the ashes disappeared into the silent, relentless wind.

"Mom?"

"I'm right here, honey." She went in and played with the still drowsy five-year-old. Then she hustled him into the shower, watching through the glass door as he made a small mountain of soap suds on his head. Well, there goes another bottle of baby shampoo, she thought. She was covering Chase with a bath sheet large enough to cover a Boston Bruin, when she heard the door of the suite open.

"You people are supposed to be ready to go. George is already downstairs waiting for us," Maggie called. "And I want to see for myself that place Jason was going on about last night."

"Okay, we'll leave right now. Chase, put on your coat."

"Mom, I don't even have my underpants on!"

They all laughed and in what seemed just moments later, they were driving along the turnpike and Jason was giving a nonstop explanation to Maggie about all she would see. Kim relaxed, watching the lovely countryside as they moved through the back roads to Dover. Soon they were climbing the long driveway, and when they stopped at the sensors, Chase told Maggie, "Smile, 'cause there's secret cameras taking pictures of us right now." Kim couldn't help laughing when she saw Maggie and Chase mugging for their unseen audience.

As the limousine pulled out of the woods, Kim was even more impressed than she'd been the night before. In the daylight, the estate seemed immense. The meticulous landscaping was now apparent. And now she could see the tennis courts and stables. As they swung around the drive, George stopped the car.

"There are Doctor and Mrs. Marchand," he said. Kate stood gesturing towards the chimneys on top of a garage that looked more like an old carriage house, complete with upstairs windows and shutters. Kim looked up to where Kate had been pointing and saw a line that looked like a crack on one side of the far chimney. I wonder if she does her own masonry too, Kim thought.

Kate took Maggie on a tour of the house while Kim sat with Jonathan in the kitchen, sharing a pot of coffee. His warmth and ease and familiar sexy good looks again made Kim's heart catch. She turned her thoughts to Kate, how she seemed to have everything. And just as she thought, "But not Chase," the little boy burst into the kitchen, followed by Kate and Maggie.

"Mom, look what Mrs. Marchand got me. Look, it's the one I don't have." Kim looked at the large toy figure Chase was holding up to her. It was Han Solo, one of the figures in the *Star Wars* mania. It was the only one he was missing from his extensive collection. Was it luck that Katherine Marchand happened to know just which one to get? Kim doubted it and guessed Maggie had been pumped for the information.

Jonathan offered to saddle up a gentle old mare for Chase and Maggie said she'd go and oversee the effort. But as Maggie turned to Kim, she saw that the color had drained from her face. And then Maggie understood. Familiar music was coming over the speakers in the kitchen. Chase, too, had now heard it and grabbed Kim's hand and looked up at her. Kim seemed to come out of her own misery, her voice uneasy, but strong.

"Chase, Jonathan says they've got a bubble covering their pool. Want to see that first?" Not waiting for a response, she turned to Jonathan who was only aware that the mood had changed.

"Sure, I'll show the way." He walked out a far door of the kitchen and Kim and Chase fell into step behind him.

Maggie sat down at the table and Kate remained standing by the counter, waiting for an explanation.

"I'm sorry, for Kim and Chase." Maggie let the words out slowly. "Kim did not mean to be rude. She just knew, for Jason, she had to get them out of the house."

"I'm afraid I don't understand."

"There's nothing I can really say," said Maggie, apologetically. "Kim is very insistent upon keeping her private life very private."

Kate sat down. "Don't feel uneasy, Maggie," said Kate reassuringly, patting the older woman's hand. "Kim should be pleased she has such loyalty from you, but I'd be less than honest if I didn't tell you I'm familiar with Kim's biography. I know it was just a year ago that she lost her husband."

"Yes," Maggie said, "that's it. And it's this song, you see, that one that's playing now. 'Chariots of Fire.' It was David's favorite, and Kim herself played it on the piano at his funeral. Little Jason sat beside her and he remembers the song, and that day, and of course, his daddy. At times, I think he's having more trouble adjusting to the loss than Kim. But then, I don't know. Kim has a very hard shell. You don't always know what's underneath."

"Well, I'll go and get this tape out of the player," said Kate, standing up. "If you go through that door and down the hall, you'll find the pool. When Kim is ready, tell her I'm in my study but there's no rush."

Kate had only been in her study a few minutes when Kim arrived. "Am I interrupting?" Kim asked.

"No, no, come in. I was pretending to work but really just enjoying the sun and the freshness."

Kim looked out at the grounds and said, "It's lovely here. Perfect really." She went to sit in a large leather chair that faced Kate's desk. "I'm sorry for seeming to be rude back there, but there was a very good reason."

Kate said slowly, "There's no need to apologize. Legitimate emotions need no apology. I know this is a hard time for you, Kim. And I'm not an insensitive ghoul. I am sorry for what you have had to go through and I understand. I also understand and respect your desire for privacy. I would never violate that."

"Thank you," said Kim, looking out. "And I wanted to tell

you that I would never take advantage either of the trust you've shown in welcoming us into your sanctuary out here.''

"Oh, Christ. It sounds like Deborah's been talking to you."

Kim laughed. She had moved to stand in the sun streaming through the French doors, and Kate could see the very strong back, the set shoulders, and the hands solidly clasped behind her back.

"Let's walk a bit, if you don't mind," said Kate, rising from her chair and, without waiting for an answer, stepping out onto the patio. "I rarely get a chance to walk these grounds and I think both of us are probably capable of walking and talking at the same time."

For almost an hour, they walked along riding paths, into the forest and out, across expanses of lawn. The entire time, Kate interviewed Kim, and Kim easily answered all the questions, from the climate of the news in New York, the type of work she was doing to what she wanted to do and what she believed was valuable. They talked about journalistic ethics, and for a moment, Kate understood what others had said about Kim being so much like her.

They were walking through a field now. The low-cut growth was just turning green, and in the distance, they could see Jonathan and Jason riding slowly together on a large horse. They were both laughing, and after a moment Kim said, "Jonathan is so good with children." And then, as an afterthought, "And so are you, for that matter."

Kate began walking. "No time, I'm afraid. One of those sacrifices that had to be made." And then quickly turned the conversation, saying, "When you talk about some of the programming in New York, you seem a little angry."

"I think that's a fair observation," Kim said. "In fact, maybe it's too acute. At times, I detest the business." There was no response, no surprise, or alarmed reaction from Kate. Kim continued. "It's so abused. We waste so much time. We're supposed to inform and enlighten but most of the time we give the viewer what some ad man tells us they want—mindless sitcoms, magazine shows specializing in how to cook pasta, interviews with the depth of a puddle, or news that spends more time on silly banter about the weather than on government corruption."

Suddenly Kim stopped and said, "Sorry, I get carried away, especially when I'm talking to someone in the business. It just galls me. Some media consultant analyzes the audience and then tells us what to do. It's such a powerful medium—and we use it to serve up junk!"

"All that you say is very true," Kate answered firmly. "Except in this town, at WLYM. We try very hard not to bow to the pressures of the ad men."

It was now Kate's turn to talk and, for the next hour, as they wound their way slowly back to the house, Kate explained the programming and principles of WLYM. It was a litany of taking chances, of integrity, of winning. Kim had checked and knew the truth of what Kate was saying. Even so, she was intrigued and awed by the degree of commitment Kate showed to her station as well as to her own principles.

As they approached the pool, they saw Jonathan and Jason working on the filter, Jonathan carefully explaining what he was doing to Jason. Jason seemed so happy that, whatever else happened, Kim was truly grateful to be away from New York this weekend.

"Where's Maggie?" Kim asked.

"Oh, Maggie went in to see if she could help Bridget with lunch," Jonathan said, joining them. "I hope it's ready. How about you, Jason? Hungry?"

As they approached the patio, they saw Bridget and Maggie working over a large glass table. "Where it's such a lovely day, even though it's so early in the season, I thought you might want to enjoy your lunch out here, Mrs. Marchand."

They all sat down to a lunch that began with a rich hot consommé, followed by a lobster salad and homemade strawberry ice cream. Jason told about his adventures on the horse and Kate confessed that she was about as graceful an equestrian as a drunk at the ballet. She described her numerous falls, and how the horses kept running away, as she clung desperately to the saddle.

"I just never made a very good Nebraska farm girl," said Kate.

"You sure don't look like a Nebraska farm girl," said Maggie.

"Oh, but I was," said Kate. "And glad not to be anymore."

"Jonathan told me I'm pretty good on a horse, Mom. And that maybe I should take riding lessons."

"Jonathan? What happened to 'Dr. Marchand'?" said Kim.

"Oh, it's easier, Kim," said Jonathan quickly. "And he *is* very good on a horse."

"Well, Maggie, what do you think?" asked Kim. "Do you think we have room for a horse in the apartment in New York?"

A few moments later Jonathan got a call from the hospital. He explained to Kate that there had been a car accident and a teenager had received a bad head injury. Then he said to Jason and Kim. "I'm sorry. I hope I get to spend more time with you. I've really enjoyed it." To Kate he added, "I don't know how late I'll be, darling. I'll have someone call you if the surgery is going to go into the night." He kissed her quickly, and she held onto his arm.

"Slow *down*, Jonathan. If you're going to be helpful, you have to get there in one piece. Drive carefully, please." Then, as he hurried into the house, she shouted after him. "And make sure you scrub well . . . you smell like a horse!"

After lunch Kate and Kim went up to the viewing room. Kate put a tape into the viewer and said, "We might as well get to the point." When Kim nodded, Kate continued, "Here's what my evening news looks like." She punched a button, and Kim saw one of the most sophisticated news opens she had ever watched. An anchor team of two very attractive people appeared, a black man and a white woman. Then, as the camera went on a tight shot of the black man, Kate froze the image and said, "Bill Halliday, age thirty-six, formerly of Chicago. Your basic street reporter out there. He was used wrong. Since arriving in Boston, he has, in two years, become not only a superb anchor, but a strong investigative reporter, and certainly one of the best liked and most respected journalists in Boston. And knowing Boston's racist reputation, that is no easy feat. It has taken a lot of work, on his part and mine, but it has paid off, and now his talent and dedication are unquestionable."

Kate moved the tape ahead until there was a close shot of the woman. "Ann Resnick, age thirty-seven, has been with the station as a reporter since before I arrived at WLYM. Once she was the princess of the public, could do no wrong. She was a hard worker and fought a good battle for the anchor position. In recent years, though, she may have become too comfortable. She rests on her laurels, although ironically she doesn't even have that many. She doesn't know it, and the public doesn't know it, and neither do my station executives, but she's dragging down the news and the station with it. Her time is over."

Kate hit a button and the set went black. She swiveled the leather chair and faced Kim. "I know you will not be surprised by what I am about to say, but even so I would like you to listen carefully." Kim turned her chair to face Kate and waited for her to begin.

"I have looked at the tape your agent sent. I have spoken to one of your colleagues. I have shared your tape with people at my station whose judgment I respect. And then I thought about what I had seen and what I had heard and, for the first time, I made a decision about an individual before I had met them. I decided I wanted you to replace Ann Resnick as soon as possible." Kate stopped. "That was before."

Kim did not let herself show any reaction to the last statement. She kept her gaze locked to Kate's.

"Now I have met you. I have spoken with you. I have listened to you talk politics and religion compassionately and sensibly. I have watched you handle yourself around total strangers. I have seen you respond to a tragedy that is still painful for you."

It was Kate who turned away first. She rose from her chair and stood looking down at the lawn. "Life dishes out good luck and bad luck very unevenly so I don't believe in dividing people into winners or losers, survivors, or nonsurvivors. It's the courageous, and the not so courageous, those are the two categories. It's a question of courage.

"It's as someone once said, 'Life is neither good nor bad . . . it's a series of predicaments.' I believe that. But people show what they are by how they handle those predicaments. And you're handling your predicament bravely and sensibly. That's one of the reasons you are here."

Kim said, "I have many battles still to go, Kate."

"You always will, Kim, just as I always will."

"I do not want to be a clone of Katherine Marchand." Kim turned abruptly.

Kate watched her and then spoke quietly. "A clone is a duplicate. How can you be my clone when you're going to exceed me?"

"If you're so sure of that, what makes you think there is room for both of us in the same market, within the same station? Sounds like close quarters." Kim's voice had a mocking tone to it.

"Because we will grow completely differently," responded Kate. "I am a manager. I am now interested only in building on that. I am a journalist only in that I keep up with the issues. But to provide the best in programming, I need someone in front of the camera who has her own goals. And you have them. You know that.

"No other place in broadcasting will give you this opportunity. I will give you the freedom to get to the top and also to be the conscience of television. You will be challenged more than you can imagine.''

"And in return, you get a face and personality that will put WLYM and your syndicates over the top,'' Kim said.

"I believe that is how it will work out.''

Kim sat down. "I would be a fool not to take this seriously but you know there are other factors I have to consider. I have a commitment to my son.''

"I consider that admirable, not an obstacle.''

"Tell me,'' said Kim, "will it be possible for me to keep both my commitment to Jason as well as to you and the station?''

"Is it possible? Yes. Whether you will do it is up to you. But believe me, I would not be putting you in this position if I did not believe in your ability to be dedicated to your personal, as well as professional, commitments.''

Kim sighed and got up again. God, she thought, this woman is smart. She looked out at Jason who was on the terrace helping Bridget and Maggie clear the table.

"What if I told you I at least wanted to wait until my present contract is up? Then we could talk again.''

"Then I would tell you to call. I will always enjoy talking to you.'' Kate's voice was like ice. "But the job will be filled by someone else. No, neither I, nor the station, has time to wait. Timing *is* just about everything.''

"Maybe you should humor me with a few details.''

Kate understood. "I am prepared to buy out your contract tomorrow morning, if you say yes. You will begin as soon as possible as the anchor, with Bill, at six and eleven. You may begin producing independent projects, as long as you work through Andrew Davis, my news director. You will be put up in a hotel suite at the station's expense until you find a home. All transportation and moving expenses will be covered, of course. Your first-year salary will be six hundred thousand dollars with stock options equaling at least another seventy-five thousand. A two-year contract, each year escalating fifty thousand dollars, not including bonuses.''

"All that, of course, needs to be negotiated with my agent,'' Kim said, but she felt it was already a difficult offer to refuse. "What would be the date at which you'd want me?''

"Ideally, I would like you on the air four weeks from tomorrow evening. Six weeks, at the most. That way you'll have the summer for transition. Both the station and you. And, of course, the public. When we hit the ratings books in the fall, I suspect you will immediately make it known, through the numbers, that you and WLYM are untouchable in first place.''

Kim turned. "You're awfully sure of yourself."

"I also am rarely wrong. In fact, I falter only when I let my emotions do my thinking for me. And I don't often allow that to happen."

Kim thought that last was said almost sadly. She sighed. "I need a few days by myself on this."

"I understand. I will be available to talk with you at any time within the next week." There was nothing more to say. They went out of Kate's office in silence and joined Maggie and Jason. The farewells were said and Kim found herself standing outside the limousine, facing Kate. For the first time since their discussion, Kate softened, or at least appeared to.

"Have a safe trip, Kim. Whatever you decide, I know I will be seeing you, or hearing about you, again. Please give this decision the same courage you have given your others." Kate touched her arm lightly, her hand pausing. "Thank you for sharing *this* weekend with us."

7

At about eleven o'clock on Monday morning, Kim parked the rental car in a deserted lot adjacent to a large, empty expanse of beach. The spring breezes of the weekend had reverted to the crisp gusts of winter and as she headed along the path towards the ocean, she pulled on some gloves she found in her jacket pocket. She was pleased to see that she was all alone, save the sandpipers darting along the sand, seemingly playing tag with the incoming tide and with the gulls swooping into the surf.

It was the first time since David had died that Kim had taken a day just for herself. No work, no friends, no Jason. She had decided that Kate Marchand's offer had to take precedence over everything else until her decision was made. She had a lot to think about, and the ocean had always been where she turned to find reason and understanding within herself. Today, at least right now, as she watched her sneakers move across the hard sand at low tide, she felt overwhelmed. Her thoughts were in a jumble: David, Jason, her career, New York, Boston and Katherine Marchand tumbling together. She kept walking, hoping that in time her mind would pull things into place and into their proper perspective.

The freedom to operate, the money and the career potential of the Boston job were, after all, superb. If those were the only considerations, the decision would be easy. But there were other factors that had to be analyzed. First, there was Deborah's warning that the balancing of her commitment to Jason and her career would be difficult. It wasn't as if this decision was not going to affect another life. It was.

The problems of transfer to a new city and new colleagues did not trouble her. Nor did a change in her life. After all, since David's death, everything had changed anyhow. And as to job and family—well, if she set limits, she could serve two masters, Jason and Katherine Marchand.

So what was bothering her? She headed back along the beach. It was growing colder and the collar of her coat did not protect her but she stopped in the wind and asked the question that she knew had been sitting in her spirit since Sunday afternoon. Can I do it? Can I be all that Kate Marchand says I can be? Do I really have the courage she says I do?

She thought of Kate Marchand's own words. "I very rarely make a mistake, and only when I let my emotions do my thinking." Well, there were no emotions here. This was a calculated business deal.

As to the other ingredient they'd discussed, well, Kim had no doubts about that. "Courage? I'll show you courage, Katherine Marchand."

Jonathan had a late surgery, and Kate sat at her desk, absentmindedly going through her personal mail. She looked at her watch, 8:45 P.M. Her eyes went to the phone. Her body was tense and stiff, and when the phone did ring, it scared her completely.

"Yes?"

"Katherine Marchand, please."

"Yes, Kim, it's me."

"Well, I hope I'm not disturbing you."

"No, I told you to call anytime." Both voices were tense.

"I'd ordinarily go through Harry on this," said Kim, "but since you went out of your way to spend so much time with me, I felt I owed you the courtesy of a personal phone call."

Kate didn't respond, but she felt her back tighten even more.

"How do I say this?" asked Kim, of no one in particular. "I have given your offer considerable thought; I've spoken with Jason . . . well, this is silly. Kate, I accept. I accept it all, the challenge as well as the commitment. I'm ready."

Kate felt a smile move across her face. "Thank you. I'm

really delighted. Congratulations. I sincerely believe you've made the right decision. And now, we'll let Harry earn his commission. Wait until you hear from him tomorrow. He and I will handle everything for you. And you and I will talk again as soon as dates have been worked out." She paused, her mind back into cold hard reality. "You know, of course, that I am going to have a delicate situation up here to deal with, so please ask Harry to keep it confidential until I make a public statement out of here. And, of course, you and I, or my PR person, Richard Blistick, will be in touch."

Kim agreed. She said, "Thank you, I'll get in touch with Harry. And Kate? The truth is, I can't wait to begin. To work with you, is what I really mean."

BOOK THREE

TECHNICAL DIFFICULTIES

"No noble thing is done without risk."

Montaigne

1

"**K**IM HAS ARRIVED, KATE."

"Thank you, Diana, send her in."

Kim pushed open the door, her head still turned, talking to Diana. They were both laughing. When Kim entered the office, Kate was pleased to see what seemed to be an even more beautiful and vibrant woman than she remembered.

"It looks like you've survived the move," Kate said.

"Thanks to Diana and a little bit of luck." Kim smiled. "I'm very grateful to Diana." As soon as Kim had accepted Kate's offer, Diana had been put at her service and had done everything from getting the movers in line to finding a school for Jason and a townhouse to rent on the waterfront.

"Are Jason and Maggie settled?" Kate asked.

"Jason thinks being able to watch boats go in and out of the harbor and at the same time watch planes take off from Logan is the greatest thing since Yoda," Kim said. "He's enrolled in a camp program for the summer and has already made some new friends. Maggie, of course, loves being near her family."

"Then we're ready to go," said Kate. "The contracts are signed and as soon as you meet with the board, the official press release will go out. I'm afraid you'll spend the next few days under siege with a lot of questions from the media. Then Monday . . . on air. Right?"

"You're the boss," Kim smiled, then grew serious. "I notice that Ann isn't on the air this week."

"Yes, I have the weekend anchor on with Bill," Kate explained. "I think it will make the transition easier for the viewer, rather than immediately switching you for Ann. I have no doubt you're going to win the public, and you should encounter very little animosity at the station. Ann was given a comfortable bonus despite the fact that since her contract was up, we owed her nothing. Also her agent will have no trouble placing her with a station that will make fewer demands on her. I don't anticipate any ugly public statements from her."

"Well, I'm prepared for a little rough sledding," said Kim. "No matter what, there are bound to be a few disgruntled people around."

"They will need fuel, Kim, and I don't think you're going to do anything to provide that. The one thing, of course, that might cause trouble, is if your salary became known. Obviously there would be trouble from the staff." Kate looked directly into Kim's eyes. Thanks to Harry Abrams's skilled negotiating, Kim had ended up costing Kate a lot more than she had anticipated. And if Kim were to do all the national syndication work Kate and Andrew Davis had in mind, her AFTRA union fees would put her salary in line with major network anchors.

"Don't worry," Kim said. "I always find money a boring topic of discussion." They were interrupted by a knock from Diana who said, "While you two are busy, I'll go down to the boardroom and meet with the board and tell them about Kim."

"What?" Kate asked.

"It's almost twelve-thirty and Andrew's out here waiting."

As Andrew, Kim and Kate rode in the elevator, Kim wondered at how thoroughly Kate had choreographed her arrival. It had basically been kept a secret. Publicity photographs, and a new video open for the news, complete with her already reporting, had been done at a major advertising house in New York. The only people who knew a new anchor was about to appear on the Boston scene were Kate's immediate entourage, Andrew Davis, Bill Halliday, Harry Abrams, Ann Resnick, and the top agency people. Now, as soon as Kim was introduced to the board, the press release would be delivered to the major news organizations. Kim had become increasingly aware that Kate wanted the communications industry to feel she was making a very bold stroke.

They were the last to arrive in the long, narrow room hung

with photographs of the major news stories of the last decade. Kate entered first, followed by Kim and Andrew Davis. The board, along with the corporate vice presidents who were present, grew silent. Kim sat in a chair next to Kate, and became aware that every eye in the room was on them as Kate pulled some papers out of her briefcase, and pushed her water glass to one side.

"Good afternoon," said Kate, smiling, as her eyes moved around the table. "I've called this unscheduled meeting of the board because I wanted all of you to know what's going on before the press gets hold of it.

"After our meeting, a press release will be delivered to the major news outlets in Boston and New York, announcing the expansion of our national documentary and investigative reporting network. The release will also inform the industry and the public that WLYM has hired a new on-air representative of that division . . . and that this individual will also be the new anchor, with Bill Halliday, on Channel Three's six and eleven o'clock news.

"It had become obvious to me over recent months that although Ann Resnick has been dedicated to WLYM and has been a dependable employee, it was time for Ann and also for Channel Three to move on . . . to reach for new and higher goals."

She looked at Kim, and said, "Ladies and gentlemen, members of the board of WLYM, America's number one station, with enormous pleasure, I present to you Kimberly Winston."

Kim stood and slowly smiled. The response was immediate. Strong applause. She nodded, and while it was still at its height, she sat down. Kate continued with a brief biography of Kim, praising her, but in a tone that was quite straightforward. She talked about the expansion of the documentary division, Kim's role, and the augmented power the new satellite would give them. She concluded her remarks and invited Kim to say a few words.

Kim rose and studied the faces in front of her. "This is all very embarrassing," she said in a tone that made Kate look up at her quizzically. "You see, Mrs. Marchand . . . I applied for the secretarial position. I think you have me confused with somebody else."

For a few seconds, the room was dead quiet. Then slowly, everyone in the room was laughing. Andrew Davis was even hitting his thigh. He couldn't remember the last time someone had made Kate Marchand the butt of a joke. And there sat Kate,

laughing with the rest of them. Finally, Kim began talking again.
"The major reason I accepted the offer of Kate Marchand," she
said, "is because I wanted a vehicle by which I could become
the best journalist in America. I believe I have found that. And
I assure you, that as you have laughed with us today, in the very
near future, you will be cheering."

Steven Merriam rose, offered his congratulations, and then
asked Kim whether she had a family and where she would be
living. Kate spoke before Kim could answer.

"For obvious reasons, Steven, I would like to keep Kim's
personal life private, right now. Let's let the fever of this announcement pass first. She will be in the newsroom tomorrow
and Friday, and available to the press from there."

"Well, it's not that the board is about to release any information, Kate, but as you wish," Merriam said.

"No, no," Kim said, before Kate could reply. "I am the
mother of a five-year-old son. And I am a widow, and we will
be living in Boston proper. Obviously I'm going to want to protect my son's anonymity—and I'll welcome any suggestions any
of you may have in that regard."

Kate smiled to herself. She couldn't have handled it better.
She rose from her chair. "Now, a sneak preview for all of you,"
Kate said, placing her hand on Kim's arm. "And this will also
be a surprise to Kim although the . . . ah . . . secretary . . . did
appear for the videotaping in New York. It's the new open for
the news, beginning on Monday."

On Kate's cue, the lights were slightly dimmed, and a countdown began on the large screen at the end of the room. Kim sat
and watched proudly what she believed was the finest news open
she had ever seen. And now she realized why the cameramen
had taken all the additional time with the lighting and camera
direction. She had never looked better on videotape. She looked
younger, but somehow more mature. The music, the scenes of
her in action, along with the shots of Bill Halliday and the newsroom, were riveting. When it was over, the people in the room
burst into applause again.

The board meeting would continue and Kim gathered her
things to leave. Kate said to the people at the table, "Let's take
a break and reconvene in ten minutes." To Kim she said quietly,
"I'll walk out with you."

While they stood at the elevator, Kate said, "I'm sorry about
those personal questions from Merriam, but I'm afraid until the

novelty of your arrival wears off, you're going to have to get used to it.''

Kim hesitated before speaking. She said, "I'm afraid that's something I'll never get used to—the prying—especially in my situation.''

Kate said shortly, "Remember our discussion. Some people rise in the face of tragedy, some people fall. But no one ever wins if they wear it.''

"If I were going to wear it, I wouldn't have come to Boston.''

"Right," Kate said, grinning. "If you need anything in the next few days, Diana knows how to find me.''

"Oh, you're not going to be in town?''

"No, it works out very nicely that I have a network meeting in San Francisco the next two days.''

"Why do you say 'it works out nicely'?''

"Because I think that you should be center stage, at this point. I'll keep up to date through the Boston papers. Your entire history, and everything from your favorite color to your bust size, along with varied suppositions about what *I* am planning, will no doubt be the major theme of both Sunday papers here.''

"So you'll also be gone the weekend?" Kim asked, and immediately regretted the question.

After an unpleasant interval, Kate asked, "Are you always this inquisitive?''

"Sorry, reporter's instincts.''

"Well, use another basic reporter instinct—respect your employer's privacy.'' Kate's voice was as harsh as she meant it to be. "In fact, I have a very hectic schedule, especially this month, dealing with the satellite and personnel changes and a greatly beefed-up documentary and special projects division. I'm flying to the coast early tomorrow where I shall argue over and over again with some gentlemen from the network who are still living in the dark ages. I'll do that for two days and two nights. In between, I'll deal with major advertisers. Then at seven o'clock Saturday morning, I'll arrive by the red-eye back in Boston, step into my car . . . and disappear until Monday morning.'' She sipped her water. "Not in Dover but in a very quiet, personal place by the sea, recharging my batteries.''

"A romantic weekend by the sea," said Kim, almost wistfully.

"No, it's a practical weekend. All alone, by my choice and with my husband's blessing. You see, a long time ago, I learned the healthiest thing for my work, my mental and physical health, and my marriage is my solitude. My solitude . . . and my privacy."

Kim held the elevator door open as she said, "As far as I'm concerned, you're locked in the office for the next four days. But tune in Channel Three Monday night. They've got a hell of a new anchorwoman."

"So I've heard. And God knows she better be: I hear she's getting paid enough to make a down payment on her own television station."

"No thanks. Remember our deal. You do the managing. I'm the journalist."

2

KATE WALKED THROUGH THE ALMOST EMPTY TERMINAL TO-
wards the overpass leading to the long-term parking area at Logan. Despite her fatigue, her spirits lifted as she felt the warm
June breezes and saw the haze on the horizon burning away in
the sun. She placed her bags in the trunk of the Jaguar and then
settled into the leather seat that had been specially designed to
fit the needs of her back.

As the car moved up Route 1, she listened to the all-news
radio station, but once she was past the commercial strip and
on the tree-lined Route 128, she inserted a tape in the deck and
reviewed with satisfaction the events of her trip. She had lured
four more stations into her syndication network, and signed up
two nationwide sponsors for the expanded documentary division.

As she approached Cape Ann, she felt her body relax. That
was always the desired, and received, effect of coming up here.
She drove through Gloucester and turned to head up to Rockport. The dunes she was passing shimmered as the sun began
to bake them dry. The morning chill was still in the air but she
pushed the button to lower the window and smell the soothing
scent of salt air.

Soon the Jaguar was on a gutted dirt road that followed
along the inlets of Rockport. She hoped that Diana had been

able to reach Murphy, one of her neighbors and the handyman for the homes along this stretch of Rockport. Most of the houses were owned by people who spent, at most, a few months of the summer here. And to the count, they were people like herself. They came here to be alone. There were no neighborhood get-togethers, no cocktail parties or Bloody Marys at Sunday brunch. This was a deserted island as far as these home owners were concerned.

It was almost three years since Kate had told Jonathan that she wanted a place that was solely her own, where she could come when he was involved in his work or when she simply needed to be alone. Jonathan had agreed and Kate contacted a few realtors on the North Shore—she knew it was the sea she wanted. She had found a house called ''The Pines,'' in a secluded section of Rockport. It was a comfortable stone and clapboard two-story home, with a large fireplace in the living room and kitchen. Upstairs were two bedrooms and a study. The master bedroom had a separate fireplace and its bathroom an oversized old bathtub on claw legs. But it was the first floor Kate loved—white stucco walls with lots of exposed weathered wood. Victorian wicker furniture mixed comfortably with glass-topped tables. An Irish wool throw lay at the foot of the couch and a huge brass vase sat in a corner, displaying wild grasses and cattails from the nearby marshes. Rough wood bookcases held an old set of the encyclopedia—inheritance of the former owners—lots of paperbacks and a collection of old decoys neatly lined up to face the sea. There was a sunroom off a very modern small kitchen and a deck overlooking the sea. The house itself sat only about one hundred yards from the breaking surf, but was protected by enormous rocky ledges.

As soon as Kate had walked through the vine-covered trellis and pushed open the large oak door, she knew Diana had reached Murphy. The windows were already open, the soft sea breezes were blowing the white linen curtains. The winter dust had been removed, and the floors waxed and polished. Through the gleaming windows she saw the twin lighthouses on the island about a mile out to sea. In the kitchen was a note from Murphy saying the refrigerator and hot water were working properly, and that some wildlife had been chased from the chimneys. There was also a vase of freshly cut flowers. She walked over to the refrigerator, opened it, and saw that Diana had also instructed Murphy to stock it with what looked like fresh shrimp and fish, along with the basics like milk and juice. She also saw several bottles of wine chilling, and smiled as she began her "Rockport ritual." It was always the same, whenever she arrived . . . day or night, sun or rain, warm or cold.

She pulled a bottle of Chardonnay from the rack in the refrigerator, opened it, took a chilled tall wine glass from the freezer, filled it and walked over to the sliding glass doors leading out to the deck. She picked up the shabby blue cardigan that was always draped over a kitchen chair, and a few seconds later, she was lying in the chaise lounge on the deck, her shoes off, her bottle of wine next to her, her glass in her hand, and the words on her lips: "To the sea and to me."

Lying back in the chaise, she looked out over the water, watching a lobsterman begin pulling pots. She let her mind go free, thinking about the life of a lobsterman, and then the quiet meal of seafood she would enjoy by herself tonight. Briefly, she wondered what Jonathan was doing and recalled how, at first, he did not understand her need for The Pines. But she teased him about how, if she wanted affairs, hotels would be cheaper. And when he saw how relaxed and refreshed she was when she returned from a day or so by the sea, he accepted her occasional need for "rest and recreation"—but a bit begrudgingly.

Jonathan had come up a few times with her, but he did not have the love of the sea that Kate did, and he missed his tennis partners. Kate knew it was more than that, though. When she was here, she was alone, in solitude, even if Jonathan was present, and he must have felt her withdrawal.

The warmth of the sun and the early morning wine combined with her lack of sleep made Kate feel drowsy. But the day was so lovely she hated to miss it. She walked up the stairs and with her wine glass still in her hand, drew a hot bath, climbed in, and reached for the nearby phone.

"Good morning," she said, sinking her body lower into the water.

"Darling! Welcome back. Are you at the Pines?"

"I certainly am," she said, smiling and taking another sip of wine. "What have you been up to?"

"Nothing since I spoke to you yesterday. Oh, I did end up having dinner with Christopher."

"Christopher?"

"You remember, darling, Chris Cerci, the new neurologist. He came out to the house for dinner. And guess what? He has a date with Kim tonight."

"Well, good for him, and good for her."

"So far, the press seems to be in love with her. Looks like it's another coup for you."

"Well, let's see if she works as hard and as well as she talks. As for me, I'm going to finish my bath, get this place in order, and take a long walk. What's your day like?"

"There's singles and a mixed doubles match at the club."

"God, Jonathan, isn't that a bit much?"

"No. Not when you consider how much rest I'll get tonight—alone in that big bed. When will you be home tomorrow?"

"Around four or five. I'll bring some lobsters."

"Wonderful. Don't push that back too hard. And Kate? I almost forgot. Diana called. No emergency. She'd just like you to give her a call when you can."

"That's strange," Kate thought when she'd hung up. Diana *never* bothered her when she was at the Pines. She had spoken to her yesterday afternoon just as Diana was leaving the office, and everything was fine. She dialed Diana's number and after an exchange of greetings said, "I presume this is important. Short of a bombing at WLYM, I hate being disturbed up here."

"Don't you think I know that?" Diana said. "It's that damned Nora Jevile."

Kate tried not to moan. The absolute last person she wanted to hear about was Nora Jevile. The last month had been very difficult with her and Kate knew she was going to have to fire the woman.

"She came literally screaming into the office," continued Diana. "I mean, I'm sure she knew you were not there but she was making all these accusations about how unfairly you paid your talent, how Kim didn't have anywhere near the experience that she had, and how Nora was being discriminated against. She said she had this background information on Kim that she was going to release to the press immediately if you didn't put her back on full contract. She said the whole station was angry at Kim's coming to Boston, and at the treatment of Ann."

"Hold it, hold it, Diana." Kate closed her eyes. "Why are you letting this woman get to you? You've seen the papers. I've seen the papers. Kim has come out beautifully. The quotes from the other staff show only delight. Apparently, she's won everyone over. Nora is grabbing at straws if she thinks she knows Kim's salary. And I know she has no information on her background that could hurt Kim."

"But the Sunday papers. They're doing whole features on

Kim. The *Herald* even got a shot of Jason in Quincy Market with Margaret."

"So what? It's a fact of Kim's life. I'm certain she can handle it," said Kate. "And remember, my dear friend, there isn't a reporter worth his or her salt in this town who believes Nora Jevile has any credibility, to say nothing of any inside sources. And if she does make an accusation, the critics in town all have your number, in order to reach me for a comment. So relax. Don't let that bitch get to you."

"I guess you're right. I'm glad you weren't there to see it. She'd been drinking."

"Then I wish I had been there, because then Nora Jevile would really have something to cry about. She'd be unemployed. See you Monday, Diana."

Kate hung up the phone and sank even lower into the bath water, refusing to waste any of her precious weekend even thinking about Nora Jevile.

The sand was cool and damp as she walked along with the receding tide. She swung her arms into the air, letting her entire body move with the motion. The beach was deserted except for an elderly couple walking a collie that chased the swooping seagulls.

Kate had left her topsiders on the deck of the house. She wore faded, rolled-up dungarees and a very worn Yale sweatshirt that had been Jonathan's when he was an undergraduate. Her hair was tied back, and after an hour in the wind and sun and salt air, the lines on her face flattened away, the creases on her forehead eased, and a brightness came into her eyes. The sea was always the best medicine for her. She loved it and was convinced the sea loved her just as much. They had made a pact together, years ago, she and the sea.

Kate was only fourteen when her grandparents took her on the exciting Christmas trip to New York City. She had immediately loved New York and knew one day she would be a part of that city. She carried with her those old unexpected impressions of the height of the city, the beauty and bustle of its people; she remembered her first subway ride to Battery Park and the trip on the Staten Island ferry past the Statue of Liberty. But though all this intoxicated the young midwestern girl, it was the ocean that captured her. They'd gone one day to Jones Beach, deserted in the winter, and she'd stood looking out, marveling at how different it was from gazing across the fields of Nebraska.

It was as if she'd got drunk on the water. On another day, despite the cold air and the rough sea, she would not go into the lounge on the ferry, crossing New York Bay. She stood at the railing wanting the trip never to end. Occasionally her grandfather would come out and try to urge her back in, and even one of the ferry hands told her it would be best for her to go inside. She remembered him warning her that a large swell could come up over the side and whisk her downstream into the ocean. She didn't really believe him but even the tremor of fear that shook her legs and made her clutch the railing seemed exciting to her, part of the sea's beauty.

When she attended the University of California at Berkeley, she had spent her spare time water skiing, or gliding across the bay in a catamaran, or swimming, mile after mile. Her friends thought she took unnecessary chances, but she always came up unscathed and smiling. In New York, she was also lured to the sea. Off Long Island, she loved to take a friend's outboard racer out beyond the surf, loving the fight to keep the bow into the breaking waves. She dared the sea, and the sea respected her skill. On assignment, she had been on an oil rig in the midst of the Gulf of Mexico when a hurricane threw a man off the platforms. Along the coast of Vietnam, she'd been on a rubber raft, sliding into shore quietly like a surfboard slicing through the sea. Exciting, frightening even, but her element, the sea—strong, unrelenting, all-powerful. And also, she knew, when it pleased, gentle and comforting.

She watched the hermit crabs scurrying across the sand and remembered how Ann Morrow Lindbergh had written that one could be like the hermit crab, shedding one shell for another when necessary. Kate wondered how many shells she had gone through in her life. Her thoughts were interrupted by the sudden cool damp breeze that signaled incoming fog. Yes, she thought as she looked out to the sea, the better part of the day was behind her. Fog would soon move in, and perhaps rain. She was too tired to make her usual swim out to the twin lighthouses. (How Jonathan protested when she did that . . . he was certain one day she'd be hit by a lobster boat or just get too tired to make it across. He didn't understand her pact with the sea.) She shed her sweatshirt and dungarees, and in her worn but comfortable bathing suit waded through the breakers. The water was still very cold, but she knew that after the first twenty yards or so, her circulation would seem to warm the water around her. She swam strongly, despite her fatigue. God, she thought, it's good to be back in the ocean, so much better than the pool. She swam straight out and then parallel to the coast and then turned back when she felt herself tire.

She came out of the water just a few yards from her clothes, and just a few moments ahead of the fast encroaching fog. She walked slowly, enjoying the fog as it enfolded her. She loved this time alone.

A few hours later, Kate was lying on the couch in the living room, listening to the fire create its own defense against the sound of the rain on the windows. She had dictated numerous memos to Diana, over a dozen letters and a general policy statement concerning the new projects of WLYM. Only then did she succumb to a nap.

Refreshed, she returned to the kitchen where she made herself a boiled dinner, New England style, of the wonderful fresh seafood Mr. Murphy had left for her. By nine o'clock, she lay peacefully in the large bed and listened to the sound of the sea on the rocks outside.

She awoke to a taunting red sun clearing the blue horizon. Looking at her clock, she thought, 'Oh shit, I'm missing the day.' It was 8:15. Dressing in corduroys and a sweater, she went downstairs and prepared a large breakfast. Poached eggs, English muffins, cereal, juice, and freshly ground coffee. The sun was baking the deck and she moved her tray onto the driftwood table and ate slowly, watching the lobster boats again. As she poured a second cup of coffee, she knew she could delay it no longer. The Sunday papers, thanks to Murphy, would be waiting on her doorstep.

As she settled in her chaise, she opted for the *Times* first. Other than the disturbing events of man vs. man, there was nothing to upset her morning. There was an article in the business section about expansion at WLYM and Kim's move from WNRB. But it was all very matter-of-fact, with exact quotes, and a line at the end of the story saying that an in-depth look at Katherine Marchand and her television achievements would be forthcoming in next week's magazine section. She put down the paper and stared out at the shimmering ocean. Well, worry about what Mike Colby would write was not going to ruin *this* Sunday.

She read the headlines of the *Globe*, then turned to the society section. The face jumped off the page. It was Kim, with her enchanting smile, on the arm of Chris Cerci. She read the caption, ''Boston's newest rising star, WLYM evening anchor, Kim

Winston, leaves Felicia's Restaurant in the North End with New
England General's Dr. Christopher Cerci.'' Kate laughed for
two reasons. First, it was wonderful publicity for Kim and
WLYM, and secondly, she knew who had recommended the
restaurant. Felicia's was one of Jonathan's favorites. She turned
to the ''Focus'' section where there was an article on WLYM,
announcing the transition and Kim's new responsibilities. Then
three pictures of Kim. Two of them in the newsroom, and one
walking across City Hall Plaza with Bill Halliday. In each picture, Kim looked beautiful, but sensible, not frivolous.

The quotes from her new anchor were what Kate had expected—full of optimism, desire for hard work and quality, and
her hope that the people of Boston would welcome her into their
homes. She answered the questions about her private life guard-
edly, not giving anything other than the basic information about
Jason, and her own widowhood. To further personal questions,
she replied that she did not think that information would be of
interest to the public, adding that she thought the sophistication
of Boston's viewers was beyond gossip and intrusion. Well done,
smiled Kate. It wasn't true, God knows, but the right move
nevertheless.

When she was asked if she had had much contact with Kate
Marchand, Kim answered, ''Of course. I would not have left
New York and come to WLYM if I did not have a tremendous
admiration for Ms. Marchand's reputation. I wanted to make
sure she was all that I had heard she was, and not some of the
things I had feared she might be.'' When asked to clarify, Kim
continued, ''It is easy to assume that someone in Ms. Marchand's position could be egocentric and difficult to work with.
Remember, I haven't been in Boston and do not know her as
well as many of you do. But I have learned that my fears could
not be further off base, and I not only feel honored to have been
picked by Ms. Marchand, I also feel a responsibility to return
the faith she has in me. In essence, I happily join the ranks of
those who respect and admire Katherine Marchand.''

Kate lay back in the chaise. Nicely done, Kim, nicely done.
Her euphoria was dampened by the front page of the *Herald*.
There was Jason, smiling merrily at a photographer in Faneuil
Hall Marketplace. She knew this was just what Kim did not
want. The caption was typical of the *Herald*. ''Exclusive photo
of Jason Winston, the well-kept secret of Boston's newest anchorwoman, Kim Winston.''

Kate turned to the article that was on page three. It was filled with pictures of Kim—once again not one bad angle. The article was not as disturbing as the caption. As usual, the paper could not back up the charge of "well-kept secret." Kim had stopped that by the simple statement, "I just want him to grow up like a regular little boy, because that's what he is. And to him, I'm just a regular mother who has a strange job."

The only disconcerting note came in the last paragraph of the article. "Although it seems that Kim has won the hearts of the staff at WLYM, there is at least some controversy. One female star, a veteran of Boston broadcasting, hinted that there was a great deal of resentment about Ms. Winston's salary and the way she was brought to Channel Three."

Nora Jevile, Kate thought. Well, the truth may soon be out, but so, my dear, will you.

3

"**W**HAT THE HELL?" SHOUTED KATE, IMMEDIATELY HITting the intercom. "Diana, in here, please." Diana came rushing in.

"What's wrong, Kate? They can hear you screaming down on the docks."

"What is going wrong with this midday news? This is the second day in a row that the tape cues have been all off, the wrong cameras are being taken. The talent doesn't seem to know what's going on."

"Want me to get Larry Keough?" asked Diana.

"Yes, but it's not the producer, I don't think. The programming quality is still there. Something else is going on."

"Martha and Tom?" asked Diana, naming the midday anchor team.

"No, it's not them." Kate looked at the screen as the wrong ID on a state representative came up. "When it's over, and that can't be soon enough, have Larry come up and also Celia Doyle or whoever is directing today. Also make some time for Andrew to see me today."

After ten minutes Diana announced that Larry and Celia had arrived. Usually, Kate would have let the matter be handled by Andrew Davis, but she found it useful sometimes to catch people off guard by having to report to her directly so that they understood how closely she monitored the station's performance.

She motioned Larry and Celia to the two chairs in front of her desk. "I'll come right to the point. Why has the midday news become so sloppy? It's looking very amateurish. The tape cues are off, wrong tapes come up, wrong chromakey slides—and that's just the beginning."

"We've been a little rushed lately," said Larry. "We've had a lot of last-minute stories."

"That doesn't explain why Martha and Tom are being cued to the wrong camera."

"Maybe you should be talking to Martha and Tom," Celia said. "I can't help it if they follow the wrong cues."

Kate stiffened at Celia's unusual defensiveness and then listened as Larry described a change in the crew schedule, which meant different cameramen, a floor director being out sick, and some problems with graphics.

Kate appeared to be giving Larry her complete attention, but she was really watching Celia. Something in her tone, the nervousness to her voice, alerted Kate.

"What about the early morning news and the cut-ins, have there also been mistakes there?" Kate addressed the question to no one in particular.

"Well, to be honest, Mrs. Marchand, I've run a little late the last couple of mornings," said Celia, smiling for no reason that Kate could understand. "Those hours are a little brutal. Don't you agree?" Again, the nervousness. Celia blew her nose.

"But you requested that shift, Celia."

"Yes, I know, and don't get me wrong, I want it." Celia knew as well as Kate that she had the lowest seniority of the directors and if she didn't do this shift, she'd be back as an assistant director. "I promise, no more running late, and I'll work with Martha and Tom on their cues."

"And the slides and tapes?"

"Yes, don't give it another thought."

"All right. Thank you both for coming up." Kate watched Celia as she left the office, then sat at her desk suddenly remembering a memo from personnel about a month before. It had notified her that two employees had taken medical leave to enter a drug treatment program. She had been troubled especially because one man was a high-ranking producer. He had made several mistakes and, she now realized, there were more mistakes. Reporters sometimes were not ready on their satellite feeds. There were false takes. The daily discrepancy sheet list-ing technical errors over the airwaves grew longer every day. And she could sense the pace of the station slowing down. She picked up a book and banged it against the ventilator. "God-damn it." She walked to her desk and buzzed for Diana.

"Diana, I want you to loosen my schedule so I have time for unannounced visits to the newsroom, control rooms, editing rooms, sales and promotion, master control, wherever there are people."

"Are you running for office?"

"Hardly, I'm about to become one of the most unpopular people in this building."

"What's going on?"

"Simple. We have a drug problem here," said Kate, rising from her chair. "Cocaine—good old cocaine."

"How do you know?"

"Celia Doyle was just sitting in my office wired to the gills. She couldn't have been more obvious if she had taken out a razor blade and mirror and done a few lines. Her eyes were flying, her nose was running, and she was as jittery as if she were holding on to a live cable. To say nothing of paranoid and de-fensive."

"Well, if it's just Celia, can't we give her a leave of absence or something?"

"That's just it," said Kate. "It's not just Celia. Believe me, it's never just one. Larry obviously knows what's going on, and all he did was throw out explanations to protect her. He's prob-ably also doing a gram here and there. I'm sure there's a major supplier for the station. Maybe more than one. It explains a lot of erratic behavior I've seen recently."

"Well, what do you do when your suspicions are con-firmed?"

"Well, druggies protect themselves and each other. The only way to deal with this effectively, is, unfortunately, to make an example of someone. In this case, I hope we can make it an example privately, within the station, and not get the police involved or break into the papers."

"Then maybe we should just wait for it to blow over?"

"It won't blow over, Diana. I've seen this happen before. If it isn't stopped soon, it will go to the very core of this station. Already, quality is being affected. I recognize all the signs. This business breeds drugs, just like the music business or Holly-wood. There's so much ego and so much room for people to be unsure of themselves. The high that coke gives them makes them feel omnipotent, untouchable. Because of their work they always have to be on. They become psychologically addicted. And believe me, it's not just the workplace that suffers. Right now, I'll bet you, we've got lives and families going under."

"Maybe you should get the vice presidents together."

"Nope, too late. I think we've already got a vice president involved."

Over the next few days, Kate could be found walking abruptly into a control room, an editing room, a vice president's office, master control. On one occasion, she brought paperwork down into the newsroom, situated herself in a corner, and spent three hours observing the movements of her reporters and managers. Another time, she walked into the mobile unit on Massachusetts Avenue near Symphony Hall in the midst of a live transmission for *Boston Live!* She didn't explain at all but clearly it made everyone nervous; and some people it made more nervous than others.

One day, she was in Studio A watching a production of *Boston Live!* Because she was near the lighting panel talking nonchalantly with one of the technicians, at first no one knew she was there. But she watched very carefully. She couldn't help noticing that the star of the show, Nora Jevile, went down the hallway to the makeup room during every commercial break. It was highly irregular. No talent, no technician, should leave the studio at any time during any program. She watched Nora return each time, hastily dragging on a cigarette.

While Nora was doing an interview, Kate went to the producer, Phil Bernelli, and asked "How long is this interview? How long before the next break?"

"Interview's about eight minutes, then Nora has a promotional bit to do on that trip to France," answered Phil, looking at the format on his clipboard.

Kate quietly left the studio, and glancing up and down the empty hallway, went into the makeup room. Since there were no makeup artists for any talent except the six and eleven anchors and reporters, the room was empty. The counter was strewn with makeup, blush, mascara, touch-up paste. What a slob that Jevile is, Kate thought, and then saw quickly what she was looking for. Without a second's hesitation, she opened Nora's leather bag, pushed its contents around, then unzipped an inside pocket. She found exactly what she expected—a small glass vial with a screw top. It was about half-filled with cocaine.

The "sniffer" Kate knew was popular among those who had to "snort and run." You shook it upside down, the white powder fell into a small receptacle, you twisted the cap to the correct angle to make a passageway for the powder. Placing it in your nostril, you could get a decent high without having to go through the trouble of laying out a line. When she was in New York, she had seen cameramen use the "sniffer" many times. And she herself had taken a few snorts many years ago.

She placed the vial into her jacket pocket, checked the time, tossed the bag back into its messy corner and walked out of the room. In a few moments, she was back in her office, asking Diana to have Timothy Hunnewell, the station's attorney, come to WLYM as soon as possible.

An hour and a half later, Hunnewell was ushered into her office and Kate got directly to the point. "WLYM has a problem, Timothy. A drug problem. I'm afraid it is hitting just about every department in the station. It's cocaine. My station is wired with cocaine." Kate sounded tired.

"That's a pretty serious charge, Kate. We all know that white powder is all over the place, but you're running a quality operation."

Kate stood up behind her desk and looked at the graying attorney. She was suddenly angry—furious. "You're damn right it's a quality operation. We pay a lot of people a lot of quality money, with which they can apparently buy a lot of quality cocaine." She pulled out the vial and slammed it down on her desk. Timothy leaned back in his chair away from the vial.

"It won't jump out and go flying up your nose, Tim."

"That's not funny, Kate. Nor is your decorating your desk with a vial of white powder that could land you behind bars and destroy the station."

"Oh, Tim, come on, relax. Let's do a few lines."

"Kate!"

"Okay, I'll be serious," Kate said, rubbing her forehead. "In the last couple of weeks, I have observed numerous members of my staff performing their tasks while obviously under the influence of cocaine."

"And this vial?"

"I took it myself from Nora Jevile's bag today."

"Does she know?"

"Well, I'm sure she knows by now it's missing, but it's not exactly the type of thing she's going to go to the lost and found about."

"Clearly, we're not going to go public with this either," Tim said. "That would be the worst thing possible for the station. On the other hand, we're dealing here with illegal activity. . . ."

"I know that. Look, I've told you where I got this vial. You are going to witness my labeling it and placing it in my office safe. Then I will continue my own investigation until I find the major dealers and get them out of here—making an example of them that everyone in this building who is using drugs will understand. Then, they will all either cease the activity immediately, or seek the proper help to get themselves cleaned up."

"First," began the attorney, still pacing, "you should not be handling this so-called investigation alone."

"Wrong, sir," Kate shot back. "I cannot trust anyone, not even a private investigator, to deal with this. I know my people, I've already got a good idea of who's using and who isn't. Cocaine, even though it's supposed to be the 'in' thing, is against the law. And no one wants to go to prison. Whoever is supplying the major portion of the cocaine to my staff—or whoever's the biggest user—will be dismissed immediately. Those within the drug circle will know exactly why. And that will stop it. People have a big stake here. And I am going to make such an example of that person that no one at this station—or when word spreads, at any of the syndicated stations where my name is on the letterhead—will ever think about snorting one more line of cocaine. I will not allow this drug to maim the people and the product that I've worked so hard to put together."

Kim moved quickly through the door of the makeup room. Bill Halliday was sitting before the gaudy mirror, flicking his script nervously against his leg while Paula smoothed a light blush across his flawless bronzed complexion. Kim had grown very fond of this extremely handsome man with his commanding, but not domineering presence.

"Hi Bill. Hi Paula." Her voice was light as she searched through Paula's makeup kit that was more like a suitcase. "Paula, I don't have time for a big number tonight. I'm trying to chase down the boyfriend of that missing coed. Can I get by with just some blush and lipstick?"

"Calm down, calm down. You can spare ten minutes."

"I'm afraid not."

"Go do what you have to and come back here about quarter to. I need that time."

"Help me, Bill, please?" She leaned over Bill's shoulder and kissed his cheek.

"Better watch it, or you'll smudge Paula's reconstruction." Then he held a hand up to her in the mirror. "Listen, Kim, as soon as I'm out of this chair, we should talk."

"Okay, I'll be at my desk." She left the makeup room and returned to her desk. She was completing a phone call when Bill tapped her on the shoulder. "I'll buy you a cup of coffee."

"If I drink, you'll have to anchor alone. Anyhow, I'm not dressed for a party." She pointed down to the jeans she wore beneath a quite elaborate white satin blouse. Like many news broadcasters, Kim often dressed only for what the camera would see—the area above the news desk.

"Come on, smart ass. We're just going to the cafeteria." He took her by the elbow, and guided her through the maze of desks in the newsroom, and then down a back stairway to the small cafeteria. They went to a corner table despite the fact that the room was virtually empty.

"What's going on?"

"We've got a problem, Kimbo." He looked at the clock on the wall: 5:20. "Forty minutes to air time and we've got a weatherman who's flying in his own hot air balloon—about thirty thousand feet off the ground."

"Oh, shit, not another one." She knew exactly what Bill was talking about. Don Bartley, the evening weatherman, was completely wired. She and Bill had discussed before what seemed to be an epidemic of cocaine use at the station. "I've never seen anything like it. Everyone's got a white nose around here. Technicians, reporters, and now the weatherman."

"I know. It's easier to get a gram of cocaine in this place than it is to get a typewriter ribbon."

"Well, what do we do about our immediate problem? We're going to have to work completely around Don. They'll have to take most of his time away, and we'll have to fill in. God, I hate this."

"While you're in makeup, I'll talk to the director, and Tony on the floor. At least they're both clean. I just wanted to warn you."

As they walked up the stairs, Bill talked about the undependable crews. "Everyone's either late, sleepy, stoned, paranoid, dealing or snorting. And on top of it all, there's something strange going on with our fearless leader. It seems that every time I turn around, she's standing there."

"I know. She came into an editing suite I was working in yesterday afternoon." Kim lowered her voice as they entered the newsroom. "You don't suppose she has any idea of what's going on around here?"

"No," Bill shook his head. "She may be a very smart lady, but she's completely protected from a lot of the shit around here."

Kim headed for the makeup room, mentally working on some intelligent small talk to fill the void that Don Bartley's problem had created.

The newscast worked because Kim and Bill ad-libbed for close to three minutes while Don's two on-camera appearances were reduced substantially. Though it had not been in her script, Kim told a story she had read that morning in the *Herald*. Since it was about people coping with the heat wave on the East Coast, it gave the viewer the impression he was hearing the weather.

Don's performance was strange. He talked too fast, missed his cues and pointed to the wrong area on the weather map twice. The director avoided any close-ups, and Kim and Bill were prepared to take over at any second.

After the broadcast, Kim said, "Okay, let's find an empty office and have a little chat with Don."

"First, we've got to find him. He left as soon as the credit roll began."

"Try the men's room."

Bill headed in that direction and a moment later he was approaching Kim with Don beside him.

"I told Don we'd like to have a chat with him. The audio booth is empty." Once in the booth, Kim and Bill quickly unplugged the microphones. Don was silent. There were beads of sweat on his forehead.

"I'll get right to the point, Don," Bill began. "You're completely stoned and you damn near made an ass out of yourself and of us in front of four hundred thousand people. To say nothing of jeopardizing your job, and throwing your entire family into disgrace."

"Don," Kim touched his arm, "what's going on? We know there's a lot of junk around, but what are you doing getting involved in this? You're a role model to kids. They love you. And what about your own three kids and your wife?"

"Kim, Bill, I'm sorry. I'm really sorry. It won't happen again. And it's no big deal." He sounded sure of himself and made them feel that they were overreacting. "I just do a little bit, here

and there. It perks me up. That way I don't get so uptight when
I have to go on.''

"What the fuck is wrong with you?" Bill shouted. "It's more
than a line or two. It's been getting worse every day."

"It is, Don, you know it," Kim said. "How many grams
have you gone through today? You're almost jumping off the
seat.''

"Lighten up, you two. All right, today was a little rough."
Don's voice was shaky. "I ended up pulling an allnighter last
night. Never got any sleep, so I needed a bit more to keep going
today.''

Kim sighed. Good old cocaine. Keeps you up forever, if you
want. Until you collapse. Suddenly she realized what she'd
heard. "Wait a minute. If you were up all night, and never slept,
where were you?''

"I was home," said Don.

"Well, where was Marilyn? Doesn't she see what's going on?
Why would she allow you to come to work like this?" Marilyn's
wholesomeness was equaled only by Don's former image. They
were Mr. and Mrs. Hometown America.

Don just shook his head. Bill was becoming impatient.
"Well?''

"Bill, don't you see?" Kim asked. "Marilyn's into it, too."

"Oh, damn it." Bill put his head in his hands. "Is it true,
Don?''

"Yeah, but it's not too bad. I tell you, we just went a little
overboard last night. It's usually just on weekends." He began
nervously playing with his tie.

"Oh, good, Mommy and Daddy get high on the weekends
and let the kids fend for themselves. What now?''

"We can just take him to Andrew," Kim said.

"No, no," Don began to panic. "He'll go to Marchand and
you know how image-conscious she is. She'll have my contract
in a paper shredder within minutes.''

"Okay, Don, but you have to do something for yourself.
Please." Kim took hold of his arm again. "Tell them you're
sick. You can't do the eleven o'clock broadcast. They'll bring
in Warren, the weekend guy. And you go home—without the
coke.''

He nodded wearily.

"Try to sleep this one off. Tomorrow morning, say around
eleven, Bill and I are going to come to your house, and if you

and Marilyn aren't straight and either willing to stop or get yourselves some help, we'll go to Davis and Marchand.''

Preparing for the eleven o'clock news, Kim found it difficult to
concentrate. She watched her colleagues on the air as if she were
looking at an old Clairol commercial. Does she or doesn't she?
Only her dealer knows for sure.

At ten o'clock Chris called and the sound of his voice bright-
ened her spirits. They had gone out three times together, to
dinner, to the theater and once on a boat cruise around the
harbor. Although there had been nothing more than a gentle
goodnight kiss, they were becoming more and more comfortable with each other. Aside from the people at work and Jason,
Christopher was the only one she spent any time with.

"So how's life as Boston's number one superstar?" Chris
asked.

"Quiet," Kim answered. "You can't go around saying that.
I have a boss who claims exclusive rights to that title.''

"Oh, right, sorry," said Chris, laughing. "Well, look, I can't
waste any time on chitchat because I have this unbearable crav-
ing for Mexican tacos. I mean the real thing.''

"So you're telling me you're flying to Tijuana tonight?''

"No, can't take the time. But I have the perfect alternative.''

"And what's that?''

"I happen to make the best all-American Mexican taco in
these here parts. And I just happen to have found all the proper
ingredients right here in Bean City. Even as we speak, the creation is going on, and they'll probably be ready right after the
eleven o'clock news.''

"Christopher, are you inviting me to a late dinner at your
apartment?''

"Is that what I'm doing? I thought I just wanted you to taste
my tacos—if you'll forgive the expression.''

"I won't touch that line," Kim said, smiling to herself.

"Okay. Here's the direct approach. How about coming over?''

"Why not save it till the weekend? Don't you have rounds at
six tomorrow morning?''

"The beans are already cooking. And it just feels right tonight . . . for Mexican food.''

"Okay, you're on, Chef.''

"Wonderful," Chris's voice jumped with pleasure. "See you
on TV, then see you right after. Bye.''

"Hold on. Chris?" Kim almost shouted into the phone. "Dr.

Cerci, I know you live on Beacon Street, but could you give me more of a hint? Or do I have to just go up and down pounding on doors?''

"Stop pounding at number eighty-seven.''

"See you later. Stir your beans.''

Christopher leaned across the bar in his sparsely equipped kitchen, trying to look seriously into Kim's laughing eyes. "You're taking this far too frivolously, Kim. Look how you're building that taco." Chris gestured at Kim stuffing tomatoes into an empty taco shell.

Kim put her half-filled taco down, folded her hands in front of her, and spoke very quietly. "Okay, you're the doctor. What is the proper protocol, sir?''

"That's better. I didn't slave over a hot stove and a cutting board for hours so you could butcher the perfect taco.'' He leaned across the bar and kissed her gently on the lips, and then, almost delicately, picked up a taco shell. He began an explanation about how the beef is chopped, never ground, and how real purists never use beans at all. He described the sauces, the seasonings, what cheeses work best, even the kind of lettuce.

"But then you have to create the masterpiece." He handed her the taco. "Now, we begin. Notice these finely arranged bowls of perfect ingredients.''

"Never mind the ingredients. I've never seen so many different bowls. Do you have any matching dinnerware at all?''

"Don't you know that's chic these days? Nothing's supposed to match. Every one of these bowls has a unique history. For example, this is from undergraduate days at Cornell. This is while I was at med school at Stanford. Here, my internship. This . . . well, there was this nurse. . . . ''

After the tacos had been constructed, they sat at a small round table in the bay window overlooking the Charles River. Chris poured Mexican Dos Equis beer for them both and, lifting his glass, said, "Welcome. *Mi casa es tu casa.*''

When Kim looked at him questioningly, he said, "Spanish traditional welcome. 'My house is your house' is what it means and what I mean.''

"*Gracias*," Kim said. "I know that much.''

"And now, the moment of truth," said Chris, raising the taco to his lips. He slowly bit into the crisp shell and after an audible crunch, a large portion of it fell to his plate. "One of the hazards," he said, laughing, "and one of the challenges. Let's see if you can get any more of it in *your* mouth."

With as much deliberation and seriousness as she could muster, Kim tried it.

"Well?" asked Chris.

"You know, it really is good. It just may be the best taco I have ever eaten. Obviously it's all in the engineering."

"And my culinary expertise," said Chris.

They continued to assemble and eat tacos, drink beer, and talk about their respective travels in Mexico. "Of course it didn't help that the woman I was with came down with Montezuma's Revenge on the second day." Chris grimaced. "It was a very romantic way to spend a ten-day vacation."

"At least David saved getting sick for the last day of our stay at Cancún. But it was a beaut of a flight back." She started to laugh and then became quiet. Chris watched as her eyes lowered to her hands. In all their time together, she had never spoken about David.

"Well, what's for dessert?" Kim was instantaneously up again.

"I thought you'd never ask. Why don't you go try out my new couch and I'll bring it right in."

Kim left the table and walked toward the obviously new brown velour couch. That, the dining table and chairs and a lovely sand-colored Moroccan rug were the only furnishings in the room. Kim chose the rug to sit on, leaning back against the couch.

"I thought it was a little warm for a fire," Chris said. He stood at the doorway from the kitchen holding two champagne glasses.

Kim smiled up at him, wrapping her arms around her knees. "Chris, what have you got there?"

"Champagne and strawberries."

"Hmmm . . . Do I go for the strawberries or the champagne first?"

Chris placed both glasses on the floor. "Maybe you should try this first," he said.

He kneeled down and brushed her hair back from her forehead, looking intently into her eyes. He then brought his lips gently towards hers, pressing firmly on the back of her head, moving his hands through her fine hair. He felt her respond as her lips parted and she placed her hand first on his waist, then moved it up across his chest and around his back, pulling him towards her.

With an athlete's grace, Chris picked Kim up. The champagne glasses stood untouched on the floor.

Only a dim light in the corner allowed Kim to distinguish that the bedroom too was quite bare. A bureau. A bed. A desk and chair in the corner. Chris tenderly placed Kim on the large bed and lowered his body onto hers, aware of the hands that were now moving through his own blond hair. He shifted to the side and pulled his face back from Kim's. For a moment he watched her face in the dim light from the other room. Her eyes were bright and watchful, and then, as if a ghost had passed between them, she shivered. Her eyes became dark and she looked away from the man above her.

She lay stiff, in another world. She had not made love with anyone since the death of her beloved David. For a long time, there had been no desire, but even now she felt deep in her heart a haunting sense that she was betraying the love she and David shared. She knew life had to go on, and especially over these past weeks with Chris, she had felt a powerful desire rising within her. Now she raised her eyes to Chris, who was watching her with patient, kind eyes. She felt his hands on her back and her arm, tracing an invisible pattern. Her body had been responding. Why had it stopped? Was she forever locked in the memories of the past? Buried, as David was?

"Kim? Kim?" Chris was saying. "He's gone." His voice was a soft whisper. "You deserve to be loved. I adore you. I won't hurt you."

She looked at him tenderly and then pulled his lips down onto hers, feeling the heat come back into her body, banishing the ghost. As the kiss grew deeper and more passionate, Chris unbuttoned her blouse and moved his hand across her stomach.

"Soft as baby's skin," he said, taking his lips from hers. She smiled at him as she reached to release her breasts to his waiting lips. Immediately, she heard her own soft moan as he let her head fall back on the bed. As he moved to her other breast, she reached down to his pants, unbuttoning the light cotton trousers, pushing the zipper down, and reaching her hand to where he eagerly awaited her touch.

In what seemed like one easy movement, he removed her clothes and his own, and then, fearful that the moment would be lost, quickly returned his lips to hers, his hand moved almost teasingly on the inside of her thigh, and then inside her. Kim had no thought for the past or for anything but the growing excitement of her body.

God, she thought to herself, I want this so much. I have wanted it for so long. Her whole body was filled with the power of Chris's touch. She wanted to let herself go completely . . . give herself completely. She felt a thirst, a desperate thirst, longing to be quenched. Suddenly the growing passion accelerated, and she shifted her body, as Chris easily moved into her. As he filled her and moved in and out of her tightness, the storm within her began to break. She pushed and pulled him into her with all her strength. Her ferocity caught Chris off guard and he was afraid he would not be able to hold on. But then he heard a sharp intake of breath and a moan as she trembled and twisted her pelvis beneath him, pulling and pushing out all the anger, bitterness, and loneliness of the past year. He let himself go with her, and with a feeling he had never known before, almost blended into the flesh beneath him.

They lay in silence for a long time, holding each other tightly. Chris thought she might have misgivings because he was certain this was the first time since the death of her husband. But then he heard a slight giggle from where her face was buried in his chest.

"What?" he asked, lifting her head up. "Was it that comical?"

"No," she said lightly, "I just can't believe I got duped into seduction by the old taco trick."

"To tell you the truth," Chris said, "I didn't think you'd fall for the etchings line."

"I may have," said Kim seriously.

"Oh?"

"Yes. You see, I hate tacos."

They both laughed, and soon they were making love again, this time more slowly, more playfully. Afterwards, Chris asked if Kim wasn't concerned about Maggie and Jason. She replied that she had warned Maggie she might be very late.

"Will you stay the night?" asked Chris. Kim looked at the clock on the bureau. It was 2:15.

"Well, it would be hard explaining the address on the cab slip—especially at two-fifteen A.M."

The next sound she heard was the shower, and she initially mistook it for the sounds of the harbor outside her condominium. She looked around her, remembered, and nestled back under the covers, smiling. Then the responsibilities of her life pushed into her mind. Chris had rounds, and she should get home before Jason was awake. She crawled out of bed, found her clothes placed neatly on a corner of the huge bed, and dressed quickly. She went into the kitchen and found her purse, and as she was pulling the brush through her hair, Chris came up behind her and wrapped his arms around her. He was in a blue terry cloth robe.

"I thought maybe you'd get some more sleep. I'm sorry if I woke you."

"No," she turned and kissed him, feeling the toothpaste freshness of his mouth and remembering she must still taste like a taco. "This way I'll get home before Jason is up. He's not used to me being away."

"I understand. I'll dress quickly and cab you home." He left the kitchen and Kim went to the refrigerator and poured herself a glass of orange juice. She became aware that she was smiling, and that despite the fact that she had probably had, at best, two hours' sleep, she was refreshed with new energy.

They decided to walk to New England General. The early morning air and rising sun invigorated them. Anyone passing would have seen they were new lovers—holding hands, stopping to hug each other, laughing. At one point, Chris picked her up in his arms, swung her around and said, "Did I ever tell you how beautiful you are? How happy you make me? How much I love to be with you?"

"How can I be beautiful with day-old makeup?"

"You're always beautiful," he said seriously. "And I will always love you."

"Christopher!" Kim jumped out of his arms. "We've never even so much as talked about *liking* each other."

"But it's true. I've loved you since I first saw you."

"Do you often drink so much and read romance novels so early in the morning?"

Chris left her side and went to stop a middle-aged man who was approaching them. Very properly dressed, he looked like a stockbroker heading for his pre-office morning constitutional around the public gardens.

"Sir, I'm sorry to disturb you," Chris said, "but I wanted you to know I love this woman. I do. I love this woman. Do you believe that I love this woman? That I always will?"

The man stared.

"Well, do you believe it? Surely a man of your esteem and wisdom knows true love."

"Yes, young man. Yes, I do believe that," he said forcefully.

"Thank you. Thank you very much." Chris shook his hand. "By the way, I'm Dr. Christopher Cerci. This is Kimberly Winston."

"And I'm Caleb Dodge. Congratulations." He tipped his hat and strode off.

Kim took Chris's hand and as soon as they were out of hearing range, burst into laughter. "You're crazy. You're absolutely crazy."

"But I'm right. And it's true. And you heard it from a man who certainly cannot be doubted. A good, upright Bostonian, Caleb Dodge. A man with a name like that certainly knows the truth when he hears it."

A half hour later when she stepped out of the shower, she was singing and feeling happier than she had felt in over a year. When she awakened Jason, he asked, "Mom, how come you're so happy? How come you're laughing so much?"

"Because I love you." She snuggled into his neck.

"But you loved me yesterday, and you didn't seem this happy."

"Well, I love you more today and it's such a beautiful day. And you've got to get ready for camp." She got him started in the bathroom, then went to get her coffee. She took it with her through the living room and then onto the small terrace that overlooked the harbor. In a few hours, it would be too hot to sit here, but right now, it was perfect.

In the kitchen, Maggie was preparing Jason's breakfast and when it was ready Jason joined his mother on the terrace. Kim and her son began an easy conversation about the movements of boats in the harbor, and the upcoming activities at camp today.

"You should see me swim, Mom. I'm the best in my age group."

"Wonderful, Chase. Maybe I'll stop by some day."

"You know what would be really neat, Mom?" he asked. "If we could go out to Jonathan and Kate's and I could show Jonathan what a really good swimmer I am now. Last time we were there, I couldn't even make it across the pool. Now I could swim the whole thing, down the long part." The accompanying arm gesture sent his milk flying, and Kim called to Maggie for paper towels.

"Sorry, Mom."

"It's okay, Chase. Just save the flailing arms for the pool."

"Well, what do you think?"

Kim was quietly helping Maggie mop up the milk.

"What, Chase?"

"About showing Jonathan how good a swimmer I am?"

"Well, honey, we have to be invited first, and the Marchands feel very strongly about their privacy."

"They certainly couldn't have been more pleasant to us," interjected Maggie. "My Lord, anything we wanted that weekend."

"Yes, and anything Katherine Marchand wanted," said Kim sarcastically. "And she got what she wanted, didn't she?"

"And didn't you, Kim? Why are you still so hard on that woman? She's made you one of the most popular people in Boston. You have a lovely home. Jason is in the best school and camp. And you seem happier than I've seen you in over a year. Come on, Jason, your ride will be here soon."

Jason got up from his seat, looking worriedly at his mother. He kissed her on the cheek. "Aren't you happier here than in New York, Mom?"

"Are you?"

"Yes, a lot, a lot happier."

"Then I'm happier, too." She hugged him as he left and then sat holding her coffee cup in two hands, watching a young woman preparing the sails of a sloop.

Why was it that she still had this undercurrent of animosity for Katherine Marchand? She had no reason to dislike her. Andrew Davis had said that Kate was delighted with her work thus far. And although they had not had an actual conversation since that day in the boardroom, whenever their paths had crossed, Kate had been polite and friendly. But Kim felt threatened by her boss. Maybe it was just the power, or the uncertainty of who Katherine Marchand was under the perfect *Vogue* exterior. Maybe, Kim thought ruefully, it was just that she envied Kate's strength.

4

"**I** DON'T KNOW, BILL, ARE YOU SURE WE'RE DOING THE right thing?" Kim asked as they drove toward Newton. "I'm almost afraid of what we'll find."

"Don't worry. I've known Don and Marilyn for a long time. I'm sure they've learned their lesson."

Bill pulled up to the driveway of a small Tudor style home. They walked up a flagstone path but before they reached the front door, Don opened it.

"My watchdogs. Right on time." His voice was light. "Come in. Marilyn's made a fresh pot of coffee."

They walked through a living room that could have belonged to any family with three young children. A few toys were scattered on the floor, a large *Star Wars* battleship station was tucked in the corner. Walking through the dining room, Kim couldn't help noticing the layer of dust on the bare table, and glasses, some clean, some dirty, sloppy on the sideboard.

But she wasn't at all prepared for what she saw in the kitchen. Bill, just in front of her, stopped in his tracks. Marilyn was sitting at the table. She looked terrible. A thin woman to begin with, she seemed to have lost fifteen or twenty pounds since Kim had met her. Her hair hung oily and soiled around her shoulders.

"Hi, Bill. Hello, Kim, it's nice to see you again." Nervously,

Marilyn kissed Bill on the cheek, and touched Kim's arm. Her eyes were dull, with dark circles beneath them.

"Marilyn, are you all right? You've lost a lot of weight, haven't you?"

"A little. I needed to. Bathing suit was getting too tight." She quickly turned back to pouring coffee. "Don explained to me why you were coming this morning. I suppose I should thank you for helping him out last night, but, to tell the truth, I think everything's all blown out of proportion. We never have anything to do with drugs. Only when Tommy, you know, Don's younger brother, is around. And even then it's just harmless. I mean, Don was absolutely fine when he got home last night. And he never does any at work. That's ridiculous. I mean, Bill, you know us better than that."

"Marilyn is right, Bill," said Don, taking the coffee from his wife's unsteady hands. "I must have been really tired when we talked last night, or at least sounded it. I mean, I don't know why I said those things. As you can see, everything's fine here."

"Wait a minute, Don," said Kim. "Do you mean to say you're denying everything you told us last night?"

"Well, yeah," he looked uncertainly at his wife. "So there's no use threatening to talk to Davis or Marchand. There's no truth to it. And what I do at home is my own business. I know there's a lot of the white stuff flying around but I'd never get involved with anything like that at work. And here, well, it's like just treating ourselves to a nice French wine on Saturday night."

"And that's going to stop anyway, because, well, Tommy's going to the Cape for the rest of the summer, and we were just kind of keeping him company. He's had a rough time lately. His girlfriend just broke up with him." Marilyn talked on about Tommy and his girlfriend until finally, Bill interrupted.

"Well, I guess we've already taken too much of your time. Kim, we'd better get to the station. We've got some more promotional shots to do."

With hurried goodbyes, they left, closing the door behind them. When they got to the end of the path, Bill grabbed Kim's arm and swung her around. "They're lying through their fucking teeth. How stupid do they think we are?"

"I'm surprised that they denied it all after what Don said, and how obviously high he was."

"And Marilyn, my God. She was literally wired for our visit. She never talks that much. And she made no sense. I've never heard a word about this brother, Tommy. And there was no way

Don was fine when he got home last night. And Kim, Holy Christ, the woman looks anorexic. She looks like she hasn't had a square meal in weeks.''

"Calm down. Marilyn obviously freaked when Don told her about our talk. She doesn't want the coke to stop coming.''

As they approached the car they heard voices from the windows of the Bartley's home.

"It's bad enough that a fucking station executive knows we're doing it. Now you had to tell Mr. and Mrs. Prim and Proper,'' Marilyn was shouting. And because the kitchen windows, only a few yards from the driveway, were open, her voice was easily heard.

"Bill and Kim aren't going to say a thing. And anyway, I'll just deny it. Remember my reputation. The audience loves me. The kids love me. Don't worry.''

There was a brief silence and then Marilyn asked, "Do you have another gram?''

"Yeah, I'll leave it with you today, and pick up more this afternoon. They're expecting a major supply. You should have seen the trouble I had getting these grams last night. She even hiked the price to a hundred and thirty.''

"You went out to the house? Did you get a little more than just the coke?''

"Come on, Marilyn, that's over. I told you. I haven't touched her since that last night.''

"I don't believe you. Why don't you go down to your little cocaine factory and maybe you can do it right on your precious weather maps?''

Kim and Bill stared at each other, and Bill gestured for Kim to get in the car. She put her hand on the door handle, then leaned across the windshield towards Bill. "Maybe we'd better push it down the driveway.''

"Yeah,'' replied Bill, and after putting the car in neutral, joined Kim to push the car easily to the street.

Both of them were shocked at what they had heard. Finally Kim spoke. "Well, once again I must defer to you. Who's the executive—the lover and the supplier? And what are we to do about it all?''

"I have no idea, Kim. I can't even begin to think. I just can't believe the whole thing. I thought they had the *perfect* marriage. It's all unbelievable.''

"I know I sound like a public service announcement, but cocaine is a killer. I saw it in New York. It destroys even the strongest people, the best marriages, the brightest careers. Trust me. Don isn't Don right now. And Marilyn isn't Marilyn.''

"Forgive me, but you sound like you speak from experience.'' Bill kept his eyes on the road, avoiding Kim's glance.

"I do, but thank God, not my own.'' She sighed, and her voice lowered. "Friends, several friends . . . in college, in the Nieman program, at work. I'm not saying I haven't tried it, I have. But it scared me so I only did it once. But people I loved got hooked and one of them, my closest friend at college, hung herself in the pool house of her parents' home in California.''

"Oh, Christ, I'm sorry, Kim. Life has thrown you a hell of a lot of stinking curves.''

"You could say that, but lately, it's been looking pretty good again.'' She smiled as she remembered Chris, and their night together.

Before they got to the station, Bill and Kim had decided that they would not rush into action on what they had just learned, but would think it over and confer later in the day.

In the newsroom now, they headed for their respective desks. As usual, the place was a sea of people rushing in various directions, of phones ringing, of orders being shouted and contradicted. The newsroom was in a state of organized chaos. Lining one wall were the wire service teletypes, noisily printing out the news of the day. There was the large assignment board, listing the names of each of the reporters, their whereabouts, and the stories they were working on. The twenty or so reporters' desks were no different than those of the dozen editors and producers. All were piled high with newspapers and wire copy, crammed together, offering no privacy. And the noise, a cacophony of voices and typewriters. But as Kim approached her desk, the room seemed to grow quieter, and all heads turned toward her.

On her desk, and on the floor around her desk, were roses. White roses, yellow roses, pink roses, even purple roses. She laughed out loud, bringing forth a number of comments from her colleagues that ranged from "Take on the whole soccer team last night?'' to "A florist wants you to do a special on roses.''

She picked up the one card that had come with the dozens of flowers. It read, "Would you please marry me? Mr. Caleb Dodge would approve.''

The smile on Kim's face faded as she slowly sat down in her chair. There was not even the remotest possibility that she would marry Christopher. She thought, I haven't even gotten over David. My heart is still entwined with him. I just spent a few hours with Chris, and we had a good time in bed. But marriage? Now?

At about five-fifty, while Kim was making final changes on the evening news copy, the phone rang. It was Diana asking Kim to drop by Kate Marchand's office after the six o'clock program. Kim felt a worried pang but had no time to think about it.

The news went rather uneventfully compared to the evening before. Don seemed in much better control, and although both Kim and Bill had trouble looking him in the eye, he acted as if nothing had happened between the three of them.

Kim left the broadcast studio as soon as the program was over. She went up to the now-deserted executive floor and directly to Kate's office. The door was open and Kate called, "Come in, Kim. Diana had to leave early—that is, at six-forty-five after coming in at seven-thirty this morning. I don't know how this station would run if she ever took a two-week vacation."

In her office, Kate thanked Kim for coming, and took a seat beside her on the far side of the desk. "Nice smooth broadcast tonight," remarked Kate.

"You make it sound like a rarity."

"Try to control your defensiveness, Kim. It's never productive."

Amazing, thought Kim, how this woman can slice you apart at the same time she builds you up.

"The fact is that I've been noticing some, let's say, rocky spots, in the evening news. What about you?"

"I'm not sure I know what you mean."

"Let me refresh your memory." Kate placed a cassette in the player. "I believe this is cued to the point in question."

As soon as the tape caught, Kim knew Kate was referring to the previous night's program. And there on the screen was Don fumbling with his pointer at the wrong parts of the weather map. Kim slumped in her chair and raised one hand to her forehead while she watched the program.

"Don seems a bit confused," Kate finally said.

"Yes, I guess he does."

"Oh, but I think you more than guess. I think you know." Kate's voice was harsh as she went to the recorder and set the machine forward until she reached the place she was looking for.

Now the tape revealed Kim ad-libbing about the heat wave in New York and then, what seemed like endless banter between Kim and Bill. Kim still thought that, to the untrained eye, this would not raise any suspicions, but Katherine Marchand was far from untrained.

"I commend you for filling in the time. But I've never liked happy talk on a news show. Especially when it takes valuable time away from reporters' stories. My math shows that almost four minutes of weather time went into ad-libbing." Kate switched off the set and returned to the chair behind her desk.

"There's really a simple explanation," Kim began. "Don didn't feel too well, and so Bill and I tried to help him out. As you probably noticed, Warren came in for the eleven o'clock."

"I noticed. But why didn't Andrew know about Don's health and replace him? Or if the weather was to be cut down, why didn't he give the reporters additional time?"

Kim wished that Bill and she had had time to talk before this "shoot-out" with the boss, but before she could frame a reply, Kate said, "That's strange. I thought I was the only ghost up here at this hour."

Because the office door was open and the floor so quiet, both women easily heard the opening of the elevator doors. Kate walked from her office and then stood quietly in the outer office. Kim was just behind her. They heard the voices of two men and when they approached Kate's door, the tone of one was unmistakable.

"Don't worry. It's probably just the cleaning staff." Just as Steven Merriam finished the sentence, he was opposite Kate's door and found himself face to face with the general manager. "Oh, Kate, I thought you'd gone. I saw Diana on the elevator before and I know she usually doesn't leave until you do."

Kate said only, "You thought wrong." She was trying to place the man with Merriam and then she remembered: Glenn Paulson, the crime reporter.

Merriam continued nervously, "I left some papers here, and coming in I ran into Glenn, and decided to catch up on the latest crime news." He paused and then said, "Oh, Kim. I didn't notice you. I've been wanting to tell you how much I enjoy you on the air."

"Thank you."

"Listen, Steve, I've got a crew waiting for me," said Glenn.

"Right. Right. Well, nice to see you two," Merriam started down the hall with Glenn at his heels.

"Ah, Mr. Paulson," Kate called after them. "Are you usually this rude, especially to your employer?"

Paulson stopped in his tracks. "Excuse me?"

"Usually one would say hello."

"Oh, for Christ's sake. I'm sorry. Hello. Hello. Hello."

Kate was too taken aback to reply. Paulson, like all the staff, had always been polite in the past.

Merriam led the crime reporter down the hall and in subdued tones, was saying something to him.

"Listen, Mrs. Marchand, I'm sorry," said Paulson from his safe distance twenty yards away. "I'm kind of tired lately and I've got this story to do. Please accept my apology." He quickly turned and entered Merriam's office.

"Is he always this uptight preparing for a story?" Kate asked Kim.

"I've never noticed it," said Kim, having made her decision, "but there's a lot of strange behavior around here lately."

Kate raised her eyebrows and led Kim back into her office, closing the door behind her. "That's what I want to talk about," said Kate, sitting down and picking up the gold pen on her desk. She began tapping it on the leather note holder. "Let me tell you what I know. You may either respond, or not respond. And I trust you will keep our conversation confidential.

"This station is awash in cocaine. It is the chosen stimulus of people in all ranks of WLYM. It goes from technicians, directors, reporters, weathermen, cameramen, and up into the management offices on this floor. I would not be at all surprised if Glenn Paulson's behavior just now was the result of being a little strung out. And I know you are aware of this epidemic that is consuming WLYM.

"I need your trust right now. Do you disagree with anything I have said?"

Kim was silent for a moment. "No," she finally said, "but I don't know if you understand the enormity of it. The number of people it has its clutches into is frightening. And it is following its usual course of ruining careers and families."

"Like Don Bartley's," Kate said coldly.

Kim made no response.

"Kim, is there anything you can tell me that can help me save some lives and jobs around here?"

Kim did not intend to lie and she did want to help, but she wanted to speak at her own pace and not be made to feel like a stool pigeon.

As if she sensed Kim's hesitation, Kate said, "Kim, this is important because of the people involved, of course, but I also am concerned about the image of this station. A drug scandal here is exactly what the other stations in town are looking for, and what my competitors across the country would love to see.''

Kim finally spoke. "And the lives involved? Don't they mean anything to you?''

"Are you saying that I am more concerned about this station and its image than its people?''

"Perhaps.''

"And I just told you, you cannot really separate the two. Most of the people here are treated very well, and in turn, they thank me by their excellent work. If WLYM gets caught in a drug scandal, it will touch everyone. Even the most innocent will not walk away unscathed. I do not want the quality of this station or the quality of its staff tarnished in any way.''

Kim was quiet for a moment and then looked directly at Kate. "Do you know one of your top executives is a supplier?''

"Yes, but I don't know who it is.''

"I don't either, but I do know it's a woman.''

"I would never ask you to divulge the names of people you know who are using coke. But I will tell you that very soon this whole rotten mess is going to blow wide open, and I am trying my very best to make certain that only those who are perpetuating this disease will feel my full wrath.''

"And the others?''

"They will be given every possible chance at rehabilitation.''

Kim rose from the chair. "Well, I do wish I could be more helpful. But I wish you the best of luck.''

"Thank you, Kim,'' said Kate, rising and walking to the door. "And by the way, I have a husband who is very anxious to see a special little five-year-old. It's supposed to be terribly hot this weekend, so perhaps Jason might like to cool off in the pool. And maybe the rose bearer would like to accompany you.''

Kim smiled. "But what about my boss's need for privacy? For space?''

"I'll worry about that. Anyway, it's been a while since we've talked. Sunday all right?''

"It's fine. Jason was actually asking about Jonathan this morning. He wants to show off his swimming.''

When Kim left, Kate called her husband. "Darling, did you reach him?''

"Yes, I did. I still don't understand why you can't use a locksmith downtown.''

"Because I trust Mike. And I can't trust any locksmith down here. When did he say he'd get here?''

"He should be arriving any minute. I told him to go straight to your office, and to dress in a suit." Jonathan's voice did not sound pleased. "What exactly are you doing, anyway? You must have a master key to all the offices."

"Yes, but not to the desks, and it would take forever to get the right keys." Kate sounded impatient.

"I guess I don't like the fact that my wife is breaking and entering."

"Drastic times call for drastic measures. The drug stuff gets worse every moment." Kate paused. "But cheer up. Jason and Kim, and I think Chris, are coming out to the house on Sunday."

"Good. I don't know what's going on between Chris and Kim, but he acted today like he won the lottery."

"Well, if he did win the lottery, he spent it all on roses for Kim," she hesitated, hearing footsteps. "I think Mike is here. I'll see you later, darling."

"Good luck, Sherlock." The line went dead.

When Kate opened her office door, Mike Sutton, the Dover locksmith, stood waiting—in a suit, holding an attaché case.

"It's my brother's," he explained, "but I've packed the tools I'll need. Dr. Marchand did say it was mostly desk locks?"

"Right. Look, Mike, I know this sounds like an awfully fishy operation but I hope you'll trust me, that I wouldn't be involved in something crooked. We've got a real problem here that I can't talk about but, believe me, what we're doing is for a good cause."

"Well, it's not the money I came into town for, Mrs. Marchand. I wouldn't ordinarily take this kind of job but I've known you and the doc a long time and—like you say—I trust you."

"And I appreciate that, Mike. Now, let's begin." She reached into her own desk and brought out a large ring of keys.

The first office she went to was Steven Merriam's. She didn't know exactly why. Maybe the old vendetta was still having its effect. After examining a number of keys on the ring, she chose one and easily unlocked Merriam's office. When she tried to open his desk, she found the top drawer and the cabinets locked. She signaled to Mike, pointing at the two locks. Mike opened his briefcase.

"Will there be any marks?" asked Kate.

"No, these are easy. It's only if something's jammed in the lock that it gets tough." Within thirty seconds, both locks were open.

"Would you mind waiting outside?"

"Tell you the truth, I'd just as soon leave."

Kate went through the center drawer first and found only the usual array of pencils, pens, paper clips and loose memos. The same was true in the side drawers. Then she went to the filing cabinets, her hands brushing through all the folders, lifting them up and pushing her hand underneath them. She found nothing. Her back ached and she thought about what a long night this was going to be. She opened the bottom file and saw the sales packet for the latest syndication project. She remembered then that she had requested a rewriting of the press release on the new satellite, and realized she hadn't seen the rewrite. She picked up the packet and shuffled through the glossies of Kim and of the satellite, and then stopped suddenly as her hand hit an unmarked envelope. It wasn't sealed and she leaned against Merriam's desk as she looked in.

There it was. A silver sniffer. Two razor blades. A mirror. And a small plastic envelope with about a teaspoon of white powder in it. She sighed. Even Merriam. She sealed the envelope, making certain her fingers did not touch any of the contents, picked up a pen, marked the envelope S.M. and placed it in a large manila envelope she had taken from her own office.

"Mike, would you come in and lock these up again?"

As she watched, and felt the fear creep into her, she worried if maybe it all hadn't gone too far. Maybe she couldn't stop it.

During the next few hours, Kate went through all the major offices of her executive staff. She found incriminating evidence in eleven of the twenty-eight offices she went through. The people implicated ranged from an uptight fifty-four-year-old salesman with grown children to one of the brightest young up-and-coming syndication producers.

It was after midnight when they approached the office of Janet Ryan. Kate initially thought of bypassing it, thinking Janet had certainly had her fill of disasters and problems in her life and would not take any further chances. Then she remembered how trouble seemed to follow some people—or else they helped create it. Though she hoped Janet's trials were behind her, she had to admit the producer had been far from productive lately.

Mike quickly opened the desk drawer and even before she heard the door close behind him, she saw three razor blades in the pencil tray. She found nothing else, though, and asked Mike to come in and lock the drawers. As she watched him, she allowed herself to relax against the bookcase in Janet's office, and to take the strain off her back, she placed her elbow on a shelf, pushing the books back for more leverage. But despite the width of the shelf, the books did not move from the pressure. Kate pulled out a few books to see what the obstruction was. Her eyes were uncertain of what they were seeing: a polished mahogany box. She pulled it out. It, too, had a lock on it.

"Mike, would you unlock this?" Mike came over, looking puzzled, and then pulled a different tool from his briefcase. It was taking longer than usual.

"It's a solid brass lock," said Mike. "I may have to mark it to open it."

"If you have to."

A few minutes later, the lock popped out of the wood, and the wooden lid lifted slightly. While Mike waited in the hall, Kate, first tenuously, then firmly, lifted the lid of the box. First, she saw scraps of memo paper, and then the shining pharmaceutical scale beneath them. Traces of white powder were visible on one of the scale's bases. The small brass weights were neatly packed in their leather pockets.

Kate examined the pieces of paper that were in the box. She had found her supplier and she had also found the list of buyers. She certainly is thorough, thought Kate. Janet had listed the names along with notations of how much each person bought, and even the different prices she charged people.

The list consisted of initials, and as Kate placed them with the appropriate names, she saw how rampant the problem really was. Janet Ryan was definitely the station's supplier. And she was the woman with whom Don Bartley was having the affair. But many low-level employees were also implicated.

She scraped into an envelope in her purse the tiny amount of powder that was visible on the brass scale. Then she put the papers back in the box and realigned the books so there was no indication of any intrusion in the office.

In the hallway, she said, "We're finished, Mike. Let me just get my briefcase and I'll go out with you." Opening the safe in her office, Kate carefully placed all the evidence inside. When she got back to the outer office, Mike was waiting for her. "Thank you for all your help," she said. "And Mike, you may be reading things in the papers in the next few weeks that will explain what I was doing tonight, but I think it's in your best interest as well as mine that you don't mention to anyone being here tonight."

"You have my word, Mrs. Marchand."

5

Early the following morning, Kate said to her secretary, "Diana, I need two things as soon as possible: First, I'm going to give you a list of names. I want you to find out from personnel how long each person has worked at WLYM, whether they're on contract, and their basic salary. Also background information, like whether they're married or have children.

"Second, and this must be done very discreetly, I would like you to tell me of the comings and goings of Janet Ryan, including the people who go in to see her. And please don't rely on her secretary for the information."

"That's going to be difficult, Kate."

"Do the best you can." She handed Diana a list that included people from all rungs of the WLYM staff—salesmen, reporters, public relations officials, cameramen, directors, technicians, secretaries, producers and associate producers.

When Kate finished, Diana looked up. "Is this what I think it is?"

"And what do you think it is?" Kate asked crisply.

"A list of possible drug users?"

"No, not possible drug users. Definite hard-core drug users."

"My God." Diana sat down in a chair, looking at the list in her hand. "It's, it's. . . ."

"I know, it's like the air conditioning system is carrying it up everyone's nose in the entire building. Please, get that information for me."

Kate spent the morning going through paperwork, dictating memos and dealing with various agents on the phone. If a major turnover was coming to WLYM, she wanted to be prepared to bring in new people. And, of course, they had to be the best. As the morning progressed, she found herself becoming angrier and angrier. How dare these people do this to her? How dare they jeopardize all she had worked for? How dare they put everyone else's careers in jeopardy?

Unexpectedly, Peter Worijik, head of promotion, came to Kate's office. She could see that he was greatly disturbed about something. "Kate, I've never had to come directly to you before, but there is a situation developing that I can't control."

"Go on, Peter."

"It's about Don Bartley. You know how he makes all those appearances before schools and colleges and civic groups?"

"All our on-air people do. It's in their contracts."

"Yes, and they're usually very cooperative. And Don always has been, except in recent months." Peter hesitated, and then just about exploded before Kate. "The son of a bitch isn't showing up! He agrees and we set it all up. Then he doesn't show and I'm left making some phony excuse that makes us look very unprofessional. He did it again yesterday afternoon, at Brookline High; a replacement appearance for a no-show two weeks ago. And once again, no Don."

Kate was now completely livid. Peter himself had rarely seen such anger in anyone's eyes.

"And what's his excuse?" Kate tried to sound calm, but the thought of her talent making a mockery of the station's reputation enraged her.

"Well, he never seems to be at home and his wife is always making excuses for him. But she has been very hostile lately and sometimes even hangs up on me. When I do catch up with Don, he says he forgot, or one of his kids was sick. It can't go on anymore."

Kate rose from her chair, back under control. "You're damn right it can't. And it won't. Do not set up any more public appearances for Don until you hear from me. How can we redeem ourselves at these schools?"

"Kim," said Peter.

"What do you mean . . . Kim?"

"We could send Kim. Everyone wants her. I know you've

told me to limit her appearances because of all her syndication work and I have. But I could really use her to help make up for Don's no-shows."

"OK. I'll tell Andrew that Kim is going to have to start doing more PR for us. And I'll handle Don. Thanks for coming to me, Peter. Don't wait so long next time. Remember, one person's actions reflect on all of us."

When Kate told Andrew Davis about Don's unreliability, he said, "It's not only his public appearances, but his television appearances too."

"I noticed that Warren filled in for him the other night."

"And tonight," said Andrew flatly. "Just before you called me, my secretary informed me that Don had called in sick today. Kate," Andrew leaned forward, his chest almost touching Kate's desk, "what the hell is going on around here?"

She looked at the searching eyes across the desk, and then slowly put her hands up to her head and let her temples rest on her palms. She spoke without looking up. "Cocaine, Andrew, cocaine. It has permeated the entire station. From top to bottom, there isn't a department unaffected by it."

"Are you sure it's that bad?" Andrew asked. "I thought there was a little bit of it around, but. . . ."

"According to records I've found, over a pound of cocaine is going through this station each week, and the problem's growing."

"You mean the supplier's in-house?"

Kate nodded, her head still in her hands.

"Are you going to the police?"

"You know that would be suicide for LYM." She raised her head. "Just be prepared to keep the news at top quality with a few, at least fewer, reporters. And wish me luck."

"Of course I do." He rose from the chair. "Let me know if there's anything I can do."

An hour later, Diana came in. "Here's all the information you asked for." She handed Kate numerous sheets of paper. "But I'm afraid that keeping tabs on Janet Ryan is an impossible task."

"What do you mean?"

"She came in this morning and at around ten-thirty told her secretary she wasn't feeling well, and left."

Kate walked over to the couch and lay down, with a pained sigh. "Diana, call Janet's home number. If she answers, just hang up."

"Do you want the ice pack?"

"No, thank you." Kate barely heard the question. Her mind was now racing, fueled by a rage she had not known for years.

"The line is busy." There was no reaction. "Kate, Kate, are you all right?"

"Yes, I'm sorry, what did you say?"

"It's busy."

"That makes sense." Kate paused briefly. "What's my schedule this afternoon?"

Diana reeled off a series of meetings, ending with a speech to the Publicity Club at six o'clock.

"Okay, cancel all my appointments except the Publicity Club. And could you meet me there? Also, cancel as many of my appointments tomorrow as you can. Get me Janet Ryan's address and call Timothy Hunnewell and tell him to stay reachable for the next forty-eight hours."

"Why, may I ask, are you going to Janet Ryan's?"

"To kick her ass back to California and to try to save this station before she destroys it with drugs." And a moment later Kate was closing her office door, briefcase in one hand, and network courier bag in the other. As Kate drove, she felt increasingly angry, less with Janet and all the other drug users at WLYM, than with herself for making such a drastic error in judgment.

Soon she was on the road marked Jameson Lane and looking for number 27. It turned out to be a modern house—all wood and glass—set far back from the road. It was an affluent neighborhood, and though Janet earned quite a bit of money at LYM, her salary was not enough to pay for such an expensive house. Kate pulled into the driveway, noticing the two cars, each with the WLYM garage sticker.

Kate felt sick. She started to question her strategy but then realized that there was no other way to avoid bringing in the police. She stepped forward and pushed the door, surprised that it was open. Because the modern house had such an open design, she could see Janet Ryan and Don Bartley at the counter that divided the living space from the kitchen. Janet was holding a razor blade over a mirror that had a pile of white powder on it. Don Bartley held a cutoff straw.

"Oh my God," Don moaned. Janet stared, her hand trembling.

Kate walked into the kitchen. It was littered with glasses and dirty dishes and empty wine bottles. She brushed them to the side, and set the wooden box on the counter.

"Is this what you're missing?" Janet was silent, her hand still shaking.

Kate said coldly to Don, "You go home and pull yourself together. Do not go near the station until tomorrow morning at nine when you are to be in my office. And, if you care at all about your job or your future, do not mention this to anyone. Have I made myself clear?"

Don went quickly out the door and when he was gone, Janet Ryan spoke. "Kate, after all you've done for me, I don't know what to say. Let me try to explain."

"I don't care about your goddamn explanations. Your career with WLYM is over. Whether I also go to the police will depend on how cooperative you are. The first thing I want to know is, where's the big supply?"

"I don't have it here," Janet said.

Kate went to the phone on the kitchen wall and picked it up distastefully because like the rest of the kitchen, it was so dirty.

"What are you doing?" Janet asked.

"I'm calling the State Police. I'm sure they'll be interested."

"No, no, Kate. No, please." Janet had jumped up and was pulling at Kate's jacket. She started to sob. "They'll arrest me. Think about my children."

"Think about your children? Why didn't *you* think about your children? Or anyone else's children for that matter. About Don Bartley's kids, for example? About all the kids, and wives and husbands?"

Janet continued to sob.

"Oh, no you don't. Cut it out. We have business to conduct and your crying isn't going to help you at all. Now, tell me, where is it?" When Janet gestured toward the refrigerator, Kate opened the freezer and saw a brown paper bag. In it was a plastic bag of white powder.

She threw it in front of Janet. "How much is here?"

"About a half kilo."

"You have a very good business going here—a new house, nice car. But I'm afraid you're going to have to go back to living on a salary—if you keep your job. Your career as WLYM drug supplier is over, as of right now."

Kate took the plastic bag over to the sink and ripped it open. Janet gasped as Kate dumped the contents into the sink, then turned on the water. The cocaine melted and flowed in a sticky white river down the drain.

"Do you know what you have almost done?" Kate asked. "You have almost destroyed a television empire and the lives of the people who work for it. You have compromised the integrity of the finest television station in America." Taking out of her briefcase the personnel files Diana had prepared for her, Kate said, "We are going to go through these names, person by person. You will tell me how heavily each one is into the drug, the problems they are having and whatever other information you have. Every detail. Do you understand?"

Janet nodded and then asked timorously, "And what will happen to me?"

"For some reason, I'm going to give you another chance," Kate said, "if only to justify my having brought you from California in the first place." Kate turned away and added silently to herself, *And to keep the city of Boston from finding out about this.*

"I have spoken to the manager of the English-speaking station in Montreal. There is an opening for an associate producer and on my recommendation, they are willing to have you."

"A job as an associate producer? I'm a vice president."

"You're lucky to get even this job. Listen, Janet, you'll do it my way, or you'll go to prison—for a long time. To tell you the truth, I don't care. Once we go over the list of your victims, you can do what you choose. Just don't let me ever see you or hear from you again."

Kate went to her bag and took from it a small tape recorder. She put it on the table and when Janet began to object, Kate said simply, "You have no choice."

They went through the list, and Kate learned the extent of the cocaine epidemic at WLYM. She heard how some of the talent had set up "cocaine breaks" in the middle of major productions. How budgets were being inflated to cover the cost of cocaine for the talent. How her mobile unit rarely left the garage without an engineer with a heavy supply of coke for everyone from the technicians to reporters. She found out who was into freebasing, crack and how heavy each person's habit was. They ranged from an occasional snort to spending as much as $1,500 a week.

"Do you mind if I have a drink?" Janet asked while they were reviewing the names. Kate shrugged and Janet poured a tumbler of vodka in front of her. A half hour later, when they had finished the list, the phone rang.

"Please don't answer that."

"But Kate, at some point, I've got to talk to people. It might be my kids trying to get me."

"Don't answer that phone!" Kate commanded. The phone rang a few more times and then was silent. "You can call your children's school if that's what's worrying you—which I doubt. But if I hear of you contacting any of my employees, you may also lose that job up there." As Kate stood up and put her papers into her briefcase, she looked toward the sink. That was almost my station, right down the drain. But she wondered, had she caught it in time?

She looked out the kitchen window, and then with an instinct she must have picked up in Vietnam, she suddenly ducked down. The glass went flying past her head, smashing against the window pane. She turned and saw Janet, her eyes glaring, her body shaking. She looked like a wild animal.

"You bitch," Janet was screaming. "Who do you think you are? God?" She screamed as she lunged for Kate but Kate quickly stepped aside, sending Janet's body crashing into the counter.

The drug paraphernalia still lay there and Kate saw Janet pick up the razor. Before Kate could move, Janet ran into the living room and began frantically riffling through a pile of newspapers and magazines, all the while screaming, "You won't destroy me. I'll destroy you. I hate you. I hate you. I'd like to kill you."

Finally, Janet seemed to find what she had been looking for—the *Times Magazine* with Kate on the cover. She kneeled down on the floor and slashed at the picture with the razor. "Bitch. Self-righteous shit." She kept tearing at the magazine, even when the razor cut into her own hand, cursing, screaming obscenities.

Kate, realizing that Janet—whether from drugs or anxiety—was completely out of control, began moving toward the kitchen door but when Janet saw her move, she shouted, "You think you can come in here and do your dirty work and leave? Not on your life."

Razor still in hand, she ran at Kate who looked quickly around and pulled the fire extinguisher off the wall. "Janet! Stop right where you are!" Kate shouted. "If I pull the tag on this thing, you'll be in really bad shape. I've seen these used for crowd control and believe me, you don't want to risk it."

But Janet was no longer listening. She lay on the floor at Kate's feet, vomiting and moaning, rolling her head back and forth in her own mess. Kate found herself retching too in disgust but just then, the kitchen door opened and Janet's two children were standing in the doorway with the middle-aged woman who was their babysitter.

"Don't worry, your mommy's going to be okay," Kate said.

The girl, who appeared to be around ten, looked at her unemotionally. "Frankly, I don't care," she said, and walked out of the room. Kate trembled. But then the little boy, who seemed to be about seven, came forward and stroked his mother's damp hair. He began to cry, and Kate put her hand on his head. "Poor baby. Poor baby."

She told the sitter, who obviously was familiar with Janet's cocaine problem, to take the children for a walk. Kate then called Diana and asked her to contact the children's grandparents and see that arrangements were promptly begun for the family's move to Montreal.

"Are you going to tell me what this is all about?"

"Well, if you get your pad and take this down, you'll have a pretty good idea. It's a memo I want to be on the desk of every employee we've got first thing tomorrow morning."

Kate then dictated into the phone fluently, punctuation in place: "Janet Ryan, vice president of programming for WLYM, has resigned as of today. She will be taking a position out of the country. I will meet with the appropriate staff members tomorrow. Please be on call to speak to me or your direct supervisor during the day."

"That's it?" Diana asked.

"That's it until the morning, when—like it says in the Bible—'Vengeance shall be mine.' "

6

KATE WAS AT HER DESK BY SEVEN-THIRTY THE FOLLOWING morning and Diana arrived shortly thereafter.

"I want you to call Hunnewell and tell him to be here as soon as possible. Try his apartment first. Then we've got a tape here that needs immediate action."

"Yes ma'am and good morning."

"Sorry, Diana, I'm going to need your patience today but you'll understand better when you listen to this tape."

Diana gave a mock salute and left the room as Kate began going through the papers on her desk. About an hour later, she heard her outer office door open and Steven Merriam came into her office, waving a piece of paper.

"What the hell is this? What do you mean she's resigned and is going 'out of the country?' You hired the woman yourself. She was working on a lot of good projects."

"The memo says exactly what it says. By the way, I want you back in my office at ten A.M." She looked back down at her papers.

"I'm in your office right now."

"Yes, you're right, Steven, but the station's attorney is not."

Merriam looked at her, bewildered, and, shrugging, left the office. Kate smiled at his retreating figure, almost enjoying the anticipation of their coming meeting.

* * *

Downstairs, Celia Doyle was between inserts into the network news. She ran into Larry Keough's office. "Have you seen this? Janet's been fired. Just like that. Did she call you? Have you spoken to her?"

"No," said Larry. "Haven't you? I thought you were buddies."

"We were. I swear she didn't know any of this was coming. I haven't heard from her, and there's no answer at her house. What's going on?"

"I hate to think. From the sound of this, Marchand's onto the whole drug business. And if Janet talked before she left, we're all dead."

Throughout the building the memo was greeted with suspicion, if not outright fear. Those who did not feel their own jobs were on the line knew too many others whose jobs were. And no one doubted the power of Katherine Marchand.

In Kate's office, Timothy Hunnewell was listening incredulously to the information Kate was presenting. As Diana and Hunnewell exchanged greetings, Kate went to the safe, motioning Diana to lock the door.

Kate pulled out the wooden box, the manila envelope, and a few smaller envelopes. "Here is the evidence taken from the desks, and this particular one, from Nora Jevile's bag. My fingerprints are on only Jevile's and they are nothing compared to hers . . . especially the nose print from this handy little device."

"Kate, I still don't like the fact that you broke into people's desks," said Hunnewell firmly.

"Tim, remember, I went to law school too. I know the risks of what I did and also the necessity for it. The management is responsible for the lives of its employees while they're in the building or doing work for us. If one of my reporters crashes in a helicopter, I am responsible. If an elevator malfunctions and falls five floors, I am responsible. So, if I have people dealing and using an illegal, life-threatening drug, I am also responsible. Correct?"

"Yes."

"Well, this evidence, and the tape. . . ." she paused, looking at Diana.

"It's all done. It's a terrible thing to hear."

"Yes, I know. Please put one copy in the safe." Kate sat down at her desk. "We will not inform these people whom we are going to see in advance. Except for the first·three. Don Bartley knows he is to be here at nine. I want you to call Nora Jevile and tell her to get in here at nine-thirty. And Steve Merriam is due at ten o'clock. Diana, will you stay and take notes? And the recorder will be going.'' Kate was interrupted by a knock on the door. "It looks like it's time to begin."

Don Bartley walked in like a sentenced man. He was dressed spotlessly, even to the makeup applied to hide the circles under his eyes.

"Sit down, Don. This is the station's attorney, Timothy Hunnewell. I'm recording this conversation." Kate pushed the buttons on the console.

"Don, I don't expect that you are going to deny that you are very actively into cocaine use?"

Don shook his head and said, "No."

"In a lengthy conversation with Janet Ryan yesterday, following your departure from her home," Kate narrowed her stare, "I learned that the disease has traveled to your wife. In fact, you and your wife are going through fifteen or twenty grams a week." Don looked down at his hands. "Don't look away from me, Don. I'll only get angrier." She leaned forward, pointing at him. "You are regarded as the best weatherman in this city. You are applauded for your work with kids and your easygoing, southern-gentlemanly manner. And now you're a cokehead. You have embarrassed this station repeatedly by not showing up for your public appearances. On top of that, you have gone on the air under the influence of that drug. These are grounds for not only dismissal, but with the evidence I have on this tape, and what I saw yesterday, police action."

Don was afraid to move his eyes from Kate's. "I know the seriousness of what I have done," his voice was shaking, "but, I beg of you, Kate, please . . . a second chance."

Kate recoiled as if she had been struck. "A second chance! What for? So you can do it all over again? So you can jeopardize everyone here, again? So there can be another affair, another drug, more embarrassment for all of us?"

Don finally found some strength in his voice. "It will never happen again. I love this station. I love this town. I love my job. And I made a mistake. Haven't you ever made a mistake?"

"Yes, a big one. I hired Janet Ryan." Kate slammed her fist on her desk. "But that's my last mistake." She leaned back in her chair. "Now I'm going to tell you what your options are. You can, first of all, get your wife into a drug rehabilitation program . . . today. Send your children off to be with their grandmother. You will go cold turkey, after spending tomorrow with a drug counselor at McLean's Psychiatric Hospital. We'll set it up for you.'' She nodded in Diana's direction. ''You will spend the day among the people who have gone mad because of drug use and alcohol use. Maybe it will help you to help your wife. And you will return to work on Monday, and be the man I hired . . . or you'll face dismissal.''

Don spoke quickly. ''Of course, I'll take care of Marilyn. The kids can stay with my mother for a couple of weeks, and I'll go to McLean's.''

''You might also try to get your finances in order. You've blown, or should I say snorted up that overrated nose of yours, over thirty thousand dollars in cash in the last several weeks. According to Janet, despite your obviously inappropriate high salary, you had to take a second mortgage on your house.''

Don said nothing, only nodded.

''And one more thing, Don. If I get any hint that you may be involved in any drug, or even drinking heavily, I will dismiss you immediately, and I will destroy you forever in the television industry. You won't be able to get a job in a television cafeteria in Eastback, Tennessee. Do I make myself clear?''

''Yes. Yes,'' Don said. ''And don't worry. I'll make it up to you, Kate.''

''You could never make it up to me, but if I were you, I'd try damn hard to. Now get out of my office.''

As the door closed behind Don, Hunnewell spoke up. ''Why didn't you let him go? He sounds like too much trouble.''

''Because I cannot break up the anchor team. I can't throw too many bodies out of here, especially not the bodies the public loves. And Don will make it. I know you didn't see it from him today, but underneath, he is strong, and he is a good person. He's not weak and evil like our next customer. See if she's out there, Diana.''

Nora came in, Kate's memo in her hand. ''I just got in and someone handed me this. Why wasn't I told? Janet was a friend of mine.''

''Why don't you just take a seat, Nora? Oh, by the way, this is the station's attorney, Timothy Hunnewell.''

The introduction seemed to stop Nora in her tracks. Kate looked out at the rain and fog over the harbor. She couldn't help herself. She was going to enjoy this. She turned and looked directly at Nora.

"Nora, as of this moment, you are fired!"

Nora's mouth went slack. "What do you mean? You can't do this. I'm calling my agent." She tried to rise.

"Sit down!" Kate's voice had the tone of a Marine Corps drill instructor. "I certainly *can* do this. You're on a month-to-month contract. It's the end of August. You are no longer an employee of WLYM."

"You have to have grounds. What are your grounds?"

"Okay," Kate said lightly, "let's see. Late for work, inability to work with producers, abuse of personnel from directors to technicians to associate producers, drinking on location and on the set. Then there's your repeated lying, your failure to prepare yourself for the show, your untrustworthiness . . . and the fact that you're just no damn good. I don't know who ever pulled you out of commercials, Nora, but they certainly made a mistake. Your ratings are terrible, and as long as I've been here, you just have never, ever, been worth the aggravation. I should have fired you long ago."

"I'll fight this, you'll never get away with this." Nora Jevile rose to leave.

Kate took the recorder from her drawer and said, "One moment please. I want you to hear something. You'll recognize the voice. It's your friend, Janet Ryan."

Nora's face grew visibly white even under her thick makeup.

"Nora, Nora Jevile," Janet Ryan's voice came through the small speaker. "She actually helped spread the word that I was a good, clean contact. And she was probably one of my best customers, though I think maybe she was dealing herself."

Kate turned off the recorder. "And if you think this is some game, here is something I believe belongs to you." She took out the sniffer.

Nora looked from Kate to the attorney. "What are you going to do?" she asked.

"I'm having you escorted from the building. Do not try to reenter it. And if I were you, I wouldn't try contacting any of your other friends at LYM." Kate stood. "That's all, you can go now."

"Diana, would you please tell Phil Bernelli, Nora has been dismissed, and that for today, Andrew will have to free a reporter or anchor to do her show. I'll talk to Phil about permanent arrangements later."

Diana left the office and Steven Merriam came in.

"What's going on around here? I just passed Nora Jevile sobbing and being escorted into the elevator by one of the guards."

"Yes, I just fired her."

"You want to explain all this firing?"

"Cocaine," Kate said.

"Listen, there's coke around everywhere. It's no big deal. So a couple of techs do a line here and there."

"We're not talking about a couple of boom operators. We're talking about producers, reporters, weathermen, hosts of shows, PR men, vice president of programming," she paused and added, "vice president of sales."

"What?" Merriam was on his feet. "What are you talking about?"

"Sit down, Steven. Diana?"

"Two-sixteen."

Kate pushed the button until the recorder reached that number. She also opened a lower desk drawer and took out the wooden box and opened it. Merriam stared at the scales. "You see, Steven, before Janet Ryan left, she gave me some information."

The voice on the recorder began. "Steven was good for around ten grams a week. I think . . . no, I know . . . he gave some of it to the advertisers, you know, to sweeten the deal, and make him look a little better."

Kate turned off the machine.

"That's just a hysterical, delirious confession. It doesn't mean anything," Merriam said.

"Oh, and all these notes from Janet don't mean anything either." She pulled out the original pieces of memo paper. "And neither does the drug found on the scales. And neither does this . . . found in your file cabinet. The evidence is irrefutable."

Hunnewell added, "And possession of this amount carries a minimum prison term of two years."

Merriam stood and threw his arms into the air.

"Well I guess that's it. You're finally going to get what you've always wanted. To get rid of me," he said.

"That depends upon you," Kate answered curtly. "Despite our differences, you have been a good sales manager. Unfortunately, you haven't been doing enough of that lately. Your whole department hasn't been. LYM could survive without you, but God knows there will be enough bodies around this place by the end of the day . . . including six of your own sales staff."

"Six? How do you expect us to sell time?"

Kate ignored the question. "Despite it all, I have a deal for you. You never touch the drug again, of course. Make certain everyone in your department knows it's a death knell to even think of snorting coke. Replace your six people with men and women of impeccable credentials . . . and within a year, increase our sales profits by fifty percent."

"Fifty percent? That's impossible."

"You know it's not that hard. We went up almost thirty percent last year. With a better staff, and you working harder, that goal will be easy to meet."

"And if it's not met?"

"The consequences will be serious," said Kate. "That's all I care to say."

Glenn Paulson came next. And so the morning went. Kate personally fired and pledged to silence each person she had chosen as irretrievable or not worth the trouble. The effect of the scales on her desk only increased the impact of her words. No one argued with her. Everyone was convinced the police had done the investigation and therefore they were all inches away from court and prison. Some cried, a few pleaded. But the answer was always the same: "Get out!"

By noon, Kate had fired two daily talk show hosts, four reporters, six salesmen, eight technicians, five producers, and four associate producers. Another twelve employees had had the fear of God put into them.

A station meeting was called for 4:45 and, by the time Kate walked into Studio Six, she felt once again in complete control of her organization. She stepped to the front of the room and faced several hundred employees.

"I'm sorry to take you away from your work, but I hope this is the last such diversion you will have. As you know, Janet Ryan's dismissal yesterday has been followed today by the dismissal of several dozen others. You and I all know why. A vicious, murderous substance became more important to many among us than dedication to their work, and their fellow employees. I have spared some of you." Kate paused for a full minute. "I did it because I believe in your strength and in your ability to beat this. WLYM will expand its drug counseling program to help any of you who desire it.

"The individuals we have lost will be quickly replaced with the finest people available. But department heads no longer have complete autonomy in hiring. I will participate in and approve all hiring for the foreseeable future.

"In the meantime, I expect you all to return to the task of delivering the highest quality programming, news and special coverage, for which this station is recognized. And I would hope that what has happened will remain a family matter. Airing laundry in public will only hurt us all.

"Be assured that the reputation of WLYM has not been tarnished. Our reputation for quality and integrity remains unchanged. And as long as I lead this exceptional staff, it always will."

The applause started slowly, but built so the studio almost rocked with it. As she headed toward the door she passed close to Kim who said, "Thank you, Kate."

"Whatever for?"

"I can't help thinking how mediocre life would be without you."

BOOK FOUR

TAKE TWO

"Success can make you go one of two ways. It can make you a prima donna, or it can smooth the edges, take away the insecurities, let the nice things come out."

Barbara Walters
Newsweek, May 6, 1974

1

KATE LET THE WARMTH OF THE SUN PRESS HER BODY INTO the smooth covering of the raft that so lethargically drifted around the pool. The events of the week had exhausted her; the pain in her back was hardly bearable.

Months earlier she had told Jonathan that short of morphine, which she did not want to use regularly, none of her medications was helping her. She had tried biofeedback and acupuncture and though they each had given her brief relief at the beginning, they no longer worked. Now she was trying self-hypnosis.

She had gone to a renowned psychiatrist who was a colleague of Jonathan's and he had taught her a technique she was now employing. As she put herself under, she remembered his words, "Lie flat, in a comfortable place. Let your eyes float up until they are looking at the sky and then, while they are still in that position, let your lids drop down over them. . . . Let your left arm dangle to the side. Take long, slow deep breaths, feeling your body sink into the mattress as you exhale, feeling it rise into the blue sky as you breathe in. . . ."

The mental pictures she had been given relaxed each part of her body and seemed to enable her muscles to let go of the pain . . . for a while.

Jonathan had come down to the pool and settled into a chaise with a few magazines. He did not greet Kate because he knew about her self-hypnosis program and could tell from the arm trailing in the water that she was "putting herself under." He tried to control his impatience: Despite some evidence in its favor, he couldn't help feeling that what she was doing was based not on scientific data but on old wives' tales. He felt extremely uncomfortable, too, that nothing he or his colleagues had been able to do gave Kate any relief. He knew that sometimes he let Kate see his frustration and he tried to control it. Comes from being a neurosurgeon, he thought. Our batting average isn't so hot so we start blaming the . . . well, yeah, we start blaming the patients. Only human nature, I suppose.

Jonathan shook his head, annoyed at himself for wasting time on imaginings that get you nowhere and might even undermine your self-confidence. He picked up a hang gliding magazine and plunged into plans for his own next trip. The club he belonged to flew out of Ascutney, Vermont, only about two hours away, and he'd arranged to drive up. What a sport, he thought. Better than ballooning, where you had so little navigational control, or skydiving where he'd seen too many spiral breaks in the legs of the practitioners. Even loving thrills the way he did, as a physician he'd decided the odds against free-falls were too great.

He glanced up and saw Kate's hand move slightly, and he saw the familiar clenching and releasing of the fist. She was coming out of her trance. He watched her body adjust to the realities of air and atmosphere, and she opened her eyes at just the point where the raft put Jonathan in their scope. She smiled warmly.

"Feel better?" asked Jonathan.

"Much," she answered sleepily. "How long was I out?"

Jonathan looked at his watch. "Almost an hour." He stood up, walked to the edge of the pool.

"Why don't you come and keep your wife company? This raft was built for two."

Without a word, Jonathan dove into the pool, leaving barely a splash behind him, and emerged next to Kate. After threatening that if he pushed her over he'd be in divorce court, she helped him onto the raft and they both lay, side by side, closing their eyes against the sun, Kate draping one leg over Jonathan's.

"So what has the world's finest neurosurgeon been doing?"

"Thinking about the world's most successful television magnate."

"God, that sounds boring and I'm afraid you haven't had much of a wife this week."

"Well, Sundays are for making up for that." Jonathan shifted his body and moved his hand across Kate's stomach and up to her breast. Beneath the thin fabric of her suit, Kate's nipple immediately grew hard under his touch.

"Why is it," she asked, tracing her finger around Jonathan's mouth, "that when men think of a woman being a wife, they only think of sex? What about keeping up the house, always being at her husband's side, taking care of the children?" The last phrase slipped out accidentally, and caused an uneasy silence between them. Shit, thought Kate, when I get too relaxed, I lose control. She raised herself up on one elbow, and after the raft adjusted to the change in weight, she closed her mouth over Jonathan's, as if to signal an end to the conversation. Jonathan responded and pulled Kate almost on top of him. This movement was too much for the raft and they both toppled into the water. Kate was laughing and pulling at Jonathan's swimming trunks.

"Hey," he said, "I'm not sure we have time to get serious. Aren't we expecting company? Didn't you say Kim and her men were coming?"

"It's only eleven. We've got plenty of time." They were in the shallow end of the pool and Kate had pulled Jonathan's mouth to her breast.

"Bridget," Jonathan mumbled. "Don't forget Bridget's probably here to make lunch."

"Damn," Kate said. "Why is that woman always around when I'm lusting for my husband?"

She took Jonathan's hand and ran with him into the house. Within a few minutes of laughing, shouting lovemaking, they both lay spent on the big bed in their room. A quarter of an hour later Jonathan slapped Kate's leg. "Let's move it, girl. Let's get this show on the road."

As they were dressing, Bridget called upstairs to say that their guests had come through the gates. Jonathan went quickly downstairs and as Kate got to the open front door she saw him kiss Kim on the lips and then kneel down as Jason hurled himself forward. Jason was hugging him, saying, "Jonathan, Jonathan, wait till you see how good I can swim."

Chris put his arm around Kim's shoulder as if to announce they were a couple. Funny, Kate thought, it's like he's reacting to Jonathan greeting Kim and Jason so warmly.

Kim did look beautiful. She already had a light tan—Kate would have to warn her not to get burned. That broiled look is hard to cover for the camera. The sun had streaked her blonde

hair with almost white lights that shone over her white tennis
clothes. Kate realized that it had been so long since her own
back had allowed her to play, that the tennis clothes in her closet
were now passé. Kim's full-cut, almost baggy shorts were longer
than any Kate had ever worn and the cut of her shirt was much
fuller but the effect was . . . well, cute, you'd have to say, sexy,
in some reverse twist of a way.

They ate their lunch gaily, a lot of the conversation focused
on Jason, as if all the adults were carefully trying to keep it
light, to avoid talking about the events of the week. But as happens whenever a topic is being avoided, the gaiety was forced
and there were several unnatural awkward silences. Finally Kate
said, "Listen, I know we're all dieting so I told Bridget to skip
dessert and bring on the coke and the straw."

Jason said, "Gee, Kate, my mom only lets me drink two
Cokes a week and I went to this birthday party yesterday and
used them all up."

Everybody laughed, Jason got his ice cream and the five of
them headed out for the tennis courts. Kim and Chris had brought
their rackets and Jason was appointed ball boy. Jonathan and
Kim played first and Chris and Kate sat by the side of the court.

Jonathan's first serve was strong but off its mark and Kate
immediately sprang to her feet. "Jonathan Marchand! If one of
those tennis balls hits that face, your own balls will be in serious
danger."

"Kate, watch your language," Jonathan shouted back.
"There's a child present."

"Whose mother has a million-dollar face I cannot afford to
have smashed!"

"That's my wife," Jonathan said sarcastically, "the great hu-
manitarian." He moved back into position on the court and
called across to Kim, "Sorry. As you could see, it was a mistake. I'll serve them easier."

"Don't you dare!" Kim said. "You'll need all the tricks
you've got in this game, Doctor."

"She's quite a woman, isn't she?" asked Chris.

"She's a hell of a journalist and a hell of a worker," Kate
replied. "I'll leave the rest of it up to you."

"You sound almost cold."

"Well, I believe in keeping a polite distance between myself
and those who work for me, or whom I deal with professionally.
But I do like Kim, and Jonathan, in particular, enjoys spending
time with Jason—and, of course the two of you are colleagues."

Jonathan was playing the net and they heard him shout in frustration as Kim lobbed a ball over his head.

"That's my girl," Chris called.

"You two seem to have a very nice relationship." Kate smiled.

"We do. I've never met anyone I felt as strongly about as Kim. I've asked her to marry me."

Kate put down her iced tea slowly and looked at Chris. "I guess I missed a few steps in there. I had no idea it had become that serious."

Chris leaned toward Kate. "I'm thirty-eight years old and I have never married for the simple reason that I never found a woman I truly loved. That first night I met Kim at your home, I knew I had found her." He laughed. "You think I'm crazy."

"Not at all. I understand all too well. You see that man out there chasing that fuzzy ball? I was sitting in a bar in Manhattan—actually, it was a seedy joint in the Village—reading the Sunday *Times*. This man walked in looking very tired and fed up with the world. He, too, started reading the *Times*. Then at one point, we both looked up, across this expanse of bar, and our eyes connected. I knew at that moment I had found the only man I would ever love. And if you ask him about it, he'll tell you the same thing. So no, I don't think you're crazy at all."

"The trouble is, Kim's the one who thinks I'm crazy."

"Maybe she feels a little rushed. It's only a year since her husband died."

Chris shook his head. "She says that's in the past. She says she loved him very much, but she doesn't talk about him at all."

"What about Jason?" Kate asked.

"Well, I really like him a lot and I think he feels the same way, but I know Kim worries. She says I've never had children of my own and don't understand the day-to-day problems."

"And?" Kate asked.

"And here come the characters in question."

Kim and Jonathan flung themselves into some chairs and Kim said, "Kate, this husband of yours has Lendl's forehand and McEnroe's. . . ."

"Don't say it!" Jonathan objected. "I didn't throw my racket down once."

Kim made a joke of batting her eyelashes. "Why, Jonathan, I was going to compare your serve and volley to his. Go on Chris, get out there and win one for the visiting team."

As Chris and Jonathan rose, Jason asked, "Can I chase balls again, Jonathan?"

"I won't go out there without you, Champ." He threw a laughing Jason onto his shoulders and the three of them headed back to the courts.

Kim sank into the chair and poured herself a glass of iced tea. "Your husband takes his tennis very seriously."

"He takes everything very seriously, Kim," said Kate, in a very friendly tone. "I think it's because he deals with life and death every day in his work. It adds an intensity to everything he does. Although I admire that, at times it makes me worry. Like when he's hang gliding or gunning his Porsche down these back roads."

"I guess I should be thankful that Chris is a neurologist and not a neurosurgeon."

"Maybe," Kate replied. "Jonathan's nerves are often strung taut after a difficult brain or spinal cord surgery. He takes it very personally and it shows on him. There are times I wish he wasn't so good and in such demand. A neurologist can diagnose and advise the surgeon, but it's the surgeon who has to do it . . . and then has to live with someone who's lost his eyesight or sense of smell, or who stays paralyzed—or dies."

"You both have such demanding work. It must be an exceptional marriage to survive it."

"We are very happy," Kate said shortly.

Suddenly Jason came running up to them, breaking the silence that lay between them. "Mom, Mom, I'm all hot and sweaty. Can I go swimming now?"

"That sounds like a great idea. We'll all go. Kim, I hope you brought your suit?" Kate was standing, Jason's hand in hers.

Kate had changed and was checking the chlorine level with Jason when Kim came out through the doors of the study. Her yellow suit was almost identical to Kate's black one. Low cut, thin straps, with a design that revealed the thigh and hip up to the waist. On both women the suit accentuated the firmness of their breasts and stomach, and the length and elegance of their legs.

"You have good taste in suits," called Kate.

"You, too," said Kim, smiling. Then she saw to her horror that her son was about to push her boss into the pool.

"Kate! Chase, stop it. Kate, be careful of your back!"

Without turning, Kate knew immediately what was coming. She dropped the testing kit, turned and dove into the pool. The twist had been painful, but a jolt from Jason would have been worse. As she surfaced, she heard Jason protesting to his mother.

"Mom, you ruined it!" Kim was now circling the pool to where Jason was.

"Young man, you don't throw people into the pool. I've told you before it is unsafe." She had Jason by the arm now, and held him angrily as she turned towards the water. "I'm sorry, Kate, are you all right?"

"Thanks to your warning, yes." She swam away as Kim returned to her reprimand.

Jason seemed confused. "But you always thought it was funny when I did it to Daddy."

"Doing it to Daddy was different," admonished Kim. "Mrs. Marchand sometimes has trouble with her back and you could have hurt her. Now go and apologize."

Jason was crying as he walked down to the end of the pool where Kate was doing some leg exercises in the water.

"I'm sorry, Kate. I wouldn't mean to hurt you."

"I know you wouldn't hurt me, honey. Come on in, and we'll both climb on the raft. It's built for two." Jason walked down the steps, wiping his face as Kate pulled the raft toward them. Soon they were both positioned on it comfortably, and Kate sent it sailing down the pool.

Jason shouted to his mother to do a flip, and Kim said, "Okay, here I go."

She went to the diving board, took three strong bounces and lifted herself into a perfect jackknife. She came up to the applause of Kate and her son, and then returned to the board for an almost perfect swan dive. By this time, Chris and Jonathan were watching. Kim said, "Come on, Jason. Show Dr. Marchand what you learned in camp."

Soon mother and son were doing simple dives, one after the other, bowing elaborately after each ascent to the board.

Chris applauded and said, "I never learned to do that. Always hated getting water up my nose."

"I'm an expert, myself," Jonathan said. He went to the board and began to joke around, doing belly flops and backward jumps, at one point holding Jason and Kim, one over each shoulder before he dove.

"Jonathan!" Kate shouted. "One bad back in this family is enough."

"To put it mildly," Chris said.

After all the others had left the pool, Kate began to swim laps.

"There's barely a splash," Chris remarked.

"That's because she's not moving her legs," Jonathan answered.

"What?" said Chris, looking more closely. "You're right. Why ever not? She trying for a body building team?"

"No. Degenerative neuritis, made worse by the presence of foreign objects. Shrapnel and bone chips imbedded from the war."

"She has to be in oppressive pain."

"She is, but she doesn't talk about it, and seems able, so far, to work through it. She's very gutsy, my wife. Single-minded."

Later after they'd all showered and changed, Kim passed the door to Kate's study and saw her boss hard at work behind her desk.

"Do you ever take any time off?"

"I have most of today," replied Kate. "But I'm sorry, I don't mean to be rude."

"You're not. Chris tells me that I work all the time myself."

"Nice man," Kate said. "And according to Chris, he has found in you the only woman he will ever truly love."

"Yes, so he's said." Kim was silent for a moment, then added, "He's a very good man."

"But it doesn't sound as if there are exactly fireworks going off in your heart."

"How can fireworks go off in a heart that feels so dead? My heart just doesn't trust happiness or love anymore." Kim's voice was soft and pained. "But I guess that's not fair to Jason, nor to Chris."

"You should trust your feelings, Kim," said Kate calmly. "You can't force yourself to fall in love if the chemistry's not right. Maybe Chris just isn't the right one."

"Yes, I know," said Kim wistfully, "but if not him now, then who, when?"

"Wait for Jonathan's clone, that's my advice."

2

DIANA PUT THE PHONE BACK ON ITS HOOK AND WONDERED again why everyone thought the world of television was so glamorous and exciting. So much of what went on involved dealing with the insecure egos of producers, directors and on-camera people, along with the hard-edged maneuvering of salespeople and promoters. And the stupidity! thought Diana. Not here, maybe, but in the industry.

Kate's buzzer summoned and as soon as Diana was through the door, Kate handed her a sheet of paper and pointed to the editorial director of WLYM who was in her office.

"Charles here has, at my request, written a strong editorial concerning the growing abuse of drugs in this country," Kate said. "However, I don't think it's quite strong enough, and I'm going to rewrite a few parts of it, and add some additional recommendations. I'll dictate the differences to you now, Diana, so Charles can see them. And then I'd like you to get some studio time for me this afternoon."

Diana paused halfway in her descent into a chair to begin the dictation. "Studio time?"

"Yes, I'm going to deliver this editorial."

"I still think that's a mistake, Kate," Charles Whittaker said. "You haven't done an editorial on camera in quite a while and

I think your presence would call more attention than we want to this whole subject.''

"There is no such thing as too much attention to this problem.''

"But with what's recently gone on here, I think it's just asking for trouble.'' He approached Kate. "Why don't we just lay low on this one? Let me make a simple statement and be done with it.''

"It is precisely because of what has gone on here that we cannot lay low on this one,'' Kate responded. "And I don't want there to be any doubts as to how I feel about this issue—inside or outside this station.''

Using the facts Whittaker had laid out for her, Kate redictated the press release and editorial. The message from it was clear: WLYM was strongly against any drug use and it would open its facilities in any way that would foster additional drug information and encourage stricter law enforcement and stricter laws for drug dealers and offenders.

When she had finished, she said, "I'll tape it this afternoon, and we should run it in the news tonight.''

Kate looked briefly at the daily itinerary Diana had given her that morning. "Looks like a pretty easy day. I'm hoping to get out of here around four-thirty and head home to a very neglected husband. Really, Diana, we have been going about twelve hours a day to get ready for the November sweeps.''

"I know,'' Diana said, a little uneasily, "and remember how I told you I thought things were going a little too smoothly, considering it's just before the ratings?''

"So what turbulence has suddenly come up?''

"Well, first of all, Leonard Mankin's secretary called, and he would like to see you in his office this afternoon at four. I checked your appointments and said you'd be there.''

"Did our esteemed chairman of the board or his secretary say what it was about?''

"No, just that it was very important.''

"Well, I don't know of anything we've done that would anger Leonard, so I'm not going to worry about that too much,'' Kate said calmly. "Is there anything else?''

"Yes. You know a Leo Fugard?''

"You know I know Leo Fugard. He's the manager of Barrington's and a major advertiser.''

"Well, it seems that there's a misunderstanding with Roger Lewis.'' Kate checked off in her mind: Roger Lewis, producer of *Happenings in the A.M.*, an hour-long talk and information program.

"According to Mr. Fugard," continued Diana, "*Happenings* has been using a lot of their items lately, things like exotic birthday presents, the latest cooking gadgets, or collections of photographs or prints."

"That's not unusual, Diana," said Kate. "Barrington's is one of the finest department store chains in the country. We often use their merchandise. Are we not giving them proper credit? Is the stuff being returned damaged?"

"No, not exactly," Diana took in a deep breath. "According to Mr. Fugard, for the first time, a lot of it just isn't being returned."

"Not being returned? Impossible. Get Roger into my office."

While Diana dialed his office, Kate thought that it all fit. Roger's immediate supervisor had been Janet Ryan. Either she hadn't noticed what was going on, or she was also part of his scam. Diana informed Kate that Roger was out of the building. "Then get me the program's unit manager and then get Leo Fugard on the line for me."

After exchanging the usual pleasantries with Fugard, Kate got to the reason for the call. She wanted details and Leo gave them to her.

"It's not as if our budget cannot withstand this, Mrs. Marchand," Fugard said politely. "It just doesn't seem fair, especially because you already do very well by us in advertising dollars."

Kate knew that Barrington's needed WLYM much more than WLYM needed Barrington's. But it was certainly wrong and, if the Federal Communications Commission found out, it could put their license in jeopardy.

Kate assured Fugard that this abuse would stop immediately and that the missing merchandise would be returned to the store as soon as possible. "This never should have happened and I assure you, it will never happen again."

Diana soon ushered in a nervous-looking man in his early thirties. "Kate, this is Sean McKinley, unit manager for *Happenings*. Kate gestured towards a chair and turned to Diana, asking her to remain and take notes.

"Sean," Kate began, "ordinarily, a matter like this would be handled by the programming executive, but because we have not yet replaced Janet Ryan, it has fallen into my lap."

"What's the problem, Mrs. Marchand?"

"*Happenings* occasionally borrows Barrington's merchandise, does it not?"

"Yes, they're always tapped into the latest craze, and they also lend us some very high-quality stuff."

"Correct me, but in recent months, you have featured from Barrington's an elegant silver serving tray, a breakfast tray, a fully equipped briefcase . . ." Kate walked over to her desk and picked up a list before continuing, "a leatherbound set of Shakespeare's classics, an antique wine rack, framed photographs of Boston in the 1880s, a wristwatch containing a television set, a waterproof Sony Walkman, a wind surfboard, diving equipment . . ." Kate paused. "Do you recall seeing any of these on the set?"

"Yes," replied Sean quickly. "I remember the hosts working with each of those items."

"I just got a call from Leo Fugard at Barrington's." Kate leaned towards Sean, who leaned away from her. "He says that these items were borrowed but never returned." Kate went to a file cabinet and quickly found the folder she was looking for. She pulled a piece of paper from it and handed it to Sean.

"Does this look familiar?" Without even looking at it carefully, he knew what it was. Every employee at WLYM and the syndicates had to sign this form upon their employment. It assured management that they would never take advantage of their position in the television industry by accepting a bribe for editorial work. It also prohibited the acceptance of any gifts from any advertiser, sponsor, or any participant in any of the station's programs.

"Mrs. Marchand, I deal with the budget. I do not deal with the day-to-day activities of the show," Sean said bluntly.

"Does that mean you have not violated this agreement?"

"I have not personally violated that agreement."

"I accept that," Kate said. "But Barrington's is maintaining that certain items were never returned to them. Do you have any idea who might be taking all this merchandise?"

"Maybe you'd better talk to the producer." The words were barely audible.

"Diana, leave word in Roger Lewis's office that he should come up here when he gets in."

"Sean, I'd also like to talk to you about some budget questions I had. I was reviewing salaries to determine bonuses and I noticed that there were a few inequities. You seem to have two distinct salary levels on *Happenings*. One is quite high, the other distressingly low. I'm talking here only about staff salaries, not talent.

"For example, you have a producer making forty thousand dollars, a coordinating producer making thirty-six thousand, and you yourself, the unit manager, make thirty-two thousand. Then the drop begins. One associate producer making twenty-two thousand. One other at twenty thousand and two making sixteen and eighteen thousand." She put down the pages and looked at McKinley.

"Well, the people who make the big money have been here for quite a while."

Kate interrupted him. "That's not true. It clearly has nothing to do with seniority. The associate producer making twenty thousand has been here for four years. She's one of the best associate producers we have. It makes my blood boil to see her so underpaid."

"I really don't set the salaries, Mrs. Marchand. Janet and Roger used to and now it's Roger making the decisions. I just do the paperwork."

"Do you think these salaries are fair?"

"Well, no, not some of them."

"I know this goes on all over the industry but I don't want it here. Some of these men and women who are making twenty thousand a year or under work harder than many full producers. They are in the building at six A.M. and do all the behind-the-scenes work and get none of the glory. They're also the ones who get abused the most by the talent." Kate slammed her hand down in frustration. "God knows that some talent make ten times what they're worth. I can't do anything about that but try to get my money's worth out of them. But I can do something about inequities like this." She paused. "You don't recall the memo I sent to all department heads about setting a base scale for all jobs from associate producers and administrative assistants?"

"I do, and I mentioned it to Janet and Roger. They said that people were so desperate to work in television they'd settle for the lower salaries."

"The saddest part about that," Kate said sarcastically, "is that you're right. People will accept slave wages to be able to say they work with Kim Winston or that they were inside a mobile unit as a live show was put together." She lowered her voice. "So what happens is that we work people sixteen hours a day and pay them nothing until they burn out. Or, we pay them a pittance, work them hard, and they end up doing all the work of their superiors and getting none of the credit. They eventually turn bitter, leave the industry, and their superiors just hire other people to exploit.''

A moment later, Diana and Roger Lewis were standing in the doorway. ''What's going on, Kate? Not another drug bust, I hope,'' Roger said.

''That's not very funny, Roger. I'm going to get right to the point. We have two problems here. One, you have violated a written agreement you have with WLYM that prohibits you from taking anything from any sponsor or show participant.'' Kate began pacing the room.

''Oh, that. These are perks from some of the companies we help advertise. We give them air time—for them it's free advertising. They make a fortune off us. It's understood that we get to keep the merchandise in return. It's not like taking a bribe to do a story or something. We decide to do the story first.''

Kate was shocked. How did this person get into her station? How many other stores and advertisers had been cheated?

''Over at Channel Eight, it's an unwritten policy,'' Roger continued. ''All the shows do it. I was surprised at how few people do here.''

Kate's face was just inches from Roger's. ''Do you realize we could lose our license if the FCC got wind of this? You have given me no choice but to remove you immediately from your position. Furthermore, you and Janet Ryan disobeyed my directive to equalize salaries in this station. After taxes, you might as well have not even bothered to pay these people.''

When the matter was settled, Kate found herself in the newsroom. Its frenzy and electricity always soothed her. She headed for the glass enclosure behind which she knew she'd find Andrew Davis. He was busy going through some teletype copy when she pushed open the door and walked to one of the chairs opposite his desk.

''Hi, Kate. Why the long face?''

''Andrew, why did I leave news? Why couldn't I be happy as a simple street reporter?''

''Because you're too good.''

''If I'm so good, how come this place is filled with such troublemakers lately?''

''Relax, Kate. Look out there,'' he gestured through the clear windows to the newsroom. "You're batting almost a thousand there." She looked out and saw people rushing with tapes and copy, Don Bartley working on a weather map, Kim typing, Bill taking dictation over the phone, and a score of other reporters going about their work. She watched and smiled, ignoring the sound of Andrew's telephone.

"Kate? It's Diana, for you."

She took the phone, saying, "What do I have, a homing device on me or something?"

"No," said Diana. "You always go to the newsroom. Listen, you may have to change your plans. I can't get studio time for you to tape the editorial. So you'll have to do it live or have Charles do it. And then you've got Leonard Mankin at four."

"Okay, I'll go live but first I'm off to my other duties." She hung up the phone and looked at Andrew. "Can you believe it? The president and general manager of this illustrious station cannot get studio time."

"All you have to do is bump somebody."

"No, it's not worth interrupting productions. I'll do it live."

"Why are you doing it?"

"It's on drugs. I think it's best I do it, just in case there are a few malingerers. Tell Kim and Bill to make room for the old lady on the set tonight."

Riding the elevator up to the fifty-fifth floor of Mankin's office building, she felt more relaxed. The city still held the pleasant warmth of summer and she was able to forget about the incident with Roger Lewis. The question now was why was the chairman of the board summoning her?

Leonard's secretary greeted her warmly, saying "The others have already arrived. They're waiting for you."

"Thank you," Kate replied. The others?

As she entered the room, she could sense this was to be no pleasant chat among friends. Leonard rose from behind his desk.

"Kate, so glad you could make it. Sorry it's such short notice, but it seemed imperative that we all get together, and it's hard finding everybody in town at the same time." She shook Leonard's hand and then greeted the other four men. First, Raymond Aronson, general manager of Channel 6, WJTH; Earl Winslow, president of the Chamber of Commerce; Herbert Corkin, general manager of WZYN, Channel 8; and Richard Pratt, the mayor's press secretary.

The cast of characters put Kate on guard. It looked to her like the group had already reached a decision and were now depending upon Mankin to convince Kate to accept it—whatever it was about.

"Kate," Leonard began, "these gentlemen have come up with a solution to a problem we're all about to face, and I think we should go along with them."

"We, as in WLYM?" asked Kate brusquely.

"Yes, Katherine," replied Herb Corkin. "Ray and I were talking the other evening about the menace of these antiabortion groups. As you're probably aware, we've already had two fire bombings of abortion clinics."

"Yes, I'm aware. It's news."

"They're planning a rally for next week," cut in Pratt from the mayor's office. "Police estimate there'll be over fifty thousand people."

"The legislators at the statehouse are being mobbed by prolifers who come in with bunches of red roses and dolls covered with blood." Earl Winslow shook his head disdainfully.

"You gentlemen are not telling me anything I don't already know," said Kate.

"What about bomb threats?" asked Corkin. "Every time Channel Eight presents a prochoice point of view, it gets a bomb threat."

"And so does Channel Three, gentlemen," Kate responded. "Last week we increased security in and around the building and on some occasions, our reporters and crews travel with a uniformed security guard."

"So you understand the problem we're facing," said Pratt. "Violence and threats of violence on both sides in what is basically a no-win situation for the press."

"And for the business community," Winslow spoke up. "This city has finally shaken its reputation of violence and prejudice. We cannot afford to have it return."

"So you are proposing?" Kate inquired.

"A news blackout on many abortion activities," Ray Aronson said. "Not the big stuff, of course. But you know the old story, the more publicity we give them, the more they'll go for."

"We pretend it doesn't exist?" Kate asked.

"No, you know what I mean. We play it down. Give it low billing in all broadcasts. Especially the violence and the marches."

"I think that's called censorship."

"No, it's called common sense," Herb Corkin said abruptly. "For the city and for ourselves. Kate, for God's sake, we're entering a major ratings period. We don't need people taking sides based on what station carries a prolifer one night or a prochoice rally the next.''

"Ah ha, I had forgotten for a moment there about the ratings period." Like hell, she thought.

"So you understand, Kate," Ray said, "it's in our best interests to play this whole issue down."

Kate stood up at her place. "If my memory serves me correctly, several years ago a group of media representatives got together and decided they would try to control the coverage of desegregation in this town. After a heated debate, the conspiracy fell apart." She did not remind them that it was because she and the news director of the Public Broadcasting station had acted together that the conspiracy failed.

"We're trying to isolate this, this time," said Corkin, "by involving only the major television stations. The others, along with radio and newspapers, don't have rating periods."

"Look, gentlemen," Kate said—thinking ironically, no ladies invited, of course—"I know abortion is a tough issue, especially in this Catholic city. And I know it's also a powder keg because we also are surrounded by some of the most liberal academic institutions in America. But ignoring it is not going to work. The public is very involved in this question and if we don't give them the information they want they'll go elsewhere for it. We'll be accused of protecting our ratings by taking away the public's right to know. And it will backfire."

"We also have to consider that the coverage can be inflammatory," said the mayor's press secretary.

"As those of us in the room who are in the media know, every time we take a camera onto the street we run the risk of inflaming a situation. That's where the responsible reporter comes in."

The room was silent.

"Kate, we kind of anticipated your reaction to this," began Corkin, hesitatingly. "And so we thought that you should know both Ray and I have gone before our editorial boards and convinced them that facing the factors we are facing, we should stay away from the abortion issue as much as possible."

Kate returned to her chair and just shook her head. The old squeeze play. Basic blackmail. Kate would be left with the only station with balanced coverage of the issue—which in her view would imply a woman's right to abortion. Conservative Boston would come down angrily on the station. Advertisers and sponsors would be skittish and her opposition would watch gleefully for a drop in her ratings.

She decided to put it squarely to her own chairman. "Leonard, after hearing what these gentlemen have to say, what is your opinion of what we should do?"

"Based on a sketchy rundown over the phone, I agreed to have this meeting. In many ways, I regret that decision. I feel that I have been used."

Kate nodded at him, but did not speak.

"I have never yet interfered with your operation of WLYM and the syndicates, and for good reason. Your management style and expertise have always proven to be beyond reproach," Leonard said sternly. "I will not interfere now, and as usual, you can count on my complete support."

"Thank you," Kate rose in her chair and looked at the other people in the room. "I'm sure it's clear that I cannot join you in this project of yours. The station's integrity is more important than the ratings book." Kate grinned, crossing her fingers behind her back.

By the time Kate got back to her office, she had to hurry to prepare to go on the air. She brushed her hair, added highlights to her cheekbones, brushed her teeth and began talking to herself. She continued talking to herself as she walked from her office and headed towards the news studio. The assistant director handed her the copy and pointed out the chair she should move into during the next commercial break.

Kate watched as Kim and Bill breezed through the news. It was like watching two fine figure skaters going through a flawless routine on ice. Then she returned to the words going through her head. Christ, she thought, this is just like the old days: You've got five minutes before you're live on the feed, and you try to assemble hundreds of words and images into a sane package.

"Mrs. Marchand, if you'll take the seat now." The floor director was at her elbow. She quickly walked over, greeting Kim and Bill as the floor director put a microphone on her.

"So now the pro's going to show us how it's done," Bill said, smiling.

"I've been watching you two. I need lessons from you," Kate said. "And anyway, it's been over a year since I've done this . . . so the least you can do is be sympathetic and not laugh when I fall off the chair." She adjusted her microphone as a camera swung directly in front of her. Out of habit, she shifted to the left. For a serious story, she had learned years ago that the head-on shot with her head slightly tilted, with her body to the left, was most effective.

The floor director spoke. "Coming out of commercial. We'll come to you direct on Camera Three, Kim, then to Mrs. Marchand on Camera Four. Your prompter's ready, Mrs. Marchand, times out to a minute and a half."

Suddenly Kate remembered. "Tell the director to kill any chromakey she may have up for me. Julie, if you hear me, kill the key."

A voice came over the loudspeaker in the studio. "We have the cocaine key up. It matches your copy. We planned on losing it after the first thirty seconds."

"No, Julie, no cocaine key. No key at all, please."

"Okay, here we come, Kim," said the floor director, his hand outstretched underneath Camera Three. "Five, four, three, two . . ." Then there was just the fierce point of his finger.

"Coming up in this broadcast, Don Bartley will tell us if summer is going to stay with us through the weekend, and correspondent Monica Huang will have a report from Washington on the effects of the president's budget cuts for New England." Kim paused. "Right now, with an editorial representing the opinion of WLYM and its syndicate stations, we present the president and general manager of WLYM, Katherine Marchand."

Kate saw the familiar red light of the camera come on, and looking beyond the TelePrompTer and into the camera lens, she calmly began. "Whatever is good about this country has been built by the courage of men and women who speak out against what they think is wrong, or in favor of what they believe is right. It is that one attribute, protected by our First Amendment, that has made us unique among the nations of the world. We all know that, at times, the easiest thing to do, the safest thing, is to remain silent, especially when speaking out may cause repercussions in our own lives. But silence or 'going along' is the most dangerous threat to our society. This country cannot survive unless we speak out.

"But sometimes it's frightening. In recent weeks, this city has been the target of antiabortion protesters and bombers. Threats have been made, and some carried out, to organizations, including news organizations, throughout the metropolitan area. WLYM wants there to be no mistake that we condemn such acts of violence. We understand very well that the abortion issue is one of the most complex moral questions individuals or institutions have to face. Feelings run high on both sides—and for very good reasons. As for us, the editorial board of this station, after much reflection and hard work, has concluded that, finally, a woman has the right to control her own destiny. We do not believe that any individual or group of individuals should have the power to deny a woman her legal right to an abortion.''

Kate's voice was controlled but passionate as she spoke, now quoting facts and statistics, reminding viewers of the horrors of the illegal abortion and the often unlivable life of an unwanted child, and the inevitable welfare cycle that began with that child.

Watching her, Kim was mesmerized. Though the studio was large, though it was cluttered with the staff and the equipment of broadcasting, Kate's presence was extremely powerful. Kim realized the effect would be even stronger on a television screen.

Then she noticed something amazing: The TelePrompTer wasn't moving. Kate was not referring to the pages the assistant director had handed her. She was talking extemporaneously. That's why she didn't want the cocaine key. She had changed the speech at the last minute from cocaine to abortion. Kim looked over at Bill and then around at the cameramen and others on the floor. The effect was the same. They were all completely attentive.

Kate was now ending her talk. ''I want to assure all of you that such beliefs will in no way influence our reporting on the subject of abortion. We will cover both arguments objectively and effectively. We will give additional time to the discussion of the abortion issue, opening up our studios to pro and con on an absolutely equal basis. Our purpose is to give you the most information on the subject we can, in order that you may make your own decision. WLYM takes the risk of speaking out at this time because we believe that it is our duty to uphold the rights guaranteed in the Constitution of the United States. To do otherwise would undermine the rights and interests of *all* our people—men and women. Thank you.'' With the slight lift of her eyebrows that had been her trademark, Kate said goodnight.

They were in a commercial, and Kate took off her microphone. ''You're slipping, Mrs. Marchand,'' came the voice over the loud speaker. ''That was two seconds over, you're usually right on the money.''

Kate laughed. ''Forgive me, Julie. I'm out of practice.''

Applause rose from the control room followed by applause in the studio.

"Thank you," Kate said, rising. "Now, I'll leave it in the hands of the pros. Thanks for letting me visit." She smiled at Kim and Bill and walked off the set.

By the time she got to her own office, the messages were already accumulating—of both anger and support. One message was from "Dr. Marchand, requesting a date with the beautiful woman doing the editorial." Kate smiled as she remembered how much Jonathan had loved to see her on camera in the old days.

Diana buzzed. "Leonard Mankin on two."

Kate picked up the phone. "Well, are you still behind me?"

"More than ever," Leonard said. "I already heard from Aronson. He's livid. He says you've beaten them to the punch and given them no choice but to cover all the abortion activities and get completely involved. He also said both he and Herb would have to go back to their editorial boards; that it would look very suspicious for them to switch policies after all your talk about the danger of silence and acquiescing to violence."

"He's right, it would," Kate said.

"But Kate, it's no doubt going to anger some of our advertisers and our viewers."

"I realized that before I spoke, but I think the way we played it, we'll be all right. I think we'll pick up as much support as we lose."

Andrew Davis came into her office shouting in a mock serious voice. "You know I hate talent going on without the prompter!"

"Oh, dear, the news director's mad at me. I changed my copy, no prompter. I went two seconds over and to top it all, I talked about a controversial matter." She wrung her hands. "Does this mean you're going to ground me? Take me off camera? Make me a production assistant?"

"No, I'm here to offer you an anchor position. Name your price."

"You already have a splendid anchor team, and anyway, the general manager of the station would never approve."

"Really, Kate, don't you ever miss it? You're so good."

"The truth? Yes, I do miss it. I miss the nervousness and the excitement."

"But?" said Andrew.

"I can't do both at the same time. And you know me, Andrew old pal. There's more power controlling what's in front of that camera than being in front of it."

3

WITH THE TIPS OF HER FINGERS, KIM TRACED THE LINE OF Christopher's shoulder. He was asleep and she lay watching the large fair weather clouds move through the rays of the late afternoon sun. The sloop rocked gently beneath her, lulling her, soothing her body and her mind.

They had left Boston just at dawn. The sloop Chris had borrowed from a friend was waiting for them in Falmouth harbor, and after a trip to the market they were ready to cast off. Kim loved to watch the ease with which Chris handled the sloop, maneuvering it through the buoys and boats until they were out in open water, then leaning back against the cushions, letting the sail out full.

They had come within a half mile of Martha's Vineyard when Chris tacked into the wind, let down the sail and dropped anchor.

"Why are we stopping here?" Kim asked from her position on the side of the deck. "I thought we were going into Vineyard Haven to have lunch."

Chris didn't answer. He took off his T-shirt and walked up to the bow where he spread a large towel. Stretching himself out, he sighed and closed his eyes under the warmth of the midday sun.

Kim knelt beside him. "Do I detect a change in plans, Captain?"

"No change in plans, everything is going as scheduled." Without opening his eyes, he pulled her down so that her head was on his chest. "You, Madame, have been kidnapped by a pirate named Christopher Cerci."

"What if I told you I had a direct line to Peter Pan?" inquired Kim.

"It's no good. I slammed the window on his head the other night. He's in intensive care at New England General."

"You're a cruel man, Mr. Pirate."

"No, I'm not. Selfish, maybe, but not cruel. If we go into the Vineyard, every place we go people are going to be saying 'That's Kim Winston, who's that with her?' You will have no privacy and I will feel like a gigolo. This way we can just float here at sea, in this perfect weather, under this flawless sky, be completely alone . . . with no interruptions but the seagulls." His voice was rocking with the motion of the boat as he undid the clasp at the back of her bikini.

With the sails down and the anchor out, the sloop drifted into the wind in the waters off Martha's Vineyard. Kim put the top of her suit to one side as she ran her hands along Chris's athlete's thighs.

"And what about food?"

"Why do you think I bought caviar and champagne this morning, to say nothing of orange juice and smoked salmon?"

"Because you know I love to eat?"

"No, because I want you alone."

She lifted her head, and looked at Chris's strong, handsome face. "We do have a great time together, Chris. At sex, I mean."

"Sex and eating, and everything else that counts, darling. We're perfect together."

"Well, let's start with the sex," Kim laughed. She climbed on top of Chris and as his hands kneaded her breasts, she quickly reached orgasm. Then, taking Chris between her hands, she said, "Don't leave, the boat hasn't docked yet." She played with his body, fondling and sucking him until he turned her beneath him and took her with a power and desire he had not known he had within him. When the final tremors left their bodies, they were covered with sweat.

"I love you," he said softly.

"I believe you do," she said lightly, "but can you swim?"

With a deft shift of her body and the kick of her leg, she sent

Chris over the side of the bow. After shouting at her, he swam around the sloop for a few minutes, then came back to the side of the bow.

"Come on in. Like they say, the water's fine."

Kim stood up on the bow and prepared to dive into the Atlantic. Suddenly Chris began laughing.

"What's so funny?"

"I think it would be great if there was someone on one of these passing boats with a long-range lens and they took a shot of Boston's number one television personality stark naked on a boat off Vineyard Haven."

Kim suddenly looked around her. What had she been thinking? She must be crazy to be standing up here like an advertisement for the pleasure of carnal knowledge. She quickly sat down and began putting on her suit.

"Don't be silly, Kim. No one can see us."

"It's a possibility, though, and one I don't need. Can you imagine Katherine Marchand's reaction if someone saw me?"

"Come on, Kim. You're only human and so is she." Chris deftly used his body's strength to flip up over the anchor line and settle again on the towel next to Kim.

"Well, I'm not so sure. My boss may invite us out to dinner, but if there was ever a question of the station versus the personal, she'd chop you dead. Even Jonathan alluded to that when we were out there last time."

"Jonathan? They have a terrific relationship."

"Well, maybe. But he does keep referring to her as single-minded and he said he'd been taking some vacations on his own, because Kate's so busy."

"I'll bet that's partly because of his hang gliding mania. Kate can hardly do that, with her bad back." He shrugged. "Luckily, it's not our problem. Let's talk about you and me, those two wonderful people. Like, for example, I know you grew up in Los Alamos, but that's about all I know about the woman I hope to marry."

"Chris, I've told you I'm not ready for that kind of talk. Let me tell you the story of my life instead."

They spread their lunch on a table on the deck. Chris opened the champagne, kissed her and said, "Okay, with the champagne to give me courage, I'm ready for your dark past."

"Well, I grew up, went to school, went to college, married, was widowed, became a television star and then was kidnapped by a pirate."

"That's a start," said Chris. "I don't suppose you could elaborate a bit?"

Kim sighed and leaned her head back, her tone soft and wistful. "My mother was your regular housewife and all-around Mom. Except she missed her calling. I think she should have been an actress. She knew all the lines of all the great plays . . . from Shakespeare to Neil Simon and Tennessee Williams. And she would act them out. Everything was a drama to Mother. Making chocolate milk was a scene out of *Cat on a Hot Tin Roof*, where Mother would play the role of Big Daddy and talk of the evils of drink. Going to sleep was Shakespeare—'Ahh, to sleep, perchance to dream.' She had an act for every moment, every event in the day. She was more alive than any woman I have ever known. And she loved us. God, did she love us."

"Us?" asked Chris, after a moment.

"Yes, us. Daddy, of course, and my twin brothers. But all the love we had was not as strong as the pollutants in Los Alamos. They make death there, in so many ways." She took a deep breath and continued. "Mother began having terrible headaches. In the middle of one of her performances, she'd suddenly stop cold, as if she had just been shot or something. I think . . . I know . . . she knew the truth. Los Alamos has a much higher cancer rate than any other part of America. There's so much radiation. And it happens so quickly. And the answer to your question is no, the finest neurosurgeon in the world couldn't have saved her. The headaches began at the end of October. She died before Christmas with a tumor inside her head the size of a grapefruit."

Kim set down her glass and pulled her knees up under her chin. "I was only fourteen, and Nicky and Charlie were thirteen. We thought our world had ended. But kids bounce back. I see that in Jason now, and I'm grateful. In some ways, he's lucky he only had his daddy for five years."

Chris reached to take her hand, but Kim pulled it away and held her arms clasped around her.

"You see, my father was a scientist for the government, no big high-level job, but enough so he wore one of those radiation tags. I never knew exactly what he did, but I know he was the most curious man who ever lived. He was fascinated with how even the simplest thing worked, from the wheel to spaceships.

"On the day of my mother's funeral, I heard him tell my uncle, my mother's brother, that he had killed her, that she had died because of all the horrible radiation he had brought into the house, into her body. Of course, my uncle said it was not his fault. But Dad changed completely after that.'' She stared ahead stonily, watching the boom rock back and forth.

"I went to the University of Texas in Austin, and the next year, my brothers followed. That year the three of us headed home on the bus for Christmas. It was dark when we arrived so we took a cab to the house. We couldn't figure out why there were no lights on but when we went in, we saw a lot of bottles of scotch around. But no Daddy. We waited through that day and through Christmas Day to New Year's. We went to the police, the neighbors, the place where he worked. No one knew anything. He just disappeared. Finally, we had to think about returning to school, so I went to the bank. There I learned all Daddy's savings had been transferred into an account in my name. It was enough to put us all through school with our scholarships. He had withdrawn five hundred dollars for himself.''

She was silent again, off in deep thought. Finally, after taking another sip of champagne, she spoke. "We have never heard a word. I'm torn between being angry and feeling terribly sorry for my father. At any rate, I think he's been selfish. I want to know if he is alive no matter where he is, whether he's a bum in a back alley or remarried. I know this sounds strange, Chris, but it's hard to grieve when you don't know exactly what you're grieving for. The loss is there, but is he gone forever? And if he is, how did he die? And God, I don't want him to die alone—or to be alone. And I want him to know his grandson.''

Chris put his arms around her but the sobbing stopped quickly.

"So you see,'' she said, "I get the actress from mother, the curiosity from father.''

They slept on the boat that night but Kim was restless, not lulled by the water's motion but kept awake by the sound of the water slapping against the hull, uncomfortable on the narrow couch that doubled as a bed. And for the first time in months, she dreamt of David—saw him and Jason at the zoo in New York. Jason was feeding the seals and David was making that funny noise his own father had taught him, that could get the seals to talk back to him. Every time he did it, Jason would laugh and laugh. In her dream, Kim was a short distance from the seal pool, leaning back against a wrought iron fence. She could feel its bars against her back. She called to them, "That's enough now. You'll get him too excited, Jonathan.''

And as she heard herself and as she watched, as if in a slow dissolve, David's features slipped a little, changed just enough so that be became . . . Jonathan.

Kim sat bolt upright, frightened and bewildered. "Jonathan?" she said softly. "Jonathan? That's ridiculous. It's just the resemblance that made me dream that."

4

KATE LEANED ACROSS HER DESK AND LOOKED AT ANDREW Davis impatiently. "For Christ's sake, what are you trying to tell me? On the one hand, you say the story will project us into the national limelight. On the other hand, you say it may be too risky and we shouldn't touch it. Since when did we stop taking chances?"

"Kate, listen to me. I just don't know if Kim's ready yet. She doesn't have a whole lot of investigative work in her background. And she's not that close to state and federal politicians yet. Maybe we ought to give it to someone else and let Kim continue to grow, along with our ratings."

"After she's done all the legwork, gathered all the facts—at the same time doing one or two stories daily, plus anchoring? And you're going to reward her by taking this away and giving it to someone else? It's unfair. It's unethical. Listen, I don't know if you've been watching your own evening broadcasts, but each day she grows stonger."

"I know that, Kate. But we are talking big, big league here. If she slips up, we could be in very hot water."

"Oh, Andrew. Stop! Listen to yourself. 'Big, big league.' We *are* big league, and if you do your job as news director properly, if I do mine as general manager, if our attorneys advise us properly, and Kim reports accurately, others will be in hot water—and from what you've told me, they deserve to be."

She stood up, her hands on her desk. "It's about time we started shaking up this town. I hate, I repeat, *hate*, playing it safe. Kim has apparently uncovered evidence that is affecting the lives of thousands. As it perpetuates, it affects thousands more. We are not going to ignore it. And if Kim wants to be the one who puts herself out front, then damn it, she's going to."

After Andrew left she sent for Kim.

"Good morning, Ms. Marchand," Kim said. "You know, I've made a big discovery I want to share with you—like they say in California."

"About the story you're working on?"

"No, ma'am. About you. I'm here to tell you that if you want it, you have a big career in television ahead of you. I'll introduce you to my agent, if you like."

"Thanks," Kate said dryly. "I hear he cuts a very good deal. Why the sudden offer?"

"Well, while I was in New York last week, I got Gary Kincaid to show me some tapes of the famous reporter, Katherine Marchand."

"Oh? I didn't know the staff was assigned to investigate *me*."

"Not investigate, *learn* from. Kate, I was impressed with your impromptu abortion broadcast here a couple of weeks ago, but I see now that was nothing compared to the impact you had in the field."

"What tapes did you see?" Kate asked.

"The burned tenement, for one. I watched you walking through the rubble, reporting on what had happened and then making it clear that a decent life for these families was over—because of the ineptitude of city officials and the greed of the landlord of that building. What was that you said?"

Kate held an imaginary microphone to her mouth and intoned, "The children who lived here, who died here, will never know again the joy of Christmas, will never go to school, will never dance or sing, will never fall in love. They fell asleep last night for the last time in a building packed with too many welfare clients . . . too many children, is what I mean. This is Kate Marchand, in the South Bronx." Kate paused, then said, "Is that what you mean?"

"Something pretty close to it. I see why the critics call you the best. You had me crying with that story and horrified with your Vietnam coverage. You sure didn't pussyfoot. I mean a couple of your stories ended with a direct accusation that the President of the United States was personally responsible for the dead bodies you were panning over. Didn't you get a lot of flak?" Kim stopped abruptly. "Oh, Kate, I'm sorry. I know you were wounded out there . . . your back . . ."

Kate's back seemed to stiffen at the reference. "That's not something I talk about, but I'm glad you think my on-camera work passed muster. Now let's get to *your* job."

"Kate, before we do, the thing that I kept wondering about is why you stopped. I mean you could have topped Barbara Walters or Diane Sawyer—or anybody."

"Well, maybe, but especially in those days, not necessarily. And as the years passed, I would have had to have had face surgery. The business was not quite as liberated as it is now—and, if you'll forgive a pun, even now the changes are only skin deep. The reality of this business is that a woman cannot grow old on camera. Yes, Walter Cronkite got away with it. But no women are about to wear their wrinkles proudly. The common wisdom has it that the public wants its female anchors to be young and attractive. Especially women viewers. They do not want to be reminded that they themselves are growing older every day. And women make up over sixty percent of the viewing public. Sure, I still make a pleasant appearance now. But what about five years from now? Where would my career be? Certainly without the opportunities I have now to be of real influence."

Power, Kim thought. She means she wants the power. And with that thought, she saw Kate turn on the power, cut off the friendly, casual conversation they'd been having.

"Andrew tells me that somehow you have found the time to uncover a scandal in this state's juvenile justice system," Kate said.

"And Andrew doesn't think I can handle it and is going to give it to someone else. I guess I'm here for you to personally tell me it may be too hot a potato."

"Tell me something!" Kate slammed her hand down on the top of her desk. "What type of complacency is going through this place. I am so sick of people thinking that just because our ratings are high, we won't take any chances." She stood up and walked around the front of her desk and stood within a few feet of Kim. "Listen to me, Kimberly Winston. You don't get any-place in this life if you don't take a chance, every now and then.

We all must take risks, personally and professionally. Otherwise, we stagnate.

"You saw the tapes of Vietnam? Did you see me sitting in a Saigon briefing room, giving the American public the pablum from the day's general report? Not once. I was always out in the field. Taking chances. But that's the only way to report the truth. . . . Now tell me about your story."

Kim leaned forward. "Well, what triggered this whole thing was that story I did on teenage pregnancy."

"I remember it. It was very good, moving."

"Thank you. While the crew was setting up, I spoke to a number of the girls and I discovered that many of them had come through the juvenile justice system. Well, 'juvenile justice system' is really a contradiction in terms. Do you remember back in the early seventies when Massachusetts closed down all its reformatories and holding houses for juvenile offenders?"

"Yes, at the time it was considered a very enlightened move. The kids then went into halfway houses and foster homes."

"That's what everyone *thinks*, Kate, but it didn't work out that way. Sure, all this money came pouring into the state and a lot of consultants were hired. Programs were allegedly being researched and set up. Psychiatrists and psychologists came in with all their recommendations and walked away with a lot of money."

"What happened to the kids? You're saying that these institutions were just shut down and the kids had no rehabilitative services available to them?"

"That's it exactly. In the whole state, there are only a few holding facilities for both boys and girls. And there are a few attempts at halfway houses. But the girls definitely get the short end of the stick. Their detention centers, before they go to court or back on the streets, are literally rat-infested dungeons, and in all of Massachusetts, there is only one halfway house for girls, and that can handle only eight girls."

"Where are the rest of them?"

"That's the best part. They're in the state hospitals, drugged into immobility, where they just sit and rock their days away. They're on the same wards with sixty-year-old schizophrenics, or the elderly who have just been abandoned.

"Except the young kids—and this is the worst part. They're at this place called the Wilkins Unit of the State Hospital System. It's funded through a lot of federal programs. I've gotten inside this unit. Five-year-olds who were just a little hyperactive are in with fifteen-year-olds who have attempted murder. There's no schooling. No counseling. Nothing. The kids are rotting. They're also being beaten. As soon as you walk into the place, you hear the kids screaming. If they're not physically beaten up on, they're locked in these holding rooms where they throw their heads and bodies against the walls.''

Kate put her head in her hands. "How did you get into these places?"

"There's an underground of people who work in different capacities—from cooks to guards—who know how wrong it all is. They trust me. I've also gotten my hands on some court records that point out, to the letter, the abuse and failure of the system. Kids bounced from one foster home to another, to the streets, to the state hospitals, to halfway houses that are a rip-off. Then back to the courts, back to the streets, to Wilkins . . . on and on. All documented.''

"You do know that juvenile files are confidential?" inquired Kate.

"Yes, I'll change the names.''

"Can you get kids to go on camera?''

"Yes, but some may have to be in silhouette.''

"What about public officials?''

"They'll try to defend themselves, but I have a judge who will tear them apart," Kim said, sounding more and more confident.

"Can you get into these places with a camera?''

"Yes, but . . .''

"But what? You've got to be able to prove your charges. It can't just be hearsay.''

"It won't be. It's just that the official policy of the state hospitals and Wilkins Unit is 'no cameras allowed.' So we'd have to go in, sneak in, under a different guise, and at some very odd hours.''

"Kim, these places are supported by state and federal monies, taxpayers' money. The public has the right to know how its money is being spent.'' Kate leaned back in her chair. It would be a superb investigative piece and it was clear Kim was already passionately involved. "What you've laid out is the mismanagement of millions of federal and state dollars, which has led to the physical and mental abuse of thousands of children. And in the end, the kids rot in the state hospitals or commit more and more serious crimes until they land in prison.''

"That's right. It's got to be done. We're losing more and more kids every day."

"Then do it," Kate said. "I'll tell Andrew to clear the decks for you. You will be assigned to this story only. I'll have public relations cut down on your personal appearances. The crew of your choice will be at your disposal. Keep Andrew notified, and make sure someone knows at all times where you are, or where you're trying to be, in the event anyone tries to get rough at these places. Then see me when you're ready and we'll figure out whether we're talking documentary, news series, special with follow-up . . . whatever it calls for."

Kim smiled. "Thank you. You won't regret this."

"I know I won't just as long as you keep the screams of those kids in your head, and do not hesitate for a second to be thorough . . . and even ruthless."

Kim nodded, wondering if ruthlessness was what it took in this business. Had Kate been ruthless in Vietnam? Or had she cared, very very much? Maybe, she thought, there's such a thing as ruthless caring.

5

TWO WEEKS LATER, AS KATE WAS RUSHING INTO HER OFFICE
after a meeting in Chicago, Diana told her that Richard Blistick,
the head of public relations for WLYM, had been into her office
twice that day demanding a meeting with her.

"What's this 'demanding' nonsense?"

"I don't know, Kate. I think he believes I'm hiding you someplace, that you're avoiding him."

"That's ridiculous. What's wrong with him? Now tell me
something important that happened while I was gone."

Diana read off a list of events, some that required immediate
attention, some that could wait. "And the best news is that John
Ponte accepted your offer as head of programming," said Diana
gleefully. "So we're back up to full staff, except for a few engineering positions."

"Wonderful. But if Herb Corkin wasn't angry at me before,
he's gunning for me now. In the last month, I've hired away
from Channel Eight his best crime reporter and now one of his
top producers. For years in this town, there's been kind of an
unspoken rule that the commercial stations don't steal from each
other. Ludicrous." She looked briefly through her mail folder,
then said, "Okay, get Blistick."

"Finally, I've found you," Richard Blistick said when he
came into the office.

"Richard, I've been in Chicago. Now what, pray tell, is going on that has you in such a royal stew?"

"Well, for openers, does the fact that the state and federal governments would like to have us shut down, and that they're both writing vicious letters to the FCC, bother you at all?"

"No," Kate said, "but it sounds very interesting."

"In the last three days, I have heard from the commissioner of mental health, the commissioner of corrections, the executive director for juvenile rehabilitation, and members of the governor's cabinet."

"Sounds like an impressive list of people. Are you in some type of trouble with the law?" Kate smiled.

"This is serious, Kate," Richard said loudly.

"It's going to be more serious if you keep shouting."

"I'm sorry. It's a little nerve-wracking when I have to hear from outside that we have a reporter, more specifically an anchorwoman, who is, with a camera crew, sneaking into state hospitals and detention centers in the middle of the night after she's been told she cannot enter. She has also harassed the director of juvenile rehabilitation while he's playing tennis. And although she has the kids' and parents' written permission for interviews, the authorities have not given it to her and she's gone ahead and done the interviews anyway. She was also found by a caretaker shooting inside one of the old reformatories. They say in some instances she is even disguising the camera."

Kate knew she was starting to smile, but she could not help it. "So what do all your big officials want?"

"They say they want Kim out of their institutions and off their backs, that she's a disruptive influence, and they refuse to cooperate with her. This is not exactly good public relations, Kate, and that's my job, you know, to guard our image."

"Our primary job is to get the story and air it. Obviously, it's because they have not cooperated with her that she has to resort to these tactics. They most definitely have something to hide."

Richard, after a moment's silence, threw up his hands. "Well, you're the journalist. You're also the boss and if you think Kim's methods are all right, I'm not about to question them."

Kate patted his shoulder, "And as soon as this documentary airs, the accolades will come pouring in."

When Richard left, Kate said to Diana, "See if Andrew has a few minutes to come up and fill me in."

Kate was surprised when both Andrew and Kim came into her office a few minutes later. Andrew was saying, "I thought

you might like to see what Kim's been up to. That *is* what you
wanted me for, isn't it?''

Kate nodded and Kim, with only a quick greeting to her employer, propped a blue and white card, about four feet by six
feet, on Kate's couch. She asked, ''Remember those court files
I told you about, that somehow fell into my hands? Well, I've
broken down one of them and charted a kid's life. This is for a
girl who is presently sixteen years old. I've changed her name
to Sally.''

Kim pointed to the card. ''Here we have Sally at the age of
two. Her mother claims she cannot take care of the child so she
goes to a foster home. Two years later she's removed from that
foster home because the social worker maintains she is being
sexually abused by the father and a brother. Goes to another
foster home. At age five, she runs and ends up in a rat-infested
detention center in the South End for a year and a half. Then to
another foster home.''

Kate interrupted. ''It sounds too unlikely. Too many things
happening to be believable.''

''That's exactly what my reaction was,'' Andrew said, ''and
then, when I went through the back-up material, I saw that this
damn chart is all too accurate.''

''Okay?'' Kim asked. ''Shall I continue?''

''Please,'' Kate said.

''At age eight Sally is picked up for purse snatching. Goes to
court but state and local authorities have no place for her so the
round begins again and by the time she's ten, she's into heroin.
She's hooking at age eleven, and picked up for prostitution. At
that point, her mother is tracked down and the girl goes home
with her. Mother's boyfriend tries to take on Sally. Sally has her
throat slashed. Spends five months in Boston City Hospital, is
released with a strong drug habit and not able to talk above a
whisper.''

Kim looked at Andrew and Kate. ''Had enough?'' she asked.
And when Kate shook her head, Kim said, ''Well, I'll try to
summarize the rest.''

''Sally was picked up again for prostitution and when she was
barely thirteen, she was placed in a state hospital on a floor with
schizophrenics and other seriously ill people. Back on the street
she was raped, beaten up and so forth until a space was found
for her in a halfway house. She actually seemed to get better,
but when funds for the halfway house dried up, the cycle began
again until eventually she was picked up for armed robbery,

bumped up to adult court, and sent to Framingham State Prison. There she was put in solitary confinement because they have no other place for her. Don't want her mingling with the hard core in the prison. So, she's locked in a cell that's right out of the Dark Ages. Food slipped under the door. No visitors. Not even a light in her cell.''

Kate had now moved from her desk and had pulled another chair next to Andrew's to stare at the chart of this girl's life.

"So she's in Framingham, and God knows who you'd have to con to get cameras in there for an interview." Her voice was cold. "The story's not over. I brought up the excerpts of two tapes for you to see. One is of Sally. We managed to grab her just before she went into court for sentencing. The other is with Judge Wintrast, the head of Juvenile Court." She picked the cassettes up from the floor and looked at Kate. "May I?"

"Of course," Kate said, as Kim went to the player. "Begin, Counselor."

"Okay, the first is Judge Wintrast, and this is at the end of a long interview. He was very cooperative, but now he's a little tired and I throw at him Sally's case history." The screen shows a picture of a charismatic, but obviously frustrated and over-worked judge.

"You don't have to go any further, Ms. Winston," said the judge, sitting forward in his shirt sleeves, his judicial robe hanging in back of him. "I know exactly who you are talking about. But if you've done your homework, you know there are hundreds, no, by now, there are thousands of these Sallys. She has been in my courtroom numerous times. And each time, I end up calling in representatives of the Welfare Department, head of foster homes, juvenile rehabilitation, the Department of Mental Health, Corrections . . . you name it. And I say to each one of them, 'What can you do to help this child? We're losing her, just like we're losing all the others.' They suggest another foster home, another detention center. But she runs. And you can't blame her. I say, 'What about all the federal money that came in last year to help these kids? I'm told it's in some programs, but not the right one for Sally, or Cindy, or Mary, or Ida . . . or any of them. Your Sally is a product of the ineptitude of the juvenile justice system in this state. I know she's in holding now. And I'll see her later today or to-morrow and once again this charade will be played. But this time, I'll have no choice but to bump her up to adult court. Because there's no other option, Ms. Winston. It's a waste and it should never happen. There is no excuse."

"Damn it!" shouted Kate, as the tape ended. "This has been going on for years. Where the hell have we been? Every day we read in the newspapers about more and more juvenile crime. Why didn't we ever go to juvenile court and find out what the hell was going on?" She was standing by the television set glaring at Andrew. "Oh, Christ, it's as much my fault as anybody's."

"Kate," Kim interrupted. "I would like to show you two more tapes, if you have the time. One, of course, is Sally herself. But remember the Wilkins Unit I told you about?"

Kate thought a moment, and then looked back at Kim. "Yes, some type of psychiatric unit for kids." Something clicked in Kate's brain. "You didn't by any chance get in there in disguise, did you?"

"There was no other way, Kate."

"I'm not criticizing, Kim, but don't tell me anything more about how or your sources . . . for your protection as well as mine."

"I understand, but I really think it was important to the story." Kim paused and her voice shook slightly, making Kate turn and look at her. Kim picked up the remote control, and as she gripped it found her own control and an unemotional voice. "When Sally was sentenced to Framingham, they couldn't take her for two nights. Solitary was full. So they locked her up in the Wilkins Unit. This tape was not shot those particular nights, but a few days before. I have no reason to believe the situation changed."

The tape began and the first shot was the exterior of an old red eighteenth-century building that looked more like a fortress than anything else. Then the camera was inside, and Kate felt she was back in the jungles of Vietnam. She saw blurred images first, but then the unmistakable image of two children, probably six or seven years old, being dragged along the floor, being kicked in the stomach and genitals. Wailing. Then they were dragged into a room, and a steel door shut behind them. A small grate in the door allowed the camera a vantage point. Another counselor had been waiting. She was holding an open pan that was steaming. The male counselor took off his belt and began beating the kids from the chest down to the ankles, at one point stripping off their pants. As they lay exhausted on the floor, the other counselor poured the searing water over their backs.

"Stop, stop, please Mr. Oaks, please," the child was wailing and sobbing.

"You promise not to talk back to anyone again? To be a good

little boy? You're lucky you're here. Your parents don't want you. No one does. If it wasn't for us, you'd rot in an alley, and rats bigger than the ones here would eat you.''

"I won't talk back anymore, I promise." The counselor hit them twice more with the belt buckle, kicked them, and started for the door. The camera immediately darted away.

The next shot was of the two counselors sipping coffee outside the locked door, as the two boys wailed and threw their bodies around, butting their heads against the door, screaming about the rats in the cell.

Kate did not speak, and did not look away from the screen. She signaled with her hand for Kim to continue.

"This is Sally," said Kim, maintaining her control. It was not exactly what Kate expected. An exceptionally attractive blonde appeared on the screen. Her face was gentle, her voice little above a whisper. The turtleneck she wore did not cover the scar that seemed to run from ear to ear.

"I tried to go straight. Many times. I really did." Her voice had the slight twang of the street, but she was amazingly articulate. Kate thought, what would have happened to her if things had been different? If that first foster home had been decent?

"And I kept asking for help. Even the judge kept asking for me. Then I gave up. It seemed easier to live on the streets. Get yourself a pimp who didn't beat up on you too much and find johns who really like young girls.

"But then you'd always get strung out. I tried to dry out a few times, but the places only keep you like four days, and then there's no place to go but back to the streets.

"Once I was at a halfway house where I got really clean. I was even going to school with my counselor. But then one day we were told it was closing down. And we all just looked at each other. We knew what it meant. Back to the streets. And this time, I knew, once I went back, I'd never get out again."

"And so it's true. I know I'm gonna end up in Framingham. And then what chance do I have? They're tough out there. They chew up kids like me and spit them out.

"I'm not saying it's not my fault. A lot of it is. But I didn't ask for this. And I never set out to hurt nobody. And I asked them to help me . . . over and over again."

The tape ended and Kate rose and walked towards the window as the shadows of early fall lowered over the harbor. Kim took the cassettes from the machine and sat facing Kate's desk, waiting for her to speak. Andrew was motionless.

Kate finally turned and sat down at her desk. Kim had not expected to see what she saw. Tears filled Kate's eyes. "Sally's dead, isn't she, Kim?"

Kim was taken aback briefly. "Yes, her third day at Framingham. They let her out of solitary to walk the corridor. When the guard wasn't looking, she grabbed a shirt off the back of the guard's chair. That night she made a noose and hung herself from a window bar." Kim gulped back her tears. "They said she was barely off the ground, so she really had to work at it. She literally had to throw herself across the room to break her own neck."

Kate rose and walked to the chart, a large thick marker in her hand. She picked up the sturdy cardboard and balanced it on her knee.

"Kim, I don't need to tell you, you have done an outstanding job."

"You've only seen part of it, Kate," Andrew said.

"I'm sure," said Kate. "Kim, I'm not in the habit of telling my reporters how to handle their work, and I'd fault most general managers for attempting or even thinking of doing such a thing. But as you know, my background is first in journalism . . ."

"I'd be a fool to shut out free advice from you," Kim said.

"First, have this art card redone. And tell me if I'm wrong, but here, at the first foster home, the government failed."

Kim nodded, and Kate then made a large circle around that incident in Sally's life. "Then here, the second foster home, then in juvenile court." And through the chart Kate went, drawing a large red circle everywhere a state or federal agency had failed. "Now shoot this chart twice. Once going through it for the history, intertwining your tape, then either by computer graphics or a plastic layover, have the art department do a chart that depicts the government failures all along the route."

"It will light up almost every turn of Sally's life," Andrew said.

"That's right," Kate agreed. "Have you started editing, Kim?"

"No, not yet. I've got a few more environmentals and interviews left."

"Is this just basic government ineptitude, or do you have proof that money is being mishandled?"

"I have proof that it's going to consultants who are friends of people in power and who have no qualifications for handling the large amounts of money they're getting. The money never reaches programs for the kids. The programs are on paper. They never happen.''

"No wonder they're running scared,'' said Kate, rising and walking behind her desk. She made some notes on the pad in front of her, and then looked up at Kim. "How about a two-hour documentary, followed up by nightly, extended reports on the six o'clock news for the next week? We'll air it Sunday night, after *Sixty Minutes*.''

Kim let out a little gasp. "That's network prime time. Prime, prime time. The most heavy television watching evening of the week.'' Kim knew how networks hated to have their prime time hours—and advertisers—taken from them. "Isn't the network going to get angry?''

"Yes, but if they have any integrity at all, their anger will come from the fact they haven't done anything this good, this important, in far too many years. I'm also going to make it mandatory that it air simultaneously in all my syndicated stations. You'll be in over thirty cities, Kim, so add a national bent to your copy. I believe that when we shut down our reformatories, Massachusetts was considered the vanguard of juvenile justice. That should be enough of a draw for other cities.''

Kate made more notes. "Any idea of how you'll open it?''

"I didn't know until a moment ago the kind of vehicle I had.''

"A suggestion?'' inquired Kate.

"Sure, please.''

"Open with a standup in front of the Wilkins Unit. Blast the whole juvenile justice system to hell. Tell them that in the next few hours you're going to prove there is no justice, and then tell them maybe the story begins here. Have the camera zoom into one of the windows over your shoulder, dissolve to the last few seconds of the beatings, the kids pleading, the sound of crying and banging heads. Then slow fade and bring up your title, your name, fade to black and into first commercial.'' Her voice was smooth, efficient.

"Don't you think that's a turnoff? Hitting the viewer over the head so early on?'' Andrew asked.

"That's exactly what you should do if we are the ones to shut down the Wilkins Unit. I want to see counselors fired. I want to see a federal and state investigation, but more important, I want to see if we can save a few of those Sallys out there. Andrew, I want you to give Kim every bit of help she needs. Don't cut any corners. Get her all the editing time she wants, the editor she wants. And then do the final run on computer editing, so she can get the most out of the effects.''

Kate paused, and looked up at Kim. "Do you have any problems? Any questions?"

"Just one," Kim said. "I like the idea of opening in front of the Wilkins Unit, but if they see me standing out in front there, well . . . there may just be a sharpshooter aiming at me."

"Just pick the right time. Isn't that what they do in the movies? When the sentries change?" She leaned back in her chair, picking up her calendar. "How about three weeks from Sunday?"

"Three weeks?" Kim shouted and jumped from her chair. "Do you have any idea how many tapes I have? The amount of editing? Copy still has to be written. You're talking two hours. It's impossible."

"Your only other job will be to anchor the news. No other stories."

"Thanks a lot."

"And you can have more than one editor if you need it."

"May I ask what's the big rush? I know it's important but why not four or five weeks, at least? I don't want to be sloppy."

"Obviously, the sooner we get it on the air, the sooner we can begin to turn the system around. Then it's already leaking—that you're snooping around. We want to avoid time for cover-ups.

"Second reason: I want it to air, let Washington know about it. I've already had pressure to stop you. It will also get to advertisers. I'm not concerned about that. I know we can go to national advertisers, but I don't want months of pressure on the sales staff. Let them sell it blind—a WLYM special. If we all keep our mouths shut before it airs, we won't get slapped with a prior restraint from any federal or state court."

Kate grinned and said, "And let's not forget. Three weeks from now is the beginning of our most important rating period. It's a sweeps week throughout the country. I want LYM and its syndicates to take the week. Your daily stories following the documentary will be satellited to all the stations. And I know by Monday morning, it will be network news."

Kim frowned. She knew, of course, that the ratings kept them in business, made it possible for this kind of story to air at all. But she wondered about her boss's motivation, about how much she had changed from that young reporter standing in the burned-out South Bronx. Power, that was what she seemed most interested in. Sure, she cared about the kids. But as much as the ratings? Kim wasn't sure. What's that Jonathan had said? That his wife was single-minded. But single-minded in what? That was the question.

Andrew had been discussing costs and schedules until Kim realized Kate was talking to her again. "Kim?" she was saying. "One last thing I want you and Andrew to do. Diana will set up a meeting with the station's attorney for some time soon. Run through everything with him, Kim, but don't back down. And Andrew, you make sure that Hunnewell doesn't get overcautious. Kim, come to me if you think your story's being compromised. Andrew, I'm willing to take some risks on this one." She looked at the blue and white art card. "We need to take some risks."

For the next two weeks, Kim worked relentlessly. She was in the office as soon as Jason was off to school. And after the final open and closing standups had been shot, she was constantly holed up in an editing room. She worked with her editor who put the intense video sequences together while Kim scribbled her voice-over copy at the same time. They edited, reedited, wrote and rewrote. Kim had never been so driven, so challenged by any project. And she discovered there were two reasons for that. First, the importance of the material, and second, the faith Katherine Marchand had put in her.

While Kim was waging her battles in the editing room, Kate was waging battles upstairs. As anticipated, the network objected strenuously when they discovered Kate planned to preempt their Sunday night schedule. At one point, they even threatened her affiliation. At that point, she left her office abruptly and told Diana to call a car for her. With her Burberry over her shoulder and her briefcase in hand, she stopped first in the newsroom and in Andrew Davis's office.

"Where is Kim?" she asked.

"She's back in 4B. Editing. What's wrong? You look like you're about to commit a homicide."

She strode from his office and down the corridor of the editing suites. Andrew followed; 4B was locked. She knocked on the door. "Just a minute," came a voice. "We've got a voice-over that has to be finished."

Kate understood the need to wait, and looked at Andrew. "Did I ever tell you the network is run by a bunch of spineless, worthless assholes?"

"Not in so many words. I take it the network is saying no to the preempting."

"Not only are they saying no, but they're saying no because they have the goddamned Miss Teen-Age America pageant. Can you believe it? They'd rather run a beauty pageant, damn it, than the solid documentary we've got."

The door to the editing suite opened and Kim stepped out. "Oh, hi. I'm sorry, I didn't know it was you."

"That's all right. I don't have time to talk. Can you give me the tapes of, say, the judge, and the Wilkins Unit? Or anything else that is very dramatic?"

Kim did not ask why, but immediately went through a stack of over thirty tapes and pulling out two, handed them to Kate.

"Thank you. How's it going?"

"Fine. Excellent. It's going to be incredible."

"Good." Kate said, "Don't worry, you'll have these back tonight."

"Where's she going? What's that all about?" asked Kim, as Kate started down the corridor.

"She's going to New York. The network is telling her not to air it." Andrew spoke nonchalantly.

"What will happen? Should I stop?"

"Of course not, Kim. She'll win. Don't worry."

Kim called to the departing figure. "Be careful with the tapes and the metal detector." Kate stopped, and slowly turned, a bemused smile on her lips. Kim covered her eyes with her hand and leaned against the wall. Why was she telling a woman who had reported from distant corners of the world to be careful of tape erasure?

"See if you can get some rest, Kim," said Kate, shaking her head and turning off the corridor.

By the time Kate arrived at the network headquarters, her anger was under control. She was led immediately into the office of Marty Rathjens, the president.

"Diana called to tell me you were en route, so I cleared the deck a bit." Marty, with his jet black hair and perfect physique, was as handsome as ever. Kate smiled and remembered a conversation years ago when Marty had propositioned her. As she had all the others, Kate had turned him down. If he was going to bend the rules now, it was going to be because they should be bent, not because of a few rolls in the hay.

"Thanks, Marty. I came because I wasn't making much progress with you over the phone."

"Listen, Kate, I don't like the pageant any more than you do, but it's a big production number. We can't afford to have the first hour of it preempted on some of our major affiliates . . . and if you're feeding your special by satellite at eight, it's going to be." He spoke kindly, but firmly.

"I know your problems, Marty, and you have an obligation to your sponsors and your programming department, but I have an obligation to my viewers in Boston. There is a major scandal in Massachusetts. I told you that. It has to be aired because kids are getting hurt. They're dying, and killing others, because of the corruptness of our juvenile justice system."

"So you told me on the phone, Kate. And you also told me that Kim Winston has a presentation that is magnetic."

"She is magnetic, and that's why I'm here. I have a couple of cassettes I want you to look at." She walked over to his cassette player, put the first one in without looking at the label, and was surprised when she saw a countdown come onto the screen. Kim had given her an edited portion.

It began with a shot of Kim at dusk walking along the grounds in front of the Wilkins Unit. It was the open to the show. Kim's voice was strong but softly modulated. She talked about the "accident of birth": Some were born to the elite, some on the wrong side of the tracks, and many ended up in a state or federal institution because they had no place else to go. Then as the camera moved in on her more tightly, Kate saw the excitement in Kim's eyes. Her voice turned harder. She talked about the hoax, the cruel hoax, that was the juvenile justice system in Massachusetts.

"There's no place for children and teenagers to go, other than the streets, and a few places like this one in back of me. It is called the Wilkins Unit, and this is where children who are unruly or hard to manage find themselves. It's a part of the state hospital system. The alternative for these kids is the streets. The streets are tough, but they may be kinder than this place. Even now, hundreds of yards away, I can hear the children crying . . . children like these two boys, six and seven, who spoke back to a counselor . . ."

Slowly, the camera moved into a window in the Unit and the cries grew louder. A quick dissolve and the viewer was face to face with the beatings. The shot froze on the two boys writhing on the floor, and the screams continued while a title came up:

"*Juvenile Justice: A Contradiction in Terms* with Kim Winston." Then the freeze stopped and the video began moving again, the children continued screaming and the following words rolled across the screen: "Massachusetts is regarded as a pioneer in juvenile justice in the United States."

Kate flipped off the tape, noticing her hand was shaking. She knew there was no need to show Marty any more. Sweat had broken out on his forehead.

"You're right. The hell with the pageant. Preempt." He was still staring at the screen. "You know I'm going to have to write a formal complaint against you and your syndicates."

"I expect that."

"And I want first dibs on all footage for the Monday network newscasts."

"Goes without saying." Kate picked up her coat and Marty stepped around his desk and helped her into it. "You know Kate, you may have finally hit upon some competition. Actually she reminds me a lot of you."

"I don't know about that. But she is good, isn't she?"

"You'd better hold onto her with an iron grasp, Kate. We're always on the lookout for talent of that quality."

"Don't worry. I have every intention of doing just that. You network boys blew your chance, Marty. Stick with the pageant."

Kate was not surprised when, a few days later, Diana informed her that Steve Merriam and a few of his key salespeople were in the outer office, asking to see her.

"We have two problems, Kate," began Merriam. "First, this special you are running. All we've been told about it is that it is a two-hour public service special, featuring Kim Winston, and that, according to Andrew, it's 'one of the most important projects WLYM has undertaken.' That's all very nice, but it's little to go on as far as luring advertisers."

"I understand the problem, Steve, and I anticipated it. I'm afraid I cannot give you more information, but I can give you permission to go to national advertisers above the network's head." She waited for the impact of what she had said to sink in.

"You mean the whole two hours is going out to all the syndicates too?" asked Merriam, suddenly feeling a little easier.

"That's right, so all your commissions go up. How much of it is sold now?" she asked.

"We're about sixty percent, but that's the second part of our problem. It seems that although we don't know that much about the special, someone out there does, and they're putting the squeeze on us.''

The bastards, thought Kate. She thought this might happen. It made the reason for the documentary even stronger, but it put the station in a financial bind. Although the documentary was not overly expensive, the station would lose the network revenue as well as its own regular spots.

Merriam gave the names of major banks that had sponsored their documentaries before, car dealerships, store chains they could always count on.

"Someone's putting pressure on them," Merriam said. "In fact, my contact for one of the major New England commuter airlines told me he may withhold all advertising for two weeks or more if this special runs. What the hell is it about, Kate?''

"You know the signs, Steven. Some important people, both in business and politics, are going to be very embarrassed by Kim's report. They think they can keep us from airing it by putting pressure on our advertisers.''

"Obviously, someone has a lot to be afraid of," an older sales rep said.

Kate nodded. "Look, I want to help you whatever way I can but I can't give you any more information. You see how risky it already is. Go to your other accounts. Hit them all. You know your staff can do it. Just remember, we're number one in the ratings. They need our advertising minutes. And when this documentary and this series push us far into the lead, you can remind them they balked.''

The Saturday before the special was to be aired, Kate came into her office to tackle a pile of paperwork. She knew if all went well, she was not going to have much time for routine. She had already spoken to her congressional contacts and the right people were ready to act as soon as the information was made public.

The promotional spots had begun airing and the newspaper and radio advertisements had also appeared. By midafternoon on Saturday all of Boston, New England and the Marchand Syndicates knew that a major scandal would be laid out before them on Sunday night.

At 4:30, Kate walked down to the CMX computer editing suite and saw Kim surrounded by rows of monitors, spinning one-inch tapes, a twenty-four-track for sound. Two of the finest computer engineers also were present. Kim was giving last-minute instructions on where a dissolve should begin and a sound track should be brought up, as Kate walked to the back of the darkened room and leaned against the heavily carpeted wall. This room alone, with the finest equipment available, was worth almost $10 million, and now it was being used to its most efficient potential. She knew that when the equipment, the engineers, and the producer/director all worked together in fine motion, the room was like a sleek moving jet.

When Kate got back to her office her private phone was ringing. It was Timothy Hunnewell who said, "I've been trying to reach you and Jonathan told me where you were. Someone has grabbed a judge off a golf course and you've got a prior restraint heading for you."

"What the hell is going on?" she demanded. "How did this happen?"

"Well, some of your government friends have arranged for Judge Frewald to hear a case for prior restraint tomorrow morning at ten o'clock."

"On what charge?"

"That you are about to air maliciously accusatory and libelous information that will cause physical and mental anguish to state employees, as well as juveniles under their charge."

"Bullshit! They're the ones who have already caused the physical and mental anguish—and deaths—damn it." Kate was shouting. "I'm not going to allow this thing to be stopped."

"If they get a prior restraint, you can't fight it, Kate. You'll lose your license."

"What can we do?"

"We fight them in court as best we can. We try to get the judge to look at the tape. Bring Kim in to testify."

"What are our chances?"

"I don't think very good. Kim would be attacked on the methods she used to get her material and they'd try to force her to reveal her sources."

Kate groaned. "And she'd probably end up in jail for a few days if she wouldn't—as she wouldn't. It's happened before to other reporters."

"I think you'd be okay on that once the program aired. The material is so powerful, whatever she did to get it—well, no one would want to challenge that. But at this point, I think you may have to concede."

"That's it," said Kate. "You just said it. Once the program

airs. They can't slap a prior restraint on a show that's already aired, correct?''

"Correct," said Hunnewell, "but this one's not scheduled till tomorrow night at eight o'clock and you say they're still working on it."

"Timothy, remember I'm not a one-station woman. If I can get a completed version up to the satellite and down to one of my other cities before ten o'clock tomorrow morning, then the prior restraint is moot, right?''

"Yes, you're technically right, Kate." His voice held a smile. "When am I going to learn to stop underestimating Katherine Marchand?''

Kate hung up and headed back to the CMX suite. This time she interrupted. The look on her face told everyone in the room to pay attention.

"Kim, how close are you?"

Kim looked at Bernie, the chief CMX operator. "We had thought the final mix would be done by midnight. Then tomorrow, we'll spruce up the effects."

"Don't worry, Mrs. Marchand," Bernie said, "this baby will be ready and perfect by eight o'clock tomorrow night."

"I'm sure it will. That's what I expect." She turned to Kim. "What do you lose if you don't 'spruce up the effects'?"

"Well, it would certainly lose something. The rough cut is rough. It would be more dramatic going through the CMX . . . and I mean, we've come this far, I really don't want to compromise." Kim was tired, and she was now a little angry at Kate. What was this woman trying to do? Kim had spilled blood over this, at Kate's insistence. Why was she pulling back now?

"Kim, listen to me. I don't want you to compromise, but we may have to lose something here," she knelt down on the carpeted floor by Kim, so the engineers could see beyond her to the monitors and keep working. "The feds are going for a prior restraint. There's a hearing at ten o'clock tomorrow morning. You'd end up testifying all day and Hunnewell says there's a good chance we may lose."

"Oh, damn," said Kim, throwing some papers up in the air. "All this for nothing!"

"Nobody said that," Kate shouted. The tapes stopped whirring and all eyes were on her. "Listen, all of you. I believe in this show as much as you do, and there's a way."

She explained her plan and Bernie said, "But Mrs. Marchand, our satellite is booked weeks in advance. They all are."

"Well, I know, but I'm going to find a two-hour hole somewhere on a station in one of our smaller cities, even if I have to burn something out. Just make sure the mix is done. Hold the final effects until tomorrow but make sure I have a copy ready to hit the satellite by midnight."

As Kate was leaving the room she heard Bernie say, "You heard the lady. She's going to do her part. Let's do ours."

For the next five hours, Kate wheeled and dealed with her own satellite, with network and cable satellites, religious network satellites, even an intermittent health channel satellite. It turned out that using her own satellite was out of the question. Her people had booked it too heavily with too much money involved. The same was true with the networks and cable. She kept upping the price, her frustration growing, until finally she found a man who agreed with her on how valuable the program was. When he freed up his satellite for two hours, Kate called her syndicate station, and told them they had a major programming change.

She walked into the CMX suite at 10:45 and realized how exhausted she must look when the room fell silent and Kim put her face in her hands.

"Now, now, come on. Wrong response," she said quietly.

"You got the time? Or did you kill the judge?" Bernie asked.

"Can you get it up to a satellite at midnight?"

"She'll be ready. What are the coordinates? Is it ours?" Bernie took the slip of paper from Kate's outstretched hand.

"No, it's one of the twenty-four-hour religion satellites. They're ready to receive at midnight straight up, and they'll send it right back down."

"Where are they sending it down to, may I ask?" Kim looked up at Kate, afraid she was going to hear New York, Chicago, or Washington.

"I thought Reno, Nevada would be a good place to set down," said Kate. "They'll air it at nine o'clock their time. Timothy Hunnewell will walk into court and tell the judge the case is moot. The show has already aired." A cheer went up in the editing room, and the two engineers, Kim and Kate came together in a huge hug.

"Well," said Kim, "this is one time God was on the side of the children."

6

THE NEXT EVENING JONATHAN AND KATE HAD AN EARLY dinner with Deborah and Robert. Now the four of them were poised around the large Sony Trinitron in the upstairs viewing room.

"I feel like we should have popcorn and Cokes," Robert said as they watched *60 Minutes* come to an end.

"Be quiet and drink your brandy and coffee," Deborah replied. She leaned toward Kate who was sitting in a large wingback chair, her stockinged feet on the hassock in front of her. "I'm glad you invited us over for this. I know how much it means to you and all you've gone through." She squeezed Kate's hand. "You don't seem nervous at all and you say you've never seen the completed copy."

"She is amazingly cool," Jonathan said. "She's usually pacing the floor about this time and ready to kill anyone who opens their mouth."

Kate said, "Sorry darling, I know I can be impossible. But I also know Kim as well as the material she's got. She's worked closely with Andrew. She's a good producer. And I'm just going to sit here like the proud mother because there's going to be plenty of time for worrying when the shit hits the fan."

Jonathan nodded. "Kim is special. You're right."

* * *

In the townhouse at the end of Union Wharf, Kim sat tensely on the deep Victorian sofa. Christopher had his arm around her, and she had hers around Jason. She had debated with herself whether or not her son should watch the program, but she knew the publicity afterwards would be unavoidable. She had explained in detail what the program was about and why she had had to spend so much time away from him in the last month and a half.

Maggie came in from the kitchen with hot chocolate for Jason, and sat on a velvet-seated turn-of-the-century rocking chair.

Jason said, in a quiet, almost scared voice, "Here you come, Mom." The television screen showed moving animation of the logo of WLYM and the Marchand Syndicates, with flashes of the more than thirty cities that would now be showing this particular program as it beamed down from the Marchand satellite. Kim shuddered nervously at the realization that, for the first time, she would be the focus of such a large, national audience. In Boston alone, the marketing people had speculated that the promotion would draw over 65 percent of the viewing audience. And after the reports of the thwarted prior restraint, well . . .

"As a public service to the people of Boston and the viewing audiences of all the Marchand Syndicates, regularly scheduled programming will not be seen tonight so that we may bring you this documentary of special interest," the announcer was saying.

The fade to black . . . and there it was. The pan down from the archaic building to Kim walking. Then the force of her words filled the air. Her heart had skipped a beat in the fade to black because it seemed a bit too long. But now the tape was running and no further changes were possible. Kim nodded at the sound of the slow rhythmic beat of a drum over the children screaming and the titles. It held the viewer so that he or she couldn't let go of what was happening.

At the first break Kim realized that Maggie was weeping. "I'm crying for those children, but I'm also crying because that's my Kim and she looks so beautiful and strong."

But it was Jason who needed his mother's attention. He had just seen boys his age being beaten and he stiffened in Kim's arms.

"It's okay, Chase, you're safe. And I'm pretty sure these boys will be safer after tonight."

The break ended and the show resumed. Chris had moved away from Kim and was leaning into the television, repeating over and over again, "I can't believe it. I can't fucking believe it. How can they do that?"

Kate had lived with rage at the injustice for weeks. More than once, at her desk, or in her bed at night, she had wept softly thinking of what might be going on at that very moment in the Wilkins Unit, on the streets, in a state hospital, or a state prison.

But now she watched the broadcast as a professional, admiring the tapestry Kim wove and her mixture of compassion and outrage. She was also aware of her own influence. Kim had used a few of Kate's tricks—lowering the camera to a child's level, so you were like a child walking through a state hospital. Pulling in music and cross dissolves of happy children at play and having them turn into the dull-eyed, drugged children on the detention wards, taking what should be and turning it into what really was. So far, Kate could find in the documentary only one flaw: It left no hope for the viewer. Well, at least not yet. Kim was still driving the viewer deeper and deeper down with the facts. Kate hoped she'd lighten up a little. You couldn't beat the viewer over the head for two straight hours.

At the nine o'clock two-and-a-half-minute break, Kate went into the study and called her office. She had asked Diana to go in and handle any calls to which Kate herself should respond.

She was not surprised when Diana answered the phone tearfully. Kate said, "Diana, you're supposed to be immune to these things by now."

"No, I'm not, Kate. You yourself said you'll get out of the business when you stop caring. I feel for those poor children and I hate those bastards so much. And Kim—she's like a cross between an angel of mercy and the fearless prosecutor."

"That sounds right," Kate said. "How are the calls?"

"The switchboard tells me they can't keep up with it, especially during the commercials. People are screaming to go after these people. Parents whose kids got caught in the same trap are calling. But so far, the calls directly to you, I've been able to handle. The usual congratulations from the syndicates. Well, she's coming back on. I'll talk to you later."

The second hour was more powerful than the first. Kim earmarked where all the money had been misspent; the channels through which it had flowed; how and through whom it had actually been laundered. Then she was back, walking the streets, talking to the kids again. The stories were like Sally's, many of them worse. Too many of the young ended up dead and unclaimed at the city morgue. And that's where Kim was now, wrenching the last tears from her viewers. Christ, thought Kate, doesn't she know you've got to let up at some point?

Then Kim was walking out of the morgue, the ugly gray building rising like an angry fortress in back of her. "I don't want you to think that there is no hope at all for these children. There are pockets of hope. There are moments of success. But long term? They must be here in this state somewhere, but from the hundreds of child counselors and officials I could talk to, I could not get the name of one child they were sure had survived the system . . . except Michael Daniels. And he wasn't easy to find."

The shot changed to Kim stepping off a small commuter airplane. The sign over the terminal read "Battle Creek, Michigan." While Kim walked up the long path leading to what looked like the administration building of a small campus, she gave the history of Michael Daniels. It fit into the pattern of the evening. Then you saw Kim watching a group of young men playing basketball, and a voice came over the "thump, thump, thump" from the court. "I know exactly what you're talking about, Miss Winston. I did it all. By age eight, I had had six foster homes. I was doing heroin. I had been beaten in that Wilkins Unit. We called it 'the hell of hell.' I had been in the state hospitals, then back on the streets. When I was eleven, I tried to kill myself, threw myself in front of a train coming out of South Station. The guy stopped the train. I don't know how. He said I jumped too soon. Anyway, this conductor let me ride to New York. Then I took a train out west. I ended up in Detroit, and was in the hospital there. I was pretty sick. They sent me to this behavior clinic down here in Battle Creek and I've been here for four years. Not in the clinic. Now I go to school. I'm a starting forward on the basketball team, and I live in a really nice foster home."

Again, the shot changed, and now you saw Michael. He looked like a regular high school jock, his gym bag thrown over his shoulder.

"Do you ever think about the past, Mike?" Kim asked, as they walked along the grass in front of the basketball court.

"Oh, I try to forget, but I never can. I still wake up in the middle of the night screaming. Sometimes in the middle of the day, I break out in a cold sweat because of something I remember. I want to forget it, but I can't."

"I know it's hard, but what's your biggest regret?"

He stopped walking and the camera came in tight. "That's not hard, Miss Winston. My biggest regret is that I didn't fill up a whole train with kids and get them out of that place. Get them away from Massachusetts to where they might have a chance. Because as long as they're there, they don't have a prayer in hell. They just live in it."

And then Mike's face dissolved through to the faces of the children back in Massachusetts. From his alive, hopeful appearance to the desperate, screaming and drugged ones back in the Commonwealth.

Kim did a final stand-up as Mike ran back to rejoin his friends. "Back in Massachusetts, thousands of children tonight will sleep in terror, on the streets, in state hospitals, in the Wilkins Unit, in abusive foster homes. And when you sleep in terror, you sleep with one eye open, watching, scared. The irony is that the men and women who create these nights of terror sleep the calm sleep of those without a conscience."

Kim walked offscreen, and after the camera had settled back on the basketball players and Mike, there was a slow dissolve to the exterior of the Wilkins Unit. Then a fade to black and the credits rolled over black, with just the haunting sounds of innocent children at play in the background.

On Union Wharf, the room was silent as the credits rolled. "Reported by Kim Winston, Chief Correspondent, WLYM, Boston. Produced and written by Kim Winston. Directed by . . ."

"What happens now, Mom?" Jason looked up at her, still hanging on to her tightly. Her response was interrupted by the ringing of the phone.

"That's what's going to happen now and probably for the next few hours, so why don't you get ready for bed, young man?" Maggie took Jason's hand and guided him toward his bedroom. Chris leaned back on the couch, listening to Kim thank whoever it was on the phone. He was struck by the two emotions he felt. First, the powerful impact of the documentary. He had never seen anything like it. And second, by the awesome talent and obvious superstardom that lay ahead of the woman he was in love with.

"That was Bill Halliday," said Kim, interrupting his thoughts. "He said it was the best documentary he had ever seen. Isn't that sweet? Other people could have been jealous."

"Jealous of all the work you put into that? The hours?"

The phone rang again, and it was Kate. "I'm sorry to call so late, but I've been on the phone taking bows for you since the end of the program."

"That's all right. My phone has been busy, too."

There was a brief silence and then Kate said "Kim, about your documentary? You have taken the word excellent and given a new meaning to it."

"Thank you," Kim said softly. "I was hoping you would call, that you would be happy. I've been told that isn't your style. You just expect the best from people."

"When people stretch themselves beyond the best, that warrants at least a phone call, don't you think?"

"Well, do you want to hear my plans for the next one?"

Kate laughed. "We're going to have to deal with the repercussions of this one for a while."

In the Dover house, Kate put down the phone and sat staring at it for a long time.

"Waiting for it to ring?" The sound of Jonathan's voice startled her.

"I'm sorry, darling. My mind was wandering." She went to him and put her arms around him, leaning heavily against him.

"Wandering, by any chance, to a reporter back in New York ten or so years ago?"

"Why do you ask?" Kate looked up into his eyes.

"Because there's no doubt that the last time anyone saw a reporter with the impact of Kim Winston was when they last saw Katherine Marchand."

"Oh, Jonathan." She pulled away from him. "I'm really getting sick of hearing that."

7

DURING THE FOLLOWING TWO WEEKS, WLYM, KIM WINSTON and Katherine Marchand were part of one of the largest publicity blitzes ever to hit electronic journalism. Kim was on numerous talk shows, and both she and Kate were the subject of various articles in newspapers and magazines across the country.

Then came the news that Kate had been waiting for. The House Committee on Government Operations was calling a special session to inquire into the charges and information revealed in *Juvenile Justice: A Contradiction in Terms*. Kate heard the news from Washington as she was leaving her office Friday evening.

She called Kim late that night to congratulate her.

Kim thanked Kate and said, "It *is* great, isn't it? That's what it's all about, when you think of it. We do a story that has a real impact on social policy. It's what we all dream about."

"Well, yes, but there's more to your job than that. I'm glad you did this story but it did take you away from a lot of your other duties for . . ."

Kim sputtered, "But you yourself said I should. Honestly, Kate, all you ever think about is your grand plan for pushing your so-called empire. Well, I like to do this kind of story and I intend to continue."

"What you continue is hardly your own decision," Kate said coldly.

"Jesus! You never did care about those kids in the first place."

"One moment, please. It was I who encouraged you and I who will continue to be the ultimate judge of what this station does." The chilly condescension in Kate's voice was almost palpable. "You have a certain talent, Kim, and your appearance is attractive. I wouldn't have hired you if that were not the case. But your career is blossoming because of what *we've* done for you. I believe you were getting about three minutes a night on the air in New York, with your little reports from Albany. It was all local stuff. You're learning, but up to now, it's I who have been responsible for whatever success you're having."

There was no reply. Kim had hung up the phone. Kate grinned and said aloud, "I guess I went too far."

That Saturday morning, after Jonathan had gone off for his regular Saturday morning mixed doubles game, she went to collect the newspaper from the table in the breakfast room. She knew Jonathan had read it because it was at his place, but he had, as usual, refolded it with a surgeon's precision so that no crease beyond those the delivery company had made could be discerned. If she were a detective, Kate thought, tracking him, there'd be no evidence here of his trail. Silly. Why track him?

On the front page of *The New York Times*, top left column, was a headline that read, "GOVERNMENT TO INVESTIGATE CHARGES OF CHILD ABUSE."

"Finally, finally," Kate said. She wished Jonathan were here to share it, then said aloud, "Funny. You'd think he'd have awakened me with the news."

She went to the phone and called Deborah. "Did you see the *Times*? It's just as I hoped, not just another documentary that would win a few awards and then be forgotten. It's going to show that television can make a difference."

"I never doubted that," Deborah said. "Why don't you come over here and celebrate with a champagne brunch?"

"Well, I'm a tennis widow again this morning and Jonathan said he's got to check on a patient on the way back."

"With his tennis racket?"

"I think he'll put it down before he examines the wound, Deb. And thanks for the invitation, but I've got to work."

Jonathan came home much later, but in the hours between the call to Deborah and his return Kate, as she rarely did, felt lonely. She supposed it was because the last few months had been so hectic. She lay down on the bed, pulling the quilt around her, and for a reason she could not fathom, started crying softly until, like a small child, she had cried herself to sleep.

Kim sat in the Planetarium at the Children's Museum of Science, listening to and watching the story of the Christmas star and what seemed like every other star in the galaxy. Jason sat next to her, fascinated. Kim at least was relieved to be in the dark. All day as they had wandered through the museum and its exhibits—whether it was watching chickens hatch or when Jason crawled inside a replica of one of the first space capsules—she had been surrounded by people congratulating her, telling her how much they liked her on television, and children, as well as some adults, asking for her autograph. It had bothered Jason when it took her attention away from an exhibit he was particularly interested in. But now, in the blackened planetarium, she was safe, only another human being straining her neck muscles.

By the time the show ended it was three o'clock, and they had covered just about every square inch of the museum. "Now let's go over to the hospital and see Chris," Jason suggested as they walked out of the museum.

"What do you mean, go and see Chris? He's probably working at the hospital."

"I know that, Mom. We had pizza together last night and that's what he told me." He looked up at her impatiently.

"Why do I get the feeling you two are responsible for the economic growth of Regina's?" asked Kim.

"Because Regina's has the best pizza in town."

"Why wasn't I told or, heaven forbid, asked if it was all right for you to go out for pizza last night?"

"Mom, don't worry. Maggie and I already had dinner, and Chris came by and said he was hungry and would I like to join him in some pizza. We tried to call you, but you were busy. What's the big deal?"

Kim felt a familiar surge of the resentment that seized her when Chris seemed to be pushing her, insisting too hard on a commitment.

"So are we going, Mom?"

"Going where?"

"Pay attention, please. To meet Chris at the hospital."

"What an idea. We're not going to bother him at the hospital."

"He *asked* me, Mom. He said in the afternoon it wasn't that busy. And I've never been in a hospital. All those times you went to visit Dad you said I couldn't come." His voice went from demanding to whining.

Kim took Jason's hand in hers and as they walked across the bridge over the Charles River leading to the harbor, she felt a cold wing of air fly directly into her heart. She herself had not stepped inside a hospital since David's death.

"You were born in a hospital, silly. Where did you think you were born—in a New York subway?" She tugged at his hand.

"No," he laughed. "Come on, Mom. Please?" She looked down at him thinking, how does one deny those beautiful beseeching blue eyes?

"Okay, but if he's busy, we're leaving." She paused. "Wait a minute. I don't even know where to find him."

"I do. I know how to get there. Don't worry." And holding hands, they walked briskly towards New England General.

Jason did know exactly where to go, thanks to a map that Chris had drawn for him. They walked through the maze of corridors. White Building. Gray Building. Bigelow. Baker. The smell and the rush of people was all too familiar to Kim, but she helped Jason with the map, and soon they arrived at a large open area with a sign reading "Ambulatory Clinic." They asked a receptionist if Dr. Cerci was with a patient, and when the reply was yes, Kim looked down at Jason. "He's busy, Baby. Maybe another day."

"Excuse me, aren't you Kim Winston?" the receptionist asked.

"Yes, she is," Jason said immediately, as if he knew his mother's fame could be useful.

The receptionist said, "Let me tell him you're here. I'm sure right after this patient, he'll be able to see you. I'll tell him you're here."

"Great! We'll sit right over here." Once again, Jason's enthusiasm carried the day. He led his mother to a chair.

Now it seemed to Kim that everyone in the waiting area was staring at her. "Come here, Chase," she said. "Crawl up on my lap. That's it. Facing me."

"This is so people can't see your face, right?"

"It would help if your head was about five times bigger. But I also want to ask you a question face to face."

Kim unbuttoned the top of his coat. "I'm curious, Chase. Why did you insist on coming here today? Why didn't you tell me earlier, when you even had a map?"

"Because Chris told me you probably wouldn't be too keen on coming, so I thought if I surprised you it would work better."

"But we usually talk these things out," Kim said, pushing the hair back from his eyes.

"I just thought we should come to the hospital, the way we used to go to the office with Dad sometimes. You know, sharing."

Kim said, "Okay, sweetie," but she was concerned about the growing relationship between Chris and Jason. She didn't want the boy bonding to someone she herself wasn't sure was going to stay in her life.

Moments later Chris's voice was saying, "I was afraid you wouldn't come," he said, looking at Kim. "I'm glad, very glad you did."

He put his arm around her, and holding Jason's hand, walked across the large waiting room. They went through a door and saw a labyrinth of other doors. First there was Chris's office, then the examining room, then a small emergency room, then a room for viewing X rays. Chris was explaining the instruments to Jason and letting him try a few. After a while Kim said she'd wait in Chris's office. As she settled down to read the newspaper, she saw in the *Boston Globe* that "The calling of the special committee meeting was precipitated by a documentary and series of reports by Kim Winston, chief correspondent for Boston's WLYM and the Marchand Syndicates."

"Chris! Chris!" She ran back to the examining room. "Did you see this? Look. Washington's really going to investigate. And they're going to do it soon." Chris took the paper from her and read the first few paragraphs of the article Kim was pointing to. He then turned and hugged her. "That's wonderful, darling. That's wonderful. You will get those changes."

"What's going on?" asked Jason.

"Remember how I told you the reason for that program was to change things so the children wouldn't be hurt anymore?" Kim asked. "Well, they're going to check out the whole mess and if it works out right, the children will be much better off."

Jason shouted, "Hooray," and Kim and Chris joined him.

There was a knock on the door. "Hey, in there," someone called.

"Oops, we're making too much noise," Jason said.

"No, office hours are over for the day."

Chris opened the door and Jonathan stood in the hallway. As soon as Jason recognized the man in the blue surgeon suit, he ran towards him. "Jonathan. Hi! Hi, Jonathan! Mom and I came to visit Chris."

Jonathan hugged the boy close and said, "I heard you were coming but I didn't know you were bringing your mother."

"I can't cross by myself yet," Jason said. "Maybe when I'm eight, if I stop daydreaming by then."

The adults could not help themselves. They stood laughing until Jonathan said, "Son, I never did stop daydreaming but eventually they let you cross the street by yourself anyhow. I tell you what, let's celebrate when that happens to you."

"What's celebrate?"

"That's what we're doing now," Kim said. "About the story in the newspaper."

"Congratulations on that," Jonathan said. "I saw that news about the special committee. It's all due to your hard work and that dynamite image you project. No one on the boob tube can touch you."

"Don't let your wife hear you call it that," Chris said. "Or this woman either, for that matter."

Jonathan said, "What about you, Jason? You going to go on TV too when you grow up?"

"Nah! I'm going to be a doctor."

"Well, you can't do that when you haven't even seen an operating room or been in an ambulance."

"Oh, Jonathan, now? Please, please . . ."

"Tell you what, you and your mom come on the grand tour with me now. Chris· is already a doctor so he can skip it." Turning to Chris he winked and said, "Give you a chance to finish up before you go out with these delicious people which—lucky dog—I assume you're going to do." But as they got to the door, Jonathan said, "By the way, Chris. Why don't the three of you drive up to Mount Ascutney with me next Saturday? If the weather's good I'm going to do some hang gliding and it might be fun for Jason to see."

"Can we Mom? Can we?"

"I'm not sure," Kim said. "It's probably too long a trip for one day and . . ."

Jonathan interrupted. "It's less than two hours and the place is beautiful. I promise you'll love it and it would be neat for me to have you come."

After the trip was arranged, Kim, Jonathan and Jason left on their tour. She wasn't sure how it had happened but Kim found herself a half hour later sitting in a parked ambulance, Jonathan's arm lightly on her shoulders, Jason in the driver's seat. Jonathan kept a running "professional" conversation going with Jason about the imaginary patient they were speeding to help. At the same time, he made Kim understand that he was aware of her presence and enjoying it. And she could not help responding. Well, why not? It meant nothing and Jonathan's warmth and savoir-faire were irresistible—to a point.

8

KIM'S MERCEDES NEATLY HELD THE CURVE AS IT MOVED OFF the exit ramp of Rte. 93 and onto Rte. 89, heading north into the Vermont mountains.

"How much longer is it, Chris?" Jason asked from the cramped back seat, interrupting the license plate game he was playing with his mother.

"According to Jonathan, it will only be another hour."

"Doesn't it strike you as odd," Kim asked, "that someone in Jonathan's position would be so involved in hang gliding of all things?"

"Odd?" Chris said, turning briefly to look at Kim. "Why is it odd? Jonathan is a very active man. You have to have some release from the pressures of the operating room."

"But why a sport so dangerous? One good miscalculation and he's sitting in a puddle of broken bones, unable ever to operate again. That is, if he survives."

"Well, neurosurgeons are a special breed. They have to be, with the kind of track record even the best of them have. They're always dealing with life-threatening problems where only the highest technical skill will work. They'd never go into that field, no less survive in it, if they weren't risk takers. But that doesn't mean reckless. Jonathan's not a reckless man."

"Well, I disagree. I think hang gliding itself is reckless. And, anyway, you'd think in his spare time he'd do something that his wife could participate in."

"When?" Chris laughed. "She's the only wife of a neuro-surgeon who has a busier schedule than her husband."

Kim sighed. "Well, that's true." Jason's hand was creeping around her neck, and Kim turned and tickled him until he was giggling uncontrollably.

It wasn't long before they turned onto Rte. 91 and then off at the exit to Windsor, Vermont. "This place seems so quiet and peaceful," Kim said, pointing to the mountains. "The day is so balmy, the sun so bright, who needs hang gliding? Even from ground level you can see for miles."

They drove through the small town of Windsor and followed the signs to Mt. Ascutney. As they drove they passed dilapidated trailers sinking into the earth as well as beautifully groomed lawns with neatly bordered paths leading to immaculate old co-lonial houses. Kim leaned back in her seat, delighting in the checkerboard of farms across the fields.

"There's the sign for Mount Ascutney!" Jason shouted. "Chris! You missed it. That's where we're supposed to go."

"Hold on, Tiger," Chris said, maneuvering the car around a sharp corner and over a small bridge. "Jonathan takes off from the mountain, but we're supposed to meet him where he lands. Kim, would you help me look for the road that Hoonts Farm is on?"

They passed through Brownsville Center—a town consisting of a general store, a fire station, an antique shop, and a real estate office—and soon found the steep driveway marked by a birdhouse mailbox that read "Hoonts."

Chris said, "Jonathan said he'd call ahead and warn them we were coming."

He parked the car next to an old tractor and when Kim stepped out she saw a man in worn overalls and a plaid shirt approach them from the barn. "Mr. Hoonts? I'm Kim Winston, a friend of Jonathan Marchand." When she stretched her hand toward him, she was struck by the kindness in his weather-beaten face and the strength of his handshake.

"The doctor told me you'd be coming," Hoonts said. Look-ing down at Jason, he asked, "Are you here to learn how to fly one of those flang dangle things?"

Jason giggled.

"I'm sorry, Mr. Hoonts," Kim said. "This is my son Jason, and this is Chris Cerci."

"You must be the other doctor Jon spoke about," Hoonts said, shaking Chris's hand, then Jason's. "You sure picked a good day. Weather started out foggy this morning. Wasn't sure it would clear."

"Mom, Chris! Look, there's one now!" Jason screamed, when he saw a hang glider move through the air a few miles away. "I bet that's Jonathan. Come on, come on." He began tugging at his mother's arm.

"Hold on, Jason," Kim said, pulling him back. "Jonathan said he wouldn't take off till noon. That's still forty-five minutes away." She turned back to Mr. Hoonts. "Is there any particular place it's best to watch from?"

"Ay-uh. Jon usually comes down in that meadow over there." Hoonts pointed to a large recently mowed field about a hundred yards away. "Unless of course he lands like he did that first time, up there on the roof of the barn."

"He landed on the barn?" Jason asked.

"He sure did, son. I was working inside and thought the roof was caving in. But it was just Dr. Marchand on one of his first runs." He smiled and turned his face back to the fields. "Now he's pretty accurate. 'Course I can't understand why a grown man wants to fly like some bird. But it's none of my business." He began to walk back to the barn. "If there's anything you need, you'll find me here and the missus in the house."

They thanked him, pulled the blankets and the lunch Maggie had packed from the car, and headed for the designated field.

By the time they were settled, there were at least a half dozen hang gliders in the air, of varying sizes and colors. Jason held Chris's binoculars to his eyes and after swinging from Kim's face to his own feet, and then up again, he finally zeroed in on a hang glider.

"I found him! That's him! That's him!"

Kim looked at her watch. "Chase, it's another twenty minutes before Jonathan said he would take off."

"What if his watch is wrong? Or yours?"

"Trust your mother, Jason," Chris said, leaning back on the blanket and closing his eyes.

"Well, how will we know it's him?" Jason demanded.

"Because we'll watch that spot where we see them taking off and then as soon as we can distinguish the colors, we'll look for Jonathan's," Chris said, not bothering to move or open his eyes. "His glider has a red and black sail and he says he wears a suit that's silver. It's for warmth, that color, Jonathan said. We'll see him, don't worry.''

The hang gliders dipped and curved above the fields and then, a few minutes before noon, Chris turned his binoculars toward the area of Ascutney Mountain where the gliders appeared to take off. Only a few minutes passed until he announced the sight of the red and black glider they were watching for.

Jason finally spotted Jonathan's hang glider. He watched with wide eyes and open mouth as it moved from the mountain, turning and gliding from east to west, sometimes taking a sudden rush up into the sky and then delicately turning and gliding downward.

"Now does that look so dangerous?" Chris asked, as Kim took the binoculars.

"From here, no," she said, "but I'm not several hundred feet off the ground." As she watched Jonathan gracefully and powerfully maneuver the glider she thought, he's literally flying like a bird. Completely free, above all these beautiful fields and farms. Yes, she admitted to herself, she was envious of the exhilaration he must be feeling.

In less than fifteen minutes Jonathan was within several hundred yards of them. As the glider slowly lost speed and thrust, he maneuvered it toward the meadow and as effortlessly as a falling leaf found his way to the ground. His body had straightened from the prone position, and he was soon running with the sail across the field until the momentum slowed and he came to a stop.

Kim, Jason, and Chris all hurried towards where Jonathan stood with the sail on the ground behind him.

"You were terrific!" Jason shouted, as Jonathan freed himself from the harness and lifted the boy into the air. "We saw you right from the very beginning. You were super! Wait till I tell the guys!"

"Calm down there, mate," Jonathan smiled. "It's not like I flew myself. I had some help from the sail."

"Oh, I think in his eyes you could walk on water . . . or fly without a sail," Kim said.

Chris was inspecting the sail and asking questions about the rigging as Jonathan took off his helmet. He showed them the various parts of the gliding rig, as well as the special features he had added: an altimeter to measure air pressure; a variometer to measure the rate of climb or descent; and a back-up karabiner, the vital link between the harness and the glider.

"Why do you have two of these kara . . . karaboomboom things?" Jason asked.

"Because if one fails, then you have another to keep you in place."

"Why? What would happen?"

"Well, you'd probably come crashing into the ground."

"Oh, then I guess it's a good idea to have two, huh?" Jason asked, as he continued examining the glider.

"But what about a parachute? Wouldn't that lessen the risk?" Kim asked.

"Some people use them, but usually for much higher and longer flights than this," Jonathan explained. "It's just too bulky for my liking. And what's wrong with a little suspense?"

"Don't worry, Mom, Jonathan can do anything. He won't fall."

Soon, they were all seated around the blanket, enjoying Maggie's elaborate lunch. Jonathan told stories of various hang gliding triumphs and a few near tragedies. "I've never found a thrill quite like it," he said. "You ought to give it a go, Chris."

"Oh, you know us California boys. We prefer the challenge of the waves," Chris answered. "I'm a surfer but I'm afraid I'm not that much of a free spirit."

"Maybe you'd like it, Chris," Kim said. "It could be a good release for you. Now that I've seen it, well, it looks absolutely wonderful."

"Want to try?" Jonathan asked.

"I admit I'm intrigued by it, but I don't think I have the time to learn. To say nothing of the fact that my boss has this problem with her talent taking unnecessary risks."

"Well, your boss isn't around now," Jonathan said, "and it doesn't take much to rig up another harness. I even have an extra helmet in the car."

"But what about a sail?" Kim asked, then said, "Oh . . . you mean both of us, together? Underneath that sail?"

"Yes, it's done all the time," Jonathan said. "You're light enough so there would be no drag. In fact, the winds are almost at twenty miles per hour. That's the perfect condition and look at that clear sky. It's just beckoning you."

"Yeah, Mom. Yeah!" Jason shouted. "You can do it. You gotta do it. So I can tell the guys. And Jonathan won't let you get hurt. Come on, Mom, it will be so neat."

Kim looked over at Chris, who shrugged his shoulders. "If you want to do it, honey, I'm sure you'll be safe with Jonathan."

"Then it's settled," Jonathan said, rising to his feet. "I'm going to go get Lester who'll give me a ride back in his pickup truck. Chris, you can follow, watch Kim get saddled up, and then we'll wait for you to get back here so you can watch us fly right back to this very spot."

Jason cheered and hugged his mother, and Kim felt a thrill of excitement. In less than ten minutes, she found herself riding in the Mercedes with Chris, following Lester Hoonts's battered truck, with the sail flapping in the back, and Jonathan and Jason carrying on a steady conversation in front.

"Are you sure you want to do this?" Chris asked, maneuvering around the ruts and holes in the dirt road. "You seemed a little hesitant back there."

"You know, sometimes I do not understand the male species at all," Kim said, opening her window and letting the breeze throw her hair back from her face. "I was hesitant before I saw it, but you yourself said I'll be safe with Jonathan and who could resist a chance like this?"

"Meaning me? Meaning I could and did decline to go?" Chris asked quietly.

"Oh Chris, for heaven's sake. Lighten up. Don't take everything so personally."

The two vehicles moved up a mountain road that grew steeper and steeper. Chris slowed the car and fell back so it would not be hit by any rocks spit up by Hoonts's truck. Eventually, they came to a small parking area off the side of the road. There were a dozen or so other hang gliders getting equipment from their cars and walking off to a path in the distance.

The sail was unloaded and Kim took a matching red and black helmet and an extra leather harness from Jonathan's Porsche. Then she and Chris and Jason watched as Jonathan hoisted the sail and its tensile tubing over his shoulder. With Jason running ahead, they set off on the path, and after a short walk, came to a flat open area above the tree line. Jonathan pointed to a rocky ledge fifty yards away where a young woman was checking her harness. As they watched, she pulled her goggles down, adjusted her hands on the side bars, and began running the length of the cliff. The glider suddenly dipped down almost out of sight and then, to the cheers of the other gliders, made a first turn and rose back up on its journey through the mountain air.

"See? That's what you're going to do, Mom!" Jason said, jumping up and down in excitement.

Kim smiled weakly and looked out at the steep drop off the cliff. "You're sure this is a good idea, Jonathan?"

"Kim, think of the position I'm in," he said as he placed the harness on her. "If I so much as put a scratch on that gorgeous 'bod' of yours, my wife will probably see to it that I'm impotent for the rest of my life."

Kim and Chris laughed and Jason asked, "What's funny?" as Jonathan set the sail, locked all the joints, and got himself into his harness.

"You two should head back to the farm," Jonathan said to Chris. "It's one-forty so you should be back there in fifteen minutes. We'll plan our takeoff for two o'clock."

Jason grabbed Chris's hand and began to pull him back to the path. "Good luck, Mom. We'll be watching." Then, as if struck by a second thought, came running back to his mother, gave her a kiss, and quickly disappeared down the path with Chris.

"Well, I can see they're really concerned about me jumping off a cliff into thin air," Kim said.

Smiling, Jonathan placed an affectionate kiss on her cheek and an arm around her shoulder. "There's nothing to worry about. You know what they say, 'after the first time, you can't get enough of it.' "

Kim's breath caught at the devil-may-care expression in Jonathan's eyes, so like the dancing light she had so adored in David's. Brusquely, she said, "You'd better tell me what I'm supposed to do once we get in the air."

"That's simple. You just hang on and enjoy." This time it was Jonathan who stared quietly into Kim's eyes. They stood caught in the silent look until they were distracted by shouting as another hang glider ran off the cliff into the brisk winds.

At just about two o'clock, Jonathan had finished his instructions and they were walking toward the cliff, side by side, their bodies touching under the flapping red and black sail. Jonathan returned the good luck wishes of the other gliders and Kim looked out over the edge of the cliff, wondering how she had managed to get herself into this position.

"Did I ever tell you I'm not the type of person who believes you have to experience everything in life in order to be happy?" Kim asked, as they waited at the far end of the cliff.

"But if you don't do it now, babe, you'll forever be wondering what you missed."

In silence, Kim conceded that Jonathan was right. She could feel the twinge of excitement move through her body. They waited a few more minutes, each with one hand on the cross bar and one hand on the side bar. It was shortly after two when Jonathan stiffened.

"Okay, babe, here comes the wind right at us. It has our name on it. Remember, just run with me and when I shout 'release,' pull your legs up, put your arm around me, and try to relax."

Kim was about to say there were many things she could do at this moment, but relaxing was not one of them—when she suddenly began running alongside Jonathan, saw the end of the rocky ledge in front of her, and heard the shout, "Release!"

For what seemed to be hours, she felt herself falling down toward the tree line. But then, with a sudden gush, the sail filled with air and jerked them up so Kim was looking at only blue sky. Her legs stretched out behind her with little effort on her part, and she placed her right arm around Jonathan as she hung suspended on the harness about six inches above him.

"You okay?" he shouted over the sound of the wind.

"I think so. When do we turn?" Jonathan had explained that the major maneuver in the flight, along with taking off and landing, was the first 180-degree turn. From then on, he had said, it was just a matter of enjoying the flight.

"We're going to do it . . . right NOW!" and before Kim could think about it she felt her body follow Jonathan's as he pushed out over the center bar and swung his legs, turning the glider back along the ridge of the mountain in what was now an ascent.

"Perfect!" shouted Jonathan, briefly lifting his hand off the side bar to pull Kim's arm tighter around him. "Now just enjoy. You're flying, lady."

And indeed she was. In what seemed a natural motion she hugged Jonathan closer and smiled into the wind. First, she watched only the clouds and the sky, but then lowering her vision to the horizon, she saw the farms along with the mountainside. The combination of the view and the exhilaration of passing through the wind, filled Kim with inexpressible joy. They hung in the air silently, part of the sky, the trees clear beneath them, a puff or two of a cloud above them in the sunlight.

They turned again, and this time with a gracefulness that made the flying itself seem like the most natural thing in the world. "And people said that man was not designed to fly," Kim said, laughing.

"Well, I don't think I'd like to do it without the help of this sail,'' Jonathan replied. He briefly smiled at her and when he turned back into the wind, she found herself once again thinking of David. The profile was almost the same, the eyes, dark and questioning, the lips, sensual and bold. Even the wisps of Jonathan's hair that curled out from underneath the helmet were the same texture and color as David's. Unconsciously, she hugged him closer but was only aware of this motion when he turned his head slightly and smiled warmly at her.

She returned the smile and kissed his cheek. But then, she had a swift reminder of who she was . . . and he . . . of reality. Still, she could not help asking, ''Has Kate ever flown with you?''

''Kate? Never! It's not worth the risk to her. One sloppy landing and she could really mess up that back of hers.''

''But her life is full of taking chances,'' shouted Kim, after they executed another perfect, delicate turn.

''She takes risks only when she knows where all the pitfalls are, only when she knows she'll win. Like in her work.''

''And with her husband,'' Kim said, wanting to pull back the words as soon as she had said them, not sure why she had said them.

''Yes, you could say so,'' Jonathan replied, as they were pulled up by a strong draft off the mountain. ''The problem there is, she doesn't know when she's won.''

Kim put it all away from her and went back to the joy of what they were doing, the excitement. Jonathan too remained silent until another turn brought them several hundred yards above some recently mowed fields. Jonathan pointed to two figures below them and Kim realized they were approaching Hoonts Farm. Chris and Jason were waving feverishly. As the glider slowed, Jonathan and Kim lowered their legs towards the ground. Then Jonathan shifted his weight slightly so that once they were on the ground, the sail would be between them and Chris and Jason.

Kim was surprised at how easy and graceful the landing was. One moment they were gliding above the meadow and the next, slowly running with the sail above them. When they came to a halt, Jonathan said, ''I dare you, girl. Tell me that wasn't the greatest feeling in the world.''

''Well, it's damn close,'' she said, smiling. And before she was quite aware of what was happening, she was looking into Jonathan's eyes again and feeling his lips on hers.

''Just a congratulatory kiss,'' he said as Kim pulled away.

Before she could respond, Chris and Jason were rounding the sail, shouting their accolades.

Jason fell asleep in the back of the car almost as soon as they left the farm. Chris and Kim were in the front and were silent until Kim said, "You must be tired. You drove up here and all over those mountains. Why don't I drive? You can have a nap with Jason."

"If you don't mind," he answered. "You don't seem to be in the mood for conversation. I guess the wind took away your communicative skills."

"What is that supposed to mean?" Kim snapped.

Chris looked at her in surprise. "I was only kidding, for heaven's sake." He pulled the car over to the side of the highway and stepped out. "Drive, and keep yourself company. Maybe you can relive the joy of hang gliding with the great doctor."

Kim could think of no reply. She knew that, despite herself, that was exactly what she would do.

9

Diana looked across her office to Judy, who was barely visible behind a growing stack of mail. She laughed and said, "Why do I get the feeling you're about to disappear? I can literally only see the top of your head. Are you making any progress at all?"

"What do you mean, am I making progress?" said Judy, standing up rather indignantly. "I have stuffed over eight thousand envelopes with those form letters we made up. But each day, another big pile comes in. And over the weekend . . . well, look at this. Why do we have to do such controversial shows anyway? We're even getting letters from Canada and Hawaii."

"You know the answer to that. The hearings on the scandal Kim uncovered about the kids—it's getting coverage everywhere. Diana walked over and picked up a few of the letters. "Sometimes I think Kate should run for office. People out there just love her."

"Speaking of our fearless leader, where is the mighty one?" Judy asked.

"She had to speak at the big annual communion breakfast the cardinal gives."

"Oh, man, I hope she brought a suit of armor. She must be a real favorite of theirs after her prochoice editorial."

"She was asked several months ago, long before the editorial.

I think they would have disinvited her if they weren't afraid she'd report it on TV." Diana, too, had thought Kate would be walking into a hostile atmosphere, but when they had discussed it on her return from Washington, Kate reassured her that the power of the juvenile justice disclosures would outweigh the abortion controversy. Or so she hoped.

At that moment, in a swirl of motion, Kate came striding into the office carrying her ever-present briefcase and also a stack of folders.

"Morning, Diana. Morning, Judy." Then she stopped halfway into her office and returned, hovering over Judy's desk. "You are in back there somewhere, aren't you, Judy?" Not waiting for a response, she headed into her office, laughing softly. She deposited the stack of papers on one of the chairs.

"What's this?" asked Diana. "The clergy give you some reading material to help get your head straight on abortion?"

"No, that's some work I did over the weekend. Some new proposals and graphs and charts for next year's projections. A lot of it's on my computer and can be interfaced with the station's, but I wanted to get a head start."

"I thought you were going to take it easy this weekend?" said Diana grimly as she went through the top pages of the paperwork.

"Well, I got a shot in the arm. Kim's story's had such great results—the committee hearings, the talk of new legislation. It's given me a new burst of energy."

"Oh, great. Just what we need is you with more energy. Can we hire another secretary?"

"I thought you said you needed more exercise," Kate answered, taking off her coat.

"How did you manage to appear humble and meek at your religious breakfast in that sable coat?" Diana asked.

"Well, for starters, I didn't wear it when I spoke to them. Didn't want to spill oatmeal on it. Can you imagine? Oatmeal. The cardinal said he likes it because it helps his digestion."

"And were you right? Did they forget about your abortion editorial?"

"For the most part, yes. They were very welcoming, except for one priest who criticized me openly on the editorial and then threw out an innuendo about a cocaine scandal. I recognized him. He's that guy who has been making inflammatory speeches on behalf of the Irish Republican Army. And so I quickly turned the whole thing around, and asked him if his parish was still condoning the violence and killing in Northern Ireland.''

"That must have pleased him."

"He actually gave me a very threatening look, shook his fist, and walked out of the ballroom. First time I've been threatened by a priest," Kate said, picking up one of the messages before her. "What's this? What does Andrew want to see me about?"

"Oh, I'm sorry," hastened Diana. "I was to call him as soon as you got in." She headed for her own phone and before Kate was finished going through the remaining messages and making notes to Diana, Andrew came in, looking pale and upset.

"What's wrong? Sit down. Calm down."

"I guess you haven't heard. I thought Maggie had called you or your husband. Look, Jason is very sick. He's been running a fever all weekend, and then he was worse last night. Kim took him to St. Marten's Children's Hospital around three A.M. and is there with him now. There's an initial diagnosis of spinal meningitis, but they're waiting."

"Oh, my God." Kate knew there was a type of spinal meningitis that paralyzed the whole body, and was eventually fatal. She turned around quickly. "Diana, get . . ."

"I'm on my way."

"I know he has surgery this morning. The minute he's finished. Tell them it's an emergency."

"Who do you want to anchor with Bill?" Andrew asked.

"Pull up Lynn Mallory. Have Tom and Martha switch off with the morning shift. And until you hear from me or Diana, this is to be kept confidential. Let's not make it worse on Kim." Kate's voice was cool and detached.

Andrew left the office, just as Diana called out, "Jonathan on line two."

Kate quickly told her husband what had happened, adding, "I suppose Chris is with her."

Jonathan answered, "I know he isn't. He left yesterday to speak at a neurological convention in Denmark."

"Terrific. Will you go over there, Jonathan?"

"I'm leaving now. I'll call you from the hospital."

"It's serious, isn't it?" Diana asked quietly when Kate hung up.

"Very, very serious," Kate said in a voice that was barely audible. Diana wondered how to decipher Kate's reaction. Concern for Kim and Jason as valued human beings? Or concern for

Kim and Jason because a tragedy for Kim could jeopardize Kate's empire? Diana wanted to believe the first.

"Kate," Diana said, "You have a sales meeting scheduled for right now. Do you want me to cancel it?"

"No, no. That's not going to help anybody." She took a folder from her desk. "Let me get my notes but make certain you let me know when Jonathan calls."

An hour and a half later, Jonathan did call. "It appears he does have meningitis, exactly what type and how severe they do not know. They've done a spinal tap, and that will give a lot of answers, but it takes time for the results—it's an elaborate process. They've also done X rays of the chest, spine and cranial cavity." His voice dipped, and Kate knew the next statement would not be good.

"Did you look at the X rays?"

"Yes. Doctor Neibuhr, who's handling the case, is one of the best in the world for this type of illness. We've also had a working relationship over the years, so he was very open and frank."

"What about the X rays?"

"Well, you know meningitis means a swelling of the membrane enveloping the brain and spinal cord?"

"Yes, yes."

"Well, if it's bacterial meningitis, it can often be treated with antibiotics if it's caught soon enough. If it's viral, it's a little trickier because it could mean anything from polio to encephalitis."

"Wait a minute, you didn't tell me about the X rays."

"Well, we don't know for sure, but according to Kim, Jason got dizzy on Saturday while roughhousing with Chris, and fell down four or five steps, knocking his head on a baseboard pretty hard. Probably as a result, Neibuhr and I both see what looks like an abscess on the brain. We're not certain. The X ray wasn't conclusive."

"Well, what does that mean?" Kate asked.

"Well, his membranes are already inflamed. An abscess can be, often is . . . fatal."

"Oh, no, Jonathan, no. Not that beautiful boy." Kate began to cry and Jonathan said, "Listen, Kate, don't get too upset yet. There are still so many variables. If the cerebrospinal fluid shows a rise in measurements of lactic dehydrogenase isoenzymes, then it's probably bacterial meningitis, and if we can get him on medication fast enough . . ."

Kate observed to herself that doctors seem to feel more in

control when they use words only they can understand. "But what about the brain abscess?"

"There'll have to be another computer scan of the brain done."

"And in the meantime?"

"I'm afraid it's one of those things you have to wait out."

"Oh, God, Jonathan, how did all this happen?"

"He was running a fever over the weekend. He was very drowsy and had some pain in his abdomen. Sunday morning he complained of a stiff neck and a worse headache. But it wasn't until early this morning that he became delirious. Kim was desperate and took him over to St. Marten's," Jonathan said, with a certain coolness in his voice that Kate did not understand. "By the way, it appears he may have caught it from another boy and that boy made it through okay. He's in the clear. That's a good sign."

"Did you talk to Kim?"

"Yes, or at least I tried to. She's somewhat in a state of shock. They've tried to medicate her, but she won't leave Jason's side. He keeps slipping in and out of consciousness, but she's completely unemotional. It's obvious she's been in this situation before. I explained a little bit of that to Neibuhr and so he's decided to just let her be." Jonathan hesitated, as if there was something else to say.

"What is it?"

"Well, I think Kim has some misdirected anger right now. She says she kept telling Chris that something was seriously wrong with Jason but he thought she was overreacting because of what happened with her husband."

"Well, she obviously wasn't. I could strangle Christopher Cerci."

"These things are difficult to diagnose. Fever, headache. Could be a flu, a cold."

"But the stiff neck? Even I know the warnings of a fever and a stiff neck. And after the fall? Come on, Jonathan."

"Listen, Chris is a top neurologist, I'm sure it's just that he didn't want to alarm Kim over nothing."

"I am so sick of you doctors protecting each other. Well, I'll go over in a few hours. Maybe I'll see you there."

For the next three hours, Kate went through the agenda of her day, feeling a little numb to the decisions she was making, the conversations she was participating in. At 3:30, she summoned

Diana. "Remember those lilies I asked you to get when Kim first came to town? When she was at the Ritz?"

"Oh, yes, I wrote that down."

"Would you please find a florist in town that has them, and tell them I'll be by in the next half hour to pick them up . . . a dozen I'd say." Kate rose from her chair, pushing papers into her briefcase.

"You're leaving?"

"No, I'm going to reach out from the seventeenth floor and pick them up," said Kate brusquely.

Once at the hospital, she realized that the doctors and the nursing staff had set up their own screen around Kim. It took a call to Dr. Neibuhr for her to get past the reception desk. When she reached Room 545, she saw what seemed like an oversize bed containing the tiny, almost yellow body of Jason. With her back to Kate, seated on the edge of the bed, in dungarees and a blue sweater, was Kim. She held Jason's left hand; the right hand was attached to an intravenous drip. Occasionally Kim wiped the child's forehead with a cloth, or rested her hand on his cheek. Wires were attached to his chest and the base of his skull. A machine in the corner let out a muted beep.

Kim did not turn at the sound of the door, nor at Kate's footsteps, when she walked over to the tray at the foot of the bed and set down the flowers. At first she thought it was a nurse checking Jason one more time, saying nothing. But then Kim smelled the familiar scent as Kate stepped up behind her and touched her shoulder. Kim moved her hand slowly from Jason's so it lay on top of Kate's, and then in almost a violent movement, she dropped the damp cloth and swung around, plunging her face into Kate's chest. Hanging on, as if Kate were a life raft in a storm, Kim was convulsed with sobs.

After a time, the tears stopped, and Kate sat on the bed beside Kim, her arms still around her. Tremors still shook Kim's body, and Kate was beginning to wonder if she should call a nurse when Kim seemed to relax a little in her arms and her breathing became more regular.

She said in a quiet, almost dead voice, "I can't take it. I can't lose him, Kate. I can't. Don't let them take him away from me."

Kate stroked Kim's hair. "It's going to be okay, Kim. It's going to be okay." When Kim began to sob again, Kate said, "Come on, let's see if we can get some circulation moving in those legs." Tossing her coat onto a chair, she put her arm around Kim's waist and walked her up and down the small room.

Kim walked stiffly as if she had been frozen on the bed for twelve hours. The only sound, as they walked, was the monitor's beep.

Once they stopped at the foot of the bed, and Kim saw the lilies for the first time. "These are the same flowers that were in the hotel suite when we first came to Boston. What are they?"

"Rubrum lilies. In biblical times, they were known as the flowers of everlasting life, everlasting love. They've always brought me good luck."

At that moment, a nurse walked into the room. "Miss Winston, you have a call at the desk from Dr. Cerci. He says he's calling from abroad and that it's urgent that he talk with you."

"Oh, now it's urgent, is it? Tell him he's a little too late."

"Excuse me, Miss Winston, but he said it was imperative."

"Kim," Kate said, "he may know something. He may have noticed something."

"He made me wait too long, maybe hopelessly long. He should have known Jason was really sick, but he thought I was just being overprotective." She suddenly burst into sobs again. "My son is *dying*, Kate. Am I being overprotective?"

Kate put her arms around Kim, holding her tightly. "No one would blame you for closing any doors on Chris but don't close them on Jason."

Kim said, "You're right," and went out of the room to the phone at the nurse's station.

When she was alone with the boy, Kate took his hand in her own, gently caressing his small, clean fingers. She remembered how they had held hands together on the raft just a few months ago, the purpose supposedly to keep the other from falling off while they both exchanged stories. And she remembered how Jonathan seemed so close to the boy, how well the two of them got along. She heard the door open behind her, and was surprised when she heard men's voices. Then she realized one of them was her husband. He was talking to a man in deep tones, interrupting the monotone of the conversation only long enough to say, "I think I saw the mother on the phone. This is my wife."

Kate nodded to the other physician and leaned back against her husband. Jonathan rubbed her back thinking he had rarely seen his wife in such emotional pain—only that time he'd been so stupid and she'd caught him. Stupid! Cruel! But she had refused to see him for many days after that, even after she'd lost their child. The doctor had told him that she'd cried incessantly but to him, her own husband, she showed only a marble coldness, a stiff control and a list of demands.

Still, he loved her and was glad they'd moved to Boston and things had held together. Watching her crying now, holding the child's hand, Jonathan was at a loss to know how to behave. He approached her gingerly, and slowly put his arms around her.

They were both experiencing the same feeling. A woman who was one of the major figures in the most powerful existing medium was helpless in this situation. And a man who daily made the difference between life and death for the gravely ill was also helpless. With all their power, they were both impotent.

"Jon, Jon, do something, please. He's just slipping away."

"Everything's being done, darling," Jonathan said, looking down at the comatose child who just a few weeks before had been giddy with joy when Jonathan put a surgeon's mask over his face.

"There has to be more that can be done," Kate said, anger in her voice.

"We can't do anything until we get that lab result, and another CT is taken, but they don't want to move him now."

"Why? Why wait?"

"Because if the tests show he'll respond to antibiotics, then they want to get that inflammation down as soon as possible. If there's an abscess, there's really little that anybody can do."

Kim had come back into the room. "Stop it! Don't say that! You're supposed to be a superior surgeon and you said Neibuhr's the best in the field. Don't give me that 'little anybody can do' business. *Do* something."

Jonathan went to her and took her hand, saying, "Kim, there are many ways it can go." His tone was calm, professional, noncommittal, but when she cried out in exasperation, he shrugged and said, "All right. Here are the facts. The worst that could happen is that the lab results will come back, and we will find out that it is a strain of meningitis that does not respond to antibiotics, that the spinal cord and brain are already afflicted. The disease will move rapidly to the lungs and heart valves and Jason will die within a few days." Kate had seen this side of Jonathan before, the completely detached doctor giving a fatal diagnosis. When he explained certain cases to her, this was how he talked: as if the patient were an eggplant. He said it was the only way he could keep his sanity.

Kim was watching him as if he were a snake and she a mesmerized small animal awaiting the strike.

Jonathan continued. "If the test results show it is bacterial, then we have a chance. If it's not too late, if it hasn't gone too far, we start pouring broad-spectrum, powerful antibiotics into him intravenously and he should come out of this coma."

"So that's what we hope for?" asked Kim.

"Yes, but there is the other problem: the potential abscess. If there is one, it will prove fatal unless removed. And it is not a simple surgical procedure. It is not the type of operation surgeons like to take on. It has a very high risk factor."

"Would you do it?" The question sounded more like a prayer.

"Generally, it's bad practice to operate on someone you know—and love."

"But you're the best. I know that. Won't you do it?"

"If Jason's team of physicians requests it, then yes, Kim, I will. But let's hope it doesn't get to that."

"If it is bacterial, and even if he does respond . . . and this is forgetting about the abscess, is there a chance of paralysis or some impairment?"

"Yes, there is that risk," Jonathan said, his voice now strained. "It's all a matter of time. How far it's traveled. How quickly he responds."

Suddenly Kim screamed and shouted. "Well, where are the damn test results? What's taking them so long?"

Jonathan stepped forward and took Kim in his arms. Kate moved in front of them, rubbing Kim's shoulder, trying to soothe her.

Jonathan said, "Let me check on where those results are, Kim. It's just about time for them to be ready."

Kim seemed to notice Kate's presence then. "You don't have to wait," she said.

"Yes, I do." They sat in silence, Kim with one hand on Jason's shoulder, her other hand absently on Kate's as it lay on Jason's hand.

"Is Chris coming back?" Kate asked.

"I told him not to, not at this point anyway. And to tell you the truth, I don't care if he never returns."

"He must be very upset, Kim."

"He is, and he should be. He knows he was wrong. I'll never forgive him for this. Even if Jason pulls through without a scar, I'll never forgive Chris. I'll never trust him again."

"What about other family? Your mother and father? Jason's grandparents? Don't you want to send for someone?"

Kim shook her head. "I just have my two brothers but we're not close. It's just Jason and me . . . and of course Maggie."

"You know that Jonathan and I will always be here for you," Kate said. "You can . . ." Kate never finished the sentence. The bed began jerking violently. At first, Kate thought the whole room was being jolted. Then she realized it was coming from Jason. His body was twisting in convulsions. His abdomen stretched up out of the bed, and then his head jumped in a violent jerking. Kim seemed paralyzed for a moment. Kate pushed the call button and began screaming for a doctor. The scream brought Kim back to reality and she threw herself across her son's chest, holding his head. Kate remembered Jonathan's words about movement and she, too, lay across the lower part of Jason's body.

The intravenous pole and bottle had gone crashing to the floor, but no one seemed to be responding to the screams. Then suddenly Jonathan came running in, saw what was happening and flung the door open wide, yelling "Code! Stat! Five-four-five." Then he was over at the side of the bed, his hand in Jason's mouth, grabbing for his tongue. The room filled with people and machines, and Kate and Kim were pulled to one side.

Kim was shaking as if she herself were in convulsions but she kept her eyes on the swarm of people around Jason's bed. Jonathan was obviously leading them, preparing to apply the electric shock to revive what must now be Jason's failing heart.

"I've been here before, Kate," Kim whispered to Kate, clinging to her hand. "I can't go through it again. I can't. I won't survive this time."

"He's going to survive, and so will you," said Kate firmly. "My husband's a great physician."

At that moment, Jonathan said loudly and imperiously, "Okay, clear the area." Nurses, doctors and technicians moved away from the bed and Jonathan applied child-size paddles to the sides of Jason's chest.

"Now!" Jason's body jumped from the shock and Jonathan studied the monitor to his side.

"Again. Back . . ."

"Oh, God," came a wail from the corner as Kim realized that Jason was in fact dying. His heart would not respond. Kate tightened her grip on Kim, feeling her own terror rise.

"Now!" Neither Kate nor Kim looked this time. Then, above Kim's soft sobbing, Kate heard Jonathan giving additional orders. She looked up at him, and from across the room, he gave her a faint smile. The nurse was placing an oxygen mask on Jason's face as Kate said, "Kim, he's breathing. He's back. You didn't lose him."

"Oh, thank God." She tried to get up and move to Jason, but Kate held her back.

"They're still working on him. Give them space."

Jonathan had come to them and was kneeling beside them. "Listen, Kim, I'm going to try to reach Neibuhr. So far we haven't had much success." His face was strained and serious. "I want to start Jason on antibiotics. On ampicillin and chloramphenicol. Those are the drugs he'd be on for bacterial meningitis. I know we don't have the test results back, but these drugs will not hurt him and he's acting more and more like it is bacterial. And it seems to be spreading to the heart valves. I don't want to risk another attack like this." He paused and touched Kim's cheek. "He barely made it through this one. We've got to start destroying the bacteria." He looked at her eyes and saw only fear. "I know Neibuhr is the attending physician. Do you want to wait for him?"

"Jonathan," said Kim, as if she was being choked, "do whatever you think is best! Do anything you can to save my son!"

Jonathan went quickly out of the room shouting commands, and, a moment later, returned with a tray of syringes. A nurse immediately began reinserting an intravenous line into Jason. Jonathan himself put several injections into Jason, then watched the nurse add a separate plastic pouch to the liquid already going into Jason's intravenous line. Then the nurses left, and Jonathan sat down on a chair next to the bed.

Where the hell is Neibuhr? Jonathan asked himself. But he knew the answer. It had been obvious from the first. Neibuhr didn't like the fact that he was dealing with Kim Winston's child who was desperately sick and might die. Bad publicity. No, Neibuhr had taken a walk on this one. And the imbeciles in the lab! Jonathan had found out they had not started the culture until the spinal fluid had been sitting there for two hours. Two hours lost. And it could mean Jason's life. And what if he himself hadn't been on the floor when Jason had gone into a seizure? It was only the expertise of the Code Team and his own appearance at just the right time that had saved Jason. So far. And what if his own last-minute gamble didn't work? He had given Jason far more than the normal dosage of drugs. But he knew that it was the only hope Jason had. Now, it was just a matter of waiting to make sure that he did not have another seizure and praying the antibiotics would kick in soon enough. Poor Kim, he thought, so beautiful even in her suffering.

The two women stayed in the room while the nurses came and went. At one point, a nurse walked to where Kate sat and said, "Mrs. Marchand?"

"Yes."

"There's a Richard Blistick on the phone outside who says it's very important that he talk to you."

"Tell him I'll call him later, but right now, all inquiries should go through the hospital. Is the press bothering the hospital?"

"We've been inundated with inquiries from all over the country. And there are more flowers and toys at the front desk than we've seen since we had the Kennedy boy in here."

"Tell the hospital staff how much Miss Winston appreciates their help. And ask them, please, to be as guarded as possible with the press."

Almost as soon as the nurse left the room, Jonathan returned. Kim ran to him and put her hands on his shoulders. "What?" she asked. "What did the tests show?"

"Good news," Kate interrupted, in an animated tone. "I can see it on your face."

"Yes. We have the lab results. It *is* bacterial meningitis."

"Oh, Jon, thank God you were here. Thank God for you." Kim had tears in her eyes. "You were right to give him the antibiotics and not to wait. Oh, thank God." The tears of relief came quickly as Jonathan pulled her into his open arms. "Thank you. Thank you," she was saying again and again.

"We're not out of the woods. He's still in a deep coma. We still don't know about that abscess. And we don't know how much damage has already been done to the spinal cord and brain."

Kim moved back to Jason's bed and began stroking his cheek and forehead. "He's still burning up," she said. "But Jonathan, thanks to you I feel hope now."

"Did I ever tell you how much I love you, Doctor?" Kate asked, from her chair.

"You have, but keep it coming," Jonathan said. "A man can't get enough of that." Kate came and kissed him, and Jonathan said, "You should get some rest, Mrs. Marchand. You still have a television station to run, you know."

Kate saw the frightened look on Kim's face and said, "No, I'll stay."

"Look, darling," Jonathan said, "I have early surgery tomorrow and it's already late. I checked with the superintendent of nurses and she said they'll set up a cot in here for Kim and let me stay in the resident's quarters."

Kate started to object, then saw the relief in Kim's eyes. "Okay," she said, "but you'd better ask Dr. Marchand here what his bill's going to be, Kim. LYM's policy certainly doesn't cover the services of a live-in neurosurgeon. I should know that."

Jonathan said, "Let me walk you out, Kate. I need to stretch my legs." Outside in the hallway, he leaned against the wall and sighed. "It really doesn't seem fair that she should have to go through this twice in her life."

"What do you mean?"

"Kate, her son is very sick."

"But you said that now that he has the antibiotics, we can hope for a response."

"You saw how violent that seizure was, Kate. His whole body. His brain. Everything is inflamed." He banged the clipboard of Jason's record against the wall. "It has to have moved into his lungs."

"What are you saying?"

"You know what I'm saying. Jason may be dying. There's a good chance it's too late, that his lungs will just stop functioning. At some point, he may very calmly stop breathing." His last sentence was spoken tearfully, and he held his wife close against him. Finally, Kate pulled a tear-stained face away from his chest.

"Shouldn't I stay?"

"Forgive me, dear, but I think one of us is enough and my presence is probably more helpful now."

10

Jonathan had left for his own hospital by the time Kate arrived in the morning.

"Long night, I'll bet," she said to Kim. "When did that arrive? The oxygen?"

"Right after you left. First, they gave him oxygen, then plasma. Then more electric shocks for the heart. But nothing helps. He just lies there like he's already dead."

"Kim, you can't give up hope yet," Kate said, trying to sound firm and sure.

"How do I know he's not already dead? He hit his head awfully hard fooling around with Chris, and he's been in this coma for over twenty-four hours. He may never come out. Oh, God, how can I stand it? He was so happy here. He loved the townhouse, the water, the planes. He had made new friends and he was finally getting over David's death. The nightmares had stopped. He had even cut down on the number of David's pictures in his room."

Kim gasped. "Is that what I have to look forward to? Pictures of my son to put next to his father's picture on the mantel? My son's ashes to scatter with his father's? My whole life over, emptied out?"

"No, Kim, no. Stop it. It's not going to be that way. We're going to make it. Jason will make it. Now believe that. Pray for that. Don't give up." And then, in a very calm voice, Kate said, "Here, I brought you a change of clothes. I'm larger than you but this sweater is, like they say, "one size fits all," and the pants have always been too tight for me." Kate laughed. "As to this article, well, I don't imagine it will matter." Kate held up a pair of very skimpy string underpants. "I thought they'd give you a lift."

Kim smiled for the first time. "Doesn't look like there's enough cloth there to lift anything, ma'am."

Kate's presence in the room seemed to allow Kim to relax her vigil. After she had changed her clothes she lay down on the cot and, within minutes, fell into a restless sleep. As soon as she saw that happen, Kate turned to keep watch over the sleeping boy, as if taking his mother's place. Jason lay still, his face waxen, the only sign he was still alive the continued action of the monitor. But then she saw a movement in his almost transparent eyelids. She blinked, then saw it again—the ever so slight movement of Jason's left eyelid. She thought, it's just a twitch, don't wake Kim. But then the fluttering became stronger and Kate was sure she saw Jason's head move slightly on the pillow.

"Kim, Kim," she called softly, and when Kim sat up, alarmed, Kate said only, "Look at him."

Kim turned towards Jason. First she shook her head for fear her eyes were playing tricks, but soon they could both see Jason's eyes moving behind his eyelids. His head was turning from side to side. Kim leaned forward, Jason's head cupped in both her hands. Her thumbs and fingers were caressing his cheeks, the creases by his eyelids. "Chase, Chase . . . it's Mommy. Wake up, Chase. Come on, wake up. I love you, baby. I love you."

Then, as if in a slow-motion movie, Jason's eyelids slowly raised. His brilliant blue eyes seemed to have a film across them and, like a blind man, he did not seem to see or focus. But then the boy blinked several times and the eyes came alive with recognition. "Mommy?" His voice was hoarse. "Mommy? Are you there?"

Kim fell to the floor beside Jason, weeping and saying his name. Kate also wept. At that moment, the door opened and Jonathan, seeing the crying women, rushed to the bedside.

"What happened? What happened? Did you try the oxygen?" Jonathan had shoved Kim and his wife aside to get near the child.

"It's all right, darling. It's all right. Jason is awake. He recognized Kim."

"What?" Incredulity was written on Jonathan's face but it was quickly replaced by a broad smile. "Okay you two faith healers, let a pro have a look."

"Hi, Jonathan," Jason said, as if he had just encountered him in a corridor at school.

"Hi, yourself. Where you been?"

"I dunno. Where have I been?"

"You've been sick. You're in the hospital now." Jonathan was busy touching the boy's face, tapping on his chest, his stomach. "My God," he said, turning to Kim and Kate, "the fever is down, and his lungs seem clear." He put the stethoscope to Jason's chest again. "His heart is a little weak, but it's okay."

"Now, Jason, I want you to move your neck, softly, easy does it." Jason did, seemingly with ease. "Did that hurt?"

"Not as much as before. And the headache isn't so bad as before."

"Okay, try to move your legs." Jonathan pulled back the sheet and the three stared at the small, pale legs. First, his toes moved a little, then his leg. But they did not move very far.

"It kind of hurts," the child said, the pain showing in his face.

"I expect it will for a while," Jonathan said, covering him again and sitting beside him. "You have a bug in your system that we're trying to get rid of. And to help you, you're going to have to stay in this hospital for a while until the medicine does its job. And before you know it, you'll be up and running around."

Kim said quietly, "What about the abscess?"

"Kim, I don't think he would have pulled through that seizure if there had been an abscess. He'd be in a lot more pain, and his mind wouldn't be so clear." He took Kim's hand in his. "I don't know how it happened. To tell the truth, I didn't think it would end this way. All the odds were against him."

Kim shook and reached for her son's hand.

"You've won this one, Kim. You and Jason have won this one." Jonathan leaned over and kissed the boy, who hung his arms around the physician's neck.

"Were you my doctor, Jonathan?"

"Yes, he was," Kim said. "And he got to you just in time."

"You mean, you thought you might lose me like we lost Daddy?"

Kim nodded her head.

"You shouldn't have worried, Mom. I'd never make you feel sad like that again."

As mother and son embraced, Jonathan turned to his wife and, holding her close, walked silently from the room.

11

TWO DAYS LATER KATE SAT AT HER DESK AND PATIENTLY listened to the mayor and the head of the Boston Redevelopment Authority discuss the importance of WLYM's involvement in the cleanup of Boston's waterfront.

Kate said, "I agree with you that we need an expanded effort to clean up both of the wharves and the pollution in the harbor, but what exactly do you want *me* to do?"

The mayor spoke. "Well, we all know the great impact Kim Winston's documentary had on the juvenile justice system here. And since she lives on Union Wharf, we thought she might have a special interest in it."

So that's what this is all about, Kate thought. They want to use Kim's expertise and popularity to spearhead this project. She half-listened to the two men as her mind wandered to Kim herself. When Kate had arrived at the hospital the night before, Kim had gone for a walk. Kate had spent a half hour with Jason and Maggie. Apparently Jason had dozed off and on all day and Kim had kept her vigil. Only late in the afternoon had Maggie been able to convince her to go out for some air.

On his way to meet Kate at the hospital, Jonathan had stopped at a bicycle shop and bought Jason a big-wheel tough-rider bike, the kind Jason had said he wanted from Santa Claus when he and Jonathan were touring New England General a few weeks before. Jonathan picked one that had all the proper pads so the boy wouldn't hurt himself, but also the one with everything from a battery-operated horn to real leather tassels. He felt like he was selecting a new Porsche and was only mildly surprised that a child's two-wheel bike could cost almost three hundred dollars.

When Jonathan wheeled the bike into the hospital room, Maggie had to restrain Jason from jumping out of his bed. He asked Jonathan to bend down so he could kiss him and then he showed off to them both how he could move his legs a little further and with less pain. And with the bike next to his bed and his hand on the black and red handlebars, he talked about how, more than ever, he wanted to be a doctor when he grew up.

Kate left a note with Maggie for Kim that simply said they had come by and were happy to see Jason doing so well. Then Kate had written: "Have attached this wire service story so you will see that the children's screams stopped the other night. Call if you need anything. Kate." The wire service story announced that federal agents had shut down the Wilkins Unit and that all the children had been moved to private hospitals.

On the way home, Kate and Jonathan were so exhausted they decided to stop for pizza and beer. In a small backroad tavern, they slid into a rear booth, and like teenage lovers, sat side by side and held hands, drank beer and ate gooey pizza with extra cheese. Then, while Jonathan was paying the bill, the waitress said to Kate, "Excuse me, but aren't you that woman with the television station? How's Kim Winston's little boy?"

Kate looked directly into the young woman's eyes. "Yes, I am and he's doing just fine." Then she smiled, took Jonathan's arm and they quickly exited.

"Usually in those situations you put on your Southern drawl," Jonathan said.

"This was different," Kate said. "I wanted to share the happy ending."

Despite their weariness, they made passionate love that night. They were quieter than usual, not making their usual post-lovemaking jokes and when they fell asleep in the comfort of each other's arms, Kate wondered if, finally, the scar she bore from her husband's affair was healed. For the first time, it seemed as if the gloom in her heart might lift.

Now, as she sat in her office, still nodding as the two men spoke, she felt the familiar chill pass over her, the familiar suspicions. Sometimes she felt she could never trust Jonathan again. Sometimes, to this day, she had all she could do—when the image of his body over that woman's clouded her vision—to keep from calling the hospital to see if her husband was indeed "with a patient."

Now she decided that she had half-heard enough of this conversation about the waterfront and began an explanation of how station policy forbids any employee to be a spokesperson for any cause. Perhaps, she added, they could work something out so that Kim could do some public service announcements on behalf of the Waterfront Revitalization and Cleanup.

As they were speaking, Kim had come to Diana's desk outside Kate's office. "Is she in?" Kim asked. "I know I shouldn't just pop up here like this. I hear people wait months for an appointment with her. Actually, I'm not even sure if she's in town today."

"Some people do wait months," replied Diana, "but I'm sure she'd like to see you. She's got people with her now, and then . . ." Diana looked at the large schedule to one side of her desk, "she'll be free for a few minutes—which if she spends with you means I won't have to take dictation nonstop."

Kim stepped around to the back of Diana's desk. "My God, look at the appointments she goes through each day."

"Oh, what's written down is nothing," Diana said. "She jams in twice as many things as are booked."

"She must have been tired the other day, after leaving the hospital so late."

"I'm sure she must have been tired, but no one would have noticed it. She went through the day just like any other. Didn't stop for a moment. She seemed no worse for wear," said Diana calmly. "Anyway, you're the mother; you're the one who should be weary and dragging. You look like you're ready to go on the air."

Kim was dressed in a pearl gray dress, with a white stripe at the neck and cuffs.

"I am. I'm back on tonight. Maggie's with Jason when I'm not there and it doesn't do him any good when I sit around and worry. He's coming along just fine."

At that moment the light went on on Diana's desk.

"What's that?" inquired Kim. "A secret signal from the allies?"

"That's supposed to be something only I see, because only I'm supposed to be in back of my desk."

"Oops, sorry," smiled Kim, moving swiftly to the front of Diana's desk.

Diana picked up the phone and buzzed Kate's intercom. "Sorry to bother you, Kate, but the news director says there is a problem with tonight's broadcast that needs your immediate attention." Diana nodded her head at Kate's reply, and then looked up at Kim. "Lest they think you may be the problem and we start more rumors, why don't you wait in the other room until they're gone?" Diana pointed to a small room in back of her and Kim saluted and quickly walked into it.

She soon heard two voices thanking Kate for her cooperation and congratulating her on all she had done for the city. Kate briskly said thank you, the men left and Kate began giving instructions to Diana about a number of things—from sales notices to a promotional graphic that should be replaced. Kim was amazed that this was the same woman who had held her and comforted her only a few days before.

"I'll see Phil Bernelli in fifteen minutes, but I'd like not to be disturbed before then." Kate's voice was a staccato instrument. Kim heard the door close and looked down at the bag she was carrying and thought how foolish she was to think she could just walk into Katherine Marchand's office. The bottom line remained: Kim was Katherine Marchand's property, a prized piece of property. That's all. Kim stepped out to Diana's desk.

"Well, I guess that ends that," she said. "Just tell her I stopped by and am returning to the air. And thank her and Jonathan for the bike."

"What's the matter with you?" Diana looked at her quizzically, then understood. "You think just because she doesn't want to talk to the mayor, she doesn't want to see you? You have a lot to learn about her."

Diana buzzed the intercom so Kim could hear. "I don't suppose you'd take an interruption from the mother of the kid who you bought that flashy bike for?"

Kate's voice came over the intercom, "Of course I will. I was just going to call her. What line is she on? Is she all right?"

"Why don't you judge for yourself? She's right here." Diana winked at Kim and nodded towards the large door. Kate was pushing some notes aside on her desk when Kim came in. She noted her anchorwoman's careful grooming, her complete control. She looks like a million dollars, Kate thought, despite her ordeal.

Kate asked, "Is Jason okay? Are you okay?"

"Yes, thank you, we're both fine."

And then, in a movement neither woman had anticipated, they walked toward each other and tenderly embraced. And though neither of them was given to casual hugging, it seemed perfectly natural to them, now, after what they had been through together.

"I wanted to thank you for everything, for that bike which is the answer to my son's dreams and for that huge donation I've just learned you made to the St. Marten's Children's Research Fund."

"No need for thanks. The bike was Jonathan's gift to his pal Jason and how I donate my money is, after all. . . ."

Kim laughingly interrupted, "I know, I know, your own business. Luckily I've learned something more about you or that statement would really intimidate me." Kim then said shyly, "Kate, there's no way I can repay you, but I did want to give you a little token. . . ."

"Not necessary," Kate said brusquely.

"No, but fun. I found out from the pro at your club what Jonathan's grip size is and sweet-talked the man into stringing a snazzy graphite Head TXP for him. He's even going to sneak it into Jonathan's locker so he'll find it there this afternoon."

"Jonathan's always talking about the advantage people have over him because he hasn't gotten around to getting a new racket. He'll be thrilled. That was a really extravagant gift, Kim."

"Nothing compared to what I owe that man. I'd do anything for him—after he saved Jason's life. And for you, Kate, well, I've noticed you never wear a bracelet. I hope that isn't because you don't like them." She handed Kate a square leather box and watched Kate's face attentively as she opened it.

In the box lay a wide gold circlet, with a surface that had been richly etched as well as embossed. It had the look of an ancient Egyptian artifact but the pattern the goldsmith had devised was abstract, intriguing.

Kate looked at Kim, her face showing her delight. "It's the most beautiful thing I've ever seen. It's absolutely unique."

"Like you," Kim said. "Like you."

"Thank you, Kim. You're one of the few people in the world whose compliments I value." Then, abruptly, she said, "Tell me, what are your plans?"

"I spoke with Andrew this morning. I need to get back in the saddle. And we worked it out so I'll do just the basic anchoring for a while. That way I can still spend time with Jason. Is that all right with you?''

''Of course it is, but are you sure you're ready?''

''Yes, and there are other reasons,'' Kim said. ''I need to stop dwelling on these last few weeks and how . . . how I almost lost my baby.'' Kim paused, then continued, ''And secondly, Chris is returning to town, and I don't want to deal with that now. I'm better off working and not worrying about my own life.''

''Well, I understand that,'' said Kate, sitting up, ''but maybe this weekend you can get away from it all somewhere, get a decent rest. Think things over. Jonathan and I will visit Jason. And Maggie's here.''

''That *is* what I need. If I were in New York, I'd find a friend and head out for the Island. Maybe I'll go down to Martha's Vineyard.''

Kate thought for a moment, and then said, ''I know what you should do. Remember how I told you there was a place I get away to? Just myself?''

''Yes, I remember. You don't even take Jonathan,'' Kim smiled.

''Right again. But listen, it's a lovely old house right on the ocean in Rockport. I'll have the caretaker stock it for you. You can relax by the fire, walk the beach, read a book, think, sleep, get drunk, whatever you like. It's completely secluded. You'll have plenty of privacy, especially this time of year.''

''No, Kate, I couldn't invade your retreat.''

''Kim, you need it. And why go all the way to the Vineyard? This is just forty-five minutes away.''

''Kate, you're my boss. I can't use your home like that.''

''Well, I would hope you wouldn't make a major announcement about it,'' said Kate firmly, and then even more firmly, ''And I am your boss, and maybe I'm ordering you to do this . . . for yourself, and also for the station. We need you in top shape around here.''

''It does sound wonderful,'' said Kim hesitantly. ''But, to be frank, I'm not so sure I want to be completely alone.''

''Well, how about the company of a bad-mannered old lady with a bad back?''

''Sounds awful,'' Kim said. ''But I was hoping you'd come.''

''Actually I could use the time off myself. I'll stay out of your way. There's plenty of room for two people to be completely separate up there but, if you need someone to listen or to share a glass of wine with you—I'll be there.''

"Kate, it sounds wonderful but are you sure you want to do this?''

"You can believe I wouldn't do it if I didn't want to. Jonathan can get his fill of tennis on his own. You and I can meet at nine o'clock on Saturday at the hospital, say our goodbyes and be on our way.''

Kate got to the hospital first on Saturday morning. After she'd greeted Jason and admired his bicycle still another time, she said, "I'm going away this weekend but Jonathan said to tell you not to eat lunch today.''

The boy's chin trembled. "More tests? Do I have to have more?''

"No, silly,'' Kate said. "He just wants you to wait for him. He's going to take you to a special place in the hospital today for lunch.''

"Where?''

"The *doctor's* cafeteria.''

"Oh, *neat*! My mom's going away too. To Stoneport.''

Kate laughed and said, "You mean *Rockport*.''

"Nope. That must be some other place. *My* mom's going to Stoneport.''

"Okay. Okay. I'll just have to get used to the name. Anyhow is it all right with you if she goes?''

"Sure, Mom needs a rest. You know I gave her a bad scare. And she really doesn't like hospitals that much.'' His voice lightened. "Anyway, Maggie's bringing some of my friends this afternoon. And Jonathan will be here and he says next week I'll be able to go home.''

Kim and Maggie arrived and after giving Maggie the phone number the two women left.

Kim was glad for the seat belt as they drove and glad too for the car's low center of gravity. As soon as they'd left the city, Kate's foot went down hard on the accelerator and seemed barely to touch the brake even on the curves. At one point, Kate leaned over and patted Kim's leg. "There's only one brake in this heap. And I've got it. You keep stamping down on that imaginary one, your foot's going to go right through the floor.''

Kim said crossly, "Sorry. But could you slow down? I'm not sure my insurance policy's in order.''

"I'm the one who should be sorry,'' Kate said and, pointing

to the speedometer said, "Under sixty-five from now on, I promise. Because of my back, I've had to give up skiing and tennis, so this and swimming are the only athletics I've got left."

They had turned onto Route 1 and after a while Kate made a sharp left turn. "There's the ocean now. I've got my life fixed so it's never far away. Wait till you see Rockport. The ocean's right in your life there."

When they got to the house Kim said, "It's *so* beautiful but it's a completely different side of you, so different from Dover or your office."

"Of course it's different. It's the place I step out of the fast lane. And . . ." Kate winked, "we begin with the Pines ritual. She took a bottle of wine from where it lay on its side in the refrigerator. Glasses stood chilling stem side up, on the rack beside it.

"Mr. Murphy rides again," Kate said, "and thank God."

She told Kim about the caretaker as they went out to the deck. The December sun was almost hot on the well-protected deck and the lounge seats felt warm to the touch.

"Mmm, Kate, this is heaven. Makes me forget all my problems."

"Are they so bad, now that Jason's better?"

"Of course not. But Kate, can I ask you something?"

"Only if you don't sound so grave."

"Sorry. It's about Chris. Did Jonathan mention anything to you about whether or not he thought Chris had used bad judgment in not having me get Chase to the hospital sooner?"

"Kim, I'll be very honest with you. Jonathan and I are very close, but there are certain things he just will not talk to me about, although I know they're there. Even if I asked him directly—and in a way I did—whether Chris had erred, he wouldn't tell me. Especially in this situation, he would not want to prejudice me, and perhaps you, against Chris. He believes it was a difficult thing to diagnose."

"And what do you think?"

"I'm not a doctor."

"Please."

"When Jonathan first told me, I was livid. Even I know a fever and a stiff neck often mean meningitis. If anything had happened to Jason, I'm afraid I would have had a hard time not killing Chris. But Kim," Kate touched Kim's elbow, "I also believe that Chris *was* trying to protect you. And sometimes when you love someone, you want to protect them too much.''

"And the result was a disaster. I think it *was* Chris's fault. You and Jonathan are so happy together, I don't think you can understand how it feels to be let down by someone you love— or were growing to love.''

Kate turned away as she felt the stab of Kim's words in her own heart. Let down? Kate thought. How about betrayed? She said aloud, "We all have things to get over, you know.''

They lay back quietly in their chaise lounges until, noticing that the wine was finished, Kate said, "I think I'm going to take advantage of this weather and stretch my legs on the beach. Would you like to join me? Or maybe you'd prefer some time alone?''

"I'd like to walk,'' Kim said, "but I don't want to intrude on your time, or your space.''

"I'll let you know when you do.''

They headed down the rocky path, moving gingerly. Kim stretched and tossed her hair in the sun, leaning back and saying thankfully, "Oh, God, free at last.'' Then with a shout, she went running along the beach, playing with the waves as they glided in and out. Kate watched for a moment, then began walking at her own pace. Above the sound of the surf, she could hear Kim shouting, laughing into the wind, and at times, misjudging a wave and running through the cold water as it drenched her ankles and calves.

After about ten minutes she came running back and tapped Kate on the shoulder, calling, "You're it.''

"I most definitely am not,'' Kate said, as they walked companionably together along the shore.

"Mind if I ask a work problem?''

"Shoot.''

"Do all my special series have to be in the Boston, New England area?''

"No, not at all,'' said Kate. "And I'd hope they wouldn't be. As long as it's a unique story or an investigative piece, you can go to Zimbabwe for all I care. I would have thought Andrew would have made that clear.'' Kim noticed that when she talked about work, Kate's tone and manner changed completely.

"I haven't had a chance to discuss it with him because of what life's been like these past weeks but I actually stumbled across this story in the cafeteria at St. Marten's Hospital. A woman was visiting a very sick Mexican boy. I overheard her talking to a man and then I asked her a few questions. It turns out the Mexican boy was there because he had been severely beaten while trying to cross the Mexican-American border. Only Children's had the means to save him, and for some reason the authorities got him out here. This woman was their contact."

"Who beat him? The border guards? I thought they were just supposed to stop the illegal aliens."

"That's just it." Kim's voice grew excited. "Right below San Diego is a place known as Dead Man's Valley, or something like that. All the aliens heading for work have to pass through it. And it's not the border guards who give them a rough time. It's the bandits."

"The bandits?" asked Kate.

"Yes, gangs of bandits that prey on the people going through this valley. They beat them, rob them, rape them and then leave them to be killed off by the rattlesnakes. *And*," she continued, her voice rising in anger, "the border guards turn their back on all this, and in fact condone it. Instead of stopping them, they often take bribes to allow the bandits access to people who are crossing, especially when they're returning from work at night and have money for their families. There are a lot of stories there, Kate."

"Go for it," said Kate firmly. "It sounds like a damn good story, from many different angles. Just be careful. It's going to be tough shooting tape in that valley. Make sure you find someone. . . ." She stopped. "I'm sorry, I'm not about to tell you how to do your work. You don't need my help. Just please be careful. I've spent enough time in the hospital with you already."

Late in the afternoon, Kim called Jason and was told, "I don't miss you yet, Mom. Call me tomorrow. Maybe I will then."

When she reported this dialogue to her hostess, Kate said, "Ungrateful wretch! Why don't you go have a little R and R and I'll try to get a little work done."

From the kitchen Kate could hear the soft chords of the piano in the living room. Though the instrument was kept in tune, no one had played it for a long time. Kate had played the piano throughout her childhood and the early part of her career, but then when she came to Boston, she never seemed to find the leisure for it. She had bought one for this house thinking that here, she would have the time. But the piano had remained unused, perhaps because she knew she would be rusty and cross with herself for not playing well. But the sound of the music cheered her as she paused in her work to look out over the darkening sea and watch the whitecaps roll rhythmically, almost in tune to the sounds coming from the house, on the edge of the rocks.

The music became a little louder and Kate tried to place it. She soon realized that Kim was playing the score from the movie *Chariots of Fire*. The score was brilliant, and as Kim played, the music grew louder and surer. Kate decided to go and sit by the fire to listen, but as soon as she stepped into the room and glanced at Kim, she knew she shouldn't make her presence known.

Kim sat perfectly erect over the keys of the piano, but her face was flushed and she was crying. Kate realized that Kim was playing the song Maggie had said she'd played at her husband's funeral. She went to sit beside her on the piano bench and gently placing her arms around the younger woman's shoulders, she said, "There's nothing wrong with crying. It may even help you to let David go, to finally set yourself free."

Later that afternoon, Kim said, "I want you to know how much I value your friendship, Kate. I know how unusual it is. What is it about the television industry? Friendships seem so fleeting and sometimes people can be so cruel."

"I know how you feel."

"You're going to tell me it's lonely at the top?"

"No, no more lonely than any other level in this industry." Kate put the fish in the oven and walked over to the small table to pick up her drink. "I've actually thought a great deal about it. Obviously one of the reasons is that it's such a competitive business. You always have to be one step ahead of the next person. It's also a very ego-oriented business, and the egos are generally so frail that people feel they have to keep proving something—to themselves, and to others. They become very self-centered and selfish. With a few exceptions, people in television are among the most insincere, insensitive people I know."

"Whew!" said Kim. "That's a pretty heavy indictment."

Kate looked out at the lighthouses across the channel. "I wish I could say I was exaggerating or being too hard, but I've seen far too many people hurt or destroyed by this industry. The business creates some real monsters." She rose from her chair and walked over to the refrigerator, taking some ice from the freezer. "Present company excepted, of course."

12

CHRIS WAS HOME, ANXIOUS ABOUT JASON, FRIGHTENED THAT he'd lost Kim. He had called from the airport the moment he arrived from Denmark and Kim had agreed to see him. She had planned carefully for their meeting and in a very calm, cold voice had told him, "I've thought it over carefully and I don't want to waste your time or mine on recriminations and the pros and cons of what should have been done for my son."

"Kim, don't shut me out. We have to discuss this."

"No, we don't. And I will not. On the other hand, Jason is very fond of you and I don't want him to feel that suddenly you're . . . cut off and out of our lives."

"And you? You and me? Doesn't that mean anything to you?"

In a much softer voice, Kim said, "Chris, I don't know what will happen to you and me. For now at least I do not want to be pushed. I would understand perfectly if it's not satisfactory to you for us to see each other with absolutely no commitments, but . . ."

"It's not what I want, Kim," Chris said, "but I want this to work. I want a chance to heal our relationship. What can I do to get us started again?"

Kim laughed. "Sounds like you're talking about an old outboard or something. In any case, I'm going to Albuquerque this week on a story I've been pursuing so any start-up will have to wait.''

Kim called Kate from the West Coast several days later.

"How's it going?'' Kate asked. Other than brief reports from Andrew, Kate had no real idea whether Kim had found what she was looking for.

"Well, we've finished shooting down here and we're going to head north and get some of the migrant farms now. The worst is behind us.''

"Is it good?'' Kate asked.

"Oh, it's good all right. I can't believe what animals there are in this world. We've made a few enemies of some people down here, including the San Diego Police Department. But if they were still my friends, that would mean I'd failed. And by the way, Willy and Ben have been marvelous.'' Kate knew Willy was one of the station's top cameramen, and assumed Ben was audio. "Willy is a little crazy. He'll go anywhere with that camera—which also got us into a little trouble.''

"What kind of trouble?''

"Well, we ended up renting a new recorder.'' She paused. "The other one seemed to have run into a bullet.''

"Christ, Kim, I thought you weren't going to take any unnecessary chances.''

"I didn't exactly plan it. We kind of got caught in the middle. I still don't know if it was the bandits, border patrol, or the police.''

"Was the tape destroyed?'' asked Kate.

"No, Boss, we saved the tape,'' answered Kim wearily.

"When are you returning?''

"Friday morning. That gives us three full days to wrap up out here—Federal officials and that sort of stuff. And the guys want to be back for the Christmas party Friday night.''

The Christmas party was all that Kate had feared it would be. The music was too loud and there seemed to be a never-ending, somewhat sickening, flow of food and booze. Kate wore a calf-length taupe dress, cut on the bias so it fell beautifully, as only custom-made clothes can. Her only jewelry was a lovely gold chain Jonathan had given her the first year they met, and the beautiful gold bracelet she'd received from Kim.

At the party's midpoint, Kate made a brief speech about the strides the station and its syndicates had made in the last year.

She gave the credit to "all of you before me who are dedicated to excellence and have no room in your personal or professional lives for mediocrity." Kate also thanked the staff for "so admirably pulling through the internal crisis that would have paralyzed a less dedicated group of individuals." It was understood that she was talking about the cocaine crisis.

Bill Halliday leaned down to Kim's ear. "You've got to admit it, the woman is in command. She knows it all. She's like a master puppeteer, a tough customer who gets exactly what she wants."

"I thought you liked her?" asked Kim, surprised.

"I do. I think she's terrific. I'm just glad I'm on the right side of her."

When Kate had finished talking and was surrounded by well-wishers, Bill pushed through them gracefully and reaching his target, smiled, bowed and led his employer onto the dance floor.

Kim watched quietly, thinking how some of Bill's graceful dance moves had to be hurting Kate's back, and as soon as the dance was over, she saw Kate move to a straight-backed chair in a corner of the room.

Kim went to Kate's side, saying, "You okay? Can I get you something?"

"No, just sit down beside me and make like we're having a very private conversation—while I do some quiet stretches."

As Kate slowly moved her head from side to side, she asked Kim, "Were you able to finish everything in California?"

"Yes and, to put it modestly, I think it's going to make a blockbuster of a ninety-minute documentary—and you'll be able to spin off a series besides."

Kate smiled. "Did someone put you in charge of programming when I wasn't looking?" She rose to leave. "We'll see you and *Chris* tomorrow night. Is that right?"

Kim shrugged. "So it seems."

Chris and Kim sat in a corner up against the wall of the large Ritz dining room. Away from the windows that overlooked the Boston Public Gardens, the table offered the most privacy in the room. The problem was getting to it. Although they had walked quickly, the fifty-foot walk to the table had exposed Kim to the entire dining room. Although she had been less visible in the last few weeks, her face had not been forgotten. In fact, if her mail was any indicator, Kim's popularity was hitting an all-time high. She had never known such recognition and, in fact, did not feel uncomfortable with it.

They ordered drinks and sat close together, obviously in harmony. It had been a nice day for both of them. The morning was spent Christmas shopping, trading Jason off to each other so each of them could pick gifts for Jason—or Jason for one of them. Later in the afternoon, Jason and Maggie had gone to a Christmas party in Southie and Chris and Kim had made love for the first time since Jason's illness. It was as if, despite the terms Kim had laid down, they were picking up some parts of their relationship.

"Jonathan said he thought they might be a little late. They were making an appearance at some benefit. Apparently this is one of his wife's favorite charities and she's on the board. But then that woman's on every board, it seems."

"When are you going to get over feeling that Kate is just some big brass automaton?"

"It's not far off the mark, is it? I mean I think she and Jonathan have a pretty good marriage but even so, there's something a little cold and ruthless about her. Jonathan, too, in a way. I don't know for sure but I think he had something going with a young resident earlier this year. Pretty girl, and smart."

"God, Chris, you have everything wrong. Naturally, people think that about him because he's so sexy and handsome. But he's really in love with Kate and, as for her, well, she's a generous friend beneath that exterior."

"And what an exterior! Turn around and watch this entrance."

Slowly Kim turned and, although she was accustomed to Kate's beauty, she was not prepared for what she saw. Kate's dark, shining hair had been pulled up and was held in place by diamond clips. Her makeup, brighter than usual, made her seem more youthful, more vibrant. Around her neck was a magnificent old choker, precious stones in a platinum setting in a design Marie Antoinette would have coveted. Her dress was stark black silk, the better to display her jewels as well as her long, beautifully contoured body. With his hand delicately touching her waist as they wove through the tables, Jonathan too was strikingly handsome in his dinner jacket. They bowed to people they knew as they traversed the room and the maitre d' led them along as if they were his exclusive property.

When they reached the table, Kim said, "You've given half

the women in this room indigestion, you look so beautiful, Kate."

"You don't look so bad yourself," Jonathan said. "When I was a kid, half my daydreams were about blond, blue-eyed girls in chiffon dresses."

"You, too?" Chris asked. "I thought Kim was the answer only to my dreams."

Kate said coolly, "Well my dream is going to be answered tomorrow when this good-looking guy and I fly off, alone at last, to St. Bart's. We're just going to swim and lie around and see absolutely no one."

"Except for the tennis pro, that is," Jonathan said.

They had ordered a sumptuous dinner and, as they talked, the courses were brought and the wine was poured with the Ritz Carlton's usual impeccable but unobtrusive service.

Kim said, "I envy you the weather. I'm taking Jason skiing but even with the hassles we had in southern California on this story, I sure appreciated that warm sun. I don't know if I'll ever get used to New England winters."

"Kate told me that you were in San Diego. How did it go?" Jonathan asked.

"At first, I thought it was going to be a nonstory," Kim said. "No one would say anything. But then one of my local contacts came through and a whole network of angry people were suddenly ready to open up." She leaned forward excitedly. "It is scandalous how the government border guards are not only breaking the law but are responsible for the injury and death of so many Mexicans."

"Death?" Jonathan asked incredulously.

"Yes, death. They support the bandits who work the border. They turn their backs—for a fee of course—and let them attack, mug, rape, and rob the people as they cross the border from their jobs in the fields.

"And, if you don't believe me, well, the camera never lies. And we have it all on tape." She paused and then angrily began again. "It's sickening the way lives are wasted out there."

"Yeah," Chris said, "especially if the life is yours."

"What do you mean?" Kate asked.

"Oh, don't worry, Kate," Kim said casually. "Just a few bullets fired to scare us off. I don't think they would really go after us. Although I'm sure they could have gotten a good price for our equipment."

Chris sat back, shaking his head. "Someone takes a couple shots at you and all you're concerned about is the equipment."

Kate laughed and said, "Listen, Chris, do you know how much one of those cameras costs?" Kim joined her laughter and Jonathan leaned over and patted Chris on the shoulder. "She's probably kidding, fella, though you can't be sure."

By the time Kim had finished her story, the dessert cart had arrived at their table. "Okay, everyone," Chris said, "Christmas comes but once a year . . . let's go for it! Kate, what will you have?"

Kate pointed to the Bouche Noel, the beautifully decorated Christmas log surrounded by meringue mushrooms so artfully rendered they might have been lying on the forest floor instead of the silver pastry platter. When the captain lifted his knife to cut a slice of the cake, Kate laughed. "No, no, just one of the mushrooms, please."

Jonathan groaned. "An iron will. My wife has an unbending iron will. And she expects everyone to be like her."

"Only the people I love, darling," Kate said quietly.

"I believe that's called blackmail," Jonathan responded. "In velvet gloves, but . . . all the same." He pointed to a tower of profiteroles on a crystal stand. "I'll have a few of those," he said to the waiting captain.

"With chocolate sauce, monsieur?"

"Why not? I'm going to get a bad grade anyhow, from Madame here. Might as well enjoy myself."

13

Cursing at the weather and still shaking snow from the upraised collar of her coat, Kate greeted Diana with a perfunctory "Happy New Year" and "It's time we relocated this operation to Maui."

"I'm ready anytime," Diana said. "How was your vacation?" At that moment, Mickey Merriam came struggling into the office carrying a large cardboard box. "Oh no!" cried Diana. "Not again, Kate!" Kate just smiled and gestured to where the young man should place the box. "Can't you ever go away and just do nothing? Relax, you know, like ordinary people?"

"I had a wonderful time. Don't I look refreshed?"

"Well, you do," said Diana, stooping over the box and picking through the first of numerous memos. "But I'll be damned if I know when you find the time."

"Without any interruptions, I can get done in four hours what sometimes takes me four days in the office," said Kate, going through the messages on her desk. "Speaking of which. . . ."

"Yes, as you requested. No appointments. You and I are locked in here for the day. But there are some calls you should make."

"I'll do that when you break for lunch."

"Oh, I get a lunch break?"

"Subject to cancellation," said Kate seriously. "Now, let's begin."

For the next four hours, Kate dictated memos, handed over rewritten proposals, recited already memorized editorials, and read the final draft of the annual report. After making the necessary corrections, she released Diana for lunch and began making her own phone calls. When Diana reentered the office, Kate explained in detail a new sales management effort that was to be launched in Europe, instructing Diana on exactly what material was to be made available. Then they went through the mail, scheduled meetings, and locked in place the final version of Kate's itinerary for the next two and a half months: trips to some of the smaller stations, appearances on the Coast, network meetings in New York, two overseas excursions and Jonathan's birthday all were listed.

"Diana, this is absurd," Kate said.

"It's very tight, but at each point, I asked you if someone else couldn't go in your stead. You delegated in very few places."

"Because there are very few places where anyone else can get what I need accomplished."

"End of argument."

"But are you sure," said Kate turning, "that I agreed to speak to the National Association of Television Programming Executives in San Francisco next month? They usually schedule that months in advance, and it's not the type of thing I do." She looked at Diana who was fidgeting with her pad and pencil. "In fact," she said sternly, "I'm having a lot of trouble remembering agreeing to this." She paused. "Diana?"

"You know, you'd think with everything on your mind, just one little thing might slip by," Diana said. "Well, I might as well confess: You had been in St. Bart's for only a few days and I thought it was too early to bother you. Paul Diamond from the executive board called and said they definitely wanted you to speak because of all the changes you've made in the industry. I told him you were away and I couldn't give him an answer till the first of the year but he also told me, completely off the record, that NATPE was probably going to give a special award to Kim for her work."

"Probably?" Kate asked. "All I can say is I just hope I don't end up watching the award go to someone other than Kimberly Winston." Kate shared a covert smile with Diana that said they both knew the award was going to Kim and Kate would be there to make Marchand Syndicates appear all powerful. Quickly, she looked at her watch. Five forty-five. "I'm going down to see Andrew. I'll see you in the morning."

"There's my dancing partner," said Bill to Kim, as he looked up from the copy he was correcting. They had both come out of makeup and were doing a last-minute check before air time. "Gosh, she looks good in a tan," said Bill, a slight whistle under his breath. "Of course, I bet she looks good in anything— or nothing."

"Bill!" said Kim. "A little respect for your superiors. Anyhow, there's a part of me that's glad she's home, running the store, especially with that Mexican story of mine soon to run."

Andrew Davis, after thanking Kate for his Christmas bonus, gave her a brief rundown on events on his floor. The new sportscaster was doing well. Kim's documentary was moving along quickly and he thought it might surpass the previous one. After discussing its progress, they decided on the Sunday night slot.

"You're going to have more trouble with the network," reminded Davis.

"I know, but I'll also win—if it's as good as you say it is." Kate looked at the date they had marked on the calendar in Andrew's office, and then called her office. "Damn," she said to her news director. "As I thought, I'll be in London at that time. We'll have to set up a contingency plan. I'll work out all the details with Diana and you be prepared to pump it up to another satellite if necessary, like we did last time. But this time, let's have it in the can a little earlier than a few hours before it airs."

"I'll make sure, Kate." He then filled her in on other series and specials the news was doing. As he took careful notes, she gave him numerous directives on subjects that should be investigated.

"What did you do, Kate," asked Andrew, "just lay on the beach and think of work for us to do?"

Kate went next to Steve Merriam's office. He was on the phone but signaled he'd be right with her. She noticed that Merriam, like herself, had spent the holidays in the sun.

When the phone call was over he rose to his feet. "This is a pleasure. You look well, Kate."

"And so do you, Steven." She smiled at the tan.

"Took the whole family to Jamaica. There's not much to sell over the holidays, Kate . . . at least not after them."

"I know, Steve. You don't have to apologize for taking a

vacation. I went through the sales sheets and I have to congratulate you. You've more than kept your part of the bargain.''

"To tell the truth, once we got organized, it wasn't that hard.''

Kate was pleased with Merriam's truthfulness. Perhaps a leopard could change its spots, she thought. "Any trouble selling the new documentary?''

"No trouble at all,''said Merriam. "Never have trouble selling Kim. She could probably sit there and read Greek and we'd still be able to sell her.''

The winter weeks went by quickly. Kate traveled a great deal, her power and influence growing daily. She found time for a few workouts at the club with her friend Deborah, but otherwise it was work, or short periods of time here and there with Jonathan. Numerous attempts had been made to set up dinners with Kim and Chris, or an afternoon with Jason, but either Kate's schedule, Kim's editing, or an emergency for Jonathan or Chris prevented it.

On the last Saturday in January, Kate was in New York meeting privately with individual board members of the network. Jonathan was home in Dover working on a medical talk he was to give in a few weeks.

He felt annoyed when the ring of the phone interrupted him. "Yes?" he asked crossly.

"It sounds like you were just bitten by a mad dog. Why don't you forget the phone rang, and I'll try again later?''

"Kim? Is that you? What can I do for you?''

"I was just calling to invite you and Kate out.''

"Kate's away, big deals cooking in New York—which I'm probably not supposed to talk about.''

"Oh, too bad,'' Kim said. "Actually I called because Jason has a hockey game out in Wellesley, and I thought we might stop by afterwards.''

"Never mind *afterwards*. I'm an old hockey player myself. Where's the rink, and what time?''

Within an hour, Jonathan had parked his car in front of the rink and walked into the chill of the ice arena. On the ice, two teams of well-padded and helmeted young boys were going through their practice, with a fair amount of difficulty.

"Jonathan, Jonathan, here I am! Over here!'' Jonathan saw a bulky blue-and-white uniform skating towards him, fast and slightly out of control. Then, with a thud, Jason's skates hit the boards and he fell in a heap on the ice.

"I still need to practice stopping," the boy said, "but I can skate real fast."

Jonathan said, "I bet you can. And you've gotten bigger too."

"Nah, silly, that's just my hockey pads."

"Keep your helmet on. We don't want any knocks on that head of yours."

"Don't worry, and I'm gonna get a goal for you. Gotta go." He jammed the plastic mouthpiece back into his mouth with a heavily gloved hand, and after steadying himself with his stick, skated off to rejoin his team.

Kim called to Jonathan then, and when he joined her he said, "I've just been talking to the future Bobby Orr."

The game began and they stood together by the side of the rink, looking through the wire mesh that separated the parents sitting in the bleachers from the players. Young bodies were skidding and colliding on the ice and the puck seemed propelled more by traffic accidents than by actual stick work. Jason was not the only one who could not stop. Most of the boys stopped by collision.

"Lucky they've got all that padding," Jonathan laughed.

"You should just try getting him dressed. It's a major feat." At that point, Jason, wearing a large 34 on the back of his jersey, broke away from a pileup and began skating wildly towards the opposite goal. Both Jonathan and Kim began shouting and encouraging. Unfortunately, Jason made it into the net, but the puck didn't.

A few minutes later Jason was again heading for the goal, in a whir of blue and white. The signal was given that a goal had been scored and the players were slapping Jason on the back.

"Oh my God," Kim cried. "His first goal. He made his first goal!"

As the proud mother jumped up and down, the son circled the ice with his stick raised. Jonathan couldn't help laughing. "He does have his mother's flair for the dramatic."

Jason had lifted the mask of his helmet, and as he skated by, Kim and Jonathan could see his beaming face. Jonathan continued to applaud but when he looked at Kim he saw a mask of pain. He put his arm around her shoulder and squeezed gently.

Kim leaned against him and bit her lip, saying, "I have to stop wishing, everytime he does something, that his father were here and could see him."

"That's understandable, and anyhow, I'm glad I'm here so he's got some man to show off to."

"You're right, Jonathan, and I do appreciate your kindness to Jason. He really adores you, more even than . . . well, a lot."

"You mean Chris? What's with you two now anyhow?"

"I don't really know what to say. I have the feeling that if it hadn't been for you, my son would never have gotten well, and if it hadn't been for Chris he might never have been so sick."

"Not fair, Kim, but I love being your hero." Jonathan still had his arm around her and hugged her closer before she stepped away.

A week later, Chris and Kim were finishing a late brunch in her townhouse and reading the Sunday papers. Each newspaper—*New York Times*, *Washington Post*, *Boston Globe*—had run large advertisements promoting Kim's special, *The San Diego Connection*, which was airing that night.

Suddenly Chris pushed the business section of the *Times* in front of Kim. "Look at this." He pointed to a headline: "KATHERINE MARCHAND IN LONDON MAKES FINAL MOVES FOR SECOND SATELLITE." Kim took the paper from Chris's hand, noticed the London dateline, and read the article about the growing Marchand syndication. She put the paper down and pushed it to one side.

"What's wrong?" asked Chris.

"Well, the documentary airs tonight. What if something goes wrong, like before? And she hasn't even seen it. We only finished on Thursday, and this says she's been in London since Wednesday."

"So, she'll see it when she gets back. What's the big deal?" Chris went back to his croissants and the rest of the paper. Kim picked up her jacket and gloves and headed out the door, saying that she'd decided to pick Jason up from Sunday school herself, rather than have him come home with one of his friends.

She didn't know why she was reacting so childishly. So Kate was out of town and would miss it. What was the big deal? She was obviously working on bigger and better things. Still her mood did not improve, and some of the excitement about seeing the documentary that evening was gone.

Later that afternoon she was walking through the living room with extra wood for the fireplace when the phone rang.

"Kim?" Maggie asked. "Are you in for a transatlantic call from Kate?"

Kim took the phone from Maggie's hand and the first words she heard were, "Absolutely incredible, Kim! I think you may have even surpassed the first one. The story, the shots, the writing. It is a masterpiece.''

''You're talking about my show?'' Kim asked. ''How did you see it?''

''You just aired overseas for the first time. *The San Diego Connection* was the first international program for the Marchand Syndicates.''

Kim eased down the wall and was now sitting on the floor. ''But according to the papers, you haven't solidified the satellite deal yet.''

''That's true, I hadn't. So I used another satellite to transmit *The San Diego Connection*. It just aired prime time. And, thanks to your excellent work, the few sponsors who were holding out are now banging down the advertising door. I knew that would happen. It worked out just the way I planned it.''

''I don't know what to say,'' said Kim softly, and she didn't. A year ago she was an ordinary reporter in Manhattan. Now she was an award-winning international figure. A year ago Katherine Marchand was only a name belonging to a formidable person. Now she was her boss, and her friend.

''Thank you, Kate . . . and thank you for calling.''

''No, thank *you*, Kim.''

14

"**Y**OU'VE GOT TO BE KIDDING," JONATHAN SAID INCREDulously as he sat on the leather couch in his wife's office. He had dropped by late in the afternoon because they were going to a performance of the Boston Symphony. "It's never before been done. It would take massive infusions of capital, to say nothing about all the regulations from the Federal Communications Commission."

Nancy Thranacite, Kate's personal accountant and financial consultant, answered him. "You're absolutely right, Jonathan, it has never been done." She had worked for one of the finest firms in New York, but when Kate came to Boston, Nancy left her company and started her own in Boston. In ten years, both women's reputations had soared and Kate was now only one of Nancy's many multimillion-dollar clients.

"But your wife has made some very strong investments in recent years, has acquired many important media outlets, and there are many investors who would love to buy into Marchand Syndicates. And," continued Nancy, "we don't anticipate any trouble with the FCC. Kate has always been very popular with them and she has no code violations on her record."

Kate sat beside Jonathan on the couch and placed her hand on his arm. "Darling, it's not going to happen tomorrow. Probably not even next year. But, very soon, unless something goes wrong.''

Nancy said, ''Nobody's going to mess up. You are already a very powerful person in the media, but when Marchand Syndicates buys out the NRB network, no one will be able to touch you. You will be head of the world's largest communications network. Worth about eight and a half billion dollars!''

''My God!'' Jonathan said, stunned. ''I had no idea we were talking about that kind of money.''

Laughing, Kate looked at her watch. ''Oh my God,'' she said, ''the hearings. Mind if we turn up the volume? I want to see the network news.''

Kate hit the remote control and didn't even try to repress a smile when she saw the opening logo of NRB come up on the screen. Yes, it had taken time, ingenuity and sacrifice, but she would soon make the ultimate power play. And how ironic, she smiled to herself, that the network she had chosen was the same network in whose fields she had once labored and made so fruitful. And the one that had stepped on her. It's true, she thought, what goes around comes around.

As she expected, the network featured Kim's testimony before the Government Operations Committee. She had been testifying for two days, and the reports were that her performance was, once again, flawless. Kate now watched as Kim talked about stumbling over the bodies of young children who had been shot in the valley outside San Diego and how she and her crew had themselves been targets of both bandits and the police. In a deep blue suit with a white blouse, Kim looked as beautiful and as intelligent as ever.

''She sure was a hell of a find, Kate,'' Nancy said matter-of-factly. ''Aren't you afraid the networks will grab her? Well, on second thought, if you own the network, you won't have to worry.''

A few weeks later, Diana was taking dictation from Kate about the sales meeting she had just returned from. If all went well, Kate would go to Chicago next and return as a major stockholder of the leading local station. It was an essential acquisition for Marchand Syndicates.

''Why don't you leave that information with me and I'll spend the next couple of hours before I have to leave for the airport going through it,'' Kate said, returning to her desk and glancing at her schedule. "According to this, I'm free until I have to leave."

"Yes," Diana said, "except that Andrew Davis called. He and Kim would like to meet with you for a few minutes today. Kim and Bill have been asked to emcee the Emmy Awards."

"What? Kim and Bill are emceeing the NATAS banquet?" Kate was pleasantly surprised. The annual gathering of the National Academy of Television Arts and Sciences was one of the most important events in Boston's television year. There was a banquet that all the top people in the Boston media attended, then a lengthy ceremony where the Emmy Awards were given out. The submissions—from best documentary to best reporter to best cinematographer—were judged by a panel from another city and then presented at the award ceremony which was broadcast live. Each year a different station took over the expensive task and this year WLYM was in charge of the production. The hosts of the ceremony were picked by the executive board of NATAS. For two people from the same station to be chosen was certainly out of the ordinary.

"Those two certainly are popular in this town," Diana said. "It may be embarrassing for Kim, though, because she's up for Emmys herself in six categories. What if she gets them all?"

"Worse things could happen, Diana. She may not get any of them. If I recall correctly, the judging committee this year is from New York. You never know how they'll react to her, especially since she came from New York."

"But they'll have to see that her work is really outstanding. No one else even comes close to her professionally."

"Diana, the whole Emmy business is so political. The judges are not always the finest critics, and often the best ends up coming in second."

"You never seem to complain when we sweep the awards every year, or at least for the past three years."

"I've never said we deserve every award we receive. We have some excellent competition in this town. Now, can we get on with the day? Tell Andrew I'll see him and Kim right away. Then I want time to study this background material for Chicago."

When he and Kim were seated in Kate's office, Andrew said, "It seems Kim has another documentary and series idea and I have a few problems with it. But before I make a decision, I thought we should talk about it."

"Andrew, since when do I become involved in your decision-making process?"

"Well, you don't, Kate, and I'm grateful for that. But I believe when you hear the details of Kim's proposal, you'll see why I consulted you."

"All right. Tell me about it, Kim."

"When I was in California, I learned a great deal about the cocaine smuggling business and how our government tries in vain to prevent it. The Customs people and the Drug Enforcement Administration trip over each other, involved in petty arguments, and the major suppliers laugh and continue to haul their stuff up. I met some of the inside people and found a couple who will talk if their voices are distorted and their backs are to the camera. I also heard about a major processing factory just under the nose of the DEA."

"It sounds dangerous to me," Kate broke in. "We're not talking here about exposing a few local officials. We're talking about getting at people who are involved in smuggling millions of dollars of narcotics."

"I know the risks, but I believe it can be done safely," Kim said. She continued the explanation, discussing the different angles and the various shooting possibilities, the cooperation she could get from ex-drug runners and even from some disenchanted federal officials. She ended with a statement about the service such an exposé would provide. Kate smiled at the mention of "service."

"So, Andrew? It sounds like an excellent series and documentary." She thought she heard a slight sigh of relief from Kim. "What's your problem?"

"Kate!" Andrew exclaimed. "Listen to what she's just said. Trying to penetrate the drug smuggling industry. That's Mafia-controlled, Kate. It's very dangerous."

"That's not the angle she's going for. She's going to concentrate on government efforts."

"But it's going to make people angry, Kate." Andrew's voice was loud and tense. "That's very rough territory. Where drugs are involved, human life is secondary. Kim's found that some of these flights from Colombia carry several million dollars' worth of cocaine. Her life could be worth nothing next to that type of money. I think it's just too dangerous."

"What are you afraid of, Andrew?"

"Isn't it obvious? A woman would be so vulnerable with these guys."

Kate smiled to herself. He had fallen into the trap. She tried to sound sympathetic and concerned. "Are you saying that you'd be more comfortable with a man doing this story?"

"Well, to be honest, yes. I would feel more comfortable if Bill did this story."

Kate whirled in her chair. "Maybe you'd feel more comfortable with a man as president and general manager of WLYM and Marchand Syndicates. I mean, there are real wolves out there. I could get hurt. Just like I could have gotten hurt in Vietnam. Or in Laos. And perhaps you'd feel more comfortable with a male airline pilot than a female? And perhaps you think a man could have done a better job in the Nixon investigation than Barbara Jordan?"

Kim could not help herself. She began to laugh and now Kate swung to look at her. "What's so funny, may I ask?"

Kim said, "Sorry, Kate. It was rude to laugh. I've just never seen you on a soapbox before—not that I mind in this case since you're on the right side."

To Andrew's relief, Kate smiled sheepishly. "Sorry Andrew, I really know your feminist credentials are in order. But I don't like the idea that we make decisions on the basis of gender."

"Of course, Kate," Andrew said. "Anyhow, Bill's involved in a series on medical malpractice."

"That's another thing to consider. Bill's strong and he's good and I wouldn't trade him for anything," Kate said. "But he has his own strengths and interests, and seems content to let Kim do the muckraking. On a project like the one he's now covering, he is excellent. No one can touch him. Kim has different ambitions, and God knows she's proven herself under fire. Literally and figuratively."

Andrew allowed himself a slight laugh. "Oh, hell, what can I say? Go for it, Kim. And I'm sorry if I'm being overprotective."

Kim answered, "Well, as long as it's not chauvinism, our boss here won't kill you."

That Friday evening Kate was sitting in the living room in Rockport taping the eleven o'clock newscast. Although she was reading at the same time, she was aware that there seemed to be something "off." Then she realized that Bill and Kim were too light, almost jocular. She didn't like that. The news is serious but so far, she thought, there had been no real damage done. The news itself was light.

She returned to her reading when the television set caught her attention again. Bill was restraining himself from laughing on the air. He was doing this while trying to read a wire story about a woman who, for her eighty-fifth birthday, had asked her family and friends to cheer her as she ran naked across the Lexington Green. Her wish had been granted and the conservative town, known for its minutemen and the "shot heard round the world," had found it necessary to arrest the woman. At this point, Bill completely lost it, and could not read the story intelligibly. Kim picked up the rest of the story, not doing much better and then falling into gales of laughter as she told the viewers the woman's family maintained the beloved "streaker was perfectly sane. She's just always had this thing about clothes."

As Kim threw her head back, she lost her balance in the chair and Bill had to reach over and catch her before she fell, which threw him off balance. They both managed to remain upright, but now were laughing uncontrollably. Kim was able to stumble out a "We'll be right back," and the director had the good sense to go to commercial.

Kate covered her eyes with one hand, as if to make the television go away. It was one of the most unprofessional displays she had ever seen.

When they returned after the commercial, Kim offered a brief apology for their "moment of abandon." And then, while Kate sat there disbelieving, Kim asked the viewing audience to consider making donations to her and Bill's careers, because if management saw their performance, they would probably be sent on the assignment of tracking Admiral Byrd's footsteps to the North Pole.

Kate was furious. The news was no place for a comedy team. These two had clearly overstepped the limits of professionalism. She dialed the studio and asked for Warren, the eleven o'clock producer.

"He's busy right now. Can I take a message?" came an unknown voice.

"He's not too busy to talk to me. This is Katherine Marchand." There was silence on the end of the line. Kate could imagine the panic in the control room.

When Warren came to the phone, she said, "I want to remind you and the entire news staff that I am always watching what goes out across my airwaves. Please inform Kim and Bill that the news is not comedy, and that I find their behavior unprofessional and if it ever happens again they *will* be reporting from the North Pole, but not for LYM or any of the Marchand Syndicates. Good evening.'' She hung up the phone and walked back to the television set. They had moved into another break. A minute and a half later, when Kim and Bill returned on camera, it was clear Warren had relayed her message. They were absolutely serious.

Kate said nothing about the incident again but she did receive flowers the following morning. Instead of a card, a sheet of paper torn from a child's notebook was enclosed and on it, about twenty times, was written, ''We'll never do it again,'' ''We'll never do it again,'' ''We'll never. . . .''

15

KIM AND CHRIS ENTERED THE LOBBY OF THE SHERATON
Plaza shortly before seven o'clock on a Saturday evening two
weeks later. They made a striking couple, both with their streaky
blond hair and delicate bone structure. Kim wore a crepe de
chine evening suit. The skirt was tulip-shaped, Carole
Lombard-style, and under the open jacket she wore a strapless,
glitteringly sequined top.

As they walked across the crowded ballroom, Chris said in
her ear, "I can tell by the stares we're getting that this outfit of
yours is sensational but I don't really see it for a wedding."

"What? What wedding?"

"Ours. Have you been thinking about that? About what you'll
wear, I mean."

"Chris, please don't do this and especially not tonight. I'll
tell you when I'm ready to talk about our relationship. That was
our bargain."

When they reached their seats Bill Halliday rose and walked
towards Kim, giving her an affectionate kiss. He shook Chris's
hand and introduced his friend Yvonne. Diana was there with
her husband, and Kate's friend Deborah and her husband Bob
were also at the table.

"Aren't we missing a couple?" asked Chris, looking at the
two empty seats beside him.

"Jonathan is here. He just had to make a call," Diana said. "But Kate's flight from Europe was delayed because of bad weather. I spoke to her around one o'clock and she was getting ready to board then, but we're not sure when it took off." She looked up and said, "Here comes the other half, at least."

Jonathan walked first to Kim, kissing her on the mouth. She placed her hand on his arm and, for a moment, thought, How strange, this is Kate's husband. But then she thought, He is also my friend, the protector of my son. She kissed him back.

"You look absolutely gorgeous, Kim," he said. "Who's the funny-looking penguin you brought with you?"

"Listen, at least I have a date for this affair. I didn't have to crash it," Chris joked.

"I don't know how Kate does it," Bill said. "Think of all the changes and new plans at the station, all engineered by her. We have a new mobile unit, the satellites, new promotion and campaigns; it seems like she must be at the station twenty-four hours a day. How can she be off in Europe and still pull all this together?"

"Bill," Jonathan said, "you've worked for my wife a long time. You know how long her reach is, and you know her work is never more than an eighth of a thought away from her."

"What I want to know," Bill's chic date said, "is when is she going to change? She can't very well show up at this function in a traveling suit."

"Don't worry, Yvonne, I'm sure she's already in the right clothes," Jonathan said. "She probably knew before she left exactly how long the delay would be and had everything planned in advance—with God."

Precisely at eight o'clock, with the cameras on and the live telecast beginning, the annual NATAS awards ceremony began. The chairman delivered his greeting, stating the purpose of the ceremony—to reward the finest in the profession—and then explained to the audience and the viewers the schedule of events for the evening.

Kim watched this man with interest. It was Herbert Corkin, the general manager of WZYN, the closest competition for WLYM. He had been chairman of NATAS for two years, and had used the position as a springboard for his own station and advertisers. But ZYN remained over four rating points behind LYM at the six o'clock news, seven points at the eleven o'clock. Kim thought about how different his demeanor was from Kate's.

Class, she thought. He doesn't have it and Kate does. That's all there is to it.

Corkin was ending his speech, saying, "Now, according to the program, I introduce the Masters of Ceremonies for the evening. I am pleased that the Academy has chosen these two people who are so skilled and so controlled." He nodded to a waiting technician at the far end of the platform. The large screen to his right suddenly came alive with the image of Kim and Bill at the anchor desk. "You all recognize these two dedicated, sincere communicators of the news."

At their table, Kim and Bill looked at each other and then at Diana who offered her best innocent smile.

"Well, that's how they usually are, but perhaps some of you missed their finest hour. It came a week ago Friday. I hear that some people now refer to it as 'Friday Night Live at WLYM.' "

The tape changed and soon the entire event unfolded before those assembled in the ballroom and the hundreds of thousands of viewers watching at home. Kim and Bill simultaneously put a hand to their eyes and looked away. The entire ballroom was soon convulsed with laughter, especially when Kim suggested they might be looking for work at the North Pole. The tape ended and Kate, who had arrived while the film was running, stepped to the microphone. Waiting for the laughter to die down, she said, "I tried to fire them but the Eskimos of the North Pole protested, so here they are, Kim Winston and Bill Halliday."

After she and Bill got to the platform and acknowledged the welcoming applause, Kim said, "I think it only fair to explain that Bill and I didn't respond so hysterically to the story for any simple reason. You see, there was another part of the story we could not broadcast. But it may be a *fait accompli* by the end of this evening, especially since this is being broadcast over WLYM." The audience was quiet waiting for Kim's explanation.

"You see, the lady from Lexington actually had two wishes. One was to streak across the Lexington Green, the other was to do a similar performance before the Emmy award ceremonies. . . ."

Kim and Bill presided graciously over the ceremonies, even when it became apparent that WLYM was going to sweep the awards. It also became obvious that Kim was probably going to walk off with all she had been nominated for. With Bill, she won Best Anchor Team. Alone, she won Best Spot News Coverage for a gas explosion piece; Best Live Event Reporting for the visit of the president; Best Public Service Series for juvenile justice. Bill won Best Information Program for reporting a medical special. The only one remaining, and the most important, was Best Documentary.

Scott Shepherd, the anchor for JTH, opened the envelope, looked up and said, "I think we all know that if this award had gone to anyone other than the person on this card, all would be suspect here tonight. But the integrity of these awards is preserved because the Emmy for Best Documentary goes to the one who stands above us all in deserving this honor. Kim, I believe this belongs to you."

Kim's heart lifted against her chest as the applause swelled. She made a short acceptance speech, praising the individual staff members of WLYM, the news director, Andrew Davis, and especially, the general manager, Katherine Marchand.

"Won't you say a word or two, Kate?" Kim asked when she had finished.

Kate rose and came forward looking elegant but extremely tired. "Thank you, Kim, thank you. One of the smartest things I ever did was hiring you. I've been watching this ceremony and I want to thank you all—for the honors WLYM has received but also for this beautiful evening. It belongs to all of us in television who strive for higher standards, free, unbiased news and personal and professional integrity." She bowed her head and quickly went to her place.

When Kim got back to the table, she said, "I never thought leaving New York could mean this."

"You know what leaving New York is really going to mean?" Deborah asked. "It's going to mean returning to New York. You're going to wake up tomorrow morning with every network after you."

"There's only one left that hasn't made an offer," Chris said, kissing Kim on the head.

Kate turned abruptly towards Kim. Why hadn't she told her? When had all this happened? She said coldly, "Perhaps it's time we looked at the terms of your contract."

"That's not necessary," said Kim, responding with the same edge in her voice. "I thought you knew me better."

Jonathan said, "Now, now, we're supposed to be celebrating. And Kate, aren't we forgetting something? Our special tribute to Kim?"

"Thanks for reminding me, darling." Kate smiled brilliantly at Jonathan and then reached into her small, antique cut-steel evening purse. She took from it a leather jewel box and held it out to Kim. "Peace, my dear, and grateful congratulations."

With Chris leaning over her, Kim pressed the tiny button that released the domed top of the box. There, on a bed of crushed velvet, lay a rubrum lily, of the most delicately painted enamel. Its outer edges and stamen were highlighted with a subtle sparkling of pink tourmaline, and it was looped onto a gold chain so fine that when she put it on the lily seemed to rest low on Kim's throat, free, held invisibly.

Jonathan said, "It looks a lot better there than in that box."

Kim, with tears in her eyes, thanked Jonathan and then went to Kate and timidly kissed her cheek. "Thank you. It's the most beautiful thing I've ever seen," she said. "It looks like a very old piece but I know it can't be."

"A wonderful jeweler on Newbury Street made it to my specifications—and did a pretty good job, I have to grant."

"How in the world do you have time for things like this?" Chris asked, surprised when Jonathan answered.

"For one thing, because my life on the tennis court leaves Kate with a lot of free time. As a matter of fact, we're going to have to leave soon. The big club tournament starts at eight tomorrow morning."

"Unfortunately, I have to get home, too," Chris said. "I'm on duty at the hospital all weekend."

As they waited for their coats in the lobby, Kate said, "It sounds like you and I are going to be on our own most of this weekend, Kim. Why don't we make the most of it?"

"Go out and pick up some other guys you mean?" Kim asked.

"Well, if that's what you want. I saw it more like private time, catch-up time. Want to go up to the Pines tomorrow morning and stay through Sunday?"

"You know," Kim said, "that would really work out well. Jason and Maggie are going off this weekend to a big family celebration her nephew's having in New Hampshire and I was thinking that, after tonight, being alone was going to be a big letdown."

"Then it's settled," Kate said. "I'll pick you up at eleven tomorrow morning."

"And Chris and I will spend a cold, lonely Saturday night," Jonathan added, helping Kate with her coat.

"Just give up your tournament, darling, and I'll gladly stay."

"Touché, Madame. It is a sacrifice I am not strong enough to bear."

Laughing, the four of them left the banquet. A scattering of applause from their industry colleagues followed them to the door.

The two women drove uneventfully to Rockport the following morning, stopping for lunch at a roadside clam bar on the way. When they got to the house they settled peacefully in, Kate reading through a stack of magazines, Kim looking through some old sheet music on the piano.

The quiet was interrupted by the ringing telephone. Kate sighed and went to her study, and a few moments later emerged with an irritated expression. "It seems it's just not in the cards for me to get away from work, no matter where I go," she said. "That was Diana with information that a very important client is on his way from Los Angeles. He will be arriving at Kennedy Airport late this evening."

"What does Diana do, run a travel agency on the side and keep you apprised of the comings and goings of everyone who does business with LYM?"

"That's a good idea, I hadn't thought of that. But the truth is we do try to catch up with this particular man. And for very good reason. He's president and chairman of the board of Bearson's Electronics. As you may have noticed, they are one of our major advertisers, and Bearson himself holds stock in two cable companies I'm interested in acquiring."

"Perhaps I've missed something here," Kim said, "but I still don't understand why you would be concerned with his personal itinerary. Is he flying on an airline you're also interested in acquiring?"

"Hmmm," Kate paused, "that's another good thought. You see, whenever I can, I try to do something special for major advertisers, especially those involved in syndicate advertising."

"And especially those who hold particular stock."

"You'll discover, Kim, that an unexpected bit of kindness can go very far in a business world dominated by the male ego. And for that reason I'm afraid I'm going to have to cut my stay short and head down to JFK."

"What?" Kim's eyebrows registered her surprise. "You just got in from Europe yourself."

"Yes, I did. And if I had known about Edgar Bearson's travel plans before this, I would already be in New York. So now I'm going to change my clothes, get back in the car, drive down to Logan, and fly to Kennedy Airport where I will meet my financial friend as he deplanes, buy him a nice late supper, offer him some good company, and then walk him to the gate where he will board his flight to Germany. I'll then go to the Pierre, get some rest, do some work and drum up another client for dinner Sunday night. I have meetings in New York on Monday anyway." She reached out and touched Kim's arm. "I am sorry, my friend. I'll miss spending the time with you, but I hope we can make up for it soon."

Kim leaned on the piano and said, "Let me get this straight. You're returning to Logan to fly to JFK to spend a couple of hours with a client who just happens to have a layover in New York?"

Kate turned and nodded. "That's right. Believe me, it will be appreciated. Bearson will be plumped up like a pheasant thinking that I would go to all that trouble to keep him company."

"I'm sure it will score points in whatever race you're running," Kim said, as she turned and headed for the stairs.

"Where are you going?" Kate asked. "There's no reason for you to leave. Chris is on call all weekend and Jason is away with Maggie. You might as well stay here and get some rest. You've more than earned it. You can have Chris pick you up when he gets off."

Kim hesitated on the stairs, felt the fatigue in her body and the ragged edge of her nerves. "Perhaps you're right. If you don't mind, I think I *will* stay."

"I'd be insulted if you didn't. Enjoy yourself. I'm just sorry I can't be here." Kate headed for the stairs and put her arm around Kim's shoulders. "You say you always find the sea so reassuring and serene. You've earned some serenity and this is one of the best places on earth to get it."

A few moments later, Kim was standing at the fireplace, adding a log. Hearing Kate on the stairs, she turned and saw her, luggage in hand, dressed, seemingly refreshed and ready for action. "I really don't see how you keep going," she said.

"Because right now, I'm in the final sprint of a race I have every intention of winning." She smiled, raised a gloved hand and blew a kiss to Kim, adding, "Relax, and don't do anything I wouldn't do." She winked and was gone.

Kim sat on the couch after Kate left. "She is going to do it," she mumbled into the flames. "She's going to do what no man could. A nonviolent, polite network takeover. They're going to think she did it all with her smiling integrity, but I bet she plays dirtball like the rest of them." Wondering what Katherine Marchand was like when she took off her gloves and bared her claws, Kim shivered involuntarily and said, "I hope I never find out."

Before she left for New York, Kate left a message for Jonathan on their answering machine, explaining that her plans had changed. She said she'd try to make it home at a reasonable hour on Monday night so that they could spend some time together.

That evening Jonathan went to the hospital. As he left a patient's room, he met Chris, who was walking with several interns towards the radiology department. Chris pulled away from the others and fell into stride with Jonathan. "You're just the person I'm looking for," Chris said. "I seem to have a damsel in distress stranded in Rockport."

"What?" Jonathan asked.

"Oh, I thought you knew. Kim just assumed Kate would have called you."

"Well, she did but I was still on the court. There was a message on the machine that she's headed for New York. What's Kim got to do with it?"

"Didn't Kate tell you? Kim's still up in Rockport. I have to pick her up tomorrow. She said it would be best to get the directions from you."

"Funny," Jonathan said, "I just assumed Kim came down with her. That damn machine we've got doesn't leave time for any long messages."

"The problem is," Chris continued, "I'm on bloody call, so Kim's up there relaxing in front of the fireplace without me. Why did I ever want to be a doctor anyway? Why not a plumber? They always get Saturday nights off."

"Because, Chris my boy," Jonathan said, hitting him gently on the shoulder, "beautiful, talented and sophisticated women do not hang out with plumbers." As he headed down the hallway, Jonathan called over his shoulder, "I'll stick the directions to the Rockport house under your office door."

Kim was playing old show tunes on the piano when she stopped to gaze at the fire and listen to the incoming tide on the rocks outside. She'd found a bottle of Dom Perignon in the refrigerator and, after making a note to send Kate two bottles in replacement, she'd taken it with her to sip while she bathed. Now, at the piano, as she poured the sparkling liquid into her glass, she was surprised to see that the bottle was almost empty. "Oh well," she said carelessly, "not much you can do with leftover champagne." And with that, she filled the tulip-shaped glass with what was left. "To Katherine Marchand," she toasted, "may you run your race and win it whatever way you can."

"I'm sure she will," came a deep voice from the door in back of her.

Champagne and glass flew in the air as Kim rose several inches off the piano bench. "Jonathan!" She leaned on the piano keys and put her hand to her breast as if to silence her pounding heart.

"I didn't mean to startle you," Jonathan said, as he knelt to pick up the glass. When he stood up again, he looked around and asked, "Where is my wife, whom you were so elegantly toasting?"

"Your wife? Kate?"

Jonathan placed his hand on Kim's shoulder and, like a concerned doctor, said, "Yes. Remember her? Brunette, about five-nine? Has this racket going running television stations?" He paused and squeezed Kim's shoulder, noticing the color returning to her cheeks. "Kim, are you all right?"

"Yes, Jonathan, I'm sorry." She patted Jonathan's hand where it lay on her shoulder. "You just surprised me."

"Where is Kate, anyway? I thought I'd surprise *her*."

"Well, you'll have to go to New York to do that. She left a couple of hours ago to meet a client who had a layover at JFK."

"Aha!" Jonathan answered quickly. "The old layover trick."

"What do you mean by that?" Kim asked, rising a little unsteadily. As Jonathan moved to steady her, she said, "I'm afraid I indulged in a bit of champagne. I'll never learn. Almost turned my wedding trip into the lost weekend. You should ask David about that." As soon as the words were out of her mouth she tried to grab them back. Flailing, she looked down and pulled away from Jonathan. "God! What am I saying? I must be drunker than I thought I was. Excuse me, while I freshen up a bit."

Kim fled up the stairs. In the bathroom, she went directly to the window, opened it and leaned out on her elbows. With a sigh, she looked out at the Twin Lights and took several deep breaths, trying unsuccessfully to clear her head. A thousand thoughts and images bombarded her. Kate wasn't here. She was in New York. But her husband was here, looking for her—and what was that crack he made about the "old layover trick?" She knew that had to be a joke. Kate didn't screw around and she wouldn't have come all the way to Rockport to turn around and head for an affair in New York. Would she? Kim shook her head. No, in fact, the only person she was sure fooled around was the man downstairs. He gave off that aura. It was as simple as that. But he was legitimately looking for his wife. Yet why hadn't Kate called him? Or had she? No, not that she remembered.

Abruptly she snapped the window closed and, turning to the sink, splashed cold water on her face.

"Are you all right, Kim?" Jonathan was shouting from downstairs.

"Yes, I'll be right down," she called through the closed door. Taking time to brush her hair, she thought about how foolish a little champagne could make her. After all, this was Jonathan, Kate's husband. Who was simply looking for Kate.

When she returned to the living room, she was surprised to see Jonathan, his coat off, stoking the fire.

"I'm sorry, Kim. I shouldn't have made that joke. I guess Kate and I missed connecting with each other. I'm just disappointed that I haven't seen much of my ever so successful wife lately." He paused and looked at her with a slight smile. "And I certainly didn't mean to scare you like I did."

"It's I who should apologize," Kim said, returning the smile. "Champagne and exhaustion just don't mix."

"Well, you know the problem with champagne," Jonathan said, turning and heading for the kitchen. "You can't stop drinking it. That's when the trouble starts. You mix too much air in with the bubbles." He waved his hands over his head in emphasis. "If I know my wife, there is more than one bottle of champagne up here. Come on, let's have a look." He took Kim's hand and playfully pulled her with him to the kitchen.

"So Kate is off to New York, leaving you to keep the home fires burning?" Jonathan opened the refrigerator door. "Well, I won't interrupt your solitude. I'll just share a glass of the bubbly with you and then head back to Dover. Ah, here's another bottle." He raised the heavy green bottle from the lower shelves. "Did my wife happen to mention when she was arriving home?"

"Actually," Kim said, "I don't think she's coming back until Monday evening."

"Damn, I wish this takeover of hers would hurry up and get moving," Jonathan said, removing the wire net from the champagne bottle. "It's not good for her to live with all this tension."

"Her back?" asked Kim, leaning on the counter as she watched Jonathan take two champagne glasses from a top shelf.

"Her back, her overall level of anxiety, and her preoccupation with work," Jonathan continued as he loosened the cork.

"You sound like the standard complaining, abandoned husband," Kim smiled.

"Is that what I sound like? I don't mean to." He picked up a towel and poured the champagne, his back to Kim. "After all, we both know that I'm one of the luckiest men in the world."

Jonathan held a glass out to Kim but she stepped back from it, her hand up in front of her. "I think I'll wait, thank you. I don't think it's such a good idea to let my boss's husband see me out cold."

"Well, just sit and keep me company a moment before I head back. Carry this for me." Jonathan handed her a glass of champagne. "In fact, it's a good chance for us to talk. Kate tells me you're still somewhat worried about Jason's illness." Leading her back into the living room, he continued, "I understand you're still plagued with doubts about whether Chris handled the case properly."

Kim sat on the couch, and, almost automatically, sipped the champagne. It was true that Chris's behavior still gnawed at her. And if she was going to consider life with him, she had better have this issue settled in her mind. As she glanced toward Jonathan she saw that the fire cast a shadowed glow on his features. A bit of champagne spilled on her fingers as she became aware once again of how much Jonathan resembled David. For a moment, she stared at the rugged and strangely familiar profile, at the elegant, but masculine ease with which Jonathan moved.

His head turned and his face in the firelight was lit by a warm, knowing smile. Kim responded by instinct, as if she were back in an earlier time when trust was whole, understanding complete, and love uncompromising.

"As far as Jason's health is concerned," Jonathan began calmly, not moving his eyes from Kim's, "you can be sure his recovery is complete. I'm fairly confident he will never so much as show a sign of having had spinal meningitis. And you know how little boys' memories are, soon he won't even remember he was sick at all."

"I don't know," Kim said, finally turning her eyes away from Jonathan. She took a long sip of champagne as if to fortify herself for the next sentence. "Jason seems to have a very good memory—almost too good."

"You mean his memories about his father? I've noticed that. David must have been a very special father. Jason has told me all about the trips to Jones Beach, like the time they went out to do some surf casting and the fog came in. . . ."

Kim remembered that day. She'd sat watching her "men" at the water's edge, and had seen Jason cling to David's leg as the fog began to envelop them. Now, staring at the fading flames, she could hear the resonance of David's voice. It was as if she were watching a family movie: David's strong arms lifting Chase, then standing the poles in the sand. Then David laughing, running with Chase along the sandbar, playing hide and seek with the approaching and receding banks of fog.

Smiling to herself, she finished her champagne. The room was dark, lit only by the dying fire, and Kim saw the face she loved so dearly, so completely, move out of the fog toward her own. Intently, she watched the eyes until they fell below her own line of vision. She felt the soft familiar kisses on her neck, and from far away heard the soft murmur of her name. Then she felt her breast respond to the knowing touch. She arched her back and let her head fall back, her arms fall to the side.

"David, David . . . oh God, David," Kim whispered from the depth of her throat.

The only response was the kisses covering her neck, the warm breath in her hair. It was Kim's mouth that now searched for the tongue playing in her ear. Hungrily she pulled the head to her and moved her arms to encircle the powerful body. Only seconds passed before she was undressed and a hardness was penetrating her. Again she arched her back to receive it.

In the frenzy of the moments that followed, Kim was aware of floating in and out of a strange consciousness. At times she seemed to push her lover away; at other moments, she pulled him into her with a blind need that made of her body a wild animal newly freed from a trap.

Finally, with a scream that mingled in the air with another dark cry, Kim collapsed back into the thick cover of fog.

16

DAWN CAST SNAKY STREAKS INTO THE SKY OF SUNDAY
morning as Chris drove Kim's Mercedes up Rte. 128. Although
still exhausted from the night at the hospital, he felt lucky he'd
been able to persuade a colleague to relieve him. Then, rather
than try to sleep, he decided to surprise Kim and head up to
Rockport early in the morning. He let his mind wander with
thoughts of awakening her, loving her, and then falling into a
peaceful sleep.

He glanced down at the directions Jonathan had written out
and then up at the dashboard clock: 5:55. He should be there
by 6:15.

About fifteen minutes later he was driving down the rutted
dirt road towards Kate's Rockport hideaway. As he rounded a
corner of thick pines, he came to the driveway he expected was
Kate's, but kept going along the road because a gold Porsche
was parked in the driveway. Kate's driveway would certainly be
empty, thought Chris. Then he remembered Jonathan had a gold
Porsche, and he quickly turned around and returned to the house.
Yes, there was no doubt. According to the directions and the
description this was Kate's house. But the Porsche? Kate must
have returned from New York and she and Jonathan come back
to the Pines. Could that be right?

He parked the Mercedes behind the Porsche and stepped out

of the car. The sun now sat above the water like an orange ball, impatient to get on with its ascent. Chris let out a long, stretching yawn, and refreshed by the salt air, walked toward the heavy oak door. He wondered how Kate would feel about an intruder at six A.M., but then, remembering Kate's energy, he imagined she might already be up. So much for a quiet rendezvous with Kim, he thought ruefully.

He put his hand on the brass knob and it turned freely. Pushing the door gently, Chris let himself into the simple, but perfectly appointed living room. He saw the piano, the couch, and the large bay windows with the ocean beyond. For a moment, his eyes fell on the two glasses of champagne sitting on the coffee table, one half full. The scent of ashes rose from the fireplace. He quietly closed the door behind him, listening for sounds in the house. Convinced he was the only one awake, he mounted the stairs to find the bedroom where Kim was sleeping. "I hope I don't walk in on Kate and Jonathan," he thought to himself.

Silently and slowly Chris moved along the upstairs carpet and approached a half-open door. Looking into the room, he was surprised to see Kim's luggage on a chair, though the bed had not been slept in. With an uneasiness that made the hairs on the back of his neck rise, he walked warily toward the end of the hall and another open door.

Chris's eyes fell on the end of the bed and he saw a man's leg outside the sheets. As his gaze moved upward, he stiffened. Jonathan's thick tennis arm was flung across the bare breast . . . of Kim. Kim's hair was matted on her forehead and her arm was draped lazily across Jonathan's back.

Chris felt a scream start to rise, but he quickly brought his hand to his mouth. He backed away and, in seconds, he was leaning against the door of Kim's car, trying to keep the bile from rising in his throat. Shocked and moving on some automatic control, he climbed back into the car, started it, and leaving gravel flying in the driveway, sped away from the Pines.

Jonathan was awakened by the sound of the car. Raising his head and looking down at Kim, a self-satisfied smile moved over his lips. He bent down and kissed her on the lips. Her response was to groan and move her head to the side, falling deeper into sleep. Jonathan glanced at his watch: 6:20. There was plenty of time until Chris would arrive but he wanted to be safe. He also . . . well, he also wanted to leave without speaking to Kim.

* * *

It was another hour before Kim slowly opened her eyes. With a breathy moan, she turned her head towards the windows, and then shut her eyes again against the bright morning sun. Kim moved her tongue to moisten her lips, but her tongue seemed swollen and covered with a stale, vile cotton candy.

"I feel awful; where is the truck that ran me over?" she asked the intruding day as she pulled a pillow over her head. As her memory crept back, she remembered she was in Rockport, at the Pines, and then she sat up and stared at the bureau, at a picture of Kate and Jonathan on the beach.

"This isn't the guest bedroom," her mind registered, and she began to moan. "No, no, oh God, no. Please let this be a nightmare, not something that really happened." In a few minutes she'd wake up from this dream . . . in the guest room, awaiting Chris. But then the scenes of the firelit room rose to overwhelm her and she screamed. Putting her hand to her mouth, she struggled out of bed, dragging a sheet as she stumbled into the bathroom. She vomited violently, first on the floor and then finally into the toilet bowl. For about half an hour Kim kneeled on the floor, her elbows bent on the porcelain, retching violently, sobbing.

Finally she rose, cleaned herself up and began to scrub the bathroom. Kate's bathroom, she thought, Kate's perfume on the shelf, Kate's facecloth on the soap dish, Kate's shower cap. . . .

Despite the relentless throbbing in her head, almost in a frenzy, Kim stripped Kate's bed and remade it with clean white sheets from the linen closet. She then ran down the stairs and flung the bedclothes into the washer so as to purify them of all traces of the night before. She aired Kate's room too and inspected it like a sergeant before she went back to the guest room and slowly lowered herself onto the bed.

Then, very methodically, she reviewed what had happened, going through every step, every move, of the night before. At first the memory was cloudy, but she admitted to herself "Yes, Kimberly, you have slept with your boss's husband, your friend's husband." She tried to blame Jonathan, remembering the playful way he opened the second bottle of champagne and his seductive reminiscing about David and Jason. He set me up, she thought to herself, with the fire and champagne and the fact that he knew he resembled David. But then she shook her head. No, Kim, whatever Jonathan's motives were, you have to face it. He didn't rape you. He didn't force you. You didn't fight him. This activity takes two people and you were the other person.

She looked at the clock: 8:45. Chris would be off call soon and on his way up. She knew she had to clean up, and went downstairs to remove all traces of their presence. Within an hour, she had thrown away the empty champagne bottles and washed the glasses. After scrubbing herself with a vengeance in the shower, she sat on the deck sipping a glass of cold water trying in vain to figure a way out of her nightmare.

She cursed herself over and over. She should have seen it coming. From the first moment she saw him, Jonathan had stirred memories of David. He had saved her son's life and become a hero to her. Then the hang gliding incident, with the not so accidental touching of their bodies and his sweet, seductive smile. She thought of calling Jonathan, telling him it was all a mistake and must never happen again. But she was afraid. What if Kate had changed her plans and returned home last night or this morning? When had Jonathan left?

Kim rushed to the phone, called the Pierre in New York and asked if Katherine Marchand was registered.

"Yes she is. Would you like me to ring her room?"

"No, no, thank you," Kim said, hurriedly hanging up the phone.

"It will never happen again," she said aloud, firmly, certainly. "Never. Never again. Never."

She resolved to erase the night from her mind, to act now, and always, as if it had never happened. Only in that way could she diminish its importance and save two people she loved from the pain of hurt and betrayal. For she loved Kate. Whatever the nature of their business relationship, Kate was her beloved friend. And Chris? Somehow whatever had happened last night had cauterized her wound, had put her obsession with David to rest, had freed her to love Chris . . . a different kind of man, but a dear one.

17

Diana stopped typing and looked up at the man standing in front of her desk early on Tuesday morning. "Hello, Christopher." She smiled, remembering him from the Emmy ceremonies. "It will probably be about ten minutes before Kate can see you. Can I get you some coffee?"

"No, thank you, Diana. I'll just wait."

In exactly ten minutes, Chris was ushered into Kate's office and seated beside her on one of a pair of chairs in front of her desk.

"It's clear there's something bothering you, Chris," Kate said, picking a pen up off her desk and gently tapping it in her palm, "because you've never come to see me in my office before. How can I help you?"

"This is very serious, Kate. I wish I didn't have to be here." There was brief silence and then Chris struck his hand on the arm of the chair.

"Spare me the dramatics, please. If you want to talk to me, please talk," Kate said.

"It's about Jonathan and Kim."

"What about them? What are you getting at?"

Chris's voice shook as he placed his hands on the arms of the chair and let out a breath. "You know that Kim was up in Rockport Saturday night?"

"Yes, of course I do," Kate said swiftly. "I brought her up there and then had to leave. I was under the impression that you picked her up on Sunday."

"Yes, I did," Chris said.

"And you quarreled?"

"No. It's not between Kim and me. It's that . . . I have to tell you, Kate . . . Your husband went up to the Pines on Saturday evening." Chris's voice was loud and tight with anger.

"What are you charging, Christopher?" Kate demanded, feeling her soul grow cold. "My husband had no reason to go to the Pines. He was playing tennis on Saturday, and was home Saturday night. He would have mentioned it to me if he was going to Rockport. And he certainly did not go up there to see Kim. I left a message for him and I forgot to tell him Kim was at the Pines." She stood and walked behind her desk, wanting it between them.

"You didn't tell him?" Chris asked.

"No. Stop worrying." She placed the pen down on her desk, and sighed. "Are you still feeling so insecure about what happened after Jason's illness?"

"You didn't tell Jonathan that Kim was in Rockport?" Chris asked, completely ignoring Kate's comments.

"No!" Kate said firmly, "and I'm tired of this game. I have more important things to worry about. If you have doubts about your relationship with Kim, you should discuss them with her rather than accusing Jonathan."

"Dammit! *I* told him. Kim didn't tell him. You didn't tell him. *I* told him."

"Chris, what are you talking about?" Kate was shouting now.

"Just this, Kate," Chris said ominously, leaning over the desk and looking Kate unwaveringly in the eyes. "Jonathan did go to Rockport Saturday night. I saw them together on Sunday morning. I got off very early on Sunday morning and went up to surprise Kim. It was I who got the surprise." He laughed bitterly. "You see, when I stood in the bedroom door, I was greeted by the sleeping and naked bodies of your husband and my fiancée—in carnal embrace, I believe you'd call it."

Kate's breath came in short gasps as she saw once again the image of her bedroom in New York, and Jonathan making love to one of her friends. Far off in the distance, she was aware of a voice saying, "I'm sorry, Kate. I'm so sorry."

All Kate said was, "Did they see you?"

"No. And I didn't mention it later when I picked Kim up. I

don't know whether to take comfort in the fact that she was suffering from a hangover.''

"Or maybe she didn't have a hangover at all," Kate said dryly. "She just wanted an excuse not to talk to you."

A long silence filled the room. Finally Chris rose and walked to the windows beside the woman who up until a few days ago he had thought had all the happiness in the world. He placed his hand on the sleeve of her jacket. "I guess I want to know what you think I should do."

Kate laughed ironically and pulled away from Chris. She sat at her desk and picked up a folder of papers. "I suggest you forget you ever saw it, Chris." The words were clipped, with a mechanical sound, as if Kate had turned into a robot. "There is nothing to be done. Should I confront my husband with this now and fire Kim? That would be nice. The press release can read like this: 'Katherine Marchand, President of Marchand Syndicates, has announced that Kimberly Winston has been fired because she is sleeping with Mrs. Marchand's husband.' Would you like me to do that? No, Chris. I will do nothing of the kind and I strongly urge that you join me in this restraint—unless you're ready not only to give Kim up but also to destroy her career and her ability to support Jason. We would gain nothing by confronting them, at least not now. My wish is not even to know that this happened. I am going to forget you came here and what you told me. I suggest you do the same. No, I beg you to do the same." She stood up and walked to the door. "Perhaps this was just an isolated incident in Kim's life. On the other hand, 'He who listens to a fool, is a fool.' " She abruptly opened the door. "It was nice to see you, Chris. Goodbye."

Chris left the office just before the door closed behind him. As he moved through the entranceway, he heard Kate's voice on the intercom, asking Diana not to disturb her for a few moments.

Kate stood at the windows leaning her head into her hands on the cool glass. She was sobbing uncontrollably. She thought she had grown incapable of feeling this much hurt, this kind of betrayal. She swore at Jonathan through the tears, and then at Kim, her friend, the only one she'd ever taken to Rockport. . . . "Fool! What a fool I am," Kate cried.

Finally, she walked into the bathroom, washed her face and refurbished her makeup. When she was finished, control had returned. She stared at her image in the mirror. "Well, Katherine Marchand, he's done it to you again," she said to herself.

"And so what? If you'd admitted it, you always knew it would happen again some day. How do you know Kim is the second one? She could be the third. Or the fifteenth." Kate could not bear to think about her own intimacies with Jonathan, how she had shared and given of herself, how happy and trusting she had allowed herself to become.

"Yes, you are a fool, old girl," she said again to the mirror, but calmly this time. She began to brush her hair and in a quite calculated way, gave up on the passion she'd had for Jonathan. He did not deserve it. Whether he ever would . . . well, it remained to be seen.

Kate asked Diana to come in and immediately went back to work. If Diana noticed anything, it was only that Kate seemed more driven than ever. At one point Kate received a call from Jonathan and arranged to meet him for dinner. Her voice was steady and gave nothing away. That was how it was going to be. Under her control.

When Diana left for the day, Kate asked her for the tape of Kim hosting the Emmys. In the solitude of her office, Kate placed the video recording in the machine and started it. She watched calmly until the moment when Kim had welcomed Kate onto the stage. She froze the image of a smiling Kim, an arm extended, ready to greet the head of Marchand Communications.

"*You,*" Kate said solemnly, "I would have expected better of."

BOOK FIVE

FADE TO BLACK

"In the end, love is purely a matter of conscience and faith."

Søren Kierkegaard

1

WHATEVER THE HORROR OF HER PERSONAL LIFE, KATE Marchand's professional life was all-consuming that August. She was feverishly putting together the final pieces of Marchand Communications, the parent company that would soon absorb Marchand Syndicates and all its acquisitions. The operation took all her time.

On Wednesday morning at 6:30, Kate leaned over and clicked off the alarm, awakened by the sound of Jonathan's car going down the drive. He had told her he had very early morning surgery. Did he? Were any of his reasons for leaving the house true? Was it Kim he was going off to? Perhaps to sneak quietly into the townhouse overlooking the harbor, then leave before Jason awoke? Damn. She felt her back stiffen and said, "The hell with it," as she slowly walked into the bathroom, put on her suit and stretched her already tense muscles.

As she swam her laps, she thought about the events of the day before. Everything had gone as planned. She had held the news conference in New York, and Marchand Communications stock opened at its all-time high and went even higher. She herself became a millionaire several times over in the space of a few hours.

She had returned to Boston in time to see Kim announce the event on the six o'clock news, along with the release of a bulletin saying that a shuttle had safely deployed a Marchand Communications satellite that afternoon. The national business news also carried the consolidation information. Thus far all response had been favorable, and as far as Kate could tell, no one was yet aware of how close she was to pulling off her "coup."

"That's what I have to concentrate on," she told herself, "not those two. . . ."

She had finished her laps and, as she stood in the water pulling off her goggles, she found herself looking up the barrel of an M-16 rifle.

"What the hell!" she blurted.

"That's no way to talk, lady." A dark-haired, muscular man, a stocking pulled over his face, slowly lowered the scope away from his eye.

"What do you want?" she asked coldly. Her legs trembled when she saw two other men behind him, their heads also covered with masks. Kate recognized the weapons they had aimed at her: Uzi machine guns, oversized pistols. She had seen them many times in Vietnam, as she had also seen the M-16.

"I want to talk about that station of yours and the people you got working for you over there." He relaxed the gun in the crook of his arm, but his colleagues kept theirs aimed at her.

"How did you get in here?"

"Easy. People in this house, they keep regular hours, every day the same. Your husband, he leaves the house at six-thirty, the maid don't come in here till eight in the morning. All we got to do is come in the same minute his car goes out and we fool that fancy machine you got down there on the road. We practiced even, all last week. Anyhow, like I said, the maid doesn't get here till eight o'clock. That gives us plenty of time."

Kate tried to swallow her panic. "Since we have so much time, may I at least get out of the water?" She began moving, and immediately the rifle was raised.

"No!" he shouted. Kate froze, and slowly the gunman relaxed.

"Who are you?" asked Kate.

"Business people. Me and my friends are in business—how do you say?—like the pharmacy business—and we don't need that station of yours or that fucking blonde you got there messing with our business."

"What are you talking about?" Kate asked. "What business? Where?"

"Importing, lady, we import stuff. All you got to know is get your nose out of it or there'll be big trouble. That Winston bitch is messing around in places she don't belong . . . dangerous places. Understand?''

The man's accent was Latin and Kate took the chance: "*Señor*," she said, "I can see you are a gentleman, *un hidalgo*. I suffer from a weak back and we could talk better if I could just lean against the side of the pool.''

He shrugged, then gestured to the left. As she walked slowly to the side of the pool, and leaned her arm on the edge, Kate said, "Thank you." And then in a motion as quick as the flick of a snake's tongue, she grabbed the small wire running along the lip of the pool. Immediately a screeching siren sounded across the estate.

The gunmen turned to look around and Kate dove under the water, swimming along the bottom of the pool as it grew deeper and darker, and into the shadows. Thanking God for her lung capacity, she stayed down as long as she could. Even when her lungs began to ache, she counted seconds, trying to calculate how long it would take for the police sirens to be heard. When she could hold her breath no longer, she eased towards the surface. She lifted her head above the water, gulped air and then quickly descended as she heard shouts in Spanish.

Where were the police? The wire went to an alarm Jonathan had insisted upon so that if Kate got into trouble swimming, she could summon help. She had thought it foolish at the time but now she blessed her husband's protectiveness.

She had to come up for air again, and this time she did so aiming for another corner of the pool, hoping to throw off her attackers. As she broke the surface, the sound of sirens filled the air and she heard car doors open and slam.

When she surfaced this time, Kenny Dawson, one of the town's policemen, reached down to help her up. "You okay, Mrs. Marchand?''

When he saw that she was, he radioed the station. "They'll get the state police after those bastards and a couple of our guys will come up here.''

An hour later, after she had spoken to the police, Kate called the security force of WLYM and ordered all security strengthened. Anyone going in or out of the building would have to submit to a body search, as well as a strict identification check. She also ordered that all equipment and boxes be examined, including cassettes.

Then she called Diana, explained briefly what had happened

and told her to get in touch with Kim. "They must be Colombians," she said. "And they're worried about the cocaine story. Let's get all Kim's tapes out of LYM and into our safe deposit box at the bank."

Kate then called Jonathan—the habit of their love and mutual concern drew her to the phone. After explaining what had happened and hearing Jonathan's fear for her, his relief that she was safe, Kate told him that he also would have to be guarded.

When she arrived at her office, Diana told Kate that everything had been taken care of but that she had not been able to contact Kim because she was attending a special parents' day at Jason's school.

At four o'clock that afternoon, with Diana and Andrew Davis at her side, Kate entered the large conference room of WLYM. The room was filled with television, newspaper and magazine reporters representing not only the local media, but national as well.

As she walked up to a stand covered with microphones, Kate saw Kim slightly to her right. She stiffened and thought, How am I to think of her? My friend? My betrayer? How are we to get through this ordeal? Especially with this new danger. . . .

She turned her head sharply away and spoke into the microphones, as usual, without notes.

"Ladies and gentlemen, I appreciate your attendance at this rather hastily called news conference. I have a news story for you, and I also have a statement that I wish to address to some very dangerous people.

"This morning, at approximately six A.M., I was personally threatened at my home, at gunpoint."

There was an audible gasp throughout the room.

"The reason for their visit was to persuade me to stop an investigation in which Kim Winston is involved. They referred to themselves as in the pharmacy business and in importing. Since Ms. Winston has been, for several months, involved in preparing a story on cocaine and the Colombia connection—well, it seems safe to assume that is what this is all about.

"The police are actively pursuing these criminals and security has been increased for everyone even remotely involved in this matter, but I want it known that we here at WLYM will *not* be intimidated. Terrorism and violence, whether in the Middle East or North Africa or in Boston, Massachusetts, will not prevail. We will pursue our task of gathering and reporting the news—carefully, of course, but diligently, ladies and gentlemen. We will continue to be stubborn in our pursuit of the truth.''

Kate stood by the windows, looking out at the harbor below, only vaguely aware of the newscast on the monitor behind her. She was retracing the events of the day when she heard Diana talking outside her office door. There was a quiet knock and Diana leaned her head in and said, ''A Mr. Thomas McCarthy from the Justice Department would like to speak to you.''

''Send him in,'' Kate said.

''Mrs. Marchand, I'm sorry to add to your already long and hectic day,'' came the deep voice.

''That's all right, Mr. McCarthy,'' Kate said. She was stopped in mid-sentence by the woman who stood beside the Justice Department representative: Kimberly Winston.

The surprise of seeing her caught Kate off guard. It was the first time they had been face to face since the weekend at the Pines. Kate stared directly into Kim's eyes, as if she were sending a powerful beam toward the younger woman.

Finally, it was Kim who pulled her eyes away. She held tightly to her shaking hands. My God, she thought, it's as if she knows. But she *can't* know. And I have to stop this.

''You look like you've seen a ghost, Kim,'' Kate said. ''You really must not let these matters get to you.''

''Well, I can see why she might be a little shaken,'' interrupted McCarthy. ''but then I guess you're also a bit shaken, Mrs. Marchand.''

''For a few minutes today, I was,'' Kate said. ''However, that was earlier. Now I'm just trying to run a television station and protect my loyal employees.'' On the last phrase, she turned her eyes to Kim, again casting a dark shadow between them. ''Well,'' Kate cleared her voice, ''what can I do for you both?''

''As I've been explaining to Miss Winston, it is very important that we know the information obtained by your station that has obviously caused this incident.'' He cleared his throat. ''We're sure you see the reason why Miss Winston's investigation must stop immediately and that all the information she has must be placed in the hands of the Justice Department.''

Kate rose and walked towards the windows, her arms closed across her chest. ''I have no intention of stopping Miss Winston's investigative reporting. If she wishes to, she can. . . .''

''I have already told him that unless you order otherwise, I am prepared to continue . . . and want to,'' Kim broke in.

"So there's the answer to that question, Mr. McCarthy," Kate
said. "And as concerns my part, I will definitely not release any
tapes or information to you or anyone else. And to save you the
step of a search warrant, the tapes are not in this building."

"Mrs. Marchand, I think you fail to understand the seriousness of this situation."

"I think I do," Kate answered. "Remember, it was I they
came to visit this morning. You should understand that while
we will not obstruct justice we certainly won't stop our pursuit
of the truth. You've heard of the First Amendment, haven't you?"

McCarthy rose to his feet. "We could demand Miss Winston
appear in court and reveal her sources and other information.
As I recall, Massachusetts does not have a shield law to protect
journalists."

"I am very aware of the backwoods mentality of a Massachusetts legislature that does not provide a shield law," Kate
said. "But you can be sure I'll fight all the way to the Supreme
Court to defend my reporters' rights to the confidentiality of
their sources." Kate smiled at the Justice Department officer.
"I really think the best thing is to get on with business, ours
and yours. Like catching these people who have threatened me,
for example. And will no doubt threaten—and maybe kill—
others."

The police came to the Marchand home that evening and told
Kate and Jonathan that they were fairly certain that her assailants
had been Colombians, probably working out of Chelsea, a city
near Boston that was known for its drug dealing. "You know,"
the detective explained, "those are nice hard-working people
there in Chelsea. They came here to make a living and a better
life for their kids. Most of them are okay. You ever been to one
of those Colombian restaurants? A lot of rice and pork, but not
too heavy, like Mexican."

The other detective broke in, "Food aside, there are a few
people there—it's the same in New York, I hear, in Queens—
anyhow they're not in the restaurant business, that's for sure. It's
cocaine they're serving; crack, now, and there's a lot of money
involved. We put one of their top guys in jail a few months back
but, to tell you the truth, nothing much has changed. You still
got a lot of action in Chelsea and a lot of drugs on the street in
Boston and in Cambridge."

Jonathan said, "And that, obviously, is why they threatened
my wife. They want to stop Kim Winston's story from drawing

attention to their operation. But you guys must be on the case anyhow, whether LYM's involved or not.''

"Right, doctor," the first detective said. "And frankly, we'd just as soon amateurs would stay out of it. We've got enough problems without some big TV people getting hurt by cocaine dealers. But then, it's a free country. And we don't control the press.''

After they left, Jonathan put his arms around Kate and pulled her close. "Oh God, darling, I'm so relieved you're all right. I went crazy when I first heard the story when I came out of surgery this morning. I couldn't stand it if something happened to you.''

As Jonathan hugged her, Kate let herself lean into him, let her body feel his warmth, let her spirit be comforted by the concern in his voice.

Jonathan was rubbing her back with one hand, holding her pelvis tight to his with the other. He was kissing her eyelids, her cheeks, and her mouth, saying, "Oh, baby, I love you so. I couldn't do without you. Here, darling, come to me.''

Kate felt her body longing for him, softening after weeks of icy withdrawal. She moved with him as he gently pulled her to the floor. "They were awful, Jonathan, awful. I was really scared.''

"I know, darling, I know. It's too dangerous." He was opening her blouse now, reaching for her full breasts, rubbing them. "Too dangerous," he was saying. "Tell Kim to stop.''

Kate rolled away from him, pushing his searching hands from her body. "Never," she said coldly. "Forget it.''

2

KATE ARRIVED IN SAN FRANCISCO JUST BEFORE ELEVEN o'clock. Her elation about the business that brought her here drove out everything else for, within an hour, she would be signing the final papers to acquire the controlling stock of San Francisco's leading independent station. The negotiations had gone flawlessly and she was surprised as she entered the station manager's outer office to be given an urgent message to call her office as soon as possible.

When Kate reached Boston, Diana said, "I'm not sure I should have bothered you with this, but—well, better safe than sorry."

"What's up, Diana?" Kate asked impatiently.

"It seems Kim did not show up this morning to meet her crew. She was scheduled for a shoot at noon at City Hall. Andrew can't understand it. He says she's never even been late for an assignment before."

"Now wait a minute. You told me yesterday that everything had been taken care of. Monday night, Kim and Bill and some others were put under police protection as well as private guards. Well, where is Kim's guard and where are the police?"

"The police say Kim and the guard went into the market area," Diana's voice was anticipating the anger at the other end. "And they lost them. We haven't heard from the guard either."

"Diana, she's only what—about two hours late? Has anyone spoken to Maggie? Is Jason all right?"

"Jason is fine. Both Andrew and I have spoken to Maggie."

Kate asked quietly. "And Jonathan? Have you spoken to him?"

"Jonathan? Well, no, I didn't think to call him. But if you're worried about him, I can tell you he's fine. The police made sure that everyone's okay, including Jonathan."

Kate thought a minute, weighing her conflicting feelings against her duties. She said, "It sounds like everything's under control and there's no reason to panic. Call me if it's necessary and if anything new develops. I'm backed up with meetings this afternoon, tonight and all day tomorrow, but you know where to find me."

"Yes, Kate," said Diana quietly.

"Oh, one last thing. I should have done it before but put a private guard on Jason. He can handle it."

An hour later, the legal papers were all signed, and the attorney was shuffling through the copies for the various parties. There was a soft knock on the door and, without waiting for a reply, a secretary briskly walked into the room and handed the station manager a piece of wire copy. She said, "Under the circumstances, the news director thought you should see this bulletin."

He read the copy, looked up at Kate, then handed it across the desk silently. Kate warily began to read:

BOSTON:

The body of a private security guard was thrown from a speeding car shortly after noon today, landing within a few yards of the entrance to the television studios of WLYM. Police said the guard, Bill Nickerson of Worldwide Security, Inc., was shot twice in the head at close range. Nickerson was assigned to protect Kimberly Winston, the popular WLYM anchor and chief correspondent for Marchand Communications. Police revealed that at this time they do not know the whereabouts of Ms. Winston or the reason for the slaying of the security officer, but sources close to the investigation believe the incident may be linked to the recent break-in at the home of the owner of Marchand Communications, Katherine O. Marchand.

Kate felt a guillotine slam down on her neck. Within moments
she had gathered up her things, ascertained that there was a
flight to Boston within the hour, and sped to the limousine the
station had waiting at the door. The security guard who had
accompanied her from New York was with her and Kate noticed
that he held his hand inside his pocket—on a gun, she presumed.
"Mark," she said, "don't lose your head. They already have
the person they want. They know Kim Winston is . . . my most
valued employee."

Fifteen minutes later, Mark was rushing her through the
crowded halls of San Francisco International Airport. As they
passed alongside a row of people watching small black television sets, Kate saw out of the corner of her eye that there was a
break in the regular programming for a bulletin. Mark tried to
pull her along, but she stopped and stared as NRB's evening
anchor began to speak:

A radio station in Boston has just announced it has received
a message from a group claiming responsibility for the death
of a security guard in that city earlier today. The recorded
voice also maintained that they are holding as hostage Kimberly Winston, the well-known and highly regarded journalist
for WLYM and Marchand Communications. Ms. Winston is
reported by the studio as missing. The murder of security
agent Bill Nickerson and the kidnapping of Ms. Winston come
in the wake of the recent break-in at the home of Katherine
Marchand, the owner of Marchand Communications. . . .

Ignoring or forgetting her guard, Kate turned and sprinted toward the gate. She passed quickly through the weapons detector
and Mark, after showing that he was authorized to carry a
weapon, followed close behind. The area was deserted but the
ticket agent stood at the entrance to the plane, beckoning her
on.

"It's all right, Mrs. Marchand. We've been waiting for you.
The pilot has been advised of the situation." Within seconds,
they were down the ramp and entering the first class section of
the plane. As they went to their places Kate heard Mark formally
inform the steward that he was armed. Kate sank into her seat
and tried to contain herself but she felt dizzied by the pictures
flashing in her mind. Jonathan's body above a woman years
ago—who now was Kim. Kim's radiance as she accepted the
Emmy. Jonathan soaring in the sky, hang gliding—and Kate,

now Kim— beside him. Then Kim—running on the beach in Rockport, swimming with Jason at the pool. Jason. It is Jason I must remember, Kate thought. That wonderful child, fatherless . . . not motherless too, not that.

She dropped her head into her hands, willing herself to think. And the thought came to her that it was her fault that this had happened. She should have told Kim to slow down on the cocaine documentary. Perhaps she should not have been so vehement in her public statement, so provocative. And she should have taken more seriously Kim's lateness this morning. And now it was because of Kate that Kim's very life was in danger; that Kim might, in fact, right now be dead.

The security guard touched her arm and told her he had arranged with the captain that the plane would stop out on the runway when they landed at Logan Airport in Boston. They would radio ahead for Kate to be picked up there and thus avoid the press and possible danger in the terminal. The police and agents of the FBI would also be present.

Kate sank back in her seat and tried to analyze her situation. By the time the jet began its descent over western Massachusetts, she had gone through every highway and alley of her life and experience, trying to find the key to Kim's safe return while still guaranteeing the integrity and credibility of Marchand Communications.

The one thing she knew was that as much as possible, she had to maintain control herself. It was Kim's best hope, as well as Marchand Communications'. If Kate faltered, she was pretty sure the board would leave the affair exclusively in the hands of federal authorities. Kate's mind clicked through the botched attempts in the past to rescue kidnap victims. No, the "experts" had failed time and again. She had to stay as active as possible and in such a way that all that she had worked for was not taken from her. There was no doubt that Marchand stock would plummet at the news of the kidnapping, the uncertainty of what ransom would be paid, the possible tarnishing of the Syndicates' reputation for "going everywhere, saying everything."

It was clear. She had to save Kim to save her empire—and a human life. Jonathan had nothing to do with that. All that could wait. Now her entire being must focus on Kim.

But when the plane landed and, behind Mark, she stepped onto the steel ramp, she saw Jonathan running toward her. Out of a deep instinct, she ran into his arms.

"Oh, Jonathan, my God, my God. I did this."

"Stop, Kate, stop," he said, whispering in her ear. "Come on, we've got to go. They still think you're a target."

And as if on cue, a phalanx of plainclothesmen swelled around Kate and Jonathan. Mark grabbed her arm, and the large group of them walked toward a black van. Out of the corner of her eye, Kate saw that there were men crouched on the ground with rifles and machine guns. A waiting policeman pushed Kate, Jonathan and Mark into the back of the van and slammed the doors behind them. Inside a light was on, and Kate sat down on one of the padded benches along the side.

"Hello, Mrs. Marchand. I'm Norman Holbrook, FBI, Washington." He showed her a leather case that she did not bother to look at. Instead she was studying his eyes. Brown and dark, like the man himself, and strong, as he was.

"Mr. Holbrook," she said, extending her hand, "thank you for being here. Is there any word?"

"Not yet."

"Where are we going?" she asked.

Jonathan explained that everyone agreed that the house in Dover could not be used. It was too difficult to protect and too well known to the kidnappers.

"The same is true of Miss Winston's townhouse," Agent Holbrook said.

Jonathan continued, "We've rented a large condominium at Lewis Wharf. Jason and Maggie are there now. That way the FBI and the police can keep track of all of us more easily and. . . ."

"And Jason needs us with him," Kate added.

"Yes, though Chris is being really supportive too."

Maggie and Jason were waiting in the second-floor apartment on Boston's waterfront. Kate hugged the frightened boy and then Jason clung tightly to her hand as they walked through a small kitchen into the living room. They could see out the windows that the entire area had been cordoned off and was under heavy police protection. The intense security precautions had extended inside. Kate was aware of numerous men with walkie-talkies in the apartment and it seemed obvious that, under their jackets, they were all heavily armed.

Gary Kincaid, to Kate's surprise, was also present. "I couldn't bear to stay in New York," he said. "I got pretty attached to these guys." He ruffled Jason's hair, "and I thought I might be able to make myself useful."

When her eyes fell on Maggie and Chris, they must have seen

Kate's pain because they both moved toward her and put their arms around her. All three of them had tears in their eyes.

Kate turned Chris away from Maggie and said quietly to him, "I'm glad you're here."

He said, "This is where I want to be, Kate. Despite everything else, it's Kim I want. It's getting her back that counts." He slowly pulled away to look at Kate. "I hope you feel the same way, Kate. I hope you do." Kate nodded and they embraced again.

"You'll find that we have our best men pursuing this investigation, Mrs. Marchand," Holbrook said. "I doubt you will find it necessary to continue with your own protection agency."

"No," Kate said, "Worldwide Security has worked with Marchand Communications for a long time. I have faith in them. They have also paid a very dear price themselves today. Like me, they have a vested interest in the outcome of all this and I think you'll find they help, not hinder you in your work." Kate paused and said quietly, "And Mr. Holbrook, I wanted to tell you that I also will be working along with you. I think that our cooperating together can only be useful, don't you?"

"We always want cooperation, Mrs. Marchand. And that's especially true in regard to your previous statements about not dealing with terrorists."

"Now wait a minute, Mister!" Chris shouted. "We're talking about somebody's life here. They've already killed one person."

"Chris," Kate said. "I'm sure Mr. Holbrook is aware of that. There can be no decisions made until we know what we're up against. But right now, we all must remain calm."

"Kate, I want you to promise me you will keep me informed of every development, and every step you and these people take."

Holbrook said, "Dr. Cerci, I think it's important that Mrs. Marchand and I talk privately."

The others were escorted from the room and Kate, as she rarely did, poured herself a straight scotch. She then returned to the center of the room and a straight-backed chair.

Holbrook sat opposite her and said, "Let me begin by bringing you up to date. It is safe to assume that these guys have been following Miss Winston for the last forty-eight hours. The Boston police now recall situations where they believe there was a tail on Kim."

"Wonderful," said Kate bitterly. "A little after the fact, isn't it?"

"Yes, Ma'am. We also believe that the security man assigned to guard her was aware of it, at least this morning. He informed Miss Winston, in front of the nanny, that he would no longer follow behind her, but would walk alongside her. Such a change in surveillance usually means an agent believes someone may make a very bold move, such as literally grabbing the person away.

"Well, yesterday," continued Holbrook, "Miss Winston went into a stationery shop in Quincy Market and briefly looked at some writing paper. We know that she was in a hurry that day and told the sales clerk she would try to return the next day.

"Whoever was following her was probably waiting outside the store watching through the glass. Then this morning, when Miss Winston went into the stationery shop again, she was met by a different sales clerk. She had no reason to think this strange nor did her guard. Do you understand that?"

Kate was growing impatient. "I am following you just fine, Mr. Holbrook. Please continue. Where were the real clerks of the store?"

"They were in the back room where they were discovered shortly after noon. According to the testimony of these women, two other women came in, nicely dressed, with foreign accents. They asked to see wedding invitations and when the sample books were brought to them, they overpowered the clerks, chloroformed them and dragged them into the back room."

"And," said Kate, "presumably played a similar trick on Kim. But the security man? Didn't he put up a fight?"

"Yes, he must have, but they apparently had a male accomplice who overpowered him. Blood samples on the floor of the back room match his, along with pieces of skin. I'm sure he put up a struggle, and may in fact have come close to freeing himself and Miss Winston. That would explain the anger behind the subsequent shots to the head."

"But it's such a busy place. How did they get away?"

"The shop is on the ground floor and backs onto a small alley. Witnesses have recalled that a gray van was pulled up to the back of the stationery shop early that morning and seeing a man loading it. We can assume Miss Winston was forced into the van and driven away. We have no idea whether she was chloroformed or drugged."

Kate nodded. "Did you find any type other than Nickerson's in the blood samples?"

Holbrook looked like he was going to hedge, but when Kate

nodded encouragingly at him, he said, "We did not tell Dr. Cerci or her family, but yes, we found some O-negative blood, her type. We also found pieces of blond hair that we believe match hers. Her handbag was left at the scene, so we are type-matching from her hairbrush. It seems likely that Miss Winston may have struggled with the kidnappers."

"Excuse me, but you're saying a lot more than that, Mr. Holbrook." Kate's voice was angry for the first time, and as if to hide it, she walked over to the bar and spoke with her back to him. "You're saying there is a chance that Kim is injured, that she may in fact not even be alive."

Holbrook said nothing, looking down at the cigarette in the ashtray, thinking his first instinct had been right: He didn't want this case.

"I can only go by my knowledge in these matters, Mrs. Marchand. They haven't asked for ransom yet but that's usually what kidnapping is all about. If they wanted to kill her they would have done so in the shop. They know that they will certainly not get any ransom unless Miss Winston is alive."

Kate asked wearily, "Do you have any idea who the kidnappers are?"

"In fact, we do. I've brought the cassette that was delivered to the radio station announcing Miss Winston's kidnapping. Please listen to it carefully."

Kate watched as he put the ordinary-looking cassette in the recorder. As soon as she heard the voice, her hand trembled. "That's the same voice. That's *him*, the man at the pool."

"All right, Mrs. Marchand, would you look at a few of these pictures?" He held out a number of glossy prints to her.

"He was wearing a stocking over his face. Didn't the police tell you? But it was very sheer—as if they bought the wrong kind—and I could roughly make out his face. I told that to the police but they didn't think I'd be able to identify him."

"Well, have a look anyhow."

Kate turned through four of five photographs and then said decisively, "This is the man behind the voice."

"You're sure?"

"Strangely, I am. He held his head a little to one side, the way this man does, and he had that same very long neck. Of course I couldn't see his features exactly, but the configuration fits. Sharp nose, and that weak chin."

"You're sure?"

"I'm sure, in fact, absolutely sure. Of course, he's just a little more dangerous looking when he's holding an M-l6. Who is he?''

"Manuel Figueroa, the brother of Carlos Figueroa, who was convicted a few months ago and is now doing time for cocaine smuggling—on a multimillion-dollar scale.''

"So when they failed to frighten me. . . .''

"Right,'' Holbrook said. "They decided to up the ante. They'd probably read about your recent financial dealings and decided you were the one who could stop Miss Winston.''

"But the killing! It seems all out of proportion.''

"We're dealing with a lot of money here and they have a big stake in suppressing your uncovering and publicizing their operation. I suspect there are some rather high-level people who do not want to be exposed.''

Holbrook paused. "And there's something else I suspect. First of all, at the pool you—a woman—outsmarted them. And then, to make it worse, you went on television and rubbed it in.''

"Machismo,'' Kate said. "I hurt their male pride.''

"Well, it would be a mistake to think that's all that's involved, but I think it helps explain some of what's going on.''

Kate nodded. "Cocaine dealers aren't a liberation army, you mean. They're not like those insane Middle Eastern terrorists trying to get publicity for their cause.''

"No,'' Holbrook said, "they want to scare you off, but they also want to show publicly that they won't be pussy. . . .'' The agent put his hand to his mouth and said, "Sorry, ma'am.''

Kate shook her head. "That's okay, Mr. Holbrook, I get the picture. They took Kim because she was working on the story. . . .''

Holbrook said, "And because she's such an easy target—a woman who moves around the city a great deal, who is popular with the public, and someone they had reason to believe you would not wish to sacrifice.''

"What happens now?'' Kate asked.

"I think they will wait until this evening to move her to a safe location, probably in the New England area, perhaps even in Boston itself. With all the publicity, they'll probably let you and the rest of the country sweat it out for a few days, let everyone get tired, desperate, and careless. Then we'll hear from them.''

"I can assure you, Mr. Holbrook, that I may get tired, but I have never been careless.'' She rose and extended her hand. "And I suspect the same is true of you.''

After the agent had left, Kate and Jonathan retired to the room that had been set aside for them. They did not speak—for fear of what would be said and because there was no longer any need for words.

Jonathan lay down and pulled Kate close to him, holding her in his arms. She was not crying but her body trembled violently, as if from a fear too deep to escape. It was Jonathan who wept.

Responding to the internal clock that had been set when he was in medical school, Jonathan opened his eyes shortly after six and was for a moment confused about where he was and the circumstances that had placed him there. He leapt out of bed when he realized Kate was not beside him.

He found her in the shower. "I take it there's been no word?" Silence was his answer. "How is your back?"

"It's had better days."

Jonathan quickly stepped into the shower with her and turned her so she was looking directly at him. "Don't do this, Kate. Don't pull yourself away from those who love you. Don't withdraw. You must believe that there's no need for it. You and I are together—in this terrible business and in everything else."

She looked at him as the shower poured down over both of them. She did not know why but she believed him. Delusion perhaps. Wish fulfillment. But she needed Jonathan now and could not afford to think of Kim as anything but a friend and valued employee—who must be saved.

And she also knew what Jonathan was talking about. *Emotional shutdown*. That was her phrase. She had only gone into it a few times—once when she returned from Vietnam, and again, in the hospital after the loss of the baby. No one had been able to get near her. She had dealt solely from logic, given no consideration to the rest of her life. There was no emotion. And she knew that's what she was doing now . . . because it was safe. But again, when Jonathan pulled her to him, she allowed herself the comfort of his arms.

A half hour later, Jonathan left and Kate stood before the mirror. Diana had gone to Dover and brought a large suitcase of clothes for the Marchands. Now Kate was dressed in gray wool slacks, a matching gray sweater. As she eased over her stiff shoulder a white cashmere jacket, she heard the sound of a child crying.

Kate went immediately to the room Jason and Maggie shared. Maggie had gone to make the boy his breakfast and he sat on the floor weeping as he pulled on his socks. The sight of his tearful face above his Boston Red Sox pajamas broke Kate's heart. She knelt down and said, "Here, honey, let me help you."

"I'm old enough to dress myself now, Kate. That's what my mommy. . . ."

He was sobbing now, saying, "I want my mommy. I want to go home to my own house with my mommy. Where is she, Kate? Why are we here?"

"What have they told you, Chase?"

"Some men just came and got me at school yesterday, and Maggie and Chris said some people have taken Mommy and will give her back soon. Is that true?" He raised his head and Kate felt her heart stop as she saw the brilliant blue eyes that were so like Kim's.

"That's true, dear." She decided there was no way to hide the facts of the kidnapping from Jason, but she softened the danger and spared him the bloody details.

"But Kate, if it's all going to be okay, how come all these people are here, and I can't go to school? And Chris was crying before and so is Maggie."

"All these people are upset because this is the hardest time . . . waiting to hear from your mommy. And you're not going to school because I need you right by my side."

He was quiet for a moment, then said very quietly, as if he were telling a secret, "I don't know what I'd do if I lost Mommy too."

"Neither do I, Jason. Neither do I." She pressed his head against her. "So we're not going to lose her. But why don't you stay with me in my room today? Sort of keep me company. Okay?"

When the child nodded, Kate said, "Get your clothes, then get changed and we'll go have breakfast." Holding back tears, she returned to her room. Jason soon came running in with his clothes. Quickly he changed into jeans and a sweater, socks and sneakers.

"I'm ready," he announced.

"Teeth and face," said Kate. "Your mommy will have my head when she gets back here and finds out you haven't been brushing."

A moment later, they walked hand in hand into the large dining room. "Good morning, ladies and gentlemen," Kate said. "It smells like the specialty this morning might be pancakes."

"Coming right up," Maggie answered.

Diana and Gary Kincaid were at the table and Kate asked Gary what the public reaction had been to the events of the day before. She talked abstractly, hoping not to alarm the child further.

"Shock, great dismay and anger. You've received telegrams from all over the world, including Prince Charles and Lady Diana."

"And the king and queen too?" Jason asked as he attacked the pancakes Maggie placed in front of him.

"Sure, fella. I just forgot to mention them," Gary said.

"And I heard from the president's press secretary last night," he continued. "He said the president sends his concern and will call later this morning."

"Well, there is one thing that must be done now," Kate said. "Someone must go through the tapes that Kim has shot and see if there is any information that may help us. Gary, you're the best judge of that. Diana, I want you to take a playback machine and monitor to the bank with Gary and help him. You should also interview Kim's cameraman and sound person."

"Isn't the government going to want to look at those tapes?" Gary asked.

"Of course they are, but without a court order, they cannot." She turned back to Gary. "If you do find something that will help Holbrook and his men, then bring it to their attention immediately. There's no sense standing on principle right now if we can help Kim by working with the government."

The day wore on. There was no word. Neither the FBI nor the police had found anything. Cocaine dealers in New York and Boston had been detained for questioning. A delegation from the Colombian community in Chelsea had made a formal statement deploring Kim's kidnapping and promising to cooperate to the fullest in finding her abductors and stopping the drug trade.

Diana and Gary left for the bank and returned a few hours later to say that they had found nothing on Kim's tapes that would lead to her possible kidnappers. There was plenty of potentially incriminating evidence, but who it led to was apparently knowledge held by only one person—Kimberly Winston.

The police also had not turned anything up. As these reports— or nonreports—came in, Kate paced the living room floor. After turning Jason over to Maggie, she had sent telegrams to every member of the board of Marchand Communications, assuring them they would be advised of any news and any planned action by her. The press was informed that the kidnappers had not been heard from.

At about noon Mark announced that the security guard on the ground floor was reporting that a Mr. Andrew Davis was requesting to see her. Andrew was positively identified, but when he walked into the room, he seemed a changed, much older man. There were tears in his eyes and when Kate said, "Come on, Andrew, you know Kim. She'll be okay," Andrew replied, "Kate, these men seem to be ready to go to any length."

"I know, but they can't negotiate over a dead woman. That's what we need to hold on to."

"The station is like a wake. Those people really love Kim and their emotions run from anger to sorrow. I don't know what to do about Bill. He just about cracked on the news last night. And to tell you the truth, I don't know myself how to cover this story." Andrew slumped into a chair, obviously exhausted.

"I'm afraid just like any other, Andrew."

"It would help if you made a statement, Kate."

"What would I say? Plead with them? Beg them? I can't do that. I can't make a move until they make theirs. They know I'm here, and I'm waiting. It would only make Kim's position more dangerous if we acted rashly." She went to the window and then turned away impatiently. "I wish these damn curtains could be opened," she said.

"Kate, a lot of people are saying that you cannot possibly give into any demands, not in light of what you've said, or what they've already done. They're saying that a television station, in particular, can't deal with terrorists." Andrew put his hand to his head. "As for me, I hope you'll remember, it's Kim. . . ."

"Oh, for Christ's sake," Kate shouted. "Don't you think I know who it is? Don't you think I wonder what type of hell she is in every moment? Every second?" She turned and headed out of the room. "Andrew, just cover the story as you're trained to, and tell Bill Halliday and the rest of the staff that if they have any guts at all, or any feelings for Kim, they'll get a grip on themselves and show to the world that a few lousy drug dealers cannot intimidate WLYM and Marchand Communications."

When Andrew left, Kate went to her room. The morning newspapers lay on the bed and from a half dozen front pages, she saw Kim's face smiling up at her. Then she saw the accompanying picture of the body of Bill Nickerson, the security guard, in front of the WLYM building. And then Kate's own picture with the caption: "Terrorism and violence, whether in the Middle East or North Africa or in Boston, Massachusetts, will not prevail."

Kate did not know what to do. She felt as if nothing was happening, no one was doing anything. If the kidnappers did not contact them, it would mean Kim was dead. Kate shuddered as she thought of the gruesome possibility that they might throw acid in her face to destroy her looks or harm her—in some horrible way—so she could not speak.

And if none of that happened, if, as the FBI man had said, they contacted Kate for ransom or made other demands, what would she do? Would she pay? Would that even save Kim? Would the Marchand Syndicates board of directors do something foolhardy? Pay before they knew Kim was safe?

In any case, if they did deal with those bastards, if any of them had anything to do with the kidnappers, her own credibility and that of the organization she'd struggled so hard to create, would be hopelessly compromised—especially after she'd vowed never to deal with them.

Kate shook her head impatiently and thought, "And, Katherine Marchand, how much of your thinking is influenced by what happened in Rockport that weekend a century ago when your husband . . ."

Aloud, Kate said, "None. That is *not* a factor now."

3

THE NEXT MORNING . . . STILL NO WORD.

Diana looked up from the desk in the large bedroom where she was sorting through the telegrams and phone messages she had picked up at the office. Kate was lying on the bed, Jason cuddled up against her, reading *The Little Prince*. It seemed strange to Diana to hear a children's book read in Kate's commanding voice. On the floor beside her bed lay the German shepherd puppy Chris had bought Jason to distract him and who, much to Kate's dismay, had been named Katey. Kate was at the part in the book where the little prince learns that the things most important are those that we cannot see. Kate explained to Jason that the writer was talking about what we feel.

"Like the love we feel for Mommy," the child said.

Diana's eyes filled with tears as she watched them. Kate, with Jason, was a different person than Diana had ever seen before, warm and demonstrative.

But fifteen minutes later, when Maggie had taken Jason off to dress him, reading the business section of the morning paper, Kate began to curse. "Goddamn it, Marchand's down four points. Those lily-livered cowards. They think we're all going down the tube because of these shit-dealing bastards. Diana, call my broker and ask her to check whether there were any major insider transactions. Let's find out if any of our own people are jumping ship. Bastards!''

It was at that moment that Norman Holbrook appeared in the doorway. He simply nodded. Kate knew exactly what he meant as the steel rod moved coldly through her soul.

Kate and Diana followed Holbrook into a back room where most of the communication equipment was set up as well as a small arsenal.

"This was dropped in a mailbox in front of your office. I guess they just assumed it would get to you." Holbrook was holding a nondescript battered envelope that had pasted on it the pictures of Kim and Kate that had appeared in the newspapers. "The postman was wise enough not to open it. He brought it to your office and then it was turned over to our people who X-rayed it. We know there are no wires and it was also checked for fingerprints."

He handed the envelope to Kate who began carefully pulling back the scotch tape.

As soon as Kate opened this envelope, she knew this was no hoax. Kim's jeweled and enameled necklace, the rubrum lily, fell into her hand.

"Oh my God," said Kate, taking in a breath, her hand beginning to tremble.

"Is it Miss Winston's?"

"She's always wearing this necklace," said Kate softly, turning it over in her hand. "There's only one like it. It was handmade, specially designed for her."

"Are you sure?"

"I'm sure," Kate said. She emptied the remaining contents of the envelope on the table. A cassette, the same common make as the one before. Holbrook picked it up with his handkerchief and placed it inside the recorder.

"I should warn you, Mrs. Marchand," he said, "the first tape from a kidnapper is usually pretty harsh, pretty mean. Don't get upset." He pressed the proper button and sat down on the edge of a nearby table. There was silence and then the unmistakable voice of Manuel Figueroa.

"*Buenos días*, *Señora*. So we're talking again and I'm holding that same gun you and me were playing with at that fancy pool of yours. Only this time, I got it stuck right in the back of this blond bitch of yours. Listen, she don't look so good right now, not like on TV. A little mussed up, see? But if you want her back, it's easy. Listen: Just tell those FBI guys all they gotta do is release my brother—that's Carlos Figueroa at the Cedar Junction prison in Walpole. And all you got to do is get together nine million dollars. That's what it will take. Just set that up, see, and Kimicita here will be okay. Otherwise—bang. That's it. You got that? *Entiende*? Okay. Tomorrow you hear from us again."

It seemed so unreal, almost like a TV crime show, except that just as his words stopped, a low moaning could be heard and then a scream . . . . It was unmistakably Kim.

Kate held her jacket closed at her throat, as if it were cold in the room. "What do you do now, Mr. Holbrook? What are your plans for rescuing Miss Winston?"

"We'll get to work immediately analyzing the tape, we'll intensify our search of the area and our questioning in the community and we'll decide what to do about the demands—especially the ransom."

"As to the latter decision, Mr. Holbrook, as to the ransom, there is no 'we.' I'll make that decision with the help of my board."

An hour later, Gary Kincaid and Diana were sitting at the kitchen table. "Kate's been in her bedroom for over an hour. What can she be doing?" Gary asked.

"She's thinking," Diana said shortly. "You've forgotten what she's like."

"But shouldn't she be getting advice from someone?"

"Kate Marchand only gets advice from herself," answered Diana. "That's part of her character. But to be fair, she knows all the variables. Her reputation, her company, and Kim's life all depend on her now."

"If word of this demand gets out, she's in serious trouble," Gary said. "Even though boards of corporations usually pay ransom demands, it's a no-win situation—just like Iran or any other kidnapping."

"The board won't pay nine million, and they'll never release that guy from jail," Diana said.

"And the alternative? Probably Kim's death. These guys will do it. I mean, the guard is being buried today."

"What time?" They turned to see Kate standing in the doorway.

"It's a graveside service at four o'clock down in Providence. That's where his family's from." Diana looked at her quizzically. "I sent flowers for you."

Kate looked at her watch. It was shortly after noon. "We'll make it in time."

"Kate," Gary said, "would you mind explaining what's going on?"

"It's very simple. We now know what the kidnappers want and it's not me. They need me free to get them what they want. Right now, Marchand Communications appears to be without a leader. That has to stop. I am coming out of hiding. I'm going to that service this afternoon and I'm going to begin negotiating with Figueroa."

"But you don't even know if Kim is still alive."

"I'm going to find out," Kate said. "Diana, call Andrew. Tell him to clear the news set for me. I'm going to tape a message to be broadcast this evening. Tell him I want as few people as possible around. Have him prepared to dub off copies for the other stations and the networks. Gary, please inform Mr. Holbrook. Also tell the press I'll be attending Nickerson's funeral. I'm sure they'll be covering it anyway. And make sure our own security people are with me."

Kate returned to the bedroom where Jason had been playing. She explained to him that she'd be gone for a few hours and that it would be better for him to wait in the apartment.

"It would be better for you, too." Kate turned and saw her husband in the doorway. Jonathan said, "Jason, go ask Maggie if she can make me a snack, please. I'll be right along."

As soon as the child left, he said to Kate, "You're not going to take the chance. I won't allow it."

"Jonathan, I have no choice anymore. Our stock's falling—another four points this morning. No one knows who the hell is running Marchand Communications. I don't know if Kim is dead or alive. I only know the kidnappers think they're beating me and I'm going to show them. As the saying goes, I've just begun to fight."

"Holbrook says you should just wait."

"Jonathan, go listen to that tape. And after you listen to it, come back here and see if you still want me to wait."

He stalked out of the room as she changed. By the time she was ready, Jonathan was back, ripping a dark suit out of the closet.

A few moments later, with Jonathan on one arm and the guard Mark on the other, a phalanx of agents surrounding them, Kate was ushered into the back seat of the limousine. Despite Holbrook's objections, she refused to go into the underground entrance of WLYM. She knew the press would be staked out in front and she wanted the world to see her walking into her studios.

When the limousine pulled up in front, the crews were indeed waiting and in the corridors of WLYM, several of her employees were shocked to see her pass by.

Andrew, Gary Kincaid and Diana were waiting in the news studio with a few technicians.

"Hello, Andrew. Sorry for the short notice."

"So you heard from them?" he asked.

"Yes, but the trouble is, I don't know if Kim is all right. That's what this is all about." Turning to Diana, Kate asked, "Were you able to fix that?"

"Oh, yes," answered Diana quickly, taking something from her pocket and handing it to Kate.

"All right, let's get this over with." Kate turned and headed for the news set. After hesitating briefly, she sat in Kim's chair.

Inside the control room, Julie, the director, put on her headset. "Okay, give me a single of Kim. I mean Kate. I mean . . . oh shit." She shook her head, trying to hold back the tears that had been flowing almost nonstop since Kim's disappearance.

"What's the problem?" Kate asked, adjusting her microphone.

Putting his hand over the mouthpiece of his headset, Eddie, the cameraman said, "We've all been taking this awfully hard, Mrs. Marchand."

Kate nodded, and knowing her mike was open, said, "I know this is a hard time for all of us, but what we're doing right now is for Kim."

"I'm sorry, Mrs. Marchand," came the voice over the loudspeaker. "I guess it's the necklace that threw me off the most." For the first time, the others in the control room noticed. Kate was wearing Kim's lily necklace, the torn gold chain knotted conspicuously near the front.

Julie pressed a button in front of her, once again activating the loudspeaker in the studio. Ordinarily she would speak to the floor director, but Andrew had said using one was not necessary, so Julie gave the instructions. "Voice check, please."

"The quality of mercy is not strained. It droppeth. . . ."

"Thank you," came Julie's quick reply. In the control room, Gary smiled to himself. That had been Kate's usual voice check in New York. Today it seemed particularly appropriate.

"Roll tape," said Julie. "Tell me when we have speed." She

listened and a few seconds later, "Pull back a little, Eddie, I want to see her hands . . . that's better. The gold bracelet looks nice against the dark suit. Okay, tell her we've got speed, anytime she's ready."

"This morning I received a taped message from Mr. Manuel Figueroa concerning the fate of Kim Winston. In this tape. . . ."

Everyone in the control room stared in disbelief. Kate's voice had cracked, her eyes had filled with tears, and her hands had begun shaking.

"Stop tape!" Julia shouted. "Switch her off." The switcher next to Julie automatically took another source so Kate's image could not be seen. Julie didn't know if she acted out of training or because she couldn't bear to see Katherine Marchand break down.

Diana and Jonathan rushed out to the studio, but Kate had already taken off the microphone and stepped away from the camera. She was squeezing her hands together and pacing. "Please," she said, "let me alone."

When they got back to the control room, Holbrook said, "I don't like this delay. Even though we have men on the entrances, too many people know she's in here."

The moments passed in silence, then Julie put her headset back on. "How are we doing, Eddie?" She listened, then said to no one in particular, "She's getting back on the set." Another few seconds passed. "Okay, take Camera Two, Willy." She smiled at the technician next to her.

Kate's image came up on the screen again. Everyone noticed something different about her, and Julie, whose business it was to study expressions through the camera, pinpointed it. "She's got it now. She's mad." And in fact, Kate did look angry.

"Okay, Julie, tell me when you're ready."

Kate began again. "This morning I received a taped message from a man called Manuel Figueroa. He says he is holding Kim Winston as hostage. He also made specific demands that I will not honor by even responding to at this time. Apparently Mr. Figueroa is under the impression that Marchand Communications is on its knees begging for mercy, willing to do anything he desires. Well, you are wrong, sir. Nothing, absolutely nothing will be done until I hear Miss Winston's voice talking directly to me. I will make no move until I have heard the voice of Kim Winston. Deliver a tape of Kim answering the following questions: What is the name of the first flowers to arrive at the hospital during her son's recent illness? Second, if you wanted to get away for a weekend of solitude, where would I suggest you go? If you do have Kim and she is well enough, she will know the appropriate answers to these questions. Get that tape to me, Figueroa, and then perhaps we will begin negotiating.''

In the control room, Julie checked the tape. After a few seconds of rollback, she spoke into her headset. ''Okay, that's a take, Mrs. Marchand. Hope it helps.''

Kate smiled weakly into the camera as she took off her microphone. As the guards directed her to the limousine, Holbrook asked, ''Are you sure she's going to remember the name of the first flowers?''

''If she's alive and coherent, she'll have no trouble remembering. And I'm hoping that in naming that place of seclusion, she'll somehow give us a hint as to where she is.''

In the car, Kate allowed herself to feel some hope for the first time. She knew that so far she had not compromised herself or Marchand Communications. And she had shown she was back in command.

As the limousine headed onto the expressway towards Rte. 95 and Providence, Kate sank in the seat and sighed. Jonathan reassuringly took her hand in his. At first she just stared at his hand. Yes, she thought, the same hand that had stroked Kim. And now, here she was, the betrayed wife, trying to save her husband's lover. She closed her eyes and clenched her teeth. I must not think like that, her brain demanded. I am saving a loyal employee. A woman whom I have pushed into dangerous journalism waters.

She squeezed Jonathan's hand and continued to hold it, not looking at him. She would take whatever comfort she could get in this crap game. Somehow, she had to save Kim. She had to save Marchand Communications.

4

THE FOLLOWING MORNING, AT BREAKFAST, JASON PUT HIS face into Kate's neck and mumbled, "I know what it means if Mommy is not on the next tape."

Kate tugged him closer to her. While Kate was at the Nickerson funeral the day before, Maggie had been busy in the kitchen and had not realized until it was too late that Jason was watching the news. "What do you mean?" Kate now asked hesitatingly.

"It means Mommy has gone to be with Daddy." He said it firmly and bravely. Kate didn't know what to say. She just held him, but his attention seemed to quickly return to his cereal. Oh God, she thought, help us all.

"Ahhh . . . hum." Kate did not turn in her chair. She knew the sound of Norman Holbrook clearing his throat. It meant there was some news, or possibly a tape. Diana got up and a few seconds later Maggie came bustling into the living room, saying she had some new dog food for Katey and asking Jason if he wanted to feed her.

Kate rose and walked stiffly back to the communications room. She looked around. Gary, Diana, Mark, Holbrook, and a few policemen were present.

"Another special delivery," Holbrook said. "The postmen are now alert for them. It's another cassette. At least we know from their response time that they're not on the other side of the earth. But then,'' he added weakly, ''they could also be any- where within a twelve-hour drive of Boston.'' He opened the envelope and handed Kate the cassette, with the handkerchief. She placed it into the recorder in front of her, and then snapped down the plastic lid.

Her finger moved onto the play button, but she did not have the strength to push it. She felt dizzy and weak and was afraid for a moment that she was going to be sick.

''Kate! Kate!'' She shook her head. Gary had his arm around her. ''Are you all right? What's going on?'' She sat upright, taking a breath and clearing her mind. The nausea did not lessen, but she started the machine. The wheels of the cassette went around. Silence. For about a minute there was no sound.

''Damn! Another prankster,'' Holbrook said. ''We thought for sure it was Figueroa because the package looked the same. Your and Kim's picture. And only the postman knows how it came yesterday.''

''And if it is from them, the blank cassette means. . . .'' Kate looked up at Holbrook, but before he could answer, there was a click on the tape and the crackling of a microphone. They all stared down at the turning cassette, and then the voice began.

''The flowers were rubrum lilies, distinct because they have two red stamens coming out from the top of the flower. For a quiet weekend, Katherine Marchand would tell me to go to a house in Stoneridge. But I would take Chase.''

Kate hit the stop button and put her face into her hands and cried openly, unashamedly. ''That's her. That's Kim. She's all right.'' Tears were in everyone else's eyes, also, even Hol- brook's.

Kate jumped up and ran from the room. ''Jason . . . Chase. . . .'' She found him in the kitchen and scooped him up. ''Your mommy's okay, honey. Your mommy's okay.'' Turn- ing to Maggie, she said, ''Maggie, she's on the tape. She's okay.'' Maggie pulled out her rosary, crossing herself. Kate carried a laughing, crying Chase back into the communications room. She smiled lovingly at Diana and Gary who were crying with relief in each other's arms.

Kate sat down with Chase, rewound the tape a bit, then pressed ''play,'' this time with a broad smile. As soon as Chase heard his mother's voice he smiled, and nodded, staring at the tape as if he were looking at his mother.

"I take it those are the right answers," Holbrook said, smiling at Jason.

"Well, it's definitely Kim's voice." Kate rose and began pacing the room. "But I'm confused. I don't know why she said Stoneridge. I would have urged her to go to Rockport, where I have a home on the ocean. Why didn't she just say that?"

"That's easy to understand," Holbrook said quickly. "She's trying to give us a lead as to where she is. Are there any towns around here called Stoneridge?"

"Not that I'm aware of," Kate said. "There is a Stoneham, but that is far too obvious. Figueroa and his people are not going to let her name where she is."

"No, of course not. But she could take advantage of their unfamiliarity with the area and name a place that is near to where she is being held. I'm sure there are plenty of towns in New England that have 'stone' in their name."

"Why would she say she would take Jason with her?" Gary asked. "Has he been to Rockport with her?"

"No," Kate said. "She's either been with me, or she's been alone." She was glad Jonathan was at the hospital and could not see her flinch as she spoke.

"Well, it seems to me she's trying to use a place that her son has been to," Holbrook said, turning to Jason, who was still happily listening to the sound of his mother's voice. "Son, can you tell me about places you've been with your mom recently?"

He looked at Kate and then looked around the room uncomfortably. "No," he said in a whisper.

"Yes you can, honey," Kate said, sitting next to him and holding him in her arms. "Remember when you and Mommy went to Vermont hang gliding with Jonathan?"

"Yes," came the quiet reply.

"Vermont. . . ." Holbrook said, letting the word dangle. "Aren't there a lot of quarries up there?"

"Yes, many," Kate said, her voice growing more excited. "And many of them have been abandoned."

"Isn't that convenient?" Holbrook smiled. "A perfect place to keep someone. A deserted quarry, where all sounds echo so you could hear someone approaching a half mile away. I think we may be onto something here. I'm going to go to the hospital and get more details about the area they were in from your husband, and in the meantime, I'll have men begin checking any city, town, or neighborhood that has stone in it."

As Kate watched the men begin to go after what appeared to

be leads in Kim's direction, she took Jason's hand and walked out of the room, towards the kitchen. Something was gnawing at the back of her brain, and she couldn't pull it into her consciousness. Stoneridge? Stoneridge? What was it about that name? And the rubrum lily, did it really have two red stamens sticking up? It didn't seem quite right to her. As soon as she delivered Jason to Maggie, she went into her bedroom and called a florist.

The days passed, and though the police and the FBI seemed to have located every quarry in the Northeast, nothing had turned up. Kate was growing more nervous all the time. She said angrily to Holbrook, "Why is nothing happening?"

He answered, "We still have a lot of ground to cover and unfortunately, we're wasting a lot of time following false leads. Miss Winston is so popular, everyone wants to help, so everyone and his uncle is calling in to share their suspicions with us. Usually people don't want to get involved. We have just the opposite situation here. She seems to be really special."

"That's why we have to keep her alive, Kate," Chris Cerci said. "The public will never forgive you if you let anything happen to her."

"What makes you think I'm going to let anything happen to her?"

"I'm sorry, Kate. I guess I don't have your stamina," he apologized. "Kim is so important to me and I'm a little frayed around the edges. But it has been five days since we've heard from her. And these guys are killers, we know that. The stories of their activities in Latin America are horrendous, and we know that the papers are full of 'drug-related murders.' "

It was late in the afternoon and both Chris and Jonathan were in the apartment. Jonathan went to stand behind Kate, his hands on her shoulders.

"Kate doesn't need any more pressure, Chris. This whole thing is as tough on her as on anybody. . . ." He paused and then said, "Kim had become her close friend, not just her employee. We should all remember that."

Kate sighed and squeezed Jonathan's hand in silent acknowledgment of the apology implicit in his words. Then she said, "It's all right. I think Chris is right. It's time to move. First thing tomorrow morning we'll issue a press release announcing a meeting of the board of directors for the following day. I think there's nothing more to be gained from waiting. It is too dangerous for Kim—they're not making any progress in finding her. Our stock falls daily, the entire acquisition plan is in limbo. . . . No, none of that counts. It's Kim's life at stake.''

Chris said, "Thank God. I was so afraid that after you made that statement about not dealing with kidnappers . . . well, that it was hopeless.''

"Did you think I'd abandon her?'' Kate asked. "In any case, people are so concerned with Kim's safety that our dealing with those people will be understood.''

By the following morning, none of this was possible. Three young teenagers had gone berserk, breaking the serenity of the Ivy League community of Harvard. They had boarded the MBTA, taken the Red Line to Cambridge, entered the Harvard Co-op, and sprayed the crowded department store with bullets. Police said the youths were apparently "stoned out of their minds'' on cocaine, on crack, and other drugs. The guns, like the drugs, were "off the street.''

Eighteen people had been struck. Twelve were dead, as was one of the perpetrators. Among the dead were six children, including a pair of five-year-old twins. The newspaper headline read, "CRACK MASSACRE.'' The mayor and the governor issued a statement that they were declaring "all-out war'' on cocaine and that anyone connected with the drug trade, in Boston or anywhere else, would be hunted down and prosecuted. A special judges' panel promised "no leniency and no mercy.''

"Oh my God,'' Kate said. "The world will never let me ransom Kim now.''

Leonard Mankin called shortly after this news hit the air. He said that he had polled the board by telephone and they were unanimous in their decision *not* to negotiate with the Colombians. When Kate tried to call Holbrook, she was told that he was out in one of two planes flying up and down the coast, searching for . . . whatever they could find.

Chris had come to be with Jason, and Kate said to him, "I assume, Doctor, that you think I should negotiate, even with this latest horror.''

Chris said, "Don't think I'm ignoring your problem, Kate. I know you want to have Kim freed. Of course you do. But there's a good chance your reputation, your credibility, will be ruined if you deal with those bastards, after what happened in Cambridge. There's a good chance you'll lose everything you've worked for all your life. But Kate, none of that is important now. The only thing that counts is Kim's safety.''

A policeman came into the living room and announced that Kate's friend Deborah Falkenstein was waiting. When Deborah came into the room, she and Kate embraced and almost at once, Deborah said, ''Kate, we're all so fond of Kim. She's wonderful. You must be going through hell.''

Kate nodded as Deborah said, ''But you know you have no choice. If you do negotiate or pay anything—the whole country will be up in arms. Think of the hard line Wall Street is taking. No one expects you to bow to the kidnappers. Everyone's saying that since those kids went crazy. Well, be thankful, this whole thing is out of your hands now. Leave it that way.''

''Leave it that way? It's *my* responsibility. Aside from any personal feelings I have—how much Jonathan and I care for Jason, for example—aside from all that, Kim was working for *me* when she got into this trouble. It was because she was pursuing a story for LYM that she got in the way of these drug dealers in the first place. We got her into it, it's our duty to get her out.''

''How, for God's sake?'' Deborah asked.

''Not by sitting around in this prison-by-the-sea, that's for sure.'' Kate got up, went for a coat and headed for the door. ''I'm going to work. That's where I do my best thinking.''

Kate insisted to the men assigned to guard her that her trip was urgent and, within a half hour, she was in her office. But once she was behind her desk, she found she could not work, could not concentrate. The huge room seemed to her as confining as the condominium. She looked around her office, and it seemed filled with symbols of the power, the empire she had amassed. But now, she thought angrily and sadly, all that power did her no good. She was basically powerless right now. Powerless to save Kim.

With her guard Mark trailing behind her, she went to the newsroom. It was shortly after four and there was the usual prenews rush going on. Bill Halliday was banging away at his typewriter. Other reporters were rushing in and out of the room from the various editing suites. The large board on the wall told the location of every mobile unit, and every reporter who wasn't inhouse. Her eyes fell on the stenciled ''K. Winston'' at the top of the board. Next to her name, there was a blank. In the corner, where Kim's empty desk was, a small vase of fresh, bright flowers sat next to the typewriter.

Kate turned her blurred gaze away from Kim's chair and saw Julie working at her center desk, looking more frayed than usual. "Is anything wrong?" Kate asked.

Julie was visibly startled by Kate's presence.

"Sorry, Kate," she said. "I guess I'm more jumpy than usual these days. If you're looking for Andrew, he's not here." She held up to Kate the news rundown. "But then, there aren't too many people here."

Kate looked around and said, "So I see. What's going on?"

"Oh, everything is legit. Andrew is worn out. He left early. It was so slow, then all hell broke loose. And of course just when we're short of producers. Like the news producers."

"Where are they?"

"As I said, all legit. One's wife is giving birth even as we speak. Another was in a fender bender on the expressway and is undergoing routine X rays. Nothing serious. The director for the five-thirty is still out with the mobile unit covering that trial in Providence. And although Susan, the associate producer, is here, she really shouldn't be. She got served with divorce papers this morning. Neglect. Husband says she spends too much time at work."

Kate followed Julie's glance towards a very harried looking woman going through the wire copy with Bill Halliday.

"Well," Kate said firmly, pulling a chair next to Julie's, "I'd say you need a producer for the news, especially if you're going to end up directing both the five-thirty and the six."

"That would certainly be a help," Julie said, wondering who Kate had in mind. Then at Kate's slight smile and wink, she realized she was looking at that producer.

"Okay, let's see where we stand," Kate said, picking up a pen and the news rundown.

Moments later, the rundown was redone, and reporters and editors were scurrying to the commands of their employer. Kate added flair and drama to the newscast by pulling in more live feeds, including a double satellite link between Washington and New York. Locally, she had microwave units go live from an oil spill in the harbor, a nursing home fire in the North Shore, a Mafia-linked murder in a nearby suburb, a budget debate at the state house, and, of course, the embezzlement trial of a bank president in Worcester. She ordered additional file footage for specific stories in order to give them more impact, and she personally wrote the national and international news wrap-up, calling out to Julie to pull the appropriate chromakey slide and piece of footage.

Kate felt alive for the first time since the kidnapping. She knew how well she was working and she was pleased that her mind could once again click into the journalistic mode, that her fingers still remembered the rough, tense touch of the Tele-PrompTer typewriter.

"Excuse me, Kate?"

As she looked, Bill Halliday said, "I thought you might want to look at the copy for the lead story. I don't exactly know where to say Katherine Marchand is or what she's doing."

Kate smiled weakly and took the copy from him. She read it through and said, "It's fine the way it is, Bill, but let me take a stab at rewriting it so it will have more emotional impact along with all the facts."

A few minutes later, Kate rose from the typewriter and handed her copy to Bill. "My feelings won't be hurt if you go with your own instead."

But as he began reading his employer's words, he saw that Kate's script was far superior. It spelled out the crisis succinctly, but the reader felt it painfully. It showed clearly Kate's situation and how little choice she had, but it did not reveal what she would do.

At 5:25, with the guard, Mark, at her heels, Kate picked up the stack of copy and walked into the control room. She casually took the producer's seat next to Julie, and stared at the monitors in front of her. She noticed that someone had taped a small placard below the main monitor. Decorated with a lily in each corner, it read simply, "The Lily Lives."

Kate expressed no emotion, knowing that the eyes of all the technicians must be on her. Julie called for the talent to prepare themselves, then for the countdown and the 5:30 open. The news was on. As the half hour progressed, Kate made a few changes, cutting some copy, adding a wire service story. But when a call came through from one of the mobile units, Kate got on the phone to the other units.

During the two-minute break before the six o'clock, Kate informed Julie that there had been major developments at the oil spill site and in Washington, and that she was reordering the formats and all the feeds. Julie looked at her incredulously.

"It's too late to make those changes. The units aren't ready," Julie protested.

"They are ready and waiting," said Kate sternly. "Follow

these changes while I go out and make corrections in Bill's copy.'' She handed Julie a rundown covered with red arrows and new outcues and times written in precise script.

Then Kate was on the monitor, on the set with Bill, flipping through his copy, changing the order of stories, and changing the leads to many of the live remote feeds.

''Tell Mrs. Marchand, 'off the set,' we're coming straight up.'' Julie's voice was strained over the loudspeaker.

Kate walked off the set briskly and immediately sat down at a typewriter and worked on the leads for later in the broadcast. They still led with the story of the kidnapping crisis but that was about all that remained as it had been. During the first commercial, Kate handed Bill the revised copy and then returned to the control room where she talked to the mobile units and asked them specifics about their feeds and even, in one case, requested that a reporter pull in another official to interview.

And so the newscast went. Kate either stood directly behind Julie and the switcher, or she paced as she called out changes. Several times, she returned to the phone for the mobile units, lengthening or shortening their feeds. She was like a master puppeteer, pulling the strings to make the perfect newscast.

When they went to the final commercial just before Bill's goodnight, everyone let out a breath.

''I don't know how we did it, Mrs. Marchand,'' Julie said.

''Because you are all the best,'' Kate said firmly.

Kate smiled as she watched the credit roll begin. The assistant director had typed into the character generator at the beginning of the credit roll: Produced by Katherine Marchand.

Her mind alert for the first time in days, Kate went back to her office. The board meeting was to be at ten o'clock the following morning and, for the first time in her life, she had not done her homework. She had no idea how she would conduct herself, what she would say. But she felt, strangely, that she would do best to postpone a decision and just to wait and see what would happen.

She knew it was useless and foolhardy to try to persuade the authorities to release Carlos Figueroa. It had always been useless but now, with twelve people dead as a result of the madness of drugs . . . Well, even the most liberal-minded politicians and officials were now demanding that Marchand Syndicates be adamant and not give so much as a dollar to the kidnappers.

As to the money, she could come up with that. But to what end? If you considered the matter less narrowly, it was clear that money was not the main concern of the kidnappers. Figueroa's release was. Showing their power. Stopping the television investigation. Kate grimaced and said aloud, "Well, they've certainly accomplished that."

Several hours later, surrounded by guards, she returned to the waterfront. Everyone, including Jonathan and Chris, sat in the living room as if awaiting some word from her. But she stared at the faces without expression and wearily turned back towards Jason's bedroom. After kissing and stroking his sleeping blond head, she knelt beside the bed as images as diverse as Kim laughing and the Harvard Square massacre went through her head.

The next morning, without a word to anyone, not even to her husband, Katherine Marchand dressed and headed for her board meeting. As cameras followed her into WLYM, network anchors and analysts told the world about what was now referred to as the trial of Katherine Marchand and Marchand Communications. They pointed out that public sentiment had shifted: At first everyone had been in favor of getting Kim back at any cost. Now there was strong feeling that the station should not deal with terrorists.

To anyone who looked at her as she entered the boardroom, Kate's eyes seemed black, almost void of life. No sooner had she taken her place and greeted the directors than someone knocked at the door.

Surprised and annoyed, Kate called, "Yes?" and the guard entered, with Agent Holbrook just behind him.

"We have another tape," Holbrook said. "It came a few minutes ago."

He carried a small recording machine but before Kate could take it from him, Leonard Mankin said, "Of course, this is *very* important and we will all be interested in hearing it. But I must tell you, Kate, that we are all in agreement that this wavering back and forth is hurting us irreparably. We must issue a statement at once denouncing Figueroa, saying that we will do anything we can to help Miss Winston—anything short of dealing with assassins."

Kate nodded and mildly said, "Let's listen to the tape anyhow, Leonard." And turning to the others at the long, highly polished table, she said, "I take it there are no objections."

When she turned on the machine, she was startled at the voice she heard. It was Kim all right, but she was speaking loudly, urgently, almost harshly: "Kate, stop treating this like a stupid game of tag. You'll take the rap for this. No pool will ever be safe for you.''

The tape ended and the board members looked at each other curiously and then back at the silent recorder.

"Well," Mankin began, "that doesn't make me very sympathetic. She sounds downright mean. Doesn't she know we've looked all over creation for her? I think we've got to face the fact there's nothing more we can do for Kim Winston. They've probably drugged and beaten her so she's useless to us anyway. In fact, sounds like she almost wants to join them. You know, like Patty Hearst did.''

The others around the table nodded solemnly. A few talked about the station's image on the world markets.

But Kate wasn't listening. She stared at the wall above Mankin's head, and pushing her analytical mind, she watched the messages from the two tapes come together.

"Rubrum lily with two red stamens." According to the florist, the rubrum lily did not have two distinct stamens. Just a varying cluster, and they are not red.

"You'll take the rap for this." Wrap it up, in television language, means, "That's it, the end."

"Stupid game of tag." Kim had rushed up to her on the beach, shouting, "You're it."

"No pool will ever be safe." So where would she swim? Where did Kim know she swam?

Suddenly Kate bolted from her chair.

"Damn it!" she said. "She told us where she was on the first fucking tape!" She jerked open the door and ran down the hall toward her office.

"I know where she is, and she's going to try to swim for her freedom," Kate shouted at Holbrook who stared wide-eyed. "She's on the island of Twin Lights off Rockport.''

"Rockport?''

"Yes, Rockport," Kate said, swallowing air in gulps. "Tell me, Holbrook, did we ever check an island off Rockport?''

"Well, no," he said. "What makes you think she's there?''

"Because she told us, on the first tape! 'Stoneridge. I'd take Jason.' Jason's the key. He never got the word Rockport right. He calls it Stoneport. She couldn't very well say Stoneport, so she came as close as she could and threw in Jason as the key.

"And 'two red stamens.' The lily doesn't have two red stamens, but the kidnappers didn't know that. But Twin Lights Island has two lighthouses that flash a red signal.

"As to this second tape. 'A game of tag.' She once ran up to me on the beach off the island crying 'You're it' in a mock game of tag." Kate was smiling now. "Don't you all see? Isn't it falling into place?" No one else spoke, all of them mesmerized by Kate's performance, as if she were a sorcerer who held them in thrall.

" 'You'll take the wrap,' " Kate continued. "That means that's it, the end, in television lingo.

" 'No pool will ever be safe.' So where would I swim? Where does she know I swim? Off Rockport, specifically to and from Twin Lights Island."

Kate grabbed Holbrook's lapel. "Trust me, that's where they're keeping her. A deserted island, close enough to Boston to get daily messages in and out with no trouble. They could simply use a lobster boat and no one would ever question another lobster boat in those waters.

"And her stay is at an end. She's got something planned. *She's* going to try to swim for it. And I bet if we check the tides we'll find there's a high tide tonight in Rockport, and Kim is going to make the swim of her life."

Diana was pulling at the pages of the paper, ripping them as she searched for the weather. "You're right, Kate. There's a high tide at nine-twelve tonight in Rockport."

"Goddamn it!" Kate cried as she slammed her fist on her desk. "She told us, she told *me*, in the first tape." Then, with her eyes blazing, "We've got to get up there. It's cold, and it's a long swim against a strong current." She turned to Holbrook. "And only if we get *her* in time, can you get Figueroa and his friends."

A half hour later, with Mark at the wheel, Holbrook, Jonathan and Kate were heading up Route 128 towards Rockport. Behind them was another car filled with agents. Holbrook had already sent others ahead to secure the necessary police and Coast Guard boats. Kate had made them promise not to make any move until she herself had explained the situation and they could see exactly what they were up against.

"You understand, Mr. Holbrook," Jonathan said, "that my wife has a house in Rockport. It overlooks a deserted island that's called Twin Lights."

"And when the tide and temperature are right, I often swim there and back," Kate said.

"How far is it?" Holbrook asked her.

"Again, depending on the tide and where you come ashore, it's about three quarters of a mile."

"You swim that distance?" Holbrook asked.

"My wife's a genius at all sorts of things," Jonathan said. "What I want to know, darling, is how you convinced the board to stay where they were in that building."

"I told them the truth, that we knew where Kim was, and that she could be rescued and the drug dealers captured by eleven o'clock, as long as we kept up the pretense that the board meeting was still in progress." Kate laughed somewhat bitterly. "Of course it didn't hurt that I pointed out that this would resolve the dilemma of whether to look bad for abandoning Kim or for dealing with the cocaine dealers—to say nothing of saving the ransom and seeing their stock soar back up."

"Mrs. Marchand," Holbrook asked, clearing his throat, "What happens if you are wrong? If Miss Winston is not on this island? Or is and we fail to get her?"

"Nothing at all, Mr. Holbrook, nothing at all. Except Kim will almost certainly die and, for various reasons, professional and personal, my own life, as I know it, will be over."

They were now on the dirt road and Kate directed Mark into the pine-enclosed driveway. She opened the door with unsteady hands, and with the others behind her, walked over to the sliding glass doors.

Kate looked out over the water to the Twin Light Island she used to find so comforting, and sighed deeply, leaning against Jonathan's body. "It's okay, darling," he said. "We're getting closer." Kate went to open the screen to go out onto the deck. Holbrook put his hand on hers.

"No, Mrs. Marchand. If they *are* there, they probably have high-powered binoculars and are constantly scanning the coastline for any type of activity," Holbrook said, looking out at the island as the sun lowered over the horizon in back of him. "Anyhow, we can be thankful there's no storm forecast—though a little fog might be nice."

"You can never tell," Jonathan replied. "This area may just accommodate you. You know what they say about the weather along the New England coast? If you don't like it, wait a minute, it's bound to change."

A detective had set up a large telescope on a tripod. "I don't see anything to indicate movement. No small boats around or anything."

"They would work from the other side of the island," Kate

said confidently. "I've walked the island. On the other side of the lighthouses, there are many inlets that are under cover from boats passing on the ocean side, and of course, no one could see them from this side."

"But we know that they went back and forth. They had to deliver those tapes," Holbrook said. "Someone would have noticed."

"Maybe not, if they used the right kind of boat. Lobster boats are continually working this area, even in the winter. One more lobster boat going around the island would not be considered peculiar at all," Jonathan pointed out.

"But they have to dock, don't they?" Holbrook asked.

"Lobstermen keep very strange hours and many of them moor their boats away from the shore and take a small dinghy to shore," Kate answered tiredly. "No, Mr. Holbrook, it's a perfect plan. I doubt if those lighthouses are checked more than a couple times a year. And you can be sure Figueroa and his friends checked that. They must have set up shop inside one of those abandoned rock fortresses where Kim could scream and never be heard."

"There are still a couple of pieces that don't fit," Holbrook said. "How does she know where she is? Most kidnappers keep their victims naked and in the dark. And even if she was being let out to walk, how would she know?"

"See the top of those lighthouses?" Kate pointed out. "At night, they flash a red light. I don't know of any other lighthouse on this coast like this one. Kim may have been just awake enough when they put her into the boat to see where she was going.

"And as to Kim being able to talk them into letting her walk outside, if you have ever seen her documentaries, you will realize the woman is capable of getting just about anyone to agree to anything." For a brief moment Kate's heart fell. Even Jonathan, she thought. Does she want him? And then, visibly shaking her head, she dismissed the idea, filed it away for when this crisis was over.

"You don't think she'd try a swim from the other side of the island, do you?" Jonathan asked.

"No. She has probably talked them into letting her walk at night. She's been watching the tides and apparently the high tide is the best opportunity for her."

"They're never going to let her out of sight. She can't just slip into the water," warned Holbrook.

"Perhaps she plans to overpower someone or trick them. I know it's a long shot, but. . ."

Holbrook and the police conferred at one side of the now darkening room; Kate and Jonathan stood looking out at the water. Finally the FBI man said, "We have a few options. We can just surround the island, use a bullhorn to let them know we're there and we'll get them all."

"And Kim Winston will be shot as soon as they catch sight of the first boat," Kate said flatly.

"Exactly," Holbrook agreed. "My colleagues agree with me that we have a little time. If Miss Winston doesn't make a move, then we can move in. But we'll try to give her a chance to get off the island first."

Kate and Jonathan were relieved as they heard the planning for where to launch a boat, station back-up police and ambulances. Kate provided information on the coast and where she thought the tide might bring Kim ashore, depending on where she was starting off from.

Kate and Jonathan crouched beside Mark, who was scanning the channel between the mainland and the island with binoculars. Next to him was a walkie-talkie on the same frequency as Holbrook's. The agent was down on the shore where his men were ready with boats and binoculars, waiting for any move.

"What time is it?" Kate asked.

"Eight twenty-five," Jonathan said, consulting the luminous dial on his watch. "The tide's still coming in, but it must be pretty close to high, especially out on the island." He put his arm around his wife. They were both shaking, from the cold and fear.

"Oh my God!" Mark's body stiffened. "I think I've got something. It could be a buoy . . . hold on. . . . My God, it's not. It's someone swimming. I've been looking out too far. She's over halfway in. The tide's taking her."

He grabbed for the walkie-talkie. "Holbrook! Holbrook! Do you read?"

"This is Holbrook," came the sharp response.

"Victim is in the water. Swimming strong. Beyond halfway mark."

"Are you sure?"

Mark went back to the telescope, then picked up the walkie-talkie again. "It's got to be her."

"Hold on. I think we've spotted her," came Holbrook's voice

over the walkie-talkie. "But we're not the only ones. There's a boat moving out from the other side of the island."

"Goddamn it!" Kate said, jerking the man to his feet and pulling him and Jonathan through the house to the car.

"The current's going to carry her and they're going to get her." They drove quickly to a rocky inlet with a small beach just down the coast from the Pines.

Jonathan brought the car to a screeching halt, almost hitting the boulders on the side of the road. As they ran from the car, they saw that fog was rolling in and now enshrouded part of Twin Lights Island. The sound of boats filled the air—more than one, it seemed.

Then, a spotlight hit the water and moved until it found something breaking the surface. Mark screamed, "No!" and from a small boat rapidly approaching, there came a red flare and the sound of an M-16.

Kate screamed and plunged into the water. Vaguely she saw the smaller boat heading away and two larger boats in quick pursuit.

"Aim the car's headlights towards the water! Radio for an ambulance," Jonathan bellowed at Mark. Angry and stunned, Mark did as he was ordered. Kate was already fifty yards from shore by the time the car's headlights lit the water around her. She could see nothing but she continued swimming toward where the spotlight had hit Kim.

Jonathan had picked up a pair of binoculars, and now he saw what Kate did not. He ran as far as he could into the water and began shouting. "Right! Right! Go right!" Mark found him in the water and in unison they shouted to make their voices heard. And, finally, Kate did hear. And a moment later, her hand struck Kim's shoulder.

"It's all right, Kim. It's all right." Kate saw with horror that blood was streaming from Kim's head. She heard the younger woman say, "I knew you'd come, Kate, I knew it." And then the head fell onto the water and Kim was unconscious.

Fighting the tide, Kate finally made it close enough to shore so that Mark and Jonathan could take Kim the rest of the way in. As she herself collapsed on the wet sand, Kate heard Jonathan shouting at the arriving ambulance.

"She's still alive. Move it! Bring a stretcher. She's also got a bullet in her back!"

Jonathan bent over Kim, trying to breathe life into her lungs as ambulance men and police cars filled the beach. He helped move her onto a stretcher and just as he put his foot up to follow the paramedic in, he turned and searched for his wife. She stood with a blanket over her shoulders and before he could speak, she called, "Go ahead, Jonathan, you're needed there. I'll be along soon."

Kate went with Mark and Holbrook back to the house. She told the men to fix them all a drink while she changed. Then, as soon as she came back into the living room, Holbrook said, "We got them all. Four of them including Manuel Figueroa. And we've got men going out to the lighthouse now so we'll have more details."

Kate smiled wanly. "Thank you for telling me but Kim . . . I didn't even ask where they were taking her."

"New England General," Mark said. "It's a lucky thing your husband was down at the beach. He called to tell you that she's alive. She'll go into surgery immediately and he gives her a good fifty-fifty chance."

"I owe you my congratulations and thanks, Mrs. Marchand," Holbrook said. "Without you. . . ."

"Please, Mr. Holbrook, I have a favor to ask."

"Under the circumstances, I can't think of anything I'd say no to."

"I've had quite enough publicity lately, enough to last me a lifetime." She sat down, exhausted. "Let's forget that I was even up here. I'm sure my board is willing to say I stayed right in that room with them tonight. Let's just say you and your men did a superb job."

"I'm sure the Bureau would be happy to go along with that." Holbrook grinned and Kate realized she'd never seen him smile before.

"Now if I can make a phone call first, could you give me a ride back to Boston?"

"It would be my pleasure." Holbrook watched Kate walk out of the room and then turned to Mark. "Didn't you tell me it was *Mrs.* Marchand who dove into the water and went after Miss Winston?"

"That's right," Mark said, handing the FBI man a bourbon on the rocks.

"But you and *Doctor* Marchand were also there."

"Well, at first I was positioning the car so . . ." Mark stopped and changed his tone. "You're wondering why Dr. Marchand or I didn't go in after her?"

"Yeah, I guess I am."

"Like I said, I was in the car and, well, Mrs. Marchand, as is her style, acted very quickly."

Holbrook just nodded and sipped his drink.

"And as far as Dr. Marchand," Mark continued, "I mean, he's a hell of a guy, and certainly cares about Miss Winston. But," he paused choosing his words carefully, "the stakes were much higher for Mrs. Marchand. She was saving more than Kim Winston. She was saving Katherine Marchand and all she represents."

5

K ATE CALLED HER OFFICE AND WITH A CALM PRECISION RE-
cited to Bill Halliday the events of the evening.

"Break in right now, Bill," she said. "Get a special report
out immediately. We don't want to be scooped on our own story.
And Bill? You can tell the board they can go now—pride and
pocketbooks intact."

Bill laughed. "Not quite yet, boss. They'll have to wait until
after we go on the air before we let them out."

Holbrook drove Kate directly to the hospital. As she walked
down the corridor toward Jonathan's office, she met a white-
faced Chris Cerci. He told Kate what she already knew—that a
bullet had hit Kim in the head and also in the back. But, he
added, it had missed the spinal cord. Jonathan was presently
using the laser to remove chips of bone from around the spinal
cord.

As they entered Jonathan's office, Chris took Kate's hand in
his, surprised at how cold it was. "He also told me, while he
was scrubbing, what you did for Kim." Tears came to his eyes
and Kate, seeing all the pain and worry of the last week in him,
hugged him close to her.

"Thank you, Kate," Chris said, pulling away from her
slightly. "How can I ever thank you?"

"By making sure Kim and Chase are always happy." Chris

nodded and then left to return to the operating room and Kate sat wondering if that would ever be possible—for so many reasons.

Kate fell asleep on a couch in Jonathan's office and did not awaken until her husband returned several hours later. "How is she?" Kate asked. "What happened?"

"The bullet just grazed her left temple, but she lost a lot of blood from it. I don't see any sign of brain damage but there's no doubt she will need some plastic surgery." His voice seemed heavy and so did his movements. "We got the bullet out of her spine. No damage to the spinal cord, but some vertebrae were broken. Everything will depend on how she heals."

"Will she be all right?"

"She's lost a lot of blood and she was suffering from hypothermia. I wouldn't be surprised if she lapses into a coma."

"A coma?" Kate's voice trembled.

"That's not necessarily bad. It might be a resting coma that would give her body a chance to repair. In any case, given the circumstances, she's doing all right." He turned off the light and lay down next to her on the large worn couch. He knew Kate should probably go someplace where she could get a good night's sleep, but he didn't want to leave the hospital in the event Kim's condition changed, and he did want to be with his wife on this night.

"Have I told you recently how much I love you?" he whispered into her ear as he pulled her close to him. But then he realized that for the first time in over a week, Kate was really asleep. Sound asleep.

When his beeper went off at seven in the morning, both Jonathan and Kate were roused from a sound sleep. Kate listened anxiously as Jonathan spoke on the phone. He said, "I'll be right there," and then quickly dressed in a clean shirt he had in his closet and into a fresh white coat.

"I'm coming with you," Kate said.

Jonathan nodded, and within moments they both stood waiting for the elevator.

"Don't expect her to be conscious yet," Jonathan said. "Even if she doesn't go into a coma on us, I doubt she'd awaken this fast."

Finally the elevator came and they descended silently to the third floor and the Surgical Intensive Care Unit. They went directly to Kim's bed and as Jonathan read the chart and talked to the nurse about heart rate, breathing rhythms and brain waves,

Kate looked down at her chief correspondent. Most of Kim's head was encased in what appeared to be thick layers of white bandage. It was even wrapped around her chin. There were bruises around her eyes and nose. Her cheeks, once so full, seemed sunken. Her complexion was a grayish yellow. Even her lips, cracked and swollen, held no color. Oxygen tubes ran from her nostrils and Kate could see wires going from underneath the gauze to a machine similar to the one that had been monitoring Jason's brain waves during his illness.

Both Kim's arms were outside the sheet and both had tubes and wires attached to them, with inflated pillows supporting them. Glancing over Kim's shoulder, Kate saw additional dressings with clear tubes coming from them. She shuddered when she realized that the tube sometimes filled with a stream that looked like a mixture of blood and cream. Several different kinds of monitors surrounded Kim. Heavy bags of blood plasma hung from steel racks beside the bed.

Kate had seen sights like this before but now it seemed unbearable. None of her anger about Kim and Jonathan remained. Kate felt that whatever had happened that awful Saturday was now behind her. The sick and broken person on the bed was her valued employee, wounded in service to Kate's company. And, Kate admitted to herself, she was her friend. So why? Why would you and Jon . . . ?

"Her vital signs are good, Kate," Jonathan was saying. "But the way her breathing pattern changed and her heartbeat, it appears that she has slipped into a coma. By now the anesthesia should have worn off and we should have seen some movement." He put his hand on Kate's shoulder. "She's strong. I think she'll be okay because we don't see injury. There could be a clot developing, or blocking something, but I can't risk moving her for a brain scan. I've increased the anticoagulants and I'm afraid we just have to wait."

"How long?" came Kate's dry voice.

"If it's from blood loss, the coma should not last long, maybe a day or two."

"You believe that, Jonathan? I know it sounds ghoulish but I have to make some press statements today. I'm afraid a lot of things depend on what I say."

Jonathan winced and said only, "I believe you're safe in saying she'll be all right." He reached up and adjusted the flow of blood into Kim. "But don't expect her back on the air for a while. It's going to be a long recuperation. Plastic surgery will fix up her head, but only time will heal her back . . . and her mind."

The weekend came and went and, to even Jonathan's surprise, there was no change in Kim's condition. She was moved out of intensive care and into a private room in Marshall House. This was the building of the hospital that was primarily reserved for the most wealthy or most well-known patients. The rooms were large, many even had fireplaces. Marshall House had its own linen and china. The meals were superb, as was the nursing care. John Wayne and the Kennedys had recuperated here and now Kim Winston lay in a bed overlooking the Charles River and the Esplanade.

But Kim was completely unaware of her surroundings. Although her vital signs remained steady, they were not growing stronger, and Jonathan and Chris were now talking of the possibility of operating again. The brain scan had shown no signs of bone fragments or clotting, but they could not be sure. Only one thing was certain: The longer Kim lay unconscious, the less the chance that she would come out undamaged.

When Kim had been in the coma for a week and another operation became more likely, Kate suggested that Jason be allowed to see his mother. Though Kim was still attached to wires and tubes and her head was still bandaged, she looked slightly better than immediately after surgery. The bruises had faded, and thanks to the care of the nurses, her lips and hands had become smooth again.

As the days passed, it was becoming increasingly difficult to keep the boy away from the hospital. Each night, the news contained an update on Kim's condition and Jason insisted upon watching. He was getting frantic, as if he were afraid she would die without him.

Jonathan himself, trying to regard Kim as just another patient, was growing uncertain. He watched these people he cared about—his wife and Chris and Jason—and spun unlikely theories. Perhaps the staff psychologist's opinion was correct, that the horrors that Kim had gone through might be keeping her mind in this subconscious state. Perhaps she simply didn't want to face, or return to the days of torture and humiliation, the kidnapping and . . . Oh, God, Jonathan thought, perhaps she was also afraid to face what had happened just before, when he had maneuvered her into making love with him.

He desperately wanted to avoid opening up Kim's head again,

but knowing he might have to, he agreed to Jason's visit. He did not want the boy to lose his mother without even seeing her once again.

The next afternoon, Jason was brought to his mother's room. He had been warned of what to expect: the bandages, the tubes, his mother's lack of response. But no one is ever prepared for a sight like that. Certainly not a child, and not a child who has only that one person on the bed left in his life.

Jason froze as soon as he rounded the foot of the bed and saw her. He was like a mechanical toy whose battery had just gone dead. He stood paralyzed, staring. He dropped Kate's hand, but not before Kate felt all the warmth drain from it.

Chris and Jonathan and Kate watched this brave child whom they all loved. For the first time, his eyes did not glow, his cheeks held no color, his lips looked gray and dried. Kate thought she was going to scream. It took every ounce of her control not to.

For reasons they could never verbalize, Chris and Jonathan left the room.

Still, Jason stood and stared.

Kate did not know how long it was until the boy finally moved his legs towards his mother's bed. Using the chair by the side of the bed as a stool, he climbed gently onto the bed and, sitting on the edge, leaned over and kissed Kim. It was a long kiss, and Kate, watching, felt that she now had seen a heart breaking.

Jason sat down close to his mother's side. He lifted her arm with its wires and tubes onto his lap, and holding her hand in both of his, watched his mother's unmoving face.

At first the words came out creakingly, but gradually, the soft voice became stronger, as the child who had been sung to so often now sang to his mother.

> "Puff, the magic dragon
> lived by the sea
> and frolicked in the autumn mist
> in a land called Hanna Lee.
> Little Jackie Paper
> loved that rascal Puff
> and brought him strings and sealing wax
> and other fancy stuff."

Tears began to flow down Jason's cheeks but he continued his sad song, not taking his eyes off the mask that was his mother's face. Kate sat down on the chair next to him. She felt the scorching tears falling like fire down her own cheeks as Jason sobbed between the words, trying to sing through his tears. He lowered himself onto his mother's chest. There was no longer any melody, just the whisper of the words:

> "His head was bent in sorrow.
> Green scales fell like rain.
> Puff no longer went to play
> along the cherry lane.
> Without his lifelong friend
> Puff could not be brave
> and Puff that mighty dragon
> finally slipped into his grave."

Jason's grief broke through and he started to wail. "Mommy, don't die. Don't go with Daddy. Stay with me. Please, Mommy, please, I need you!" He was clutching her and almost shaking her. Kate picked him up and pulled him onto her lap, wrapping her arms around him as he sobbed and trembled, and she remembered almost a year before when she had held Kim while she pleaded for Jason's life.

Jonathan and Chris had run into the room when they heard Jason's scream, and now as Kate looked up through her tears at Jonathan, she saw terror in his eyes. At that instant, he lunged for Kim's head to keep it still during this new convulsion.

Knowing what was happening, Kate pressed Jason's head into her neck and ran from the room. This time it was Kate in the hallway, hanging onto Jason, shouting for help. The nurses saw her and soon bells were going off and the corridor filled with carts and running people.

Jason had been crying hysterically, but when he calmed, they went to sit quietly in a small waiting area. Jason was silent and still on her lap. Kate's mind was blank.

Finally Jonathan appeared. He said that Kim was stable for now. Chris said he would take Jason home, and the boy, still dazed, took his hand and walked with him. Jonathan sat beside Kate and took her cold hand in his.

"Chris agrees with me that her only hope now is if we go in and try to find the trouble. She won't survive another convulsion."

"What caused it?"

"It could have been anything. Maybe a part of her mind heard

Jason's voice and she tried to respond, but she couldn't make it. I don't know. It was probably just her heart. It's been working very hard.'' He sounded defeated.

"Is it strong enough to get through surgery?"

"Hellman, the cardiologist, is with her now."

They waited in silence until Dr. Hellman appeared. He told Jonathan that he thought Kim's heart could make it, if the surgery was not too long. While Jonathan went to arrange for the surgery, Kate returned to Kim's room. It seemed to her that Kim looked a little better, but she assumed that was only because she had expected her to look worse. She sat on a chair beside the bed, holding Kim's hand, watching the sun set over the Charles River and singing quietly, her mind blank with grief and confusion.

> "His head was bent in sorrow.
> Green scales fell like rain.
> Puff no longer went to play
> along the cherry lane. . . ."

Kate leaned abruptly towards Kim as she looked down at her own hand. She knew she had felt it. Kim had squeezed her hand. Not strongly, but she had felt it. "Kim! Kim! It's Kate! Squeeze my hand if you hear me. Please, Kim! Please!" She looked at Kim's hand, willing it to move. She touched Kim's face. Pinched her arm. Pleading for a response. Anything.

Kate reached for the buzzer and had Jonathan paged. A moment later, he came running in. Excitedly, she told him, standing and gesturing at Kim.

He pulled her into his arms. "Darling, darling, I really don't think she can hear you. She's just gone through cardiac arrest. Her nerves and reflexes are bound to react."

"But it wasn't a reflex!" Kate shouted. "She *squeezed* my hand!"

"Listen, Kate," Jonathan said. "You've gone through so much these last weeks. We all have. Believe me, there's no sign of anything new."

Kate nodded sadly but then, as if hit by lightning, her whole body jolted. She pulled at Jonathan's arm and pointed at Kim. Her eyes were open, open wide. Kate tried to speak, but she couldn't. She thought, my God, she just died, it's a death stare. She tried to say Kim's name but she could not.

"Kate . . . Kate . . . forgive me," came a rasping voice.

"Oh, thank God," Kate cried. "Oh, Kim, dear girl, welcome back. There's nothing left to forgive."

"Kim?" Jonathan went to the side of the bed, his heart lifting as he saw Kim's eyes follow him.

"Hi, Dr. Marchand."

With a small flashlight, Jonathan looked into Kim's eyes, then checked her heartbeat. "We were about ready to take you back to surgery," he said.

"I know," Kim said. "I had to wake up. I . . . I couldn't stand the sound of Kate singing anymore."

There was a knock at the door and a stretcher was wheeled into the room. Jonathan said, "I don't think we're going to need that. It looks like the patient is going to be just fine." He smiled back at Kim. "How do you feel?"

"I don't know," she said weakly. "My back hurts."

Jonathan laughed aloud again. "That's the best news I've heard in weeks."

Chris came running into the room. "When I got back after taking Jason home, the nurses said. . . ." He froze as he saw Kim, her eyes open, and moving, with a slight smile, her hand in Kate's. "Oh, dear God . . . you're alive. You're alive . . . ." As he came toward the bed, Kate withdrew her hand from Kim's.

Slowly, she felt the life come back into her but then she shouted, "Jason. We've got to tell him!"

Kate rushed to the condominium and picked Jason up from the floor where he sat watching *Sesame Street* on television and eating Cheerios.

"Why are you in your pajamas?" she asked. "Get up you lazy thing. Your mommy's waiting to see you."

"What do you mean?" Jason asked.

"I mean," said Kate, spinning around with the child in her arms, "your mommy's awake! She's okay! Your mommy wants to see you! All our troubles are over, baby." She held the child tightly, silently thanking the heavens.

The euphoria lasted about three months. Figueroa and his people were indicted and the police department decided that there was no longer any need for around-the-clock protection for Kim and Kate. Kim's recovery progressed enough for her to resume some of her duties at the station.

Her first project was the completion of the cocaine documentary. Despite the publicity surrounding the kidnapping, the documentary was anything but old news. It revealed the inroads cocaine smuggling had made in almost every major industry. The documentary led to specific state and federal investigations that resulted in the arrests and indictments of heretofore upstanding members of the Boston and New York business communities. Again, Kim testified before Washington subcommittees and her testimony became the catalyst for change in the Drug Enforcement Administration and the narcotics arm of the Justice Department.

Although she never revealed the treatment she received at the hands of the kidnappers to anyone but the FBI, it was obvious from her expression whenever the Colombians were mentioned that the ordeal had been filled with torture, humiliation and unrelenting fear.

Kim Winston had become the heroine for a nation at war with drugs. A presidential commendation and citations and awards were added almost daily to her professional biography. But slowly, as the clamor died down and public attention turned to other matters, all of them—Chris, Jonathan, Jason, Kim and Kate—settled back into the day-to-day routines of their lives. And beneath the veneer and the celluloid, the truth was that the damage that had been done over those previous months had not yet been repaired.

A wall of cold air kept the Marchands from any real contact with each other. They went to public functions, they slept together . . . they even had sex. But they no longer made love.

Jonathan never mentioned the night at Rockport with Kim. He never really knew that Kate had found out about it, but neither did he make an overture to Kim again. It was Kate who dwelt upon it, whose imagination was inflamed by the old pictures of Jonathan years ago, on top of that other woman in New York, and by the fresh nightmare of Kim and Jonathan together. It was not that she distrusted Kim. Instinctively she understood that whatever had happened, it was not an ongoing thing. In a way, she felt that the kidnapping had put an end to whatever possibilities there might have been. But each time she saw Kim, the newsreel in her brain began again: the house in Rockport, Jonathan and Kim asleep in Kate's own bed, Chris watching them at the door. Kate felt that if she were the strong woman she was purported to be, she would leave Jonathan, but she was so passionately and intricately involved with him it was almost impossible for her to sever their connection . . . at least for now. Yet his behavior felt like a deep burn on the tissue of her heart.

Kate handled her obsession by working, working constantly,

ruthlessly and very effectively. Marchand Communications stock was at its all-time high, now selling at $103 a share, up sixteen from where it had been while Kim was being held by the kidnappers. The possibility of the network takeover was being reported in business columns around the country and it had been mentioned as a tip on *Wall Street Roundup* the previous Friday night. The only "weak link" the communications specialist had mentioned on the television show was the low ratings on the last sweeps of the California affiliate. That station was apparently in bad shape, but, the commentator said, Katherine Marchand "is known not only for her business acumen, she also knows television talent. You can be sure, once she gets in there, some heads will roll and new ones will be crowned. She did that in Boston and made it the most commercially successful as well as the most prize-winning station in the country."

The Saturday night following that broadcast Jonathan and Kate were entertaining their friends Deborah and Bob Falkenstein. Deborah had taped the financial show for Kate and the four of them watched the segment in which Marchand Communications was mentioned. As soon as the segment was over, Deborah said, "Well, I suppose I should congratulate you but, as your friend, I think the cost is way too high."

"What do you mean?" Jonathan asked. "What cost?"

"Have you looked at your wife lately, Doctor? She looks like hell." Then, turning to Kate she said, "You know I've always envied how thin you've stayed over the years—but this is too much. You must have lost fifteen pounds in the last few months."

Kate shrugged. "You know what they say. You can never be too rich or too thin."

"Listen, Kate," Bob said, "I'm an old Marchand ogler from way back, and I have to agree with my pleasingly plump wife here. You're not looking your best, sweetie. You're frowning a line between your eyes and you seem nervous, edgy. No business deal is worth it."

Kate laughed off her friends' concern but Jonathan remained silent during the conversation. He brought it up later that evening and Kate said only, "Don't worry about my work, Jonathan. That has nothing to do with any change Deb sees in my appearance. LYM is fun. The takeover is stimulating and completely absorbing. My work, unlike other parts of my life, gives me a lot of happiness."

Jonathan did not pursue it. He did not take her up on the implicit invitation to discuss what lay between them.

They saw very little of Kim but one day Maggie called. She said that she had dialed their number for Jason who wanted to speak to them. When Kate picked up the phone, Jason said, "Hi Kate. Tell Jonathan to go listen on that white phone in the bathroom. The hanging one."

Kate laughed and gave Jonathan his instructions. When they were both on the line, Jason said, "I'm shooing you an invitation."

"You're what?" Kate asked.

"Issuing, Kate," came Jonathan's voice. "We're being invited to something."

"That's right, Jonathan. Well, this is it . . . next week is my mother's birthday and I'm building a party for her. Maggie's helping and Chris is going to keep Mom out of the house until it's the right time. Pizza and ice cream, that's all we're going to have. That's her favorites—but a lot of both of them. So can you come?"

Kate loved the child and she felt a mixture of laughter and tears as she listened to his voice. But to go to an intimate party for Kim? Seeing her at the station was one thing—though, as a matter of fact, Kate had been so occupied with corporate matters since Kim had been back, even that contact had been minimal.

Jonathan was talking to the boy, saying that it "was up to Kate, Jason. She's very busy now."

"Oh please, Kate, please. I'm only asking the specials . . . only you and Jonathan and Chris and Maggie and my friend Nicholas and his mom. He doesn't have a dad either but his dad divorced himself last month so that's why Nicholas can use a party. Okay? So please say you'll come."

"Of course we will, sweetie. Just put Maggie on and we'll get the details."

The next morning, Kim was working at her desk at home on Union Wharf. Suddenly, Maggie burst into the room and said, "Turn on the TV, quick."

As the network came out of commercial, the morning anchorman began: "What has been rumored for several months has now been confirmed by the president of NRB. Martin Rathjens revealed in a press conference today that final negotiations were underway for the sale of the network to Marchand Communications. It is the first time in the history of television that a major network has been taken over by another communications outlet.

"The person responsible for this event is Katherine Marchand, president of Marchand Communications. In recent years, she has acquired numerous cable systems, newspapers, production companies, as well as television and radio stations that are now a part of her syndication empire. Sources say that Marchand will soon make the official bid of several billion dollars for the network. According to Rathjens, the NRB board and the majority of the stockholders and staff are enthusiastic about coming under the umbrella of Marchand Communications.

"Katherine Marchand herself has become one of the most admired women in America. Marchand is a former correspondent for NRB. In 1974 she went to Boston to become the executive producer of the WLYM news and later became general manager of that station and began syndicating programs throughout the United States. She has since expanded into the European market, syndicating and acquiring various media concerns. In the meantime, associates say she remains actively involved in the operations of WLYM, which in recent years has become one of the finest local stations in the United States.

"A woman of ruthless integrity, some observers felt her professional aspirations were in serious jeopardy when several months ago the anchor and chief correspondent for WLYM, Kimberly Winston, was kidnapped by members of a drug ring and held for ransom. . . ."

The report continued with pictures of both Kate and Kim and a final word that Katherine Marchand, as she was leaving New York today, said she had no comment on Mr. Rathjens' announcement.

The announcement ended with a shot of Kate at Logan Airport. The man behind her, his hand protectively on her elbow . . . Kim's heart leapt. Despite herself—though never, ever, would she take the slightest action on it—despite herself, her heart leapt when she saw Jonathan.

Jason did not have to go to school the next day. Kim felt she couldn't keep up with all the holidays at his new school. Considering what tuition was, if you counted up the vacations and winter and spring breaks, and protracted summer vacation—well, Kim thought, the daily rate for actual class time approached the salary of a highly paid anchorwoman.

Because Jason could sleep later the next morning, Chris had taken him off to a Celtics game. The two of them were getting along better all the time. Chris was more patient than he'd been with the child's rambunctiousness and Jason seemed to be warming to this slim, blond man who was so different from his father.

As Kim lay on the couch, an open book on the floor beside her, she heard voices in the hall. "You guys win?" she called.

Jason, pulling off his coat, said in a superior tone, "We didn't *play*, Mom. We *watched*."

"That's all?" Kim asked. "I'm disappointed."

"Well, we cheered too. Chris knows how to make this loud whistle when you put your two fingers on your front teeth. That's what he has that space there in his mouth for. You know?"

"You know? You know? When are you going to outgrow 'you know'?"

"Stop criticalling, Mom. I have to go to bed."

After Jason was asleep, Kim sat with Chris on the cushioned window seat, looking out at the lights in the harbor.

"Kim," Chris said, taking her hand. "I have something I've been wanting to talk to you about but I'm afraid I've left it too long."

"You're married," Kim laughed.

"No . . . I wish I were. That's the subject we've been avoiding for months, isn't it? We've both had a lot to think about. . . ."

Kim looked sharply at Chris. He had been such an ardent suitor she hadn't realized he also had reservations about their relationship, things to think about. She listened attentively as Chris continued speaking.

"I learned a lot about myself," he was saying, "during the kidnapping. The only thing I cared about was your safety. All I wanted was to have you back and to have the three of us—you and me and Jason—together. Whatever else had happened, that's what counts."

"Happened? What do you mean, Chris?"

"I know, Kim. I know about you and Jonathan . . . at Rockport."

"No! No! Oh my God, no! Oh my dear God!" Kim had her head between her hands and was rocking back and forth. "How? How do you know, Chris? Chris? Oh my God."

Chris leaned across the window seat and pulled her trembling body to him. "It's all right, Kim. It's all right. We all make mistakes and Jonathan's a pretty persuasive guy. I know that."

Kim sat up and pulled away. "You must believe me, Chris. I

was a person completely outside myself. I was so confused I didn't even know who he was.''

"What do you mean by that?" Chris asked coldly.

"David . . . I thought it was David. I was up there alone, I'd had a lot of champagne and I completely let down my guard. Oh, Chris, I am so ashamed.'' Suddenly she stood up and began pulling at Chris's jacket. "Kate! What about Kate? Does she know?''

Chris lied. He thought about it only a second and then, with a very sure voice, said, "No." He felt that, with all she had been through, this woman he loved could not survive any other answer.

They talked for an hour until finally Chris said, "Honey, let's put this behind us. Let's think about the future. It's become a pressing question, to tell you the truth.''

"That sounds ominous.''

"No, it's a good problem. You know I've felt restless here because there's been no time for me to spend on my research. That was part of the understanding when I came here from California, but New England General's such a big place, so busy and there are so many problems. Well, I can see I'll never have time for the lab.''

Kim nodded. "I feel so selfish. I didn't realize you were having this trouble.''

"Well, we've had other things on our minds that sort of needed immediate attention—like you in a coma, for example. The point is, something *has* happened that changes my professional status. I've been offered a top-flight job at Stanford, all sorts of perks, star money and—and this is what I care about—most of my time would be allotted to research. I'd supervise a couple of postdocs who would be assigned to my lab and I'd teach one course a semester—and that's it. The clinical stuff would be minimal, only when I chose to get involved or when a consultation would be especially helpful in a tricky case. I've told Jonathan I'm considering it.''

"Chris, it sounds wonderful." Kim's voice wavered. "I don't know what to say. I guess it never occurred to me that you'd leave, that you'd go back to California.''

"I wouldn't go, Kim. I probably wouldn't even consider it if I could look forward to your being my wife. If that required staying here, I'd stay. But I don't know what's going on between us. I feel you leaning away from me.''

Kim looked at Chris's face and felt within herself the same

sadness and confusion that marred his usually buoyant good looks. What was she to do? Chris deserved better. He deserved a chance to do what he truly wanted. But then, what about her career? She knew she was now one of the most highly regarded journalists in the country, that every network had approached her agent, even though she had said her loyalty lay with Marchand Communications. But like an animal scratching at a door, the memory of the night in Rockport dug deeper and deeper into her heart. Chris knew, and now she wasn't so sure Kate also didn't know.

What tangled webs we weave, she thought. . . . Her hand caressed Chris's hair and neck lovingly, and, looking deep into his hopeful eyes, she promised him an answer as soon as possible.

6

On SATURDAY AFTERNOON, IN A PLOT WITH JASON, CHRIS insisted that Kim accompany him to Louis, the elegant men's store on Boylston Street. He said, "You know how I only wear the same suit every day until it's in shreds and then buy another one? Well, I'm determined to change my ways."

Kim groaned. "I've noticed, Doctor. And I've also noticed how all your shoes are the same style—brown or black, thank God—but exactly the same."

Chris laughed and pinched her cheek. "You sound just like my mother, scolding my father. Well, it's up to you. Do you want approval rights on my new suit or not? If you don't come, I might buy something green, or Reagan brown."

"You win, you win," Kim said with mock resignation. When she told Jason she'd be home in a couple of hours, the child giggled uncontrollably.

"What's so funny about that?" Kim asked, as Chris pulled her out the front door. "Why is he so hysterical?"

It was two and a half hours before Kim and Chris returned and when Kim stepped in the front door she was greeted with cries of "Surprise! Surprise! Happy Birthday!"

She saw Jason first and his friend Nicholas and Nicholas's

mother and Maggie. And then she felt her heart pounding as Jonathan and Kate stepped forward to greet her.

Kim kissed each of them on the cheek and acted as happy and welcoming as she could, but her gaze was pinned on Kate. Every time Kim turned away, she would be drawn back to watching her, covertly staring at her. For Kate looked terrible. Always in good shape, fashionably slim, she now looked almost emaciated. And though she was beautifully groomed, as always, her clothes did not fit her properly. And her face? Kate looked older, there were dark smudges beneath her eyes. And then, while Kim was watching Kate, Jonathan said, "You look wonderful, Kim. Even my professional eyes don't detect any sign of what you've been through."

Kim saw Kate's face go leaden, pale so much that she seemed completely drained of pigment.

"She knows," Kim thought. "She knows. Oh dear God, she knows."

Kim turned away from Kate and felt her whole body grow cold. She realized that she was visibly shaking and quickly headed for the bathroom. As she leaned against the sink, her mind swirled with a series of images. She and Kate together. She and Jonathan together. Chris, Jason. Kate . . . Kate . . . looking like the wrath of God, at a time when she should be so happy, when her dream was finally coming true. But that was the trouble, wasn't it? That happiness takes more than dreams. Kim lifted her face and stared at her own image in the mirror. A moment later, she knew what she had to do. But first, she had to get through this party.

As she emerged from the bathroom, Jason ran up to her and announced it was now time to open presents. She smiled as well as she could and, avoiding Kate's eyes, walked to the couch, sat down, and began with a large package from Jason. It turned out to be one box after another, with Jason laughing joyously as each box led to another box. Finally, she reached the present. It was a gold bracelet, similar to an ID bracelet. On the front it read, "To the Greatest Mom." On the back was "Love, Chase."

"Chris helped me pick it out," Jason said, as he folded himself into her arms. "You can wear it all the time, just like you used to wear that nice necklace. You know, before."

"Yes," Kim said, kissing his blond head. "Before." She looked up briefly and saw Kate's eyes watching her, almost sorrowfully. Again, Kim trembled.

She moved on to the next package. Beautiful pearl earrings

from Chris, and a silver jewelry box. There was a sweater and a robe from Maggie and then Jonathan moved forward, with the gift from Kate and him. Kim pulled off the wrappings and found an elegantly framed collage of photographs from her documentaries. In the very center was a picture of her, smiling on the news set. She thought to herself, That was during the good times.

Kim thanked Kate as well as she could without looking directly at her. Kate said simply, "Well, we have all your awards and Emmys at the station. You should have some remembrance here."

Because Jonathan had been tied up at the hospital all day, Kate and Jonathan had arrived at Kim's house in separate cars. Kate had told Jonathan she had "personal business" to attend to that day and because of the coolness between them, he had not pursued the question.

Because Kate felt she no longer could spare the time to drive herself, she now used a long black limousine, equipped with tape decks, monitors, a computer, and a telephone. Diana had referred to it simply as "another office on wheels." Along with the limousine came Kate's personal driver/bodyguard—Coby, a 31-year-old Australian who was formerly an Olympic wrestler.

Now as Kate walked out of Kim's condominium, she turned to Jonathan and said, "Would you mind following me? There's something I would like to show you."

"This late?" Jonathan protested. "I've already put in a killer of a day."

"Please. It won't take long." She stepped into the limousine, giving instructions to Coby who was holding the door for her. Jonathan shrugged and headed for his car.

A few moments later, they were pulling up in front of the condominium on Lewis Wharf that had been their headquarters during the kidnapping.

Jonathan stepped out of the Porsche. "What are we doing here?" Kate did not reply, but walked swiftly to the door, unlocked it, and moved into the hallway with Jonathan at her heels.

She turned on the light and led her husband into the living room where she watched him survey the room. There was the leather couch from the study in Dover, the lounge chair he always sat in, other pieces of furniture from their Dover home, and on the walls, paintings and pictures he had either picked out himself or especially admired.

Kate watched his face move from surprise to anger until he roughly brushed her aside and headed into the bedroom. She heard him opening drawers and closets. He then reappeared, holding his tennis racket.

"I hope this isn't what I think it is," he said.

"And what's that?"

"Stop playing games with me, Kate. This place is filled with my stuff. There is nothing here that is yours." He paused and then, with a twisted smile, asked, "Is this the way the new network president tells her husband she's found someone else and their marriage is over?"

"*I've* found someone else?" Kate laughed. "Be serious. You know that's not my style."

"Well, then why this? You know you're the only one I care about. . . ."

"Stop it, Jonathan! Don't make an ass of yourself." Kate shouted. "Don't add lying to the list."

"What list? What is this? Am I still being punished for your New York reporter? I told you. I promised you, never again."

Kate's voice cracked as she felt the tears and anger choke in her throat. "Hang on to what dignity you have. At least be honest." She walked towards him and grabbed the tennis racket. "Isn't it interesting that of all the memorabilia here, you pick up the racket given to you by. . . ." Kate turned her head away, throwing the racket to the floor. Desperately, she tried to hold back the tears.

"You know?" Jonathan asked weakly. He then sighed. "Of course, your friendship with Kim."

"No, Jonathan, nothing that easy. This time Chris was the lucky one. You see, Chris went early to pick up Kim. He saw you together, in *my* bed, just like before." The tears now let loose. Jonathan moved toward her but when she stiffened, he pulled back and lowered himself into a chair.

"No wonder he's been acting the way he has towards me. No wonder you. . . ." He stopped and put his head into his hands.

"Yes, this latest liaison of yours—if it is your latest—has hurt quite a few people. Chris, me, I'm sure Jason in some ways, and I believe even Kim. Her expression today was a picture of pain. It must have made her ordeal with the kidnappers twice as miserable."

"But wait," Jonathan interrupted. "You have to have just found out about this. Surely you didn't know before the kidnapping."

"Oh, Jonathan, sometimes I think you barely know me."
She walked over to the windows. "Of course I knew before the
kidnapping. You think I couldn't have known, because I struggled so hard to save her? Even knowing you think that makes it
hurt more." Kate shrugged and then continued. "No, Kim was
my friend and a valuable person. I still believed in her. Perhaps
it was you I couldn't believe in."

"You never have," Jonathan said standing, his voice crack-
ing. "Ever since that incident in New York and the miscarriage,
you've closed a part of yourself off to me. Even Kim and Jason
were able to get closer to you in some ways. Don't you think
I've suffered too?"

"I've thought about that, Jonathan. How my distrust of you,
my holding something back, could have prodded you into the
arms of other women." She paused and shook her head in confusion. "No, I cannot blame it all on you. Whether it was just
Kim or a dozen other women."

Jonathan walked towards her and put his arms on her trembling shoulders. "It was just Kim, and it was just that once.
Please believe me. It never happened again."

"Maybe with the kidnapping, it just didn't have time to happen again."

"No, Kate, no, I swear." His voice was like a whisper. "You
are the only woman I've ever loved. The only woman I will ever
love. Please believe that. Please let me into your heart again.
Please trust me, let me love you."

Kate pushed away from him, hot tears falling down her
cheeks. "Trust you?" she cried. "Trust you? All I've ever asked
of you is your love, your faithfulness. And what did I get in
return? I got kicked in the teeth. Not once, but twice. Do you
really think I deserved that? Was I that horrible a wife?"

"Kate, please. I never meant to . . . you yourself have said
you held something back," he pleaded. "For God's sake, in
some ways, you were even closer to Kim."

"*Were*, Jonathan. You ruined that, too. When you throw a
rock into a pond, don't expect just one ripple." Kate's voice
rose in passion. "*You* did this to us. *You* put the scars across my
heart and it was a heart that belonged to you, that loved you
unconditionally." She straightened her back, breathed deeply,
and then said calmly, "You are a liability I can no longer afford,
my dear husband. I have a lot to do and I can't go on tearing
myself up over this, constantly wondering who your next 'patient' will be. Not now, at least, not now."

"So you're just going to discard me, just throw me aside."

"I'm going to free myself, and give us both time. The house in Dover is in my name. I'll rent it for a year and I've bought an apartment in New York where I probably will stay when I'm not traveling."

"But what about LYM? Aren't you going to return to Boston at all?"

"Yes, and there is a company suite at the Ritz." She paused, her voice shaky. "Although, if things improve . . . perhaps, eventually, you and I can be together, perhaps . . . even here."

"So you're not divorcing me?"

"No, Jonathan. In a way, I wish I could, but I cannot." She turned and looked directly at him. "I'm still in love with you. I just can't seem to turn that off."

"Then why, Kate? Why are you doing this?" He moved to embrace her but she slipped out of his arms.

"Jonathan, can't you see? I don't want to do anything final yet. I want to see if our marriage can be saved, if there's anything worth saving. But I cannot stay with you—not now—because I cannot live with the constant fear of betrayal.

"No, I've finally set myself free, free of your shadow. But I understand that what's happened isn't all your fault. Let's give each other time to heal and to reassess our lives." She sighed wearily, walked to Jonathan and handed him the key. "Don't worry, that's the only one. I didn't make one for myself."

"That's a cheap shot."

"You should know, Jonathan." She walked past him, slowly closed the door behind her and hurried into the limousine.

The following Monday Kate returned from a business lunch with a client and stood in the outer office delivering instructions and deadlines to Diana and Judy. While they were working, Diana took a call and told Kate that it was Harry Abrams, Kim's agent.

"Well, we know what that's about," Kate said, as she walked into her own office. "Her contract has just two months to go and Harry's going to take me to the bank. Might as well take the call and begin the negotiations. See how many millions our million-dollar baby is going to cost us."

A few moments later, Kate held the phone in her hand, staring at it. She was in a state of shock. What Harry had just said made no sense at all.

"Are you still there, Kate?" the agent asked.

"Yes, Harry, I'm just having trouble digesting your information."

"You think *you're* having trouble?" Harry said sharply. "Think of the commission I've lost."

"Harry, are you sure you have the information correctly?"

"I walked in this morning. There was a message to call her. Of course I did. She's one client I don't keep waiting, if you get my drift." Kate understood perfectly. This contract could be worth twenty-five to fifty thousand dollars to him. Without really thinking, she absently opened her side drawer and gently picked up Kim's rubrum lily necklace.

"We chatted for a few minutes," Harry continued, "and then she drops the bomb. She says she doesn't want to renew her contract at any price!

"At first I thought she decided to go with another network. Between you and me," Harry said quietly, "they've both told me they're willing to bid as much as three million for her, with mixed packages as far as documentaries and specials. And the perks! Limousines. Clothes. You name it. Actually I was looking forward to a good tangle with you. I know you don't believe in perks and people being treated like superstars."

"Sorry to disappoint you, Harry," Kate said. "Tell me again what her reason was."

"She didn't give a reason. She just said she was going to bow out of the industry for a while. The woman's *crazy*! I couldn't believe it. I figured you already knew."

"Well, quite obviously, I didn't," Kate said.

"But you're going to talk to her now, aren't you? Talk some sense into her. Really, Kate, my dear, you can't let this woman just walk away from her career. The lady's a star. And worth a fortune!"

Kate assured the agent she'd talk to Kim, and then she hung up. She went to her couch and eased herself down. The news had made her back ache and her head spin. She knew it would be a blow to her network, but there were many capable people there. The business would survive. On a personal level, she was unsure of what she really felt—upset, confused, that was the only thing she was sure of.

Shortly after seven o'clock, Kate heard a quiet knock on her door. She called "Come in," the door was pushed open, and Kim Winston and Katherine Marchand were face to face.

"Hello, Kate, I received a message from Diana that you wanted to see me."

"Yes, please sit down. I spoke to Harry Abrams today and he told me some startling news."

Kim was silent and Kate said, "Look, when you came to work here, Harry only took care of the technicalities. It was you and I who made the basic decision. I think now you owe me more than a phone call from your agent."

"Chris and I are getting married. He has a research appointment at Stanford that is too good to refuse. And, well, I need a rest. And I can do without the East Coast winters." Kim spoke in a monotone, no emotion in her voice.

The only thing in Kate's mind at that moment was the waste. She knew how rare a talent Kim's was and she valued it so much that, without thinking of any other considerations, she said, "You're making a mistake. You love this business. It's in your blood. Anyone can see that. You glow on the air. With us, you could be the network anchor, the first woman to hold that singular position." Kate paused. "And you know you can write your own ticket anywhere, with the Emmys you've won—to say nothing of the Peabodys and your own heroic reputation."

"I don't know why we have to keep beating a dead horse," Kim said abruptly. "I told you my plans. It's time . . . it's more than time." In a harsh tone, Kim said, "Kate, stop staring out of the damn windows. Look at me. I'm leaving LYM, Kate. As soon as possible."

Kate held up her hand as if to ward off a blow—or words she did not wish to hear. "If you don't want to work for me, then go to another network. They're standing in line with blank checks, waiting for you."

Kim rose and went to stand beside Kate at the windows. "You should know me better. Whatever else happens, I would never go to work for your competition." She put her hand on Kate's sleeve. "I'm going to California so Jason and I can be with Chris. That's all there is to it."

Kate forced herself to respond to Kim's touch, to look directly into the face that was only inches from hers. She said, "You made up your mind at the birthday party, didn't you?"

"Yes."

Kate only nodded, but she felt again the stab at her heart like when she'd seen Kim that day, in the same room as Jonathan. Not that she feared . . . no, it was only that Kim was—and would always be—a living reminder.

Kim was talking and Kate's attention was caught, not by what she was saying, but by the dullness of her tone, the flat dead sound coming from this animated woman. "And I'll have the leisure to find a good school out there for Jason and to find the right house and. . . ."

"*Decorate* it, maybe?" Kate asked sarcastically. "Christ! Is that what you're going to do with what could be a brilliant future? Instead of on a national television screen, you'll look at your image reflecting off the floor wax?"

This time Kim stared out the windows, waiting for the knot in her gut to ease. "Actually," she began, "there was one thought I had. There's a lot of talk about KJNA in San Francisco. Critics say it's the weak link in your network."

"The critics are right," snapped Kate. Then realizing what Kim was leading to, she lowered her tone. "You mean you'd consider reporting, anchoring at KJNA?"

"I'd consider anchoring. Your anchor team needs help."

Kate said nothing.

"And I'd also want a free hand to do documentary work of my choosing."

Kate sat down behind her desk. "I don't like it. It would be a step down for you, Kim. Damn it! You're wanted by the networks!"

"It's not for you to say what's right for me and what isn't. I'd still be working for you. I'd still be working on the side of compassion and excellence." Kim turned and looked at Kate. "We began with you offering me the supposed chance of a lifetime. Well, I've taken that chance . . ."

"So move on, move up," Kate interrupted. "Go to New York where you belong. *Go* to the networks."

"You're not listening, Kate. I'm going to San Francisco with my family. I'm offering you my services *there*. This time, the decision is yours."

"I'll have to think about it," Kate said quietly, feeling somehow defeated.

"Please tell Harry your decision as soon as possible." Kim walked towards the office door, then hesitated. "Oh, one last thing. Do you know what happened to my lily necklace?"

"No," Kate said, in a manner that ended their conversation.

Kim walked out of the office, closing the door gently behind her. She felt the tears lock in her throat but did not succumb. She was doing a special taping tonight at the Symphony and she couldn't afford to smear her makeup.

Inside the office, Kate slammed her fist onto the desk top and then lowered her head into the shadows of her hands. She was too angry to cry.

Four weeks later, Kimberly Winston made her final appearance on WLYM. Shortly before airtime, Diana delivered an envelope to her. In it was the rubrum lily necklace, repaired and polished. This time, the tears did fall as she read the note that was enclosed: "Thank you for your courage. You have given far more than was given. Go in peace, dear friend."

Upstairs, as the sky darkened, Katherine Marchand—now president of the most powerful network in America—sat alone watching the Friday evening newscast. Kim Winston, wearing the lily necklace, said farewell to her Boston audience and announced she would soon be appearing on the anchor desk of KJNA in San Francisco.

With grief and an almost overwhelming regret, Katherine Marchand watched the woman who was so close to becoming one of the most important, most respected journalists in the country say goodbye. Still, Kate told herself, Kim was so unique, so able, there really was no way to predict where her career or, for that matter, her life would go.

She shrugged slightly and said aloud, "In any case." Then, pressing the intercom, in a voice crisp and businesslike, she added, "Diana, please get together all the résumé tapes of the candidates for the evening news. We'll run them now—I know how you like to think you are picking the new talent."

About the Author

PAMELA BULLARD is a former producer and anchorwoman who has worked at several Boston TV stations. She was also a producer for the *McNeil-Lehrer Report*. She currently lives in Boston.